F*CK STEAL KILL

KRIS BUTLER
xoxo

F*CK STEAL KILL

KRIS BUTLER

xoxo

CONTENTS

BLURB

It's only a game… until someone gets hurt.

In a town known for the macabre and bizarre, it didn't provide many options for women outside of marriage. Working as a maid in a themed hotel hadn't been my dream, but at least I got to do it with my two best friends—Lacey and Joy. To help with the boredom of living in a town with no future, we started a game.

*Select three people and cast them into their lots—to f*ck, steal from, or kill.*

At first, it was all hypothetical, but after an accidental murder, it became so much more.

It became our escape.

And with it, the birth of the XOXO killer and a way out of Foolshope for good.

But when three gorgeous guys snagged my attention, it appeared our luck had finally run out. Someone was after us. It looked like we'd discovered another way out of this town after all—in a body bag.

One thing was certain: we would be leaving this town —either as another foolish victim of hope or covered in the blood of our enemies.

Go ahead, underestimate us, and see which list you end up on.

XOXO.

This is a why choose romance, meaning the FMC will end up with three or more love interests. There is no cheating, and it ends in a HEA. This series is an NA medium-high burn with MM, MFM, and MFMM meant for 18+ readers. Some themes may be triggering for some readers. Please read the foreword for information on triggers and content.

FOREWORD

This book has sexual scenes meant for adults. It is a why-choose romance that has bi-awakening themes. The steamy scenes are steamy, and you might need new batteries by the end. Sorry, not sorry. This book uses the F-word as well as other foul language.

Recap: The first eight chapters were originally included in the Dark and Stabby Anthology. There have been 2k words added to those chapters, so I'd suggest reading them again to reorient yourself to the FSK world, and ensure you have the most up-to-date information on the characters and world. But if you want a recap, check the end of this section.

TROPES/CONTENT:

- Multi-Pov
- Badass females with sassy mouths

- hurt/comfort
- found family
- public sex
- Pegging
- Dirty talk
- Praise
- Group sex
- Possessive, growly men
- Bi-awakening (light MM, all exploration is with FMC)
- FF (in Joy's chapter only)
- Positive female friendships

SENSITIVE MATERIAL:

- murder/violence
- Death
- Bad people doing bad things (off-page)
- Vengeance/revenge
- Kidnapping
- Stabbing/fighting
- 'God, Jesus, Hell, Damn' is used casually or in a sexual context
- PTSD/panic attacks

RECAP OF CHAPTER 1-8

Potential spoilers can be found below. Do not read beyond this point if you do not want to be spoiled.

Last warning.

I mean it.

<u>Spoilers below.</u>

Holland introduces us to the game, the town, and her friendship with Joy and Lacey. Her first murder was an accident, but it showed her an opportunity. With her friends, they created the XOXO app to help others. Requests can be either for fucking up someone's life/reputation, stealing something, or killing (career, reputation, or life). Later get a request from a Hopeless Savage that they're not sure what to do with.

Grady, Max, and Quentin arrive in town on the hunt for the XOXO killer. Quentin encounters Holland at a bar and fingers her in the restroom, taunting her to not think about him when she's with "weasel face." Grady catches her eyes and feels something for the first time in years. Max meets her at the hotel when she's dropping off towels. Later, Max takes Q to meet his crush, and they both realize it's the same person.

Holland goes back with them to their room, gets some messages, and goes to the bathroom. Their dark web contact alerts them that someone is looking for them, asking questions. While she's in the bathroom, someone comes into the room, and she overhears him saying "Savages" and "looking for a killer." Holland bolts out of there, encounters all three guys she's felt an attraction to in the same room, acts drunk, and leaves.

A group called the Savages is following Grady, Max, and Quentin and decides to keep tabs on Holland after seeing her leave their room. The Savages are a ruthless mercenary gang that have taken someone from Max, Grady, and Quentin.

But really… You should check out those chapters again. Besides, do you really want to miss Quentin growling and that hot scene with Holland in the bathroom? So go ahead and read those chapters again; the added words are worth it.

It might be odd to dedicate a book on unaliving to friendship, but this book embraces the purest form of friendship — the ride-or-die besties.
The type of friend who doesn't question if you need help, but asks if they need to bring a shovel.
The ones that are there for you in your darkest moments, cheer for you in your best, and hold your hand in your worst.
The ones willing to hold your hair back when you're sick, and then tease you about it the next day.
The type of friend you can be silent with but still feel you had the best conversation with.

So, this book is dedicated to those who fix our crowns without first telling the world it was crooked, who never expect anything in return, and who love us with a love so powerful that it changes us forever.

I hope you have a friend like that, and if not, don't give up hope, as you never know when you might meet them.
Until then, you can be part of the XOXO squad.

XOXO

CHAPTER 1
HOLLAND xoxo

THE FIRST TIME I'D KILLED A MAN, IT WAS AN ACCIDENT.

Now, how would a girl like me, one who seemingly on the outside had it all together, find herself in a situation where she had to classify her *first* murder as an 'accident'?

But as the saying went, you shouldn't judge a book by its cover—and mine was covered in blood.

"Earth to Holland," Lacey bellowed, snapping her fingers in front of my face.

I turned my head and glowered at one of my best friends. Lacey lifted her ice-blue eyes at me, daring me to challenge her. Her long dark hair was in her customary top-knot, piled high on her head. Her lips twitched as she waited me out, and I ignored how my white-blonde hair had stuck to my dark purple lipstick in the move.

When she didn't budge, I sighed and gave in, earning a triumphant smile from her.

"What?" I groaned, spitting out my hair as I tried to pull it away from my face.

I'd been zoning out all day while we'd been working, lost in the boredom and routine. It was just another humdrum Wednesday at The Secret Keep Inn.

"Your turn," Joy, the third member of our posse, said, her sweet voice drawing my attention. Glancing around the lobby of the Inn, I picked out three people for the game after only a cursory glance.

"Baldie, button-up, and beer gut," I said through a yawn.

Joy giggled at my accidental alliteration. She placed her chin on her fist as she debated, twisting her lips back and forth. Her delicate features reminded me of an angel, triggering my protective instincts. Her honey-brown hair fell softly around her heart-shaped face, her big brown doe eyes allowing her to get away with just about anything.

For not the first time, I marveled at how different we were, even just sitting around a table. Joy had a soft and romantic style, wearing dresses and skirts in floral patterns. She was tiny, barely five feet, and often seemed to float as she walked.

Lacey was the exact opposite, always flopping down into chairs and stomping everywhere she went. She was the tallest of the three of us, topping off around 5'9", and dressed like she could go to a biker bar or rob a bank at any given time. So much black leather in her wardrobe that I often wondered if she was colorblind.

And then there was me. Average height, average weight, and dressed like a punk rock hobo. Mostly because I didn't care about clothes and also because I liked to shock people. Too many years of living up to other people's expectations had a way of doing that.

Lacey glared at the table next to us, their eyes shifting quickly at her look, causing me to snort. She shrugged, taking another swig of her coffee as she spread her legs out like she didn't have a care in the world; though the smirk growing behind her cup said otherwise. Lacey liked scaring people; it was her thing. Not that they'd given her much of a choice.

If you met the three of us separately, you'd never expect us to be friends. But small towns had a way of putting together people who normally wouldn't socialize with one another. And Ms. Hutchinson's third-grade class had done just that. It was the year everyone came down with chicken pox except the three of us.

In a classroom with only three students for a week, we bonded, forging a lifelong friendship that had stood the test of time despite our differences.

Joy was the town's sweetheart. She volunteered for everything and would bring you soup if you were sick. She was goodness incarnate, and if she hadn't met Lacey and me, she would've probably become a nun or something. I almost felt bad about that.

Lacey, on the other hand, was the town rebel and resident slut—her words. Her zip code was considered to be the wrong side of town, and she was constantly in trouble. Though that was just what she let people see. Lacey didn't let many people in, but once she did, it was for life. She also loved to bake and volunteered at animal shelters to play with all the cats and dogs no one wanted. But hardly anyone saw that side of her. Mostly because of their own biases and partly her own self-preservation.

If Joy was considered the town angel, Lacey was definitely the devil.

Which left me—the town nerd with an alcoholic mother, a deadbeat father, and a tragic past. *Go me for hitting the trifecta.*

The three of us made little sense to most people, but to each other, we were a tribe. And nothing came between us and our bond.

Not even murder.

"Fuck Baldie, steal from button-up, and kill beer gut," Joy said after deliberating. She gave herself a nod, her honey-brown strands falling into her face.

"Ugh, so boring," Lacey whined, making Joy and me turn to one another. Lacey always had an opinion about our selections. "I'd fuck button-up. He might know how to handle me," she said, licking her lips.

Snickering, I glanced at the guest list, knowing we needed to get back to work. There were still a few rooms to finish cleaning before they checked in to the Secret Keep Inn.

"Come on, break's over," I moaned.

They both sighed and tossed away their trash as I gathered the cart. Being a cleaning lady at the Inn wasn't a glamorous job, but it was one of the easier ones in a town that catered to the bizarro.

"How much more do we need?" Lacey asked, pushing the cart as she walked next to me.

"Ten thousand, four hundred, and twenty-two cents," I answered automatically. Lacey sighed dramatically before nodding in acceptance, and I pulled out the master key card as she neared the next room.

"We're getting closer," Joy cheered, her shiny optimism a constant presence.

The three of us had a joint savings account where we put the majority of our earnings. We had plans to leave this town together and only needed a little bit more to make it plausible.

Patting her hand in encouragement, I grabbed rolls of toilet paper off the cart and followed Lacey into the Egyptian room.

The Secret Keep Inn wasn't a five-star hotel, but what it lacked in high-class, it made up for in uniqueness and intrigue. Each room had a different theme, catering to a variety of fantasies.

And if there was one thing the Secret Keep Inn did well, it was to keep a secret.

"This dude was disgusting," Lacey shouted from the bedroom. "Was he on our list? Because he should be."

I glanced at the clipboard, trying to remember if Room 103 had made it onto the list the day before. "Christopher Roberts," I mumbled, trying to recall. "I don't think so."

Looking up, I spotted Lacey standing in front of me with a used condom on the end of her pen.

"Eww! Why would you show me that?" I screeched, closing my eyes and stepping back.

"Because if I have to suffer, then so do you," she teased.

"Whoa. The guy has an impressive cum load," Joy said, peering closer at the used condom like a science experiment.

"Double eww, Joy! Just why?"

She shrugged, smiling at me as she went about cleaning the bedroom, singing softly to herself.

Joy might be the sweet one of the group, but she had a dark sense of humor, often finding delight in the obscure and macabre. And now, apparently, cum.

"And people think I'm the crazy one," Lacey muttered, dropping the condom into the trash.

Regardless of how adamant Lacey was about the things people in town said about her, Joy and I knew differently. Lacey was sensitive despite her tough outer exterior.

"We all have our roles to play," Joy hummed, twerking her hips as she made the bed.

Lacey and I shared a look, giggling to ourselves at Joy's moves. She was right; the town had slotted us into our roles from an early age, and not much could change them. It made our bonds all the more special because they were authentic.

Peering into the depths of a person's soul and knowing what they were truly capable of was a rare gift few received. And the three of us, we'd all been there for each other at our darkest and most depraved moments, accepting them as who we were.

Some people bonded over books, others their

favorite sports team or rock bands; for us, it was murder.

But like I said, the first time, it had been an accident. The many times that followed… Those had all been planned.

You might wonder how three girls from different backgrounds ended up murdering people.

And like most out-of-character things, it started as a game… as a fantasy.

Stuck in a touristy town with no escape, it was either find creative ways to pass the time or lose yourself to the madness. Because in Foolshope, the options for women were limited to marrying young, marrying rich, or…

Actually, that was it—just marriage.

And marriage, well, that wasn't an option for the three of us for various reasons. Which was why we were still stuck in this town at twenty-eight, praying we didn't become another statistic of Foolshope: divorced, drunk, or dead.

But not for much longer. We had a plan, and we were so close to leaving.

"Speaking of the list, who's on the agenda tonight?" Lacey asked, fluffing up the pillows.

"Joy's in room 504 for stealing, you have room 230 for killing, and I'm in 110 for fucking," I said, reading off the clipboard.

Lacey rubbed her hands together in excitement, a rare smile gracing her face. "Yes! I have some energy I need to expend. What am I killing this time?"

The game was simple. You selected three people and put them on your list to either fuck, marry, or kill. Since the three of us were opposed to marriage, we'd altered it to steal—Fuck, Steal, Kill.

In the beginning, it was all hypothetical. We'd list people around town, guests at the Inn, or the occasional celebrity. It was stupid, yet a fun way to pass the time and break up the boredom.

Over time, it evolved into three kinds of lists. The first was hypothetical, like earlier in the lobby, where we threw out three randoms and made a snap judgment. They were usually funny and entirely fantasy.

The second type was like a wish list. That one consisted of people we held a grudge against, wanted to fuck, or prove a point to. If the opportunity to fulfill those desires ever presented itself, then the three of us were obligated to help make it happen.

For instance, I was still waiting on the chance to fuck my childhood celebrity crush. It was unlikely that Joshua Jackson would ever grace the streets of Foolshope, but if he did, I had no doubt that Lacey and Joy would be there going along with whatever plan I'd concocted.

Which led us to the third type of list. This one evolved after a fatal night when one of the men I'd gone home with had become a little too handsy, forcing himself on me, and not taking no for an answer.

As I lay there, trying to figure out how to get away from him, I missed the fact that he was having an allergic reaction until he collapsed on top of me, gasping. I'd barely managed to crawl out from under him before he suffocated me, and I knew I had a decision to make. To help him, or let him suffer.

It was my hesitation, my need to see him *hurt*, that killed my first victim.

I was so tired of men using me, of taking what they wanted without any thought to what I needed. So, I stood there, watching him struggle to breathe, his hands scrambling as he searched for relief and salvation.

And I felt *powerful*.

For the first time in my life, I felt like I could actually change my course. And that was an addictive feeling.

Blinking, I pulled out of the memory and looked up at the girls, remembering Lacey had asked a question.

"Just his career," I said, placing the clipboard onto the cart. "The request asked for photos of him naked, with drugs and alcohol present. He's some religious leader who's been preaching one thing and doing the other. The requester wants his congregation to know the real man behind the cloth."

Lacey's grin widened as she tied the trash bag, heading out of the room with Joy and me following behind.

"My favorite type of killing," she said, locking the room and doing a little shimmy.

After that fatal night, I knew we needed to move the game from hypothetical to reality. I never wanted to feel powerless again.

Since I was the brains of our trio, I saw an opportunity to not only take matters into my own hands but help others find that same hit of power and justice. It started with just Joy and Lacey, but I soon saw the far-reaching aspects of our endeavors. In doing so, we finally found a way out of this town that didn't include marriage.

My mother always said I was the enterprising type. Though, I doubt this was what she had in mind—God Bless her soul.

Working in the hospitality industry as maids, we had access to personal details of guests' lives and entry into their rooms.

By day, we met their needs with a smile. (Okay, Joy met them with a smile. For Lacey and I, it was dependent on a very precise formula that consisted of the time of day, the amount of coffee, and the number of complaints received. Simple, really.)

And by night, we snuck into rooms, fulfilling the desires of strangers *and* ourselves.

Not every person on the list was a job, and not every kill ended in murder. Despite what it sounded like, we did have a code and vetted each request that came through our app.

Fucking was for pleasure, stealing for gain, and killing for sport.

We took turns, covered our bases, and always ensured we wouldn't get caught.

Between the sweetheart, the rebel, and the brains, we made one badass killer.

As we turned the corner to head to the elevator,

Lacey spoke up, pointing at Joy. "Your turn. Who does Holland have to FSK?"

Joy grinned, turning to look out into the lobby as we passed. Instantly, I spotted three men who made my insides go haywire. They were new, each mysterious in their own right. Something about them drew me to them, and I couldn't take my eyes off them.

One of the men glanced up as the elevator door started to close, locking eyes with me. His light blue, almost gray in color, orbs held mine captive, and in that few second's flash, I felt them sear across my soul like a brand. I didn't know who that man was, but he made me feel dangerous things—things I didn't know how to handle.

Blinking, I broke the connection as the door closed, shaking my head to try to clear it. My lungs burned, and I realized I'd been holding my breath. Exhaling, I coughed as I tried to regain my equilibrium, swaying against the side of the elevator.

"Ooh, who was that?" Joy cooed, bouncing on her feet like a puppy.

"Who?" I feigned, turning to her with a blank face. She rolled her eyes, knowing me better than that.

"I'll let you off the hook for now. But don't think I didn't notice that hot eye fucking."

Scoffing, I leaned back against the wall to steady myself as the elevator rose, hoping for—and dreading —-the next time I saw him.

The challenging part, I didn't know where he fell on my list, and that was the most frightening part of all.

CHAPTER 2
GRADY

THE MOST ENIGMATIC WOMAN I'D EVER SEEN JUST vanished right before my eyes. I blinked, hoping she'd reappear, but all that remained was the silver metallic of the elevator door.

"Anything?" the gruff voice in my ear asked, bringing me back to my mission.

Tilting my mediocre cup of coffee up, I scanned the hotel lobby for the millionth time in the past hour.

"No," I grunted, meeting the dark eyes of one-third of my team. Quentin narrowed them, knowing I wasn't sharing everything. His hard mouth slanted into a frown, his forehead creasing as he assessed me.

That was the advantage and disadvantage of working with the same two men for over five years. You knew each other inside and out, often not even needing to say what you were thinking. Which meant when you were trying to hide something, they were the first to know it.

"Later," I mouthed, spinning and observing the middle-aged man with brown hair sitting at the bar.

Nothing about him stood out. Simple clothes, basic looks, and often overlooked by the other guests. He fit the profile perfectly of the killer we'd been sent to track, but something about him didn't make my gut kick in.

Sighing, I drained the last of my coffee and stood, tossing my paper cup into the trash. I headed toward the elevator, spotting the last of our team as he ducked around the corner. Maxwell's dark head of hair was a mess, his fingers having run through it while he worked on his computer. His olive skin was visible beneath his geeky t-shirt, contrasting with my pressed button-down. A backpack rested on his shoulder, his laptop stowed away now that we'd vacated the lobby.

I gave a subtle nod as he stepped into the stairwell, entering the elevator as it arrived a second later. No one would ever expect the three of us to be a team considering we were as different as night and day. But it was part of why we worked well together, blending into the crowd around us.

The ride was quick, and I couldn't help but glance both ways as I exited, hoping to spot a white-blonde beauty on the same floor. But the hallway was empty, sending my heart flutters back into my stomach. The door to the room next to mine clicked shut as I walked past, and knew Max had made it in.

Using my key, I stepped into the Viking suite I'd been placed in since it was adjoined to the room next door. Latching the chain, I double-locked the bar before heading to the connecting door. Walking through, I spotted Quentin stepping in and going through the same routine to secure the door as I had. Once he was finished, he joined Max and me further into the Alamo Saloon suite.

These fucking crazy themed rooms.

"What do you have to report?" I asked my team, leaning against the dresser and crossing my arms. I didn't make any small talk, nor did they expect it from me. My focus was completely on the job at hand.

Bullshit, my inner thought scoffed. But I ignored it.

Max pulled out his laptop and readied himself for any information we might have found to enter into the database. He looked up, waiting for someone to speak.

Quentin stared at me, not saying anything as he watched me with his arms crossed. He'd leaned against the wall, his all-black attire stood out against the wood walls of the saloon. He stayed radio-silent, waiting me out and putting pressure on me to share first.

Yeah, not happening, Q.

Snorting, I shared a look with Max, both of us hiding grins at how ridiculous he looked against the wall. I kept expecting a *Sesame Street* character to pop out from behind the wall and ask, "Which one of these is not like the other?"

"What?" he bellowed when he couldn't stand being out of the loop and snickering any longer.

"Would you like a sarsaparilla?" I asked, quirking my brow as I kept a straight face.

Quentin scowled but moved away from the wall and leaned against the window instead. "Are you going to share with the group what caught *your* attention, Chief?"

Rolling my eyes at the nickname, I dropped my arms and clasped my hands in front of me, staring at the ground. I had to say something, or he'd never let it go. But the trick was saying just enough so he'd drop it and not ask follow-up questions. Unfortunately, the words tumbled from my lips before I could stop them.

"It was… just a woman."

"A woman?" Max asked, spinning toward me, a goofy grin on his face. "Someone caught your eye, Grady?"

"It's nothing." I straightened my posture, re-crossing my arms. "We're here on a job. Work first; that's the motto."

My eyes seared into each of theirs, making sure they got the memo. I wouldn't mention it again until we found the person we'd been sent to retrieve. Max focused back on the computer, typing something before looking up.

"What did you make of the man?" he asked.

I sighed in relief that the briefing had been refocused. Tapping my fingers on my knee, I leaned back as I formulated my response.

"He fits the profile, but something's off about him. List the facts again. I'm missing… something."

"Mid to late twenties, knowledge of the area, and has the ability to go unnoticed. More than likely, he's strong, tall, and smart. *Very* smart. This person has managed to go unnoticed for at least two years, with over six kills. They're either very patient or are only getting started."

"Why do you think they're tall again?" I asked, rubbing my chin as I rolled the facts over in my head. That was one piece that felt wrong.

"Based on some of the victims, our target would need strength and height to carry out their kill. It's just not physically possible for someone short to be able to manage victim #3 or victim #5 on their own. As there's no intel that they work with a partner, we're looking for a man who can handle the heavy lifting independently."

"Sound reasoning, but let's not rule anything out until we have solid facts. Our first mark fits the profile, but didn't make my gut tick."

"What about the girl... did that make your *dick* tick?" Quentin lobbied, lifting his eyebrow in a challenge.

Rolling my eyes, I ignored him. Quentin might be one of my oldest friends, but he was still an asshole. Sometimes, I just had to ignore him and let him get his grumblings out.

"Don't mark Keith off the list, but I want us to focus on the others until we gather more intel. Who's our next potential lead?" I asked Max.

"David Johns. He's the town handyman. He's known to visit the local watering hole and the bowling alley when he's not at home."

Perfect.

"Quentin, stake out the bar. Max, set up surveillance

for the house, and I'll take the bowling alley. Remember, this is intel gathering only. Do not approach until we have more to go off of. Our employer wants to remain hidden as long as possible to not warn them of our arrival."

Quentin grunted, still upset with me for ignoring him and not sharing about the woman. Max, ever the peacekeeper between us, nodded, focusing back on his computer screen. His fingers moved faster than I could keep up with. The kid was talented, and I was glad he was on our side.

"We have a few hours until we're needed. Take a nap, shower, eat some food, whatever you need to do to prepare. We'll touch base after."

Rising, I didn't wait to see if they had any questions. Our team was efficient, and we each knew our roles at this point. There was no need to waste words or time by sitting around.

The three of us worked well together, partly because we knew when to give each other space. When you spent ninety percent of your time with the same two people, you learned to appreciate the alone time when you could.

Thankfully, as the pseudo-leader, I got my own room. It helped in situations like this one when we needed to keep a low profile of our association with one another.

Closing the adjoining door, I left it unlocked but trusted they wouldn't come through unless it was an emergency. If there was one thing we respected, it was privacy.

Removing my suit coat, I tossed it onto the dresser that was made to resemble a block of ice. Even though it wasn't real or freezing in this room, the decor and ambiance convinced your brain it was. My body shuddered at the fake temperature change, and I reconsidered putting my coat back on.

But what I really wanted was a shower.

Stripping the rest of the way, I grabbed my shower kit and headed toward the en suite. Our last case hadn't ended well, and we'd quickly jumped into this one. Partially because we wanted to forget our failure to subdue our last subject, allowing him to kill three more kids before he took his own life.

Despite knowing he couldn't kill any more innocent children, it felt wrong he'd gotten off so easily by offing himself. The man deserved to be beaten and raped over and over in prison.

And the other reason we accepted this one was the same reason we accepted them all—we needed revenge.

Turning on the water, I almost twisted the knob completely off with my ire as I recalled our incompetence. We couldn't afford to fail again. My pride wouldn't stand for it.

The water sprayed out, heating my skin as it warmed. I dropped my shoulders and closed my eyes as the water ran over my body.

I trusted my team, but I still carried the weight of

our failures on my shoulders. I never wanted them to worry about anything; they were my family, after all.

But with each job we took, it felt like I was losing more and more of myself.

Soon, I worried there wouldn't be anything left of me to give.

Except, that millisecond that my eyes had locked on hers, a spark ignited within me. Something had shifted, lighting my insides back to life. Her eyes called out to mine, their green a color I didn't know existed outside of nature. They were vivid and dark, a world of emotions in their hidden depths. Her white-blonde hair highlighted her tanned skin, accentuating her dark lipstick.

I couldn't remember what she was wearing, or even what her body looked like. It was her eyes and lips that had captivated me, promising me things I hadn't known I'd wanted.

My body responded in full force now that I'd relaxed, no longer on guard. Within seconds, my dick was heavy, bringing my attention to it. Blinking water out of my eyes, it cascaded down my cheeks as I took in the offending appendage.

Now was not the time to be distracted by a woman, but my cock had other ideas. I ignored it, refusing to give into the desire to lose myself, to let go of control.

Grabbing my soap, I lathered it and coated my body as the smell of bourbon and spice filtered around me. Steam billowed in the enclosed space, encompassing me in a warm hug. It was enough to derail my thoughts, and before I knew it, my hand was wrapped around my cock, squeezing. Hard.

My other hand fell forward onto the tile, holding me up as I leaned against it, the water rushing over my head. Now that I'd given in to gripping my dick, I was a captive to its demands. Though I couldn't picture the elevator girl's body, her eyes mocked me, flashing with a challenge. Her lips beckoned me, her tongue teasing out at the corner seductively.

I couldn't stop as my hand stroked up and down my shaft. Suds ran over my body as the water rained down, providing a natural lubricant for my aching dick.

My free hand turned into a fist, slamming gently against the tiles as I lost myself to the sensation. Her smirking eyes and flirty lips were all I had to go on, but it was more than enough. When I envisioned those lips wrapped around my cock, her eyes beckoning me to test her limits, I was done.

"Fuck," I shouted, my cum exploding out and splashing onto the tiled floor beneath me. My breaths quickened as my heart raced, my body feeling like it had run a 5K in a matter of seconds.

Rinsing off the remaining suds, I grabbed my shampoo and quickly applied it, massaging my scalp and trying to put the woman out of my mind. I'd succumbed to her temptation, hoping it would push her out of my thoughts now. I couldn't afford to think of her anymore. Not until the mission was completed.

Turning off the water, I quickly dried off, avoiding

looking at myself in the mirror, worried about what I'd find there.

Shame and disgust? Or worse, desire?

Dressing for the bowling alley, I wore a flannel shirt, old jeans, and a backward cap. I still had an hour before needing to rejoin the guys, so I grabbed my wallet and phone and headed to grab food. My phone rang as I took the stairs, and I glanced at the ID, despite knowing who was calling.

Stopping on the landing between the first and second floors, I answered the phone as I leaned against the wall.

"Jackson," I said, not elaborating.

"Grady," he barked, his rough voice filling the tiny speaker. "Any updates?"

"Nothing of significance. We're going out this evening. Will report in tomorrow."

"Good, good. I want this guy, Grady." Something pounded against a hard surface through the phone, jolting me against the wall. "If you bring them in, you and your team can have that extended vacation you've requested. Understood?"

Swallowing, the thought of our request finally being approved filled me with hope. This could be our chance. No more hotels for a while. My own bed, home-cooked meals, and, best of all, peace and quiet.

"Understood, sir. We'll get him."

"No screwups. I'll wait for your call." He hung up before I could respond, but it was for the best. There was nothing more I could say, anyway.

We had to get this guy or pay the price. It was as simple as that.

Putting my phone back into my pocket, I continued on my way, a little more determination in my step and a promise to avoid any green-eyed, blonde women, no matter how enigmatic they were.

CHAPTER 3
HOLLAND *xoxo*

The hookup I'd selected for the night was turning out to be a total dud, and I didn't understand why. He was tall and attractive, with a bit of an "I just came straight from the farm" look about him. His muscles were earned by hard labor, and my fingers itched to see what was beneath his flannel.

He had a kind face and a gentle spirit, making him generous with the drinks, and giving me a nice buzz. I twirled my finger around the pink wig, trying to entice him one last time. I hadn't had to work this hard for dick in years.

"You know what would be fun, Patrick?" I asked, giggling at the end. I leaned closer, placing my hand on his thigh and rubbing my thumb close to his groin. Patrick gulped, his breath hitching as he watched me.

"Wha-a-a-t?" he asked, licking his lips.

"Let's do something crazy and go back to your room." My fingers began to walk up his thigh as I moved closer. "I always wanted to go to Paris. We could get naked under the Eiffel Tower... *together*."

Patrick coughed, his face flaming bright red. This

guy made me question my ability to flirt. But with how often he blushed and stumbled over his words, I was halfway to believing this was his first time away from home and perhaps… a virgin.

How had I missed that?

"Oh, um, well, I…" he spluttered, his eyes wide with shock.

Sliding off the stool, I stepped in between his legs. My hand grazed his groin, finding his dick hard. Okay, I could work with this. He was interested, just a little shy.

Wrapping my arms around his neck, I played with the hair at the back of his nape and stepped even closer. Pressing my boobs against his chest, I grinned when I caught his eyes dropping to my cleavage.

Winner, winner.

He gulped again, and I wondered if that was his trademark response.

"Do you not like me, Patrick?" I purred, my lips so close to his that I could almost kiss him.

"No. I mean, yes, I like you. I just—"

"Then I'll make it easy for you. I want *you*, Patrick."

"It's just." He shook his head, his words dying on his lips.

"What is it?" I tilted my head, my eyes catching the man sitting next to him. He watched me, a curious tilt to his lips as he drank his whiskey.

His eyes were pools of darkness, making it difficult to decipher the emotions swimming there. His hair was jet black and shorn close to his scalp, accentuating his light brown skin. He was gorgeous in a completely deadly way.

He was the type of man I was putty for but often avoided, choosing to stay more in control of my sexual exploits after the last time I'd been with a man like him. Though, I didn't know if there were any men *quite* like him. He had an air about him, an energy I'd never felt before. It was electric, drawing me in like a bug-zapping machine.

My eyes lifted back to his, finding them trained on me. He sipped his drink, a challenge forming in them as I continued to stare, his smirk growing with each second we held each other's gaze. It was only when he motioned toward my date with his glass that I remembered I was busy.

My cheeks heated, and I returned to Patrick, despite how my body was now responding to the man behind him. It only highlighted the dullness I felt to the man I currently stood in front of.

Moving my fingers in his hair, I licked my lips and peered into Patrick's dull brown eyes, nowhere near as magnetic as the stranger's behind him. He seemed shell-shocked, and I suddenly found the whole seduction exhausting.

He might be safe, but if I was honest with myself, I knew I'd end up pleasing myself with the toy hidden in my purse afterward.

Why was I working so hard to get him to take me back to his room? For what? A few bumbling kisses and thrusts just so he could have a story to take home to his buddies? Leaving me to ensure my own happy ending… alone.

"Okay," he finally mumbled, pulling me out of my spiral. He nodded like an enthusiastic puppy, looking overly excited now, and I inwardly worried he'd pee on my leg in his excitement. Not my kink.

Typically, the feeling of persuading them fulfilled me and pushed me to carry out the deed, even if it was a bit lackluster. But tonight, with one look from a sexy stranger, I was left feeling empty and exhausted.

"Perfect. I just need to step away to the little girl's room for a second. I'll meet you outside?" My voice was strained, panic gripping me for some unknown reason.

His brows furrowed, but he nodded, focusing back on my cleavage. I waved my fingers, pivoting as I swung my hips, the tiny shorts I'd worn accentuating my butt as I hurried away to freak out in peace.

I didn't know why I'd mentioned needing a minute, but I was glad I had. Unease and panic continued to grip me as I neared the restroom, and I slammed into the door, stumbling over my feet. I'd worked so hard to never feel helpless again that I didn't want to slip now.

Turning on the cold water, I shoved my hands under the faucet and let the cool temp calm the raging turmoil inside of me. I stared at my reflection in the mirror, looking for the crack in my composure, but I couldn't find anything. The black eyeliner swooped out in a flawless curve, the dark lipstick fully covered my pouty lips, and my pink wig sat perfectly in place, not a hair out of place.

It was only my green eyes that seemed off. The fierceness I typically carried was gone, leaving a dullness behind.

"Alright, time to buck up and get it back. It's time to rock this guy's world and remember who you are," I whispered to myself, lifting my chin. Sucking in a breath, I pivoted on my heels, shocked when the door opened, and a man stepped through.

It only took me a second to realize it was the stranger from the bar. My heart galloped as I gaped at him. He was even sexier in full view. Dressed in all black, his jeans and shirt were plastered to his body, adding to his appeal. This man would know how to treat a woman in bed. There was no doubt in my mind. Even this stranger's pinky toe had more sex appeal than stumbling Patrick at the bar.

One time would never be enough with him, and knowing that terrified me. He was the type of man that would ruin you for others. And considering no one ever stayed in this town, that wouldn't work out so well for me.

"Excuse me, this is the ladies' room," I said, shifting on my boots and narrowing my gaze. I didn't want him to know how affected I was by his mere presence, which meant I had to bring out my bitchy side.

Crossing my arms, I unintentionally pushed my breasts out more, and when his dark eyes scanned my body, touching each inch with a lover's caress, I shivered. His hot gaze left goosebumps in its wake, spreading across my skin like a riptide. A tug, low in my abdomen, pulled at me, and I sucked in a breath at the intensity.

I wanted this man something fierce.

"Is that how we're going to play this, baby?" he drawled, the first words out of his mouth. It shocked me. So much had been said already between us without any words.

"Play this?" I gasped.

He stalked closer, bringing his dark, seductive smell with him—leather, whiskey, and a hint of mahogany.

I stepped backward, hitting the sink counter when I couldn't go any further. He didn't stop until he was entirely in my space, his hands landing on the counter next to me. Every atom in my body screamed for me to wrap my legs around his waist and kiss him until I couldn't breathe. My fingers itched to touch him, my nose to smell him, and my mouth to lick him. I wanted there to be no space between us, so I didn't know where I ended and he began.

I wanted to be consumed by him.

"This is your last chance to stop this," he whispered, nuzzling my neck with his nose, his breath sending shivers straight to my clit.

I sucked in a breath, but words didn't escape. He gazed into my eyes as his hands lifted to touch me. They were wide and rough, gripping my hips with authority. Hoisting me up, he placed me on the counter between the two sinks, spreading my legs open so he could step between them.

Absolutely nothing inside of me wanted to stop this.

We were on a crash course headed for ultimate annihilation, and I had no desire whatsoever to stop it.

This man would wreck me, and I willingly threw off my seatbelt as I beckoned him nearer, cursing myself for not wearing a skirt.

The sexy bad boy leaned into my space, his hot breath fanning against me. I was weak to stop him as he nipped my neck, leaving a trail with his teeth along my collarbone. My arms ached to reach out and touch him, but the last shred of self-preservation I had reminded me I'd be a goner if I did.

His calloused hands brushed my legs, moving under my shorts. His fingers teased my panties, grazing the thin material as he stared into my eyes, watching me. When I didn't stop him, he moved my panties out of the way. One second he gently skimmed my clit, and the next, he plunged his thick digit into my core. My back arched as my head fell against the mirror, my hips bucking up to meet him.

There was no way to hide the fact I was soaking wet for him.

A loud moan left me as my hands, no longer able to stay down, gripped his shoulders. My nails dug into his skin as I held him, his thick finger moving in and out of me with ease. I was so aroused by him and this encounter that it was almost embarrassing.

"That soft weasel of a boy doesn't deserve your honey. You need a man who knows how to wring out pleasure in you until you can no longer walk."

Gasping, I knew I needed to say something, but his

thumb stroked across my clit, making me speechless outside of my moans. His hot mouth landed on my skin, and I held him to me as he sucked. My body quaked, my pussy quivering with need as it begged for something more to fill it.

Too quickly, I came, my hips jerking around his fingers as I rode out my orgasm. He withdrew slowly, a smirk growing and making him even more ruggedly handsome, if possible.

"Now, at least you'll have something to think about when you're pretending to enjoy your vanilla sex with the weasel." He stepped back; his eyes focused on me as he placed his fingers in his mouth, sucking them dry.

He never broke eye contact as he walked to the door, winking before he unlocked it and stepped outside, and leaving me in a whimpering heap on the counter.

A second later, the door flew open, and a woman entered, eyeing my position. Sliding off, I fixed my clothes and washed my hands, needing the cool water to reground me again.

When I glanced in the mirror this time, my eyes glittered with excitement; the fierceness had returned tenfold.

Drying my hands, it wasn't until I turned to leave that I spotted his parting gift. Right on the top of my left breast was a giant hickey. One that had clearly not been there before. Shit.

He was either sending me a message or daring me to try to explain it if I went through with the weasel—I mean, Patrick.

I had to hand it to him, and not just because he had excellent fingers, but because he'd made it almost impossible for me to continue down my path tonight.

If I went through with it, I'd be thinking about him just like he suggested. And if I didn't, he won, successfully distracting me from my pursuit. Either way, the man without a name made sure his face was the last one I saw tonight.

The sad part was I was too high off my orgasm to care.

Strolling out of the bathroom, I headed for the front door, my eyes sweeping across the bar but not spotting Mr. Magic Fingers.

Patrick waited outside the door, sighing in relief when I exited. I smiled, debating my next move. Torn, I decided I didn't want to be a dick tease and looped my arm in his.

"Lead the way," I giggled, falling back into my role.

As Patrick fumbled through the next twenty minutes, I cursed Mr. Magic Fingers for making me replay our bathroom encounter in order to pretend I enjoyed it. Patrick lasted longer than I'd given him credit for, but had been a total bore otherwise.

Kissing his cheek as he drifted to sleep, I quickly dressed and pulled out my phone, hopeful I could catch Lacey or Joy with their evening endeavors. I needed a distraction.

Holland: Anyone need an extra hand?

Joy: Nope. I'm already back at our place with the goods and contacted Rose for drop-off.

Lacey: I could. He was harder to drug than I expected. Just now getting it set up for pics. I'm afraid he'll wake up at this point.

Holland: On my way!

I practically skipped my way toward the stairs to head toward Lacey in room 230. *This* was what I needed to end the night—ruining a man's reputation.

Knocking on the door, I slipped inside quietly as she opened it. I could've used my keycard, but it was always better not to leave a trail.

"Come on, I have it set up. If you can take the pictures, that will help speed up the process."

I walked into the room decorated like a Vegas casino, laughing at the irony. The middle-aged man was naked on the bed, a mirror of white dust and some empty bottles of tequila spread out next to him. Lacey pulled on a red wig and hid her face as she lay next to him in lingerie.

Making sure there wasn't anything to identify her by, I snapped a few photos, blurring out her body.

"Got it. Clean up, or leave it, so he panics?" I asked, sending the photos to the contact through the app.

"Eh, leave it. It's always fun to watch them panic."

Snorting, I helped her dress and wiped down the room for any of her fingerprints. We'd do a thorough cleaning tomorrow morning too, but we didn't want to leave anything behind just in case he called someone before we got to it.

Walking out with Lacey, I wrapped my arm around her, feeling lighter than I had an hour ago.

"So, are you going to tell me about the giant hickey on your boobie, or are you going to make me beg?" she teased, poking me in the side.

"Oh boy. Do I have a story to share! Let's wait until we're home. Joy will want to hear this, too."

Giggling, I was glad to have these two in my life, knowing I'd never be alone as long as we were together.

CHAPTER 4
QUENTIN

After leaving the women's bathroom, I couldn't focus on my subject anymore, so I left.

Not that the guy I'd been observing had been all that interesting, to begin with. He'd nursed the same beer for an hour and ate the free peanuts the bar placed out. He didn't talk to anyone or even glance at a single soul while there.

David Johns was a true loner, but I didn't think that made him a killer. Not a sophisticated one, at least.

I'd been about to head back when she had walked in and sent my world upside down.

Focusing on the brick wall of the building, I pressed my knuckles into the ridges, relishing the pain as it gradually eased the lust.

That damn woman had me under a spell.

I'd broken protocol following her into that bathroom and leaving my post. But something about her had me walking toward that door before I knew what I was doing.

Blood dripped down my knuckles, and I pulled back, staring at it. Most people didn't like the sight of blood, but for me, it was calming. Living the life we did, blood reminded me I was still alive.

"You all right, man?" a voice asked from my left.

"Yeah," I grunted, not looking up to see who it was. It didn't matter, anyway. I wouldn't remember their faces once I left this town.

Shoving my hands into my pockets, I took off in the opposite direction of the voice, hoping to avoid any further conversations.

I didn't like to talk to people. They expected too much and confused things. It was easier in my line of work if they were just an obstacle to avoid.

The gravel crunched under my boots, the sound loud in the quiet night. The sounds of the bar faded away the further I walked, reminding me I was alone.

Our job wasn't for the faint of heart. We traveled more than we stayed places, always on the go. The only two people I cared about were with me, and some days, even that was questionable when Grady got in his moods.

This job suited me, though, and it was the reason I stayed.

But lately, I felt that itch under my skin when things became too much to process. The job wasn't distracting me the way it typically did, feeling that void within. I'd grown bored with the chase; all the perps were too easily caught and dealt with lately. Outside of the last mission. That had been a clusterfuck.

But the fact remained, I needed something more. I just didn't know what that was yet.

My phone buzzed, pulling me from my spiral of thoughts. Lifting it to my ear, the smell of the pink temptress filled my nose, bringing my lust straight back to the forefront, and my cock hardened against my leg.

"Q, you there?" Max asked, reminding me I'd answered my phone.

"Yeah." I didn't elaborate, mostly because I was unable to. I'd stopped in my tracks, the hotel a few blocks away.

"Did you discover anything?" he asked. Suddenly, I was paranoid he'd been spying on me through cameras or listening through my phone.

"Excuse me?" I growled, the thought of him watching me with my pink-haired temptress upsetting. But not in the way I expected.

Shove that thought far back.

"David Johns. Was he there?" I heard shuffling. "His house was dark, and I completed the surveillance there. So, I'm back at the hotel already. Grady hasn't checked in yet, so I hoped it meant one of you had found him."

Exhaling, I remembered I was supposed to be on a hunt and not distracted by pussy.

But fuck, it had been top-grade pussy.

"It's not him," I said, not offering an explanation.

"Damn. Okay, you headed back?" he asked, something shifting in his voice as it went higher.

"Yeah." I hung up, his voice replaying in my head as I attempted to decipher what it was about.

When you spent all your time with two people, you tended to pick up on their quirks. Like earlier with

Grady, I knew he was hiding something, and now with Max, something was on his mind.

Sighing, I pushed my pink temptress to the side and marched the rest of the way to the hotel. Despite what most people believed about me, my role in this team included being the team communicator. While most people found that funny since I said the least amount of words possible and often wore a scowl, it was true.

I was selective with my words, but it didn't negate the fact I was excellent at getting my meaning across. Most people hid what they were saying in flowery messages and subterfuge. I'd learned at an early age how to dig through the bullshit and find the true meaning of what they were saying without really saying it.

It seemed stupid to waste time and words, so I didn't.

Now, no one could bullshit me. I was the ultimate BS detector, making me a valuable team member when finding bad guys and keeping us together as a unit.

Though sometimes, I loathed my role.

Being attuned to your teammates' emotions 24/7 was exhausting. It was probably why I locked mine away so much. It was more comfortable to focus on theirs and ignore my own.

And that was too much deep shit for me tonight. Time to shove it into the recesses of my mind and focus on Max.

The hotel lobby was quiet as I passed through, with only a few patrons sitting around the bar area as the TV blared the local news. No one of interest stood out, so I kept walking toward the elevator. It arrived instantly, and I stepped in, hitting the floor for our rooms.

Leaning back against the wall, my face became distorted in the reflective surface across from me. Something was different about my face, but I couldn't put my finger on it.

The door opened, dispelling my contorted face, and I brushed off the weirdness of the encounter. Within a few feet, I was at the door of our suite, pulling my key out of my back pocket. The card slid in smoothly, beeping as the door unlocked. The door stopped an inch open, and I smiled, glad Max had followed protocol.

His feet pattered toward the door a moment later, and the door fell closed as he disengaged the locks from the other side. When he opened the door, I slid in and immediately grabbed him by the throat and shoved him up against the wall. He let out a slight whimper, his eyes wide as he stared at me.

"What did you do wrong?" I growled, stepping closer into his space and pressing our bodies flat together. Max licked his lips as he tried to think. I flexed my hand around his throat, his pupils dilating at the pressure.

"I didn't check it was you," he gasped, and I released some of the pressure.

"One of these days, you're not going to check, and someone's going to shoot you in your trusting face. Is that what you want?"

My breathing was heavy as I pictured stepping into a room with Max on the ground, a pool of blood around him. I squeezed my eyes closed at the image.

"No-o-o," he stuttered, shaking his head. "I'm sorry, Q. I'll do better," he wheezed, his body vibrating against mine.

Letting go of his throat, I stomped away, needing some space between us before I crossed a line. Slamming the door to the bathroom, I leaned against the counter as I tried to regulate my breathing.

It was too late, though, and a panic attack seized me as flashbacks pounded my brain, not letting me forget what happened to people I cared about.

Blood coated the floor, and my feet slipped on it as I raced through the house, calling out for my mother. A man stood over her prone body, a blood-slicked knife in his hand. A hood covered his face, casting it into shadow. I froze, my steps faltering as I took in the scene.

My lip began to tremble as I realized my mother was dead.

The hooded figure stood slowly, keeping me in his sight. Backing away, he retreated, not dropping my eyes until he came to the door.

The whole time I'd been frozen in his trance, watching... waiting... The moment he turned, the spell was broken, and I raced to my mother's body. She was still warm, blood sputtering out of her mouth. Gripping her hand, I cried, begging her to stay with me.

"Mommy, don't go. Mommy, no. Mommy, I need you."

Her hand squeezed mine slightly, my eyes jumping to hers. I leaned forward, praying she'd tell me what to do. Instead, she whispered her last words, the name of the family responsible.

The name that haunted my dreams and life still to this day.

The Savages.

The most ruthless, cutthroat mercenary family of my generation.

And they'd killed my mother.

I didn't know much as an eight-year-old child, but I knew I wouldn't stop until I avenged her death. It was the defining moment in my life that I held onto with everything I had. It both terrified and spurred me onward toward my goal.

It was why I didn't get close to people, knowing what the future held for me—nothing but blood.

The guys understood the score, both on this team for their own reasons with the Savages. But it hadn't stopped me from caring about them, and occasionally, my need to protect them would be triggered, sending me into a tailspin.

But especially Max, my brain whispered.

Ripping off my clothes, I staggered into the open shower, turning on the water and not caring what temperature it was. I needed to shock my system and regain my composure.

The cold water beat down on my skin, stinging me as it ran over my corded muscles. The scars I'd earned from years of training and combat seemed to rise, reminding me of who I was.

I wasn't that timid little boy, too frozen in his fear to stop the man from murdering his mother. No, I was a lethal weapon sent out to destroy those who considered themselves above the law.

I'd become the nightmare.

Shivering, I regained my footing in the present, sucking in a large gulp of air. Water ran over every inch of me, washing away the last remains of my panic and fear.

I couldn't allow myself to feel those emotions anymore. They were a weakness I wouldn't accept.

Turning off the shower, I stood there as my body dripped water, shuddering from the cold temperature. Slowly, I turned, finding a towel extended toward me.

I wasn't surprised Max was there. I'd heard him enter when the shower started, but I'd been too caught up in controlling my emotions to do anything about it.

And now, I was too exhausted to yell at him. Something he knew all too well.

"I'm sorry, Q. I'd followed your progress on the app, so I knew it was you. But I still should've checked. It could be a decoy. I'll be more careful. I promise," he whispered, his voice soothing my raw nerves.

Nodding, I allowed him to help me dry off, my limbs too exhausted from the imaginary battle they'd fought to disagree.

Max was gentle, taking great care to be soothing as he patted me dry. When he was done, he handed me some clothes and helped me dress in black sweatpants and a black tank. Like a zombie, I followed his prompting, too dazed to fight.

He handed me a toothbrush, and I automatically brushed my teeth, spitting when I was done. Next, he placed the mouthwash into my hand, lifting it up to my mouth. The sting of the mint helped me focus, and part of my brain returned online.

When everything was done, he scooped up my old clothes and shoes, took my cell phone out of my jeans, and handed it to me. With his free hand, he clasped mine and dragged me out into the hideous suite.

"Fucking Alamo," I mumbled, hating everything about this room and place. The fact we hadn't been able to ID our guy yet or find any lead was weighing on me. The only thing that had saved this place was my pink-haired temptress, and it was doubtful I'd ever see her again.

Max chuckled at my displeasure, sitting me on the edge of the bed. He walked over to the minibar, pulled out two beers, and returned next to me on the bed.

"Here." He handed me the opened bottle, not saying anything else. This wasn't the first time I'd had a panic attack; this dance was familiar between us.

Taking a sip, I focused on the cold beverage as it traveled down my throat, the hops and citrus flavors rolling over my tastebuds. I kept drinking it until my limbs felt a little less tense, my body relaxing into the bed.

"That one lasted longer," he whispered, keeping his voice calm and mellow.

Grunting, I lifted the beer, finishing the last half in one go.

"Thanks," I grumbled when I was done, knowing he didn't have to put up with me, but so grateful he did. Max was my solid ground.

"Come on; we can discuss the case in the morning."

Gently, he pried the bottle from my fingers, guzzling the last of his as he placed them in the recycling. I sat, waiting on the edge, my body numb as the alcohol whirled through it.

Max took my hand and helped me under the covers before turning off the lights and crawling under himself.

"Is the door locked?" I asked, my body beginning to tense up again when I realized I hadn't checked.

"Yes." His warm hand landed on my arm, soothing me back down with his touch. "We're safe. Get some rest, Q."

Turning on my side, I closed my eyes, trying to do as he suggested, but my mind was too busy with thoughts.

In his infinite wisdom, Max wrapped his body around mine, locking me to him and finally allowing my mind to settle.

It wasn't until the moment before I fell asleep that I remembered something had been off with him.

CHAPTER 5
HOLLAND
xoxo

Despite trying to forget my encounter with the bathroom bad boy, I couldn't get him out of my head. Nor had I forgotten the mysterious man from the elevator with the sad eyes. Both men lingered in my mind, causing me to zone out and lose myself in the moment.

My phone pinged, drawing me out of my man haze. XOXO—the app we'd developed to monetize our FSK deeds—had a new notification.

Joy created the coding, Lacey the graphics, and I contributed the math for the algorithm. The idea came to us when we decided to branch out our game and use it to add to our "Get out of Foolshope fund." It had proven to be more successful than we ever could've imagined.

Clicking on the notification, I scanned through the newest entries. After a few failed attempts when we hadn't researched the requests, we added a section that ran a basic background check so we didn't find ourselves in any other sticky situations.

We might murder people, but we had morals.

"I need your help," I read aloud, stopping what I was doing to sit down. My eyes scanned the message, my heart racing as I read the rest to myself.

My family's dangerous. They hurt people for fun, not caring who anyone is. In all honesty, they scare me. If I wasn't the daughter of the president, my life would've already been over.

I'm not like them. I can't hurt anyone.

There have been so many times that I've feared for my life, only to have my father spare me at the last second. He's determined to marry me off, using me to advance his pursuits. It won't be a marriage of love.

I'll be beaten, raped, and killed.

It's not the future I want.

Nor do I think I can do the things they'll expect of me.

I'm desperate. I don't know if you can even help me, but I had to try.

I overheard my father talking about a new group, one that seemed to be morally gray. I'm hoping that means you have a conscience or a soul and don't kill for the thrill of it, like the men in my father's organization. It took my friend a while to track you down, and I hope this plea doesn't fall on deaf ears.

I guess… I guess I hope you won't turn around and sell me out to my father.

You're my last chance to escape. I just need something to change. To get out of here.

If you think you can help me, I can give you $50,000 once it's done.

I hope to hear something from you soon, if not, I'm sure you'll read about me in the papers.

Sincerely,

A hopeless Savage

"Yo, Holland! You going to clean anything today?" Lacey shouted, causing me to jump.

In the process, I dropped the phone, and it skidded across the floor. Standing, I ran to grab it, but Lacey beat me to it.

"You looking at nudes?" She chuckled, checking out the screen. When she didn't see a penis like she'd expected, she frowned and looked up at me once she read through it. "What is this?"

I shrugged, taking the last step to take my phone back. "It sounds like someone who needs help. I just don't know with what."

Lacey tilted her head, tapping her lip as she thought. "Let's discuss it with Joy. Something about it calls to me."

"Yeah, same. I... I dunno." I shook my head, confused at what I was feeling. Lacey pulled me from the bed and dragged me to the cart. She handed me a bottle of cleaner and a rag, pushing me toward the bathroom.

"Your turn!" she sang, laughing as I stomped away.

As I cleaned the bathroom, the message kept replaying over and over in my head. I didn't even know what they wanted.

Kidnapping? Not in our wheelhouse.

Kill their father? While we did that, I wasn't sure we could pull it off if her family was a group of ruthless killers.

In the big leagues of murderers, we were still in the Pee Wees.

I felt as hopeless as the poster, but I wanted to do something.

I might not know this girl, but I knew her emotions. I'd felt them. Hell, I'd lived them. In a way, Lacey and Joy had as well. It was why we did what we did, so we wouldn't ever have to feel that way again.

Knowing there was someone out there in the same position with no way out made me want to find one. I just wasn't sure how.

Finishing up, I picked up the trash and walked out of the bathroom. Lacey and Joy were also done, and we made our way out of the room.

"Did you tell Joy?" I asked as we moved on to the next room.

"Tell me what?" Joy chirped, smacking my butt.

"Here. It's easier if you read it." I handed her my phone, and the app opened to the message. Lacey and I knocked on the next door. It surprised me when it opened a crack, and a cute guy was standing there. His dark hair was ruffled, his emerald eyes wide as he stared at me.

"Housekeeping. Do you need anything? We can come back later if it's a bad time," I offered, stepping back to move on to the next room since most people dismissed us.

"Wait!" he said, shutting the door to unlock it before opening it wider. Lacey and Joy gave me a knowing look, wiggling their eyebrows before stepping to the side.

"Yes?" I asked, smiling.

The door opened, and he came into full view. He had on a graphic tee, flannel shirt, and dark jeans with holes in the knees. His brown hair was messy, sweeping down into his eyes a little. He gave a little smile, the sweetness of it catching me by surprise. He was one of the men I'd spotted in the lobby yesterday. One I'd been drawn to.

"Oh, um, could we get some extra towels?" he asked, fidgeting.

"Absolutely." Smiling, I reached down and grabbed a stack of towels, pulling a few of the shampoos and soaps as well. "Here you go," I said, turning to give them to him.

In my exuberance, the soaps tilted, sliding off the cotton. Moving forward, I attempted to grab them with my other hand, shifting my weight. The cute guy seemed to have the same idea, and we bumped heads, causing the entire stack of towels and soaps all to topple to the ground.

"Shit, I'm so sorry. I was trying to help," he said, rubbing his head. "Are you okay?" he asked, leaning forward.

We'd both crouched down in the exchange, our bodies imperceptibly closer at this angle. His hand brushed against my temple where we'd bumped, his fingers soft against my skin. It was electrifying, sending sparks through me at his gentle care.

"I'm okay," I whispered, something weird coming over me. I felt more shy and unbalanced in his presence than I had in years, and I didn't know why.

We stared at one another, our eyes locked in a battle I wasn't sure how to win.

"You okay there, Holland?" Lacey asked, stepping back toward the cart from the other room. Her voice broke whatever spell we'd fallen under. I cleared my throat, blinking as I stood.

"Yeah, just dropped something."

The cute guy stood slower, a little more on edge now that Lacey was here. I didn't like it for some reason. Was he suspicious of us, or was he hiding something he didn't want her to know? Either way, it was curious and something I needed to remember.

"Let's try this again. Here are the towels and a few extras," I said, smiling, though it didn't reach my eyes this time.

"Thanks… Holland, was it?" he asked.

I nodded, casting my eyes to Lacey. She winced, throwing her hands up as she backed away so she wouldn't accidentally give any other info away.

"Yeah. And you are?" I figured if he got to know my name, then I should know his.

"Max." His whole face lit up as he grinned at me, his green eyes twinkling. I liked how the edges of his eyes crinkled, a sign of a lot of smiling. I didn't know what it felt like to smile that much, to be that carefree with my grins.

"Well, Max, maybe I'll see you around if you're here for a while." I winked, turning back to the cart. As I pushed it to the next room, I couldn't help but put a little extra sway into my step, shaking my butt.

"I'd like that," he called after.

I couldn't stop myself from glancing back, finding him partially in the hall as he watched me. His eyes met mine, making me think he'd been looking at me, and not my butt. Huh.

Giving him a little finger wave, I headed through the propped door of the next room, needing some space between me and the sweet guy who unraveled me with a smile.

Leaning against the wall of the next room, I took a few minutes to breathe, wanting to cool my cheeks before I faced my friends. Not that it mattered, since they immediately started teasing me as I entered the Frozen Tundra, otherwise known as the Viking suite.

"Oooh, someone has a crush," Joy sang as she made the bed.

"He's cute in that boy-next-door kind of way," Lacey added. "Is he getting added to the list?" She lifted her eyebrow, waiting for me to respond.

I shrugged, picking up the discarded towels and trash. I went about my job, refilling things as I thought about what she'd asked and how I couldn't answer.

Was it because of Mr. Magic Fingers?

Or perhaps Max was someone I didn't know if I

could fuck and pretend to be someone I wasn't? He had a way of looking into my eyes and seeing my soul. I was worried if he looked too closely, he'd find all the dark and twisted things I'd done in my life in order to survive and wouldn't like me then.

Though that wasn't entirely accurate. It hadn't always been merely to survive. A certain percentage of me enjoyed punishing bad people, stealing from the corrupt, and fucking without feelings. It kept things clean and simple. I only had two people I cared about in my life, and they were in this room.

"So, should I reach out to our hopeless savage?" I asked, wanting to change the subject.

"Might as well. Never hurts to get more information. In the meantime, we need to pick our next three for the week. Who are the contenders?" Lacey asked, pulling out her tablet.

Joy kept dusting, ensuring not to touch any of the occupant's belongings. She was humming a song, almost like she was in her own world.

"There were three kill requests," I said, keeping an eye on Joy. I had a feeling I knew which one would make the list this week, but as part of our rules, I read them all off to be voted on. "The first is for a cheating boyfriend. The requester wants him to lose an appendage."

"My favorite type," Lacey said, rubbing her hands together. The sound caught Joy's attention, and she turned, looking between us.

"What did I miss?" she asked, blinking her big eyes.

"A reverse pig in a blanket. I haven't gotten to the other two yet."

"Ah, those are always fun," Joy said, chuckling. She sat in the chair next to the bed, motioning for me to continue.

"The second one concerns a woman whose boss continues to deny her request for time off so she can take her sick child to his chemo appointments."

"What a bitch. I'd do that one for free," Joy said, sitting forward. I had a feeling she'd feel that way. She had a penchant for sick kids, having been one herself.

"She just wants her boss to have some payback. Her car towed, her identity stolen, suddenly gets bed bugs, etc." I shrugged. "The basic bitch package."

"So, what's the last one? These have both been usual winners, which means the last one has to be a doozy for you to leave it," Lacey surmised, eyeing me as she typed in her notes.

"You know me," I said, smiling until I remembered the request. "A flying-the-coop request came in. A woman's husband continues to beat her every time she tries to leave, to the point she doesn't know if she can. We're her last hope before she takes things into her own hands and ends her life. We need to fake her death and help her escape with a new identity."

They both cursed, sitting forward. "What do we know?"

I filled them in on the details that had been sent over. As we finished the last of the room, we created a system to dig for more information so we could do all of them. Taking on multiple jobs at one time meant we all had to agree and have a solid plan in place or risk making an error. And mistakes got you killed, caught, or hurt.

We'd be busy over the next few days, drilling in the reality of our lives. Murdering schemes didn't leave extra time for relationships, and why fucking was part of the list. So, I pushed thoughts of cute nerdy guys, bathroom bad boys, and mysterious elevator men aside so I could focus on my job.

I was a serious businesswoman, after all—even if it was at murdering people.

CHAPTER 6
MAX

Placing the new towels on top of the other ones, I picked up the shampoo and conditioner, smiling at them. When I realized I was grinning at hair care products, I stopped, trying to control my face.

But *she'd* given them to *me*, and that was something. Women didn't often notice me, so the fact she'd flirted back had felt nice.

Pocketing them, I decided to hide them so Q wouldn't know I opened the door. Not that he could have ignored the beautiful woman standing there, either. It was just easier sometimes to follow Quentin's rules. It kept us safer, which was important in our line of work.

As I fiddled with the bottles, I knew it was something more than that. For the first time in our friendship, I wanted to keep something purely for me.

Q had been my best friend for so long that it was hard to remember a time when he didn't know everything about me. It was a blessing and a curse. I sometimes worried he only saw me as that scrawny kid who needed him as a protector, not the man I'd grown into.

There was something about Holland that felt special, and I wanted to protect it. Not listen to him ruin it by listing all the cons of why it would never work. Why relationships weren't for us.

I couldn't help being the only hopeless romantic in our group, refusing to hook up with strangers in every town we traveled to like they often did. Or at least, I assumed they had. It wasn't like we sat around and talked about our sexual conquests.

Sighing, I sat back on the bed, pulling the longest relationship I'd ever had onto my lap—my MacBook. My computer had never failed me, and I could always count on code to lead me to the right answer.

"Alright, psycho killer, time to set a trap and see if we can get you to come out of hiding."

First, I checked the locations of Grady and Quentin, finding them still at the local attractions they'd chosen to investigate for the day. This town was so odd, but I liked it in a weird way. It had a unique concept, making it more alluring than most cities, even if their best attraction was a massive toilet bowl.

Scouring my database, I still couldn't figure out how this person picked his victims. They ranged from young to old, men to women, and covered all socioeconomic backgrounds. The only common factor we could identify was that they were all despicable human beings. From child abusers, rapists, to drug addicts, the world was a better place without them around.

Which was why we were here in this odd town of Foolshope. Someone taking the law into their hands and bestowing their own form of justice was dangerous. It was only a matter of time before other people discovered what this person was doing and wanted to use them for their own gain.

The pressure to successfully secure this person was insurmountable. It was our last chance to prove to our boss we were ready to take on the Savages.

"You like bad people, so let's see how bad I need to be," I mumbled into the quiet room, typing in a few things onto a dark web message board. I didn't know how to get this guy's attention, otherwise.

> User19740: My usual haunt has become dry as of late. I'm headed to Foolshope. Does anyone know if there are any circles? I'll pay top dollar. I like them young.

Shuddering, I worried I'd give myself nightmares from this message board alone. I had a bot running to scour them and find users we needed to monitor. It saved me from reading through some despicable things I wouldn't be able to get out of my head and cut my time in half. I was filtering through some of the lines of code when a message popped up.

> User89173: I know someone. They will only meet if you can show proof of what you're requesting. A trade per se. They don't want to be set up.

> User19740: Whatever they need.

User89173: I'll reach out and get back to you for a fee.

They signed off, and I realized my heart was pumping. My hands shook slightly, and sweat had beaded along my brow. This was why I often stayed behind the computer. I wasn't good when it came to interacting with people. Taking a deep breath, I rechecked the guy's location to ensure I still had time to research. Finding them both still where they said they'd be, I closed out the dark web browser I'd been in and opened a new one.

The other night, I'd finally stumbled upon something. I'd been digging more and more into the Savages, hoping to find something new to use against them. Grady and Quentin wouldn't approve—especially Q— citing it was too dangerous, so I kept my search quiet.

But then I discovered something. I just wasn't sure if I could use it or not. Was our vengeance worth ruining an innocent's life?

I could hear Q asking how innocent a Savage could be, but I had a feeling even he would hesitate at this one. At least, I hoped.

Ava Savage, age 17, daughter to Alec Savage—known to most as Viper, head of the Savages.

Viper was the leader of the Savages and the man who'd killed Q's mom, my uncle, and Grady's fiancé. Camila had been his last victim before taking over as head of the family. We all had a reason to hate the Savages, especially Viper, but was this too far? It felt like it was.

I worried Q and Grady wouldn't think so. They were often singularly focused on their revenge, assuming once the Savages were gone, they'd feel better.

But I knew nothing would bring back the people we loved, and killing a teenage girl felt a step too far over the line into Savage territory.

Staring at Ava's social media page, I couldn't help but wonder how she fit into that world. She looked sweet. She played the flute and supported her local animal shelter. While there were several pictures of her with kids her age, she never looked like she belonged. More like she was there, but not part of the group.

I could relate to that.

Until I met Q, I'd always been on the outside, looking in. And often, the punching bag to anyone bigger.

Her dark eyes held the truth, and I didn't believe she was anything like the rest of her family. Just another victim of the Savages.

Which was why I hadn't shared this information yet.

Would they hesitate or just go after her to prove a point to Viper?

If they did, I didn't know if it was something I could live with.

I wanted to trust and believe in my team to be better, but we'd all been hurt by this man, and it would be the easiest way to pay retribution. But would it make us any better than him in the end? I didn't want to gain vengeance just to lose my soul.

The door beeped open, catching as the deadbolt activated. Closing my browser, I wiped my history and put my computer away before hopping off the bed and headed to the door. I peered through it, despite knowing it had to be Q.

"Password?" I asked, just to be an asshole.

"Dickwad," Q grunted, though I could tell he was pleased.

Pushing the door closed, I unlocked the deadbolt and chain, opening it with a smile. "Hey, you find anything?" I asked.

He didn't answer, moving forward to make me step into the room. Once he was clear, he locked the door back, headed to the adjoining door, and opened it. Grady stood waiting there.

I took my place on the bed, picking up my laptop, not offended he hadn't answered. That was Q. He'd tell us both when he was ready. Settling back with the device on my lap, I realized I didn't know how to act without it in front of me. Not only was it my longest relationship, but my computer was also my security blanket.

"Any updates from Jackson?" Grady asked, stepping into his leadership role.

"Nope. Nothing else in the chatter, either. I set the trap and got a potential bite. I should know more later."

"Good. The toilet bowl was a bust. I followed

suspect number five all day, and he showed no signs of suspicious behavior. He was just out with his family. He might be sleeping with the nanny, but I don't think he's our guy. Q?"

"Nothing," he said, not elaborating. Grady accepted it, knowing by now that if Q had anything to share, he would. Otherwise, his words were few. I was the only one he really talked to, and even then, it was scarce he shared real information. Typically, he berated me for not following some rules he'd set.

"So, we're still stuck on square one with no potential suspect. This guy is even better than I anticipated," Grady grumbled. His brow furrowed as he concentrated on something, rubbing his chin.

"What's our next move?" I asked, wanting to know the plan for the day. A hopeful part of me was eager to leave this room so I could bump into Holland again. It was unlikely I was her type, but she'd seemed interested and had flirted. It was enough to make me wonder if she was thinking about me.

"Let's hold tight until you hear back from the contact. Maybe if we lie low, he'll come out and leave a breadcrumb."

"Does that mean we have the night off?" Q asked, surprising Grady and me.

"Yeah, sure. Just don't cause a scene or get arrested. I'm not bailing you out if you do."

Quentin rolled his eyes, but I caught the corners of his mouth as they twitched. He was up to something. Or, more than likely, *someone*.

"Sure thing, chief."

"It's nice to see you showing some respect," Grady quipped, slapping Q on the shoulder as he walked back to his room.

If people actually ever saw all three of us together, they'd probably think we had a dysfunctional relationship. And perhaps it was, but when you were in the business that we were, the only type of relationships that tended to last weren't all that functional.

Grady paused before he closed the door, peering at us both in the eyes. "Be safe."

We didn't respond, the notion foreign to Q to do anything other than be safe. But I knew it was Grady's way of saying he cared. Just like with Q and his ridiculous procedures for safety.

"You going out?" I asked once the door shut, and it was just the two of us.

"Maybe. You?" he asked, assessing me closely.

"I was thinking of checking out the local pub."

"You're hiding something," he narrowed his eyes, moving from the wall.

My cheeks heated, and I shook my head no, despite knowing he was right and wouldn't stop until he discovered something. In an attempt to throw him off, I blurted out the first thing I could think of.

"I met a girl!"

Quentin stopped his forward progress, staring at me, frozen in his tracks. It would be hurtful if it wasn't so comical to watch. "A girl?"

"Yeah." I nodded and swallowed, begging my heart

to slow. "I don't know if she'll be at the pub, but I figured it was a good start."

"What's her name?" he asked, crossing his arms as he continued to assess me.

"Holland."

That stopped him; the name apparently too unique for me to have made it up on the spot.

"What does she look like?"

I smiled as I leaned back on the bed. "She has hair that's somewhere between the color of the sun and lightning. Her eyes are as green as the grass, and her smile makes my heart race. I met her today, and she didn't make me stutter all over myself. She flirted, and it was easy. I don't know; there's just something magical about her."

Quentin kept staring at me, making me nervous. I licked my lips, hoping he had bought it.

"I'll go with you. We'll leave in thirty." He headed to his suitcase, grabbed a different black shirt, and walked to the bathroom. I sighed in relief, happy I'd been able to ward him off for now.

"Oh, and Max, I know there's something else. You said you'd met her today, but something was bothering you last night. So, let me know when you're ready to spill the beans."

The door shut, and I cursed, flopping back on the bed. Why did he have to be so good at reading people? Especially me.

Deciding I'd ignore his statement and hope he'd forget, I changed into a different shirt. Maybe I'd passed for nerdy cool? A few minutes later, Q exited the bath-room and nodded at me as he headed for the door. Grabbing my wallet and phone, I followed as nerves settled into my stomach.

"Stop fidgeting," he said in the elevator.

"I can't help it. She's so pretty and nice."

"Then trust that she likes you."

Groaning, I nodded, following him to the pub a few blocks over. My anxiety ramped up, wondering how stupid I was for expecting her to be there, knowing I'd probably have one beer and be back, settled in the room in thirty minutes.

Stepping through the doors, I froze as I locked eyes with her, and she smiled, making everything in me come to life. Maybe this girl would be different.

"There she is," I whispered, pointing. Quentin followed, taking in Holland as she danced. She spun, staring him in the eyes, and I saw the moment I was screwed.

There had been a flash of heat in both of their eyes.

"Fuck," Q hissed, stomping toward the bar. "We have a problem."

Waving, I tried not to let my smile drop as I approached the bar, my hopes and dreams firmly in Q's hands.

CHAPTER 7
HOLLAND

THE MOMENT MY EYES MET THEIRS, MY PULSE skyrocketed, and my legs trembled. For precisely two seconds, I believed my night was about to get considerably more interesting.

"Shit," I cursed when reality sank in.

How did Mr. Magic Fingers and Max walk in together? Did they know one another? With the way they quickly made their way to the bar, it seemed like they did. Was the bathroom bad boy able to recognize me without the pink hair?

Joy pulled away from the girl she'd been making out with, looking at me with concern. I'd been dancing, avoiding advances from the male population all night while Lacey and Joy got their groove on with their respective partners. I'd been about to call it, not finding much enjoyment when I didn't want to sleep with any of the guys here.

Which was the first red flag of the night. The second was when two of the guys I couldn't quit thinking about walked in together. The third was when Max waved me over, offering to buy me a beer.

His counterpart kept staring, sipping his beer as he watched me. I debated whether I should take my chances or just leave and try again another day.

The magnetic pull between them and me was too much to ignore, though.

"I'll see you girls later," I mumbled, my feet moving toward a terrible idea.

Max kept smiling, though it wasn't quite as bright as when he first spotted me. It had to mean his friend told him about our bathroom adventures. Or maybe he didn't recognize me but was warning him off me. I couldn't blame Mr. Magic Fingers if that was the case. I would probably destroy sweet Max.

Even knowing that was the inevitable end, I kept walking over to them. Max filled me with sunshine, and I enjoyed feeling that warmth.

I just needed to ensure I didn't fly too close and burn my wings.

"Hi, Max," I said when I was closer. I glanced at the bathroom baddie, looking for recognition. His eyes were firmly on me, but I couldn't decide if it was because he recognized me or not.

"Hey, Holland. I'm so glad to run into you," he said, his eyes wrinkling at the corners with his genuineness.

"Oh?" I asked, glancing between the two. "Do you two know each other?" I added, unable to let it go on without knowing.

Max swallowed, then nodded. "Yeah. We work together. This is Quentin. Q, this is Holland."

Quentin. The name suited him. It was dark and

mysterious, just like my bathroom good time. I smiled and decided to see if he'd spill the beans. It seemed like my brattiness reared up when placed in awkward situations.

"It's nice to *officially* meet you, Quentin. And you were right about last night."

"On what?" he asked, one corner of his mouth turning up. He leaned back against the bar, not giving anything away. Max watched us both, his eyes bouncing back and forth as he tried to put the puzzle together.

I winked, grabbing the beer bottle out of Max's hand and taking a sip. "If I have to remind you, you're not the man I thought you were." I turned to Max, putting Quentin at my back, and looped my arms around his neck. "Now, how do you feel about sharing, or are you going to make me choose?"

"Um, what?" Max asked, coughing, his eyes wide. The few sips of alcohol I'd taken warmed me as they traveled through my bloodstream, waking up my libido in the process. All night I'd been bored, not interested in the men around me. And now I knew why. My body wanted things it couldn't have.

So, did I throw caution to the wind and go with it, knowing it would likely end in disaster?

Yeah, why the hell not?

Angling my body so I could see both of them, I set the beer bottle on the counter. The whole time I could feel Quentin's eyes on me, and I watched his smirk grow as his eyes flashed with heat. It helped push me to a decision.

Reaching up, I grabbed Max's neck and pulled him to me. He appeared shocked at the move, falling forward to meet my lips. I kissed him, his lips soft and pliable. I could taste the beer, so I licked him, making him gasp and open more for me.

I'd only intended on shocking him and kissing him briefly, but the more I kissed Max, the more I *kissed* him.

It sounded stupid in my head, but it was precisely what happened. I couldn't bring myself to stop. Max responded tenfold as his hands grasped my waist, and he pulled me closer.

Only when a body pressed to our sides did I remember we were in a bar. Breaking the kiss, I stared at Max, his pupils as fully blown as I expected mine to be. His lips were puffy, his cheeks red, and I couldn't bring myself to look away.

A throat cleared, and we both turned toward it, finding Quentin staring at us with a heated look.

"I knew you were a temptress. I just had no idea you would lead me here."

"Max, are you in?" I asked, ignoring Quentin for a second as I focused on my cute boy next door.

"If it involves you, I'll follow you wherever," he said, clearly smitten and pulling on my heartstrings. I almost got lost in his eyes again, but I remembered the broody bad boy next to us.

"So, what's it going to be, Mr. Magic Fingers? Are

you going to show me your skills outside of the bathroom, or…"

"Or what?" he growled, stepping closer to tip my
chin up, his eyes ensnaring mine.

I sucked in a breath, my mind going blank for a
second. I was losing control of the situation quickly and
needed to find it again.

"Or," I emphasized, "Max's name is the only one I
scream tonight."

Quentin's nostrils flared, his pupils blowing even
more as he stared down at me. His jaw flexed, and I
watched the battle in his eyes. Max's hands tightened
on my hips, his groin bumping into my stomach, the
hardness spurring me on.

Time seemed to stand still; the three of us locked in
that decision.

"Fuck it," Quentin growled, sealing his lips to mine
for a brief second. "Let's go."

Weightlessness overcame me as we moved through
the pub, my feet feeling like they weren't even touching
the floor. The two men surrounded me, making it hard
to gauge where I began and they ended.

It wasn't until the cool night air hit my cheeks that I
registered we'd made it out the door. Max took my
hand, stepping beside me as Quentin led the way. I
watched as he scoured the streets, almost like he was
looking for danger. It was something I usually did, but
not tonight. Not with them.

For the first time since I'd killed a man, I began to
question my actions. What was I doing? I didn't know

these guys. They could be criminals for all I knew. Which was shitty of me to judge them for, but a girl had to look out for herself. Thus, leading me to my next set of racing thoughts.

We hadn't vetted that they were safe. Nor had I told Lacey or Joy where I was going. Could I defend myself between the two of them? Probably not.

Shit. Shit. Shit.

The app might be boring, but at least they were safe.

Panic consumed me, and I stumbled. Max squeezed my hand, pulling me closer to him, and wrapping his warmth around me. The awareness of his presence grounded me, reminding me I felt safe in his arms. As I had with Quentin.

I was being so risky, but I'd also learned to trust my gut, and these guys felt safe to me. I couldn't explain it, but I knew they wouldn't hurt me. Not physically, at least.

My breathing evened out, and I could focus on my surroundings instead of my thoughts as we entered the Secret Keep Inn. I ducked my head to shield my face, not wanting to be seen with guests. It wasn't a written rule—more of an unspoken one. The implicit part was to not get caught.

We took the stairs, that frenzied feeling from the bar building the closer we neared their room and the promise that lay behind it.

"If you're not comfortable, we don't have to do this," Max whispered, shocking me. "I'd be happy just sitting and talking, getting to know you."

Blinking, I was taken aback by his words. Guys never wanted to do that if sex was on the table. I faltered in the middle of the hall, a few doors away from his room.

Quentin paused with us, somehow instinctively knowing.

"As much as I want to hear you scream my name, Temptress, we'll only step through that door if you want to. You have control." His whiskey smell swirled around me, and I knew I trusted him. That his words were sincere.

"I want to." I swallowed. "And Temptress, is it?" I teased, my words full of confidence.

In all my years of taking back control, of writing my own narrative when it came to sex, I'd never felt as assured as I did right here. This was what true control felt like. They valued me, respected my word, and we'd only met. Why weren't more guys like that?

These two men, one soft and one hard, made me feel things bigger than myself.

And yet, there was still one thing missing. I couldn't quite put my finger on what it was or how I could tell, but I knew. There was one more piece to this dynamic.

Despite my head telling me none of this made sense, and it was too fast to feel anything for two strangers—I did. Something extraordinary was brewing between us, and I wanted to uncover it.

In the blink of an eye, I was pulled forward, that weightlessness falling over me again as they dragged me to Max's room. His lips landed on mine, stealing my breath as we fell into the room, a tangle of limbs. Quentin directed us, leading me to the bed, and I fell on it with Max, neither of us breaking apart until the bed dipped and Quentin sat on my other side.

"What are you doing to us, Temptress?" he asked, stroking my hair. It was tender and sweet, something I wasn't accustomed to. A feeling stirred to life, rising up through my abdomen and sprouting in my heart. What? Huh?

"I need to pee!" I shouted, jumping off the bed and racing into the bathroom. At least I knew where it was, having cleaned this room a thousand times. I shut the door, sliding down as I took in some air.

"It's okay. It's sex. You can do that. You want to do that. Leave all the feelings and mushy stuff out," I whispered to myself, hoping to convince my heart to shut up. It didn't get a say in this.

It did not work.

My phone vibrated in my pocket, so I pulled it out, expecting it to be the girls. Except it wasn't. Our contact from the dark web had sent us a group message.

Phantasm: Are you girls being careful?
I'm seeing things that make me think
someone is on to you.

Joy: So careful. We know the rules.

Lacey: What are you seeing?

Phantasm: There was a post today looking for a kiddie circle in your area. I traced it back, and it seems to be connected to an organization. I'm just not sure which alphabet they belong to yet.

Phantasm: On top of that, a mercenary group has been asking questions. The Savages. Have you come across them?

Holland: We got a message but haven't done anything yet.

Phantasm: I'd stay away. You don't want to mess with them or get on their radar. They're ruthless and know no boundaries.

Holland: Isn't that the type of person we should be going after, though? Why we started this?

Phantasm: No one can outrun the Savages. If you pursue it, it will be your death I hear about next.

Joy: Message received. We'll steer clear. Should we worry about the kiddie circle? Is that viable? I thought we got rid of them.

Phantasm: I'll keep digging, but for now, I'd stick to F and S. No more K for the time being.

Lacey: Ah, man. I had so many plans for the reverse pigs-in-a-blanket.

> Phantasm: The amount of pain I feel
> right now is immense. You scare me,
> Lacey.

> Lacey: That's the sweetest thing
> anybody has ever said to me.

> Holland: We'll lie low. Thanks for the
> heads up.

> Phantasm: You know I have your back,
> girls. Be safe.

I was just about to open a chat with Joy and Lacey when another male's voice entered the room, surprising me. I leaned against the door, the acoustics working to my advantage as it carried their voices.

"There you two are. What's the update on our trap for our killer? Any leads on the Savages?" a deep and commanding voice boomed.

I could hear Quentin and Max shushing the owner, making me even more curious about what was happening. What did he mean about a trap? Why would they be looking for a killer? Just who were these guys? And the Savages?

That was the third time I'd heard that name in twelve hours. That couldn't be a coincidence.

Flushing the toilet, I pretended I hadn't heard anything as I stepped into the saloon, ready to play the role of drunk girl.

"Hey, sorry, I think the beer went to my head more than I realized," I slurred, stumbling as I walked to the bed. I swayed, looking up to clock the third man with the deep voice, and instantly froze in his pale blue gaze.

"It's you," he said, sounding breathless.

I glanced around the room; something wasn't adding up. Three guys who had nothing in common yet had captured my attention on three separate occasions. Something was amiss here, and that didn't happen to me. Add in the conversation I wasn't meant to overhear, and it added up to one outcome. I'd been played.

The feeling of trust and safety vanished, and I hardened myself, knowing what I had to do next.

"Do I know you?" I asked, blinking. Turning my head, I looked at Max, knowing if I looked at Quentin, he'd see right through me. I didn't know how I knew he could, just that he would.

"I think I better go. Rain check?" I asked, already backing to the door.

No one said anything, so I took that as my chance to escape. Waving, I hurried out into the hall, my heart bottoming out with each step I took away from them, ignoring the lone tear slipping down my face.

CHAPTER 8
THE SAVAGES

I watched as the blonde girl who'd been with two of the Shadows scampered down the hall, away from their room. I didn't know if she was part of this or an innocent bystander, but I'd keep an eye on her. She could be the opening I'd been waiting for.

She had managed to get between two of the smartest and deadliest agents in the game. Two men I'd been following for a while, waiting for the perfect moment to ruin their lives.

My phone vibrated, and I knew who it was without looking. "Boss."

"Updates?" he asked, not offering any pleasantries. The Viper didn't need to.

"I think so. One in the shape of a blonde bombshell."

"Excellent. Keep me posted. I'm ready to unveil my new venture, and I don't need any Shadows lurking around."

"Understood."

He hung up without saying goodbye. Again, why would he? He was the boss, and I was just the gun.

I watched the blonde bombshell hurry out of the Inn from my perch and followed out of the Inn. I trailed behind her for a few blocks, having to duck and loop back a few times when she appeared to sense me. She hadn't made a direct path to anywhere, leading me to believe she was drunk and lost… or smarter than I'd initially assumed.

She stepped into the all-night diner, meeting two other beautiful women inside. I followed her in, sat at the counter, and ordered a black coffee and pie, smiling to myself as I ate.

This boring town had just gotten a whole lot more interesting. It was time for the Savages to come out and play.

CHAPTER 9
HOLLAND xoxo

I HUNKERED DOWN BEHIND THE BUSH, PRESSING THE binoculars against my face. After I'd come clean with the girls last night about my extracurricular activities, we'd devised a plan to uncover information about the three mysterious strangers who'd snagged my attention.

God, I loved them both. Instead of berating me for being careless, they grabbed a shovel and asked how deep to dig. My besties were simply the best.

We'd been following Boss Man, the one I believed to be in charge. I refused to call him mysterious eyes until I knew more about him. Giving him a cutesy nickname felt more familiar and intimate, and I couldn't have that right now. He was just another mark we were gathering intel on.

Joy had hacked into the Inn's system, discovering the names their rooms were under, but there wasn't one ounce of me that believed he was a Bill. This man had a name that, when you moaned it, you felt it in your toes. No offense to any Bills, but that name just didn't do it for me.

So far, the girls and I had followed him to the laundromat, bank, and now the grocery store. I suspected he knew we were watching and was leading us on a wild goose chase. No one did that many errands while on vacation.

"He's placed a toothbrush, a jug of OJ, and a bag of hot chips in his basket so far," Joy whispered over the comms. We'd figured she drew the least amount of attention in town, so she'd followed BM—okay, a funny nickname didn't count as intimate—all morning. Joy was having fun changing her wig and appearance for each place she went. At least she was entertaining herself.

"Boss Man's on to us," Lacey grumbled. "No one buys those three things together on purpose. OJ and hot chips?" She shuddered. Lacey was perched on the hill with me, the grocery store below us. I was on the lookout to see if the other two joined him. So far, he'd been alone.

"Maybe, but it doesn't mean he won't reveal something. If anything, he's trying to throw us off, which means there's something to hide. He mentioned a trap and the Savages, exactly what Phantasm warned us about minutes earlier. We need to find out more."

"I highly doubt this was what Phantasm meant about lying low," Lacey muttered. I rolled my eyes, used to her attitude. She didn't like to get dirty but was too volatile to tail someone.

"Technically, you're lying high since you're on a hill, and I'm standing low," Joy replied, making me chuckle.

Lacey rolled her eyes, but I caught her smile. Typical Joy swooping in to keep the peace.

"We might have to split up tomorrow and tail the three separately if we don't find anything."

"Are you sure you're not overthinking this?" Lacey asked, turning to me. "It's one of the few times you've liked someone, even if there are three of them. How do we know this isn't a cry for help and you've gone full stalker? Or worse, you're self-sabotaging and blowing it before it becomes anything. There's only room for one of us to do that in our friendship, and I nabbed that fun little defense mechanism back in middle school." She tutted at me, her eyes boring into the side of my face. My cheeks heated, but I kept my focus forward.

"I promise you I'm not doing any of those things. I did like them, but it was the way he said killer and then mentioned the Savages. They're hunting someone, who could very likely be us, and after the same people mentioned on XOXO. It's not a coincidence. You're just crabby we've been out in the sun this long, my little vampire."

Lacey tilted her head, nodding in agreement. "Eh, you might be right. God, I hate the outdoors. Why are there things that can crawl and sting? Seems like a waste. God should've used his skills to make nail polish that doesn't chip or fade and make it instinctual that every man knows how to give good oral sex. I've had enough sloppy tongues for a lifetime. Just one of those things would be better than bugs."

Her body convulsed as I muffled a laugh. Lacey was

one of the toughest people I knew, but put a bug in front of her, and she'd scream and run away crying. I guess we all had that one thing we were scared of.

"It's why you should only get oral from another woman. It's way better," Joy said over the comms, reminding us she was there. "Oh, he's talking to someone. Let me see if I can get closer," she whispered.

"I wish we had eyes inside," I grumbled. I hated not being able to see where Joy was, but since we didn't know his movements, it hadn't been possible to set anything up beforehand. Surveillance outside the building was the best we could do.

"What if they're not the bad guy?" Lacey whispered. I glanced at her out of the corner of my eye, wondering where she was going with this.

"What makes you think they're not?"

She shrugged, picking a leaf off her sweater and jumping back when it fluttered. "You have the best bull-shit detector out of the three of us. If you were genuinely attracted to them, enough to break your rules and let them see your real face *and* know your real name, it has to mean something."

The rebuttal stopped cold on my lips as I let her words penetrate me. Had I? But that would mean… I shook my head, not wanting to entertain *those* thoughts.

"Max and the boss saw me at work. Not like I can hide who I am there. Quentin met me as a persona. I didn't know he knew Max or that they'd come for me that night. And you said my name in Max's presence," I reminded.

She grimaced but didn't stop. "Yeah, but *you* still went back to the Secret Keep with them as yourself."

She had a point there. But it wasn't enough to stop me from figuring out who they were and what they were doing here. I needed to know everything before I could make a decision. It was a flaw, my brain crawling over all the facts and always needing more.

"My BS detector doesn't work anymore. That's how this whole thing started, remember? I thought Calvin was a nice guy, and look where that got me. He tried to rape me and only failed because I'd eaten peanut butter for lunch."

"By nice guy, I think you mean bland and boring," Lacey said, ignoring the rest of my sentence. A man's voice became clearer over the comms, meaning Joy was nearer to him. Zipping my lips, I rolled them in to stop myself from talking. I didn't want to distract Joy. It had nothing to do with hearing his voice.

"Oh wow, that's a long time to live in a town. What's your favorite thing to do here from a local perspective?"

And there it was, that deep, dark, and delicious voice. It rolled through me, traveling down my body to my toes as they curled back from the sound. I pressed my lips harder, not wanting to embarrass myself by moaning in front of the girls.

The other voice was too quiet to pick up everything, but it sounded like Old Man Steve. Lacey tapped my hand, mouthing his name for confirmation. I nodded, pressing the comm further in my ear, hoping to pick up more.

"I'll have to try it out. You seem like a man who knows things, so I was wondering if you could tell me anything about one of the maids at the Inn? I kind of have a thing for her, but I don't know if she's attached to anyone."

"Oh sure, I know everyone," Steve said, clearer now. "Been around the block myself a time or two."

"I had a feeling you would." Boss Man laughed, the sound just as decadent as his timbre, hitting me squarely on the clit; the fucker. I pressed my nails into my palms, making crescent indents. "You got that look about you. I'm sure if I had time, you could tell me a story or two."

Steve chuckled, enjoying this man's attention. Hell, I couldn't blame him. BM was hella sexy. Add in that voice and those eyes, and I was a puddle on the floor. He was the type of person who made you crave them, and you didn't even know why half the time. He was just that dynamic.

But I also felt like he'd make me want to punch his stupid face just as equally, and it excited me more than it should.

With the way he'd worked over Steve so easily, I knew he was a pro. Lacey could say I was overthinking this all she wanted, but gathering information in a small town took skill. And this man had Old Man Steve eating out of his palm. He would likely give this stranger our life story and not even realize it.

"Shit, he's good," I whispered. I tapped the ground, debating how I could thwart his plan. I didn't want him to know anything about me.

"Who is it that's caught your eye? There aren't a lot of available women. Most of the girls marry young, right out of high school, and move out to the bordering counties. The ones that stay, well, I'm sure they have their reasons. But I'm guessing it won't be hard to identify her. There's only a few who work at the Inn."

"She's got white-blonde hair, about this high, and eyes that pierce your soul."

Sucking in a breath, I met Lacey's eyes, shaking my head not to say anything. I couldn't think about his words right now. Not until I knew what he wanted, why he was here. I wouldn't let any man come between the girls and me. Their protection came first.

"Oh, you mean Holland—" Steve stopped, clearing his throat, and I exhaled. "Excuse me; I just remembered I need to feed my neighbor's dog. It was nice talking to you."

"Wait—" Boss Man shouted, the sound growing quieter, and I knew Joy was on the move.

"Thank fuck. I'm assuming you got Steve to stop?" I asked.

"One second. I think he spotted me. I need to shake him," she whispered, my heart rate increasing. A door opened and then closed, a latch falling into place. "Time for a switch-a-roo."

"Lacey, run interference. You're on distraction duty."

"Finally, something fun," she groaned, standing and dusting off the dirt and leaves she'd collected in the grass. She happily trotted down the hill toward the store now that she had a mission. That or she was that excited to get away from the bugs.

"How are you doing, Joy?" I asked once Lacey entered the store. "Lacey's inside. Tell us when you need your window."

"Almost done. Time for baby," she sang. I heard the elastic as she strapped the fake belly on herself. "Okay. I'm ready. Tell me when."

"Now," Lacey whispered before her voice got louder. "Excuse me, why are you creeping into the women's bathroom? That's weird as fuck, man. Security! This man is loitering around the woman's bathroom!" she bellowed.

"No, I'm not. I'm waiting for someone."

"Uh-huh. Waiting for your next victim is more like it. I've seen those TV shows. I listen to true crime podcasts, and you, sir, are everything they warn women like me about."

"Clear," Joy said, a giggle in her voice. "Nice job. I'm almost out of the store."

"Sir, do we have a problem?" another voice asked, who I had to assume was security.

"No, just a simple misunderstanding."

"If by misunderstanding you mean thwarted abduction, then okay, Chad."

"Ma'am, do you have reason to suspect this man?"

"Just look at him! He says he's waiting for the ladies' room. But we all know what that means."

"You can't just accuse people for standing outside a door, ma'am."

"Fine, then I'll go and shop somewhere else where they care about women's safety."

Only a few seconds later, Lacey burst out in giggles as she raced out of the store. Joy was already clear and sitting in the dry cleaning van we'd borrowed.

"That was epic, Lacey. Oh my god, I almost lost it when I exited and saw what you were wearing."

"You should've seen his face. He was distraught and confused. Say what you will, Hols, but that guy seems like a good one."

Lacey climbed into the back of the van as Boss Man appeared. I watched him through the binoculars, wondering if there was any validity to Lacey's words.

He glanced around the parking lot, a crease between his eyes as he scanned it. When he found nothing, his shoulders dropped, and he looked worried. He pulled out a cell phone and made a quick call before walking to a rental car and pulling out of the lot.

I waited another ten minutes before crawling out of my spot and heading to the van. I opened the side door and climbed in, freezing when I spotted Joy and Lacey. A laugh bubbled out of me before I could stop it. They looked ridiculous.

Joy had on a red flowery dress, her fake baby bump on display. She wore a bright red wig with a straw hat. Lacey had placed a cap on her head to conceal her hair.

But what made it funny was the mullet that seemed to be attached to the back of it and the fake teeth she wore.

"You look like *America's Next Top Hillbilly*, and you a *Teen Mom* reject." I laughed, setting them off until the three of us rolled around the back as we cried from laughing too hard.

"Okay, okay," I said, wiping my face. "We know he's definitely looking for me, so I need to lie low for the next few days until we know more."

"Then it's a good thing I put a bug on him, isn't it?" Lacey said, a smug look on her face.

Jumping across the van, I tackled her to the ground in a hug as I kissed her face.

"You're brilliant."

"It's one of the disposable ones that Joy made, so it will only last for twelve hours, but it might give us a little more intel. Especially if he talks more freely without other ears around."

"I love you, guys. Thanks for helping me clean up a mess once again."

"Always. You're stuck with us forever," Joy said, squeezing my hand.

Feeling rejuvenated, I climbed into the front seat and turned the key, singing with my two best friends as we drove home.

CHAPTER 10
GRADY

The door to the gas station slammed behind me as I stalked toward the rental with a scowl on my face. I'd spent the better part of the day out looking for a ghost. Or at least that was what she was turning out to be. The second she'd emerged from that bathroom, her hair disheveled and eyes wide, I knew I was fucked.

Those green eyes pierced right through me, grabbing hold of my dead heart and squeezing it back to life. That close to her, I'd been able to see all the various shades of green that swirled in her eyes. Her dark lipstick covered her plump lips, my cock standing up as it took notice. I'd barely had a second to take in her body, my eyes scanning her curves before she turned and escaped out the door.

The second it closed, it felt like the sun had been taken from the room.

Reality crashed back into me, leaving me panting in front of my two team members as I realized my mistakes. I'd barged in talking about sensitive topics without checking it was clear, effectively blowing our cover as strangers. But what might have been worse was the knowledge that the only woman to interest me in years had also caught their eyes, enough for them to break the rules and bring her back to their room.

The paranoid part of my brain instantly assumed it was a setup, and she'd been sent to mess with the three of us, potentially by the very men we were hunting. It was much easier to believe she was a spy than entertain the notion that if she had to pick between the three of us, it wouldn't be me.

Dragging my hand over my face, I tilted my head back as I stared at the sky. Pinks and purples filled the space as the sun set across the horizon. I'd been all over this city, and no one claimed to know her outside her name. I couldn't decide if that meant the town was loyal to their own, or if she really was a plant to tempt us.

Quentin and Max disagreed with me, stating they'd met her separately under various circumstances, but I couldn't put the thought out of my mind. I needed to find her to know for sure.

My pocket vibrated, and a groan left me, knowing who it would be. I didn't want to deal with him today. Not when my head wasn't in the right place. But he'd keep calling until I answered, so I might as well get it over with.

Tugging it out of my pocket, I held it up to my ear as I twisted around to take in my surroundings. I didn't say hello, wanting to fuck with him a bit.

"Grady? You there?" his deep voice bellowed across the phone.

"Yep. What's up, Captain?"

"You missed the security call-in last night. Care to explain why, since you sound fine to me and not taken hostage?"

Rubbing my temples, I silently cursed, kicking the ground with the toe of my boot. "Sorry, Jackson. I lost track of the days."

He grumbled, the rough sound sending shivers down my spine in a panic. "Do I need to send someone else in, Grady? I thought you were ready for this case. Perhaps I was wrong."

"No, sir. I'll make sure this doesn't happen again. I'll set three alarms if needed."

"You remember what is on the line here, don't you? We can't afford to screw up." I could hear the *'you'* and *'again'* without him even saying the words.

"I know," I gritted out, my molars clenching down so hard I could hear them cracking. My dentist wouldn't like that. Good thing I didn't care what he thought. "I'm fully aware. You don't have to lecture me."

A gush of air came through the speaker, and I could picture Jackson sitting at his desk, rubbing his temples. I wanted to feel guilty about creating stress in his life, but at the end of the day, the only two people's opinions I cared about were the men on my team.

"Just get me the report tonight. I need updates on the targets and what you've found. The big boss believes this person could be the key to stopping the

Savages. And based on the latest intel, we're running out of time."

Fear gripped my chest, my heart being squeezed inside of me as the air in my lungs left me. I'd been chasing the Savages for so long I didn't know how to do anything else. If they were making moves, then it wasn't good. Anytime we caught wind of their dealings, there was always a massive trail of bodies to clean up.

Images of bloody corpses threatened to overtake me as the memory of coming home to find my fiancee, Camila, lying on the floor in a puddle of blood, her body mutilated.

Squeezing my eyes tight, I pulled on the tips of my hair, needing the pain to distract me. If I gave into the memory, I'd be useless for the rest of the day. And that wasn't a luxury I had.

"Noted. I'll send over our findings."

"Grady…" Jackson paused, and I braced myself for whatever he was preparing to say. "They're giving you a week to find this person and flip them. If you can't, then they're sending in Ryan's team."

"Fuck," I hissed, knowing what that meant.

Within the Shadows, there were several types of teams with varying degrees of skills. The three of us vetted the threats, evaluating their capacity for empathy and compliance before recommending them for recruitment or turning them over to the authorities to pay for their crimes.

And when that couldn't be done, or the person was

too far gone to reason with, a kill team came in and took care of the problem before it escalated.

Whoever this killer was, I had a gut feeling they could be valuable based on the information we knew and how they selected their victims. To have them subjected to Ryan's team felt like a waste, but I knew the Shadows would never allow them to continue as they were—killing whoever they saw fit.

So as much as I didn't want to see someone with potential taken out, I understood the rules—comply or die.

"I look forward to reading your report," Jackson said, his voice softer now.

"Yes, sir."

He hung up without saying anything else. I stood there, staring across the vacant parking lot. The sun had dipped lower, casting richer purples and pinks through the sky. I took a second to inhale the fresh air, hoping it would be enough to help me focus. This job had become even more critical. I needed to find my ghost.

Tapping on the door, I waited until Quentin opened it from his side. I lifted my brow, ensuring the space was free of civilians this time. Huffing, he rolled his eyes as he took his spot against the wall, his eyes focused on me. I could feel them cataloging every little nuance as he took in my day. Q was so attuned at times I wondered if he could read my mind.

"Any luck?" I asked, not caring about how gruff I sounded. I leaned back against the dresser, my arms crossed against my chest, and cast my eyes to the floor. I couldn't look at my team right now. Everything felt too fresh, too close to the surface, and I worried I'd see pity or disappointment in their eyes.

"I gathered her name from the Inn's system, and from there, I searched her social media and the local paper. Her name's Holland Kyler. She's about to turn twenty-nine, has lived in Foolshope her whole life, and has worked at the Secret Keep Inn for the past four years. She graduated at the top of her class with scholarships to several universities, yet chose to enroll at the local community college instead. She dropped out after two years and then completed a general studies degree online. All intel points to her being a local, *not* a Savage spy." Max's voice dripped with disdain, shocking me. It seemed I'd messed up even more than I realized if the puppy of the group was mad.

"What are your thoughts, Q?" I asked, taking a chance to glance up at him.

"She's hiding something, but not what you're implying. She used a different name and wore a disguise the first night I met her. But I don't think she was running a con, more like giving herself an ounce of anonymity with the tourists."

"What I don't get is why she stayed here," Max mumbled. "According to her test scores, she's brilliant and could've gone anywhere. Not only did she choose to stay, but she didn't finish. The degree she completed is practically useless. She could've been anything, but instead, she cleans rooms for a living." Max stared off into space, his brain working a mile a minute as he turned over the information in his head, looking for the pattern.

"Whatever it is, she's obviously beloved. No one in this God-forsaken town would tell me a single thing about her." I dropped my arms, gripping the edge of the dresser behind me. "For now, we drop our search into her and get back on track with the job we came here to do. I spoke with Jackson before I came in here."

"And?" Quentin demanded, apparently picking up on my body language.

"We have a week to find the killer and recruit. If not, Ryan's team will eliminate all the potential targets to stop them."

"Shit," Max cursed as Quentin stewed silently. They both knew what it meant to lose this asset.

"While you were out, I got a hit on the message board I posted on yesterday. It should catch the attention of our guy based on the type of people he chooses as his victims."

"Good." I nodded, trying to regain my leadership among them. "Set something up and let us know when it's ready. In the meantime, we need to buckle down on the three suspects we have left. We can't afford to let this person slip through our fingertips, not to mention the unnecessary deaths of the others if we can't identify them."

"Are you going back out tonight?" Quentin asked,

his eyes narrowing at me with suspicion. I held them as I debated how to answer.

A fierce need to keep looking for her thumped heavily in my veins. I knew it was dumb, but I couldn't stop thinking about her. If I didn't take her for myself, then I owed my team to find her. To unfuck the cluster I'd created. But that soured in my stomach; not liking the thought of not having her.

Both objectives warred within, and I didn't know which would win out. I wanted her with a fierce obsession, a possessiveness I'd never felt. The fact she made me crazy and careless with my job should've been enough to keep me away. But I knew I wouldn't be able to. She was too dangerous. It would be best to keep her away from all of us. She'd already cost us a day in our hunt; we couldn't afford any more distractions.

I closed off my emotions, shrugging in response to Q's question. "Doubtful. I need to finish the report to send to Jackson. In the hubbub of last night, I didn't get it sent over, and now I'm on thin ice."

"Hmm," Quentin hummed, his eyes assessing me. Fucker never missed a damn thing.

"You?" I asked, challenging him to deny he wouldn't be doing the same. We were both alike in that regard.

"I have a lead on Matt Donaldson, so I planned to check it out."

The lie was delivered with such precision I almost bought it. Out of all of us, Quentin was the best liar, but unfortunately for him, I knew his tells. And right now, his pinky finger tapped a rhythm against his leg that could only mean one thing—he didn't want me to know where he was going.

I held his eyes for a long moment, debating how I wanted to play this. I had my own secrets, so I knew it wasn't fair to hold his against him. But if it involved her, how could I let him get closer?

No, I needed to be the one to find Holland and keep her as far away from my team as possible. Our lives, and potentially hers, depended on it.

CHAPTER 11
HOLLAND xoxo

THE GIRLS OPENLY STARE AT ME FROM ACROSS THE TABLE AT our house, emotions I couldn't decipher swirling in their eyes. We'd gathered around it to listen to the bug Lacey had placed on Grady—whose name we knew now thanks to the phone call with his boss, and it fitted him so much better than Bill.

"So, it's clear to say they're definitely an organization looking for the XOXO killer," Joy said, her eyes watching me. "And that they know something about the Savages."

"But it didn't sound like they were okay with the Savages, more like they were enemies or competition?" Lacey asked, her brow furrowed. "I mean, they thought that you were a Savage spy, so it doesn't sound like they're in league with them."

"Yeah." I cleared my throat, tapping my fingers against the table. "I agree with that assessment. So who are they and the Savages to each other? And how did we get tangled up in their mess?" I queried, processing my thoughts out loud.

"I did some digging, and the Savages are a ruthless

gang of mercenary killers. They will take any contract and have no morals, just as the girl said. There's talk they're looking to expand their reach and get in the, um, human trafficking business." Joy grimaced, her eyes shiny with tears.

Bile rose up my throat as my stomach dropped. There was no way we could go up against someone like that. *They'd kill us.* We were amateurs at best, and they were professionals.

We were little girls playing at something we had no right to mess with.

The horror of our reality took over, and my vision blurred. Gripping the edge of the chair, I sucked in breaths as my heart tried to beat out of my chest. My lungs burned, and I couldn't suck in any air quickly enough. Dots danced around my eyes as my vision blurred.

Something sharp struck my face, knocking me out of the chair and onto the floor.

"Ow!" I cried, tears running down my face as I glared up at my so-called friends. "Who did that?" I jerked back as I touched my face, the area hot and stinging.

"Me," Lacey said, her face hard and unyielding. She bent down, offering me a hand. "You were having a panic attack." This time her tone was soft and reassuring, and I placed my palm into hers.

Placed back in my seating position, a cold glass was pressed into my hands. I lifted it to my mouth, swallowing the cool liquid and letting it ground me back in the moment, the world slowly returning to me. I blinked and spotted both of my friends sitting next to me.

"Sorry, I..." I shook my head, attempting to dislodge the panic. It had been a while since I'd had an attack that severe. "Most days, I can ignore what we're doing because the people deserve it. There's that part of me that likes to punish those who pick on others and gets excitement from watching them squirm."

"We feel that too. It's why we joined you. It doesn't make you a bad person, Hols," Joy whispered, clasping my hand.

"I know. I didn't mean it like that."

"You're worried now that we have people coming after us. That we're not safe," Lacey said, wrapping her arms around Joy and me.

"Yeah. In our little town, the XOXO killer is equivalent to the football God in a small town. But in the real world, we're still a nobody, barely a blip. I don't like feeling that way, that I could be nothing again." I sucked in a breath, letting it out slowly and keeping my heart rate steady. "We didn't consider we could attract someone in this way. That they'd be after us, and not in a jail-type way. I'd accepted it as a possible outcome, but not this... not being murdered or trafficked ourselves. XOXO was our way out, our chance to do something beyond Foolshope."

"Who says we still can't?" Joy asked.

"It's too dangerous. People are looking for us!" I

panic-whispered, my stomach clawing up my throat again.

"No…" Lacey drawled out like she was talking to a child. "They're looking for a man. You heard it yourself. They don't suspect you or us in the slightest. I mean, they thought you might be a Savage spy, but after their little recon today, they've ruled that out. So, really, we're back to where we started, except this time, we have the upper hand."

Lacey's no-nonsense attitude soothed me, and I nodded. She was right. We now knew more than they did. The feeling of power returned, and a coy smile formed on my lips.

"Okay, yeah, you're right. I'll avoid them until they're gone then. That should be easy enough."

Lacey and Joy shared a look across me, and I knew I wouldn't like what they had to say next.

"Well… it might not be a bad idea to keep tabs on them. And since you already made contact, you'd have an easier time," Joy said, fluttering her eyelashes. It made her look more innocent, but I knew the devil she was underneath despite her angelic appearance.

I opened my mouth to protest; the thought of being near all three was too much to handle. I'd already let myself get too close and had almost compromised our entire operation.

No, it would be best if I stayed away. They'd ruin me and then leave like everyone else did in the end. My hands clenched, another wave of anxiety hitting me in my chest.

"Unless you want us to divide and conquer. Joy can take the sweet one and corrupt him up real nice. And I'll take the hot boss. I have a secretary outfit I could wear. I wonder if he likes to spank? A good bending over a desk does a woman good," Lacey hummed, licking her lips.

"The fuck you will," I hissed before I could stop myself.

Lacey leaned back, pretending to blow on her nails before wiping them on her shirt. Rolling my eyes at myself, I huffed and laughed at falling into her trap.

"And my job here is done."

"Ugh, fine. I like them, and that scares me. I threw out all my rules when I was with just two of them. So now I'm worried I'll confess everything if I was with all three."

My eyes grew big as I pleaded with them to understand. It wasn't just about me and my fear of commitment, but their safety, too.

"Nonsense, Hols. One, your gut isn't broken, no matter what you think. And two, you'd throw yourself in front of a bus before harming either of us. When you love, you love hard, which is why I think these three scare you. They're not like the normal fuck guys," Joy vowed, her words so confident I paused and reassessed her.

What had I missed? Was I making it into something bigger than necessary? Was it only the fear stopping me? Because I didn't let fear control me. I stared that bitch in the face and screamed, daring it to underestimate me like everyone else in my life. So why was this time different?

"I'm not sure why I'm so scared," I admitted, my hands fidgeting in my lap as I stared down at them. The earlier panic attack had stolen all my bravado, leaving me vulnerable and insecure.

I could feel them silently communicating over my head, but I didn't care enough this time to look up to see what it was about.

"We'll figure this out together, Hols. We always do. In the meantime, I think a plan of action and getting out of the house could do wonders for you. You get cranky when you're cooped up," Lacey said, patting my back awkwardly.

She wasn't big on personal touch, so that small action meant a lot. Blowing out a breath, I nodded and straightened my back.

"You're both absolutely right. We know Q will be watching Matt Donaldson, Max will be in the hotel, and Grady's doing some reports. Though, I don't doubt for one second that Grady was giving all the details. He's a slippery one."

"His cleverness is a turn-on for you. Admit it," Joy cooed, nudging my shoulder with hers. My face heated, so I ignored her, not wanting to lie.

"What do we do about the other team? Not that I want us to be caught, but they're three guys who haven't earned death as far as I can tell," Lacey said, bringing us back to the topic.

"We only know one name. Do you think we could hack their systems?" I asked, turning my head to Joy.

"Unlikely. If they're an organization, they're probably on Phantasm's level. I'm good, but I don't have all the gadgets or keys to hack into anything secure-secure."

Biting my lip, I placed my head on my hand as I thought. "They said they wanted to recruit... why?" I mused.

"Because we're badass, obviously," Lacey answered, sitting back and crossing her legs. "Tonight, Joy and I will finish our jobs, and you go try to distract Quentin."

"With your pussy," Joy chimed in, giggling, so I smacked her.

"Ugh, fine. I'll seduce the one man who can read me better than I can. Should I go in disguise or as myself?"

"Make it fun. Go in disguise. It might help you stay in character and not give anything away," Lacey suggested as she stood. She cracked her knuckles, her signature predatory look coming over her face. She was about to go feral on her target from the looks of it. Knowing it was the domestic violence asshole, I didn't blame her.

Lacey pulled me and Joy up from our chairs and threw her arms around us for a hug. "I love you, bishes," she whispered before letting go and stomping into her room without looking back. Too much emotion shown for one setting.

Joy kissed me on the cheek, skipping her way to

hers and leaving me standing in the living room with a decision to make.

Just who should I be to make Quentin fall to his knees?

A little while later, I sauntered into the bar on the outskirts of town, my skirt swaying against my legs with each step. It had taken me a bit to track down Matt Donaldson. Thankfully, since he wasn't actually a killer, he'd been talking all day about his plans, so I only had to ask the right people to find his whereabouts.

Hello, small town gossip chain!

After learning everything I could about Matt Donaldson, I was offended they thought he was us. I mean… the man was a certain height and weight and had a criminal past. But other than that, he had nothing about him that would make me think killer. He was sloppy, loud, and a terrible thief. He'd been caught each time he tried to steal something, never making it away with the goods.

So why had they tagged him, and what were they hoping to gain? Maybe he had ties to the Savages, and they were hoping for a way in. It was the only thing I could remotely think of that would make sense.

Which made this intel gathering even more important. Activate sexy spy!

My red wig was long, the ends tickling my bare back as I continued toward my post. I'd clocked Quentin and

Matt the second I'd entered, so I placed myself between them. I had no intention of interacting with their suspect. He was of little use in this game we were playing. The only thing I needed from him was his location, and I had that.

Now it was time to reel in the big fish.

Leaning across the bar, I giggled to get the bartender's attention, showing off my cleavage while kicking up my legs to flaunt my ass...ets. Would Quentin leave his post to deal with me? My skirt barely covered my bottom, and the shirt was cut low in the front and tied in the back, displaying a lot of skin. Combined with my ankle boots, there was a lot of bare me to take in.

I wouldn't normally wear this little clothing, but since I had a desired outcome in mind, one where the man in question would jump to my rescue, it seemed like a calculated risk to take.

"Hey, gorgeous," I purred, my laugh tinkling as I continued to play the part. "What's a girl gotta do to get a drink?"

The greasy man, who was not, in fact, gorgeous, smiled my way as he left the customer he'd been with to greet me.

"You're a sight to behold, darling. We don't get many girls like you in here."

"Oh, what type of girls do you get?" I asked, twirling a piece of my red hair.

"Harder," he grunted, "and older." He licked his

lips, his eyes trailing all over me. The urge to punch him was strong, but I had to stay in character.

"What is this place? I heard some guys talking about it, so I thought I'd check it out. But, no offense, it looks just like a bar."

"Most of the patrons come to try to prove themselves in the fights below."

My eyes widened involuntarily. In all the time I'd lived here, I never knew illegal fights were a thing. I needed to make sure Lacey didn't hear about it, or she'd accidentally kill someone in the ring.

"Whoa. That's so cool," I gushed.

The guy looked me over again, something in his demeanor changing as he shifted to more concerned instead of predatory. He leaned closer, but it wasn't to flirt.

"You should leave now. This isn't the type of place for a pretty thing like you."

I pouted, sticking out my lip. "But I want a drink. Can't I have a drink?"

Movement from the corner caught my eye, but I kept my eyes forward, focusing on the bartender. His eyes shifted to my left, and I knew I'd succeeded in capturing my prey. My bait had worked—Q had a thing for redheads.

His heat hit my back, his presence engulfing me as he caged me in, his hot breath skirting over my neck.

"Temptress, you shouldn't be here," he growled, the possessiveness and heat bringing goosebumps to my skin.

I ignored him, focusing on the guy in front of me. "I'll have a double shot of tequila."

The bartender looked at Q, swallowing whatever he was about to say, and rushed out a panicked plea. "I'll, uh, let you two settle this." He backed away, returning to the customers at the other end and leaving me alone with Mr. Magic Fingers.

Huffing, I pulled back from the bar and crossed my arms over my chest, pushing my boobs together in the process. Glaring at Q, I ignored how his eyes raked over me, pure unadulterated lust brimming in them. My pussy throbbed from his eyes alone, and I shifted my legs, needing the friction.

Fuck he was good-looking. His possessiveness made me want to lick him all over instead of running the other way like I should.

His hand reached out, jerking my body to his, and I fell into his arms easily. His nose ran up my neck, his breath tickling me and sending shivers through my body. Goosebumps spread all over, the seedy bar disappearing as all of my concentration centered on the man in front of me.

I hated how much of an effect he had over me.

But I loved it too. No one had ever made me feel so irresistible before like they couldn't possibly continue to breathe without me.

"Are you going to do as I say, Temptress, or do I need to show you what happens when you don't listen to me?"

"That's the beauty of this, MF. I don't have to do

either. Now, unhand me and let me go. I have a dick to find."

His nostrils flared at my words, and his eyes heated as his pupils blew, encapsulating the dark brown color to molten chocolate.

"Over my fucking dead body."

His body vibrated, and I worried for a split second I'd pushed him too far. But then his lips crashed into mine, and everything around me disappeared.

CHAPTER 12
QUENTIN

Over the past two days, my mind had been consumed with Holland. First as the pink-haired pixie and then as the girl my best friend and I were crushing on. Neither Max nor I could find her after Grady royally fucked up and crashed into our room, spilling secrets like a newb. When she'd turned and ran from us, I accepted I'd never see her again.

It was for the best since she'd already gotten under my skin so deep that I knew I'd never want to let her go if I had her. So better not to have her.

But then she walked into this shithole, looking like the answer to every horny man's prayers. I'd given up watching the mark. He hadn't been doing anything interesting anyway, and if I had to guess, his eyes would be on her anyway, like every other asshat in this place.

Eyes on what was *mine*.

I'd stayed on my barstool for as long as I could until the desire to claim her won out, and I'd bolted, barely remembering to drop some cash on the sticky bar top before I stalked over. Narrowing my eyes at every man I passed, I sent promises to remove their eyes and dicks if they didn't look away.

My cock pressed more against my jeans the closer I got, almost like a sensor, alerting me that danger was ahead. And if there was one thing my temptress was, it was dangerous.

I didn't for one second believe she was a Savage spy. There was a purity, a vulnerability, about her that none of those fuckers had. She covered it in sass and lipstick, but I saw it. I craved it, just like I did from Max. The beast in me, the part I often had to cage, roared in delight at finding something new to protect.

But it was so much more than that.

Her body enticed me, her words challenged me, and her eyes soothed something broken in me. I couldn't decide if I wanted to fuck her, punish her, or wrap her in cottonwool and never let her see the light of day.

Who was I kidding? I wanted to do all three.

The second I neared, my mouth took over, spouting out demands I had no business making but was powerless to stop.

"Temptress, you shouldn't be here."

She ignored me, but her body responded, telling me everything I needed to know. She wanted me, and I'd wager my bonus that she'd come here looking for me. How she knew I'd be here, I didn't know, but I was confident she'd never been in this place before, only my presence drawing her here.

My nostrils flared the longer she engaged with the slimy bartender, my fists clenching as I worked my jaw back and forth. His eyes flicked to mine, and he retreated, knowing he was the prey in this situation.

Holland turned, her eyes narrowing as she attempted to act pissed off that I'd interrupted her. Her breath quickened, goosebumps spreading over her skin despite the warmth of the place. I watched in rapt fascination as she crossed her arms, pressing her tits up, and I wanted nothing more than to slide my dick between them. Holland shifted her legs, a tiny whimper leaving her throat as she glared at me.

But it was all for show. She wanted me as much as I wanted her. I had no doubt she was as wet as I was hard at this moment.

Jerking her toward me, I ran my nose up her neck, breathing in her intoxicating scent. I didn't know what it was, but I craved it, wanting my whole body to smell of her. She shivered in my hold, her hands gripping my black t-shirt like a lifeline. My dick pressed against her, attempting to find a way through both of our clothes so it could find its home between her legs.

"Are you going to do as I say, Temptress, or do I need to show you what happens when you don't listen to me?"

I didn't know which answer I wanted from her, the need to claim *and* punish her battling inside of me.

"That's the beauty of this, MF. I don't have to do either. Now, unhand me and let me go. I have a dick to find."

Her words were empty, but they had the effect she'd wanted, sending me over the edge. No longer was I a cool-headed shadow among the patrons of this bar but a man possessed by the need to claim his woman and teach her a lesson in the process.

"Over my fucking dead body." I'd gritted out the words, the sound like gravel from my throat as all sense of safety, duty, and preservation left me. It was only her and me at this moment—the rest of the world be damned.

My body vibrated with the need to spear my cock so deep in her she'd think twice before being so reckless again. Slamming my lips into her, I stole her breath, needing her to rely on me for oxygen. My hands gripped her ass as she melted into me, her breasts pressing into my chest. I was two seconds away from plunging my fingers into her warm pussy, but I had the wherewithal to remember our surroundings.

None of these fuckers got to see any piece of her a second longer.

Lifting her up under her ass, her legs wrapped around me, and I stalked out of the place, not giving a second look to any of those patrons or Matt Donaldson.

I knew without a shadow of a doubt he wasn't our killer, so there was no sense in wasting time when I could be balls deep in Holland.

"Put me down, MF," she hissed, despite no attempts to thwart my handling of her. I didn't know if she was still playing a part or if, for her own conscience, she had to pretend to fight me.

That's okay, baby. I like it when you fight back.

"I'll put you down once no one else is around and not a second before."

She huffed in protest, but her legs squeezed around my hips, and I stumbled, my cock twitching between us. I pushed out the door, leaving that disgusting bar behind us. I needed three showers to wash the stink off me.

Glancing at our surroundings, I debated fucking her up against the brick wall, using it to punish her as my cock sunk deep inside, but the thought of marring her perfect skin was out of the question.

Letting out a frustrated growl, I stomped to my bike and sat her on the back. She let out a surprised breath as her ass made contact with the leather. I grabbed my helmet and secured it on her head within seconds, not giving her time to question me. Her doe eyes blinked up at me, and I gave into the impulse to hold her gaze, despite the worry I'd find fear there.

Lust and safety stared back, setting my heart racing again. Her trust was my kryptonite, and I was two seconds away from coming in my pants.

Throwing my leg over my motorcycle, I started it and revved the engine, walking it forward before I took off like a shot into the night.

The air did nothing to quell my arousal, probably because Holland's body pressed tightly to mine, her heat seeping into me and making my mind play out a million different scenarios. Her hands lowered to my thighs, one rubbing the length of my dick. My eyes shuttered, and I jerked, remembering I was driving us both.

Looking around where I was, I spotted a deserted section up ahead with trees filling the space. Without hesitation, I pulled over and placed my feet on the ground to steady the bike before releasing the kickstand.

Reaching behind me, I yanked Holland around my side to the front, her look of shock at the move making me grin as I unhooked her helmet. Her eyes were wide, her mouth slightly open.

"Holy fuck, MF. That was hot, but not as hot as your smile. You need to weaponize that thing. Take out some insurance and get a warning label. You can't just go around throwing out smiles willy-nilly."

I didn't let her continue, stealing her words with my lips again. My hands gripped her thighs, pulling her closer to where I wanted. Her body vibrated against mine, coming alive with my touch as I caressed her skin with my thumbs. In this getup, I had so much more access to all of her, and I wasn't going to waste it.

Holland moaned, rocking forward, and I knew I was done waiting. Shoving her soaked panties to the side, I plunged my fingers into her dripping pussy, growling into her mouth at how wet she was. She let out a moan that went straight to my dick, threatening to combust in my jeans.

"Fuck, baby. I love how wet you are. This better be for me and no one else in that shitty bar."

"Only. You," she whimpered, her voice croaking as

she rode my fingers, no longer fighting me on what she wanted.

"We'll talk later about why you were dressed like this in a dirty place like that. I'll show you how upset it made me when you walked in without a care in the world."

Her eyes opened, searing into me, and I knew whatever she said next I wouldn't like.

"I'll wear whatever the fuck I want, MF."

"Like hell, you will," I roared, my possessiveness raging out of control at any other man touching what was mine. The hand gripping her thigh shot up, collaring her throat as I pressed the sides, mindful not to squeeze.

"You're fucking mine whether you like it or not. But I think we both know you love it."

Her eyes held a challenge, and I knew I needed to fuck the brattiness out of her.

"I'd give the orgasm you gave me a 5 out of 10. Might want to work on your skill," she snarked.

Oh, I so wanted to play this game.

Smirking, I rubbed my thumb on the outside of her neck, feeling her pulse jump with each plunge of my fingers. She was a fucking liar. My hands were drenched. I had no doubt the leather beneath her would be as well. I'd be smelling her on me for weeks, and I couldn't fucking wait.

"Good girls don't lie, Temptress. If you want to be a brat, fine." I withdrew my fingers, her eyes bulging, and she whimpered at the loss. Taking my time to lick them clean, I kept my eyes on her as I stuck my tongue out, rolling it around each digit. Her breathing quickened, her pulse racing faster the longer I took.

Grinning, I let go of her neck, placing both hands on her hips. I watched for a brief second as she pouted at the loss of my touch before I flipped her over, her ass landing in my lap.

"Hands on the bars," I ordered.

She followed my direction, her body trembling with need as she waited for what I would do next. Lifting her skirt, I smoothed my hands over the round globes of her ass. Taking a handful, I squeezed, watching the tiny fingerprints forming before disappearing. My cock twitched again, liking what he saw. Taking her panties into my hand, I pulled them up, gathering the fabric into my fist.

Making a thong out of them, I tugged on the material, pulling it over her sensitive areas in the front. Holland moaned, moving her hips to get more friction from the action.

"Stop. You can move when I tell you."

Her jaw clenched, and she turned her head to stare at me. "If you don't fuck me, I'm returning to that bar and grabbing the first man I see."

My hand smacked down onto her ass quicker than she could follow, her eyes widening before she let out a breathy moan. Her pupils dilated even more, and she licked her lips.

"I didn't stutter," she said, attempting to regain control.

Leaning forward, I whispered into her ear. "The only one fucking you tonight is me. So, stop suggesting otherwise. Hold on to those bars while I punish you for walking your hot ass into trouble with no regard for your safety. Then, when I'm satisfied you've learned your lesson, I'm going to fuck you so hard you won't be able to walk or sit tomorrow without thinking of me. *You're mine, Holland.* It's time to get with the fucking program."

Drawing back, I didn't give her time to respond, taking her body's reactions as my cue. Her hands gripped the bars, her knuckles turning white, and I slapped my palm on her ass in quick succession, then smoothed away the sting in a soft caress. She whimpered, rocking her pelvis against the seat, telling me everything I needed.

She liked it and needed a release.

Unzipping my jeans, I pulled out my thick cock, stroking it a few times as I stared at the beautiful woman before me with her ass still pink from my handprint. Taking out a condom, I rolled it on and lifted her hips, slamming into her a second later without warning.

"Fuck," she moaned, the sound echoing around us.

Her tight heat enveloped me, squeezing me to within an inch of giving in and coming right then and there. Taking a deep breath, I focused on her pleasure, wanting to give her the release she desperately needed.

Her walls twitched against me, and I moved, not needing any more time to adjust. The sound of skin slapping joined our moans as I rammed my dick in and out of her. The bike tilted with the force, so I braced my legs on the ground, knowing it was up to me to keep us both safe from falling over.

"Fuck, fuck, Q. Shit. You're so big, MF. Oh, god," she cursed, her words jumbled around moans. "Shit, I'm coming, I'm coming!"

My hold on my orgasm left me as I felt her tremble around me, her walls squeezing me tighter as her body quaked. Lifting her body flush with mine, I wrapped a hand around her neck again, bringing her mouth to mine. My other hand found her clit, rubbing it fast as I pumped in her, my cum spilling from my cock into the condom.

Our lips pressed into one another, our tongues tangling as we rode it out, her body shaking in my arms.

Not once did either of us look away, our eyes fixed as the broken pieces in our souls connected, fusing us together now whether we liked it or not.

CHAPTER 13
HOLLAND xoxo

The emotion combined with the pleasure my body felt wracked with was too intense, and my eyes fluttered closed to escape the things I hadn't been prepared to feel. This was too much, too soon. I'd come out here to get closer to the guys so I could uncover intel, not have one completely wreck me as he consumed me.

And he had consumed me—heart, body, and soul.

The hand on my throat squeezed, reminding me how helpless I was to his commands. That should've made me feel powerless, scared he'd take advantage of me. But perhaps what was more frightening was knowing it didn't.

Quentin made me feel safe, cherished, and adored. His desire and possessiveness were hot, and I'd already become addicted, tumbling headfirst into his arms. My walls had crashed down around me to smithereens, and now I felt flayed open…vulnerable.

"Don't hide away from me, baby. Open your eyes and be with me in this moment."

My eyes instinctively obeyed his command, despite my desire to do the opposite of what he said. His dark orbs stared back, offering me comfort and safety I hadn't known how to ask for. I swallowed, his thumb rubbing over my pulse point.

"You're mine now, Holland. Do you understand?"

I nodded without thought, then stopped as I frowned. His grip tightened, not uncomfortably, just enough to make me look into his eyes again.

"What's wrong?" he asked, his eyes searching mine for the answer.

I licked my lips as questions tumbled. How did I bring up his friends? Or mine, for that matter? What did being his actually mean?

My pussy very much liked the idea of being his, her walls tightening around the very hard dick still inside me. His nostrils flared at the move, but he waited for me to answer. Thankfully, those few seconds had allowed my voice to return, and I remembered who I was.

Holland Kyler. I didn't belong to anyone but myself.

"I'm not going to run away with you into the sunset. I'm not the marrying type. I won't be tied down to one man. *Ever*. Not even if your dick is like the gold medal of dicks. My pussy has too many disco sticks to ride in her future to be happy with one for the rest of her life."

Quentin's eyes burned with an intensity I'd never witnessed before; his stare liquified me to the spot. My body quivered, but not one ounce of me feared for my safety, which shocked me.

"Who else?" he gritted out like the words tasted sour to him.

His eyes never left my face, his hand still around my neck, and his cock still hard inside me. The position alone should've caused me pause, but it didn't. If anything, I wanted him more. But I couldn't let him win.

"Whoever the fuck I want," I taunted, licking my lips.

His eyes shuttered closed for the first time, and I worried I'd pushed him too far. His hand flexed, his nostrils flaring as he took in a deep, stuttering breath, letting it out slowly. It was only his dick twitching that clued me in that he wasn't done with me. At least not yet.

Apparently, I'd upgraded my gut bullshit meter, and my pussy was now a cock lie detector.

The longer he was quiet, the more my need to test people to see if they would leave was triggered, and I buckled down, tightening my walls around him.

What do you say, Q? Up for a game of pussy chicken?

Quentin sucked in a breath, his eyes flying open, and my heart settling now that he was staring at me again.

"Max and Grady only then," he growled, my body shivering with need at the level of lust and hunger in his voice. "Tell me you understand so I can fuck you again for trying to push me away."

This time, I sucked in a breath, and the wall I'd been trying to rebuild crumbled at my feet. There was still so much to discuss, but it didn't seem to matter at this point. Nothing but the feel of him in me did. I was so screwed.

"Yes," I said, my voice husky.

Like lightning, he released his hold on my throat and pulled out, my body whimpering at the loss of him. Why did I feel so empty now he was gone?

Before I could explore my line of thinking, hands lifted me and spun me around until my back lay against the warm metal of the motorcycle beneath me. My legs were sprawled across his thick thighs, his hands clasping down on them. The skirt was up, and my panties were in tatters around me showcasing my bare pussy on full display for him.

Quentin's gaze bored into me, licking his lips as he flexed his hands on my thighs.

"Hold on to the handlebars again."

He yanked off the condom and then froze in place, his wide eyes meeting mine.

"Shit. Fuck. Goddamn it!"

I blinked at him, not understanding his frustration.

"Sorry, I only had one condom."

I stared back, and despite only knowing him for a few days and it being a foolish idea, I said the words anyway.

"I trust you. I'm covered. If you're clean, then we don't need one."

Quentin gazed at me long and hard, his dark skin shimmering in the night with sweat. Glancing down at my pussy, he stroked his finger through my folds, my body responding immediately to his touch. Cupping me, his palm rubbed against my clit as he met my eyes.

"I want to make sure you very clearly understand what you're offering to a man like me. I already couldn't walk away from you, but if I fuck you bare..." His nostrils flared as he devoured me with his eyes. "You could run to the ends of the earth, and I would follow you and bring you back to my bed each time. You'd have to kill me to get rid of me; *that's* how obsessed I will be after this. Do you understand what you're offering me, baby?"

My breath caught, and a thousand thoughts ran through my mind. Was I ready for this? Did I want that? What about the girls? What about XOXO and our plans? Could I really give all that up right this second for some dick?

"I..." My eyes dropped, and I bit my lip as I debated.

Fuck it. I'll deal with the consequences later, like usual.

Q pulled my lip from my teeth, his thumb brushing back and forth over it tenderly. I glanced up, his expression soft and soothing.

"Not tonight, Temptress. I want you to have all the answers you need when you give me that gift. I want there to be nothing between us, emotionally or physically, when we go there. Not a drop of doubt in sight. Okay?"

I let out the breath I'd been holding, nodding as I relaxed back on the bike. I knew it was the right answer, but I couldn't shake the disappointment, either. It had been easier to let myself go there if I did it impulsively. Now I'd be thinking about it, rationalizing and over-thinking it until the day I died.

Quentin pulled me up, kissing me slow and soft, and taking his time as his tongue swirled with mine. It was sensual and had my toes curling all the same. When the kiss ended, emotions I hadn't expected flowed through me—admiration, compassion… love.

Hold up. Shove that one into the far back.

Quentin held my head reverently in his hands, brushing his thumb over my cheek. "Do you want to come back to my place?" he asked.

My phone buzzed, startling me as it vibrated against my chest. Q lifted a brow, looking over my body as he tried to locate it. Grinning, I reached in and pulled it from my bra. Outside of the skirt around my waist and my soaked panties, I was fully dressed, so he hadn't noticed where I'd stashed it. *Stupid, no pockets.* He chuckled, shaking his head as I glanced at the messages from the girls.

Joy: Done with the boss. There was a new job posted that needed a quick turnaround. Anyone up for it? I would, but met a guy and a girl, and we're going to their room.

Lacey: Damn, have fun. I'm also done. Boy, do I enjoy a good chopping.

Lacey: I could do it, but I'm at least an hour out until I'll be home, and then I need to shower, so I'm not spreading evidence.

Holland: I can do it. Send me the info, and I'll head there.

Joy: Awesomesauce. Laters taters.

Lacey: Be safe. Holler if you need backup.

Locking my phone, I knew it was for the best I had to leave. Things were too messy, and I needed some space before I jumped in without looking.

"I need to go home. My roommates need my help. Can you drop me off? I took a rideshare to the bar."

He studied me, his eyes taking in every inch of me like he was committing it to memory. "Yeah. But give me your phone. Come to my room tomorrow for breakfast. We need to talk with Max."

"I have to work in the morning."

"What time?" he asked, typing in his contact and then sending himself a message.

"Nine."

"Stop by at seven, and we'll have plenty of time to talk. Or text me after you're done tonight with your roommates, and I'll pick you up. Your choice."

He quirked an eyebrow, not leaving any option for me to deny. Q meant business.

"Yeah, okay. I'll be there in the morning."

I gulped; the promise that he wasn't running did

stupid things to me. Tucking my phone back into my bra, I stepped off the bike to right my skirt while he tucked his cock back into his jeans. Picking up the helmet he'd tossed to the ground, I placed it back on. Shifting on my feet, I kept feeling how wet my panties were, and the thought of wearing them on the bike home made me cringe. With his back still turned, I slipped them off and slid back on the bike, tucking them into his pocket as I adjusted my legs.

The second my hands were wrapped around his taut muscles, he revved the engine and took off. When we got closer to town, I pointed out where to turn, leading him to one of our dummy locations. The lights were on, and I thanked Joy for installing timers. It was easier to shake him if he believed someone else was home since I was supposed to be helping the girls.

Sliding off the back, I unclipped the helmet and handed it to Q. His hand reached out and gripped my forearm, pulling me into his hard body. Quentin tilted my chin up, his fingers gripping me.

"This isn't over, Holland. Don't forget you're mine. There's no return policy, so I'll see you soon."

He kissed me hard, withdrawing a second later and putting the helmet on his head. I stood there in a daze as he drove off, my heart beating a mile a minute as I watched him disappear.

Climbing the steps, I unlocked the door and headed into the room where we stashed extra clothes in. Changing into all black, I pulled my hair back and placed a cap over it to keep it secure. Pulling up the information Joy had sent, I scanned the fast work request from Phantasm.

> Phantasm: I know I said to lie low, but this is urgent. A teenager has been kidnapped by her stepdad. The mother called it in after the police said they couldn't do anything. Mom is worried he's become obsessed with her daughter and will rape the teen. I tracked his credit card and found a location. He's staying at the cabins in the next town over. You have a short window before they move. Can you do it?

> Holland: Send the address and name. I'll text when I have the girl. This one might get bloody. Do we have clean-up on standby, or am I on my own?

> Phantasm: I'll have someone in the area awaiting your text.

Grabbing a bag, I filled it with some tools and headed out the back door. Slinking around the side, I checked that no one was out front before I crept along the fence line to the car a few houses down. Once inside it, I pulled up the GPS on the secure server and made my way there.

The whole drive, I replayed the conversation over and over with Quentin. Was he serious? Did he actually like me? Or was it a game?

It didn't feel like a game. It felt real.

I made it to the cabins easily, ditched the car on the

side of the road, and stalked through the woods the rest of the way. These rentals were used by a lot of nefarious folks, so it wasn't the first time I'd been here, which helped in a quick job since I hadn't had time to research the layout or the man. Peering into the window, I held back the urge to vomit as I noticed the girl. She lay limp on the bed, her hair mussed and her clothes ripped.

I wanted to cry for her, for what she'd been through already at such a young age, but that wouldn't help right now. All I could do was get her out of there so she didn't go through anything more.

The man in question snored beside her, his flaccid dick lying against his leg. If it wouldn't be as traumatizing for her to watch me cut it off, I would. Lacey wasn't the only one who loved a good chopping.

Plan made, I used my lock pick to open the back door and walked slowly down the hall, keeping to the shadows.

The door to the bedroom was open, so I continued in on silent feet. The perp snored, not bothered by my presence in the slightest. Walking over to the girl, I nudged her gently to wake her. Her eyes snapped open immediately, and I lifted my finger to be quiet. She nodded, the motion practically wooden as she stared at me blankly.

I helped her from the bed, making sure not to wake him in the process. When her feet were on the floor, I bent down and whispered in her ear.

"Your mother sent me. I'm going to save you, but first, I need you to hide in the bathroom. Lock the door and don't open it until I tell you it's me. I'll use the code word octopus. Okay?"

Again, she only nodded. She was so checked out, hiding within herself to forget the horrors she'd experienced. I just hoped she'd be okay while I took care of the trash. Once the door was closed and locked, I got to work.

The asshole was so out of it that he made it easy for me to lock his wrists and feet and cover his mouth as I debated my next course of action. Tapping my finger on my chin, I smiled when inspiration struck. Placing the phone over his face, I opened the notes app and typed out the world's worst suicide note.

I'M SCUM AND A DESPICABLE HUMAN BEING. YOU'RE BETTER OFF WITHOUT ME.
DENNIS

I drew the face mask down completely so it covered my entire face and kept my identity hidden. Pulling my gun out of the holster, I moved toward the bed.

It was go time.

Adrenaline spiked in me, a crazed sense of rightness and justice flowing through my veins now that I had him in my sights. I'd make him pay for hurting her. I'd ensure he could never hurt another girl ever again. My heart thumped loudly, a grin spreading behind the mask. Now the fun began.

Pointing the barrel at his head, I pulled the hammer back, the sound echoing around the room. His eyes fluttered, but they didn't open. Poking him with the gun, I placed it on his head. And yet, he still didn't stir, so I questioned my plan and debated whether I should just kill him in the bed.

But no. I wanted him to feel scared. To know what it had felt like for that little girl. *For me.*

"Wake up," I growled, the built-in voice modulator making my voice deeper and more masculine.

His eyes popped open, his breath hitching when he realized someone was standing over him with a gun to his head. He tried to move, but with his hands tied and duct tape over his mouth, he was unsuccessful.

"Get up. If you try to run, I'll shoot you. Understand?"

He nodded, his eyes panicked as he sat up, glancing around and noticing the girl was gone.

"I already shot her. You're next."

His breathing quickened as he stood on shaky legs, his dick curling inside him like a turtle, keeping it from my view. *Thank the stars for small mercies!*

"Walk."

He stumbled with his feet locked together. I'd only given him enough width to waddle. It was funny to watch, but also necessary to minimize my risk. He was bigger and stronger than me, so I had to use what I could to my advantage. Plus, I really wanted this to look like suicide. As much as I wanted to kill him in a bloody fashion, if I could avoid attention to a murder while Quentin and his team were in town, all the better.

Besides, dead was dead at the end of the day.

The child molester shuffled out into the hall, my gun still pointed at his head and a Taser on his back. I was prepared to incapacitate him if he decided to be an asshole.

Thankfully, the pedophile followed along, moving where I told him without a fight. Opening the door to the attached garage, I shoved him inside, keeping the light off. He whimpered as I pressed the gun harder, demanding he get into the car. I'd already grabbed the keys from the nightstand earlier, so I unlocked it as he slid in.

"Turn it on," I growled, handing him the keys. They shook as he worked to find the spot, the car coming to life a second later.

Taking another zip tie, I tied his hands to the steering wheel, locking him in place. I'd have the clean-up crew remove all evidence later so it looked like he'd done it.

Taking out a piece of cloth, I stuffed it into the muffler so it would fill the car quicker with CO. With one quick salute, I headed back inside, locking the door so he couldn't enter if he managed to get out somehow.

Running back to the bedroom, I gathered my bag of goodies and did a quick scan of the room for anything the girl might need. Finding a bag of clothes, I grabbed it and the money out of his wallet. Taking a deep breath to slow down my adrenaline, I knocked on the door.

"Hey, octopus. It's me. He's gone. It's safe to come out."

The lock was slow to turn, the door opening only a

crack. I waved, trying to reassure her that it was safe. I stepped back so she could see the bed was clear as well. When she realized I wasn't lying, she opened it more, pulling her arms over her chest.

"I have your clothes. I'd let you take a shower, but I think we should get out of here first. Do you need any help?" I asked.

She shook her head, grabbed the bag, and pulled out a pair of pants and a hoodie. She tucked the nightgown she'd been wearing into the pants and slipped on some shoes. Holding out my hand, I waited as she debated taking it.

"I know I'm a stranger, but I promise to protect you and get you safely back to your mom. You just have to trust me a few more steps."

She took a deep breath, nodding.

This time, I didn't need to be quiet or stealthy, so we jogged through the house and exited back the way I'd come, locking the door. The trek to the car was slower, but we made it, and I helped her get into the backseat.

"There are some parts where I'll need you to lay down flat so that no one spots you on cameras, okay? We're going somewhere safe, and your mom will meet us there."

"What's your name?" she whispered, the sound so lost and hollow.

I hesitated, never having given my real name before. But she'd already lost so much tonight; it felt wrong to give her something else fake.

"Holland. What's yours?"

"Meredith."

"You ready to get the hell out of here, Meredith?" I asked, turning on the car. Her nod was quick, and she laid down in the seat. Pulling out my phone, I texted the clean-up crew and Phantasm to tell her mom where to go.

It was jobs like these that reminded me I couldn't stop. If XOXO didn't exist, her life would've been over. I wouldn't let that happen to anyone if I could help.

Taking a second to let out another breath, I focused on the next steps of getting her back safely. I knew if I didn't, I'd run back there and shoot his brains out, fall apart in tears myself, or probably the worst one, run straight into Quentin's arms.

CHAPTER 14
MAX

I STARED AT MY SCREEN, WISHING I COULD HEAR WHAT WAS occurring with the little dots. Quentin's icon mockingly flashed at me. The darn red dot had been stationary for a while now, and I didn't know why. He'd left the bar an hour ago, then had pulled off to the side of the road where he'd stayed since.

Was he having trouble with his bike? Had someone apprehended him? Was someone else in danger?

The questions left me helpless to act, much like I had been most of my life, and I didn't like it. I needed to do something. I wasn't a weak teenager anymore, no matter how much Q thought I was.

The Shadows had made me strong, giving me every type of training available. I'd toned my body and mind, promising myself I'd never be in another situation where I feared for my life.

I could handle myself, despite Quentin's paranoia that I'd get shot. I just chose not to most days. It wasn't my preferred method to assist the team. I found the computer easier to manage than dealing with social interactions and having to second-guess myself.

But just because I didn't know what to say at times, it didn't mean I couldn't throw a punch or incapacitate my enemy when needed. Perhaps I needed to remind Q of that.

Tapping my fingers on the keyboard, I debated whether to leave and check on him, or stay here like I was meant to. If he were in trouble, he'd welcome my assistance, but if he wasn't and I ruined whatever he was doing, then I'd never hear the end of it.

"Screw it. I'd rather know," I said aloud, putting my computer aside to get dressed in something other than my stained t-shirt and holey jeans. Throwing on my black tactical pants and a shirt, I pulled on my boots and checked the location.

"Of course, you're moving now," I grumbled, sitting on the bed.

The dot was now headed toward a side of town we hadn't been to yet. Curiosity bloomed, but there was nothing to do now but wait. Minimizing Quentin's window, I checked on Grady, finding him still down at the Inn bar. He'd stumbled around in his room for a few hours before he retreated. He hadn't gone far, claiming he would try to gather information on Holland with a different shift of people.

I couldn't tell yet if his obsession with her was out of intrigue or something more sinister. While I was eager to find her myself, it seemed to be for a different reason with Grady. I'd have to keep an eye on him because I didn't want him to scare her off. I had a connection with

Holland that was rare for me, and I didn't want to lose it.

Besides, she'd fit perfectly between Q and me, and I wanted it back. Desperately.

Falling back into my research, I spent time surveying her social media, along with Ava Savage's. I didn't know how Ava fit into the picture, but something told me she wasn't part of it. I could feel she was a vital key to this, but I needed solid evidence and a solution before sharing it. There was no way I'd put her in the crossfire without a way to save her.

A knock at the door startled me, and I jerked, pulling up the minimized window. Sure enough, Q was back. Hopping up, I raced to the door.

"Password?"

"Horseradish," Quentin's deep voice replied.

Disengaging the locks, I opened the door and stepped back. Quentin strolled in like usual, but something was different about him. He eyed me, taking in my change of clothes as he relocked everything.

"I thought you were in trouble and was going to head over to assist you. But then you moved before I could," I said to his unasked question.

His eyes traveled over my face, cataloging every detail. Satisfied with my answer, he stepped into the room, taking off his boots.

"I found Holland," he said flatly, his tone suggesting he was getting a root canal, not delivering the best news I'd heard all day.

"What! You did? How? Where? Tell me!" I shouted, my whole body vibrating with happiness.

Quentin leaned against the wall, crossing his ankles over one another. He rubbed his hand down his face, stalling when his hand neared his nose. I watched him, his nostrils flaring wide as his whole body shuddered, heating mine at the same time. Damn, what had that been?

I swallowed, taking a seat on the corner of the bed, hoping to conceal my reaction to him. When I was situated, I peered up, and Q responded, his voice far away as he recalled the events.

"She walked into that filthy bar like she didn't have a care in the world. I watched her, fighting my instincts to grab and haul her out of there."

I chuckled, the sound rough and deep. "I'm surprised you didn't."

"After about ten minutes, I couldn't take it, and I walked over, aiming to tell her to go, but instead, she pushed and pushed until I broke, and I had to shut her up."

"With your mouth?" I asked, smiling, knowing him well.

His eyes narrowed, but there was no malice behind them. If anything, there was a little heat. He smirked, moving his thumb over his plump bottom lip, and my tongue darted out to mimic the movement.

"It worked." He shrugged. "I left with her, intent on bringing her back here, but she had other ideas."

"You fucked her."

It wasn't a question; I could tell by his demeanor. Sadness and longing tumbled inside me as I dropped my eyes, my head suddenly feeling too heavy to hold up. I rubbed my hands on my pants, wishing I'd still had on my jeans. They felt nicer, more soothing. And I needed to be soothed. Dammit.

It wasn't the first time a girl had wanted Quentin over me, but it was the first time I cared. At least when we'd all been together, I got to have a part of her. But now that was gone, and I had to set my obsession aside.

"You're wrong," Quentin said, his voice soft and closer than I remembered. His rough palm grabbed my chin, tilting it up to meet his eyes. They were soft, swirling with understanding, and something I couldn't place.

"No, I'm not," I barked, angry I cared this much. Holland wasn't a girl he would just fuck. She was different. I'd lost my best friend and the girl. Fuck. Using my anger, I spat out the words. "It's written all over your face, Q. Don't try to deny it. You practically orgasmed standing there when you smelled her. You got her, and now that's that."

Quentin sighed like I was frustrating him with my denseness. *Welcome to the club, buddy.*

"No. You're wrong in thinking it means she chose me."

"But you just said..." I waved my hands between us, not wanting to repeat the words. They hurt too much to say out loud again. His grip tightened on my chin, and instead of being pissed, it did the opposite, calming me as the pain stabilized the panic and fury within.

"I've claimed her, yes, but she told me she wouldn't commit to one person. She likes you, Max. And though neither will admit it, she and Grady have a connection, too. She was the girl from the first day, the one he eye-fucked like she was the cure he needed to survive." Quentin sighed deeply, his hold loosening as his thumb brushed across my chin in a caring gesture, soothing me better than my favorite jeans.

That... felt nice.

"She's coming to talk with us before her shift in the morning. I can't let her go. She's mine... But she's also yours. And Grady's if he removes his head from his ass."

I blinked, unsure if I'd heard him correctly. She'd wanted me too? And he was willing to share?

"How will that work?" I asked, my mind racing with the need to solve this puzzle. I didn't want to lose her.

"That's what we'll talk about in the morning. She had to go do something with her roommates."

The question I couldn't ignore slipped through before I could stop it. "Why did you agree to share?" I whispered. It was so out of character for him; I needed to know his reasoning.

Quentin's dark eyes blazed into mine, his jaw ticking as he fought himself.

"Because I know how much you like her, and I can understand how she might help three broken men. Or even that she wouldn't be happy with just me. She's a force that can't be contained, and I'd only destroy her if I tried." His hold on me loosened more, a physical sign of withdrawal. No. I didn't want that.

Leaning forward, I gripped his thighs with my hands, squeezing them hard so my nails dug into him.

"Don't run from me, Q. Not on this," I demanded, pushing further into his space so he couldn't retreat. Our noses touched, hot breath fanning over each other as we stared, the tension that was always there sizzling to life.

Quentin might've rescued me from the bullies when we were younger, being my fists when I couldn't protect myself, but I'd saved him from his own emotional turmoil, showing him how to let go and be vulnerable.

We were two sides of one coin, pushing and pulling the other through the murkiness of life. We worked better together, closing the gaps in one another's weaknesses. And right now, Q needed me to show him it was okay to feel new things, even if they were scary.

Quentin licked his lips, his eyes dropping to my mouth before meeting my eyes again, and some of the turmoil lessened. The muscles in his face relaxed, his body sagging under the pressure my touch provided, reminding him I was there.

His hands slid to grasp my hair, bringing our foreheads together. Quentin squeezed his eyes closed, tugging at the strands of my hair as he fought himself. I increased the pressure on his thighs, my fingers wrapping around his thick muscles. I took in a deep breath, waiting for him to follow.

In and out, we breathed together, the action so natural it didn't take long for his heart to slow. Q leaned back an inch, spearing me in the eyes with his truth.

"You always know when I'm about to spiral and how to bring me back. I don't like to admit it, but I need you, Max. Probably more than you need me nowadays."

He sucked in another shuddering breath, letting it out slowly. I didn't respond, knowing he wasn't finished and needed to get this out. It had gone on too long as it was.

"I know I treat you like you're incapable of keeping yourself safe, and I'm sorry for that. It's easier for me to accept your help when I feel it's equal. Plus, the fear of something happening to you is overwhelming at times. Max, you're my family. You're all I have left. You and Grady, but especially *you*. Do you understand?"

I nodded, releasing some of the pressure on his thighs. His body shuddered again, his eyes closing before he took a deep breath. A thrill raced up my spine, liking that I'd affected him the same way Holland had.

I stayed quiet, hoping to give him the space to say what he felt, knowing he couldn't move forward until he'd overcome this. We stared at one another for a long time as emotions swirled in his eyes. So many beautiful emotions.

"What I'm failing to say is… I love you, Max. I don't know what that means or how that affects us, but I do. And I think having Holland between us made it easier for me to accept what has grown between us with a safe way to explore it. Because I need you both, and that scares the shit out of me, but I do. I need her to challenge me and push my buttons, and I need you to remind me it's okay to feel things. That being safe doesn't mean going through life like a zombie."

I swallowed, his words more poignant and powerful than I could've anticipated.

"Say something," he begged, his grip tightening in my hair.

"That was beautiful, Q. I'm just trying to process it all."

"Do you not… feel the same?" he asked, anxiety and sadness coating his words.

"I love you too, Q. I always have. You saved me back when I couldn't save myself, and after my uncle was killed, you became my family. I've always been scared to look at what our friendship meant because I didn't want to lose you. So, I went along with your requests, knowing it gave you control, and I'd be there for you when you needed me." I took a breath this time, the words tumbling freely from me now that we'd opened the door.

"When I thought you were going to keep Holland for yourself, I knew I'd lose you both, which terrified me. This job has shown me the horrors of life, but Holland gave me a glimpse of something bright, of a future that was more than blood and death. If you say you want us all to be together, I'll happily agree because I know she's special and I think we can be great. I just didn't want it to be a pity thing."

I dropped my eyes, biting my lip as I held myself together. I'd never been that vulnerable before, and I didn't want him to regret anything he said. To change his mind. Quentin's thumb pulled my lip from my teeth, smoothing the pad across it as he stared at it. His touch sent electricity through me, my body waking up and responding to things I'd long ignored.

"No moment with you has ever been out of pity, Max. You gave me a purpose when I was lost, someone to protect when I needed to feel like I could. I'd failed my mom, but I wouldn't fail you. How you described Holland, that's how you are to me. You brought light back into my life, pushing away some of the shadows. At first, it was your awful jokes making me laugh when I'd forgotten how. But now it's the way you know what I need when I'm too afraid to ask. I've been scared my whole life of you waking up and realizing how much better off you'd be without me and my crazy rules. So, no, Max. It's not a pity thing. It's never been."

My eyes shuttered closed, the emotion in his words too big and grand to dismiss. I let them settle in me, filling the holes and cracks of doubt and fear that had seeped in over the years and covering them in his love. My shoulders dropped as a weight lifted, my body buzzing as energy flew through me. Feeling lighter, I opened my eyes, finding him still watching me.

"What do we do now? What does this mean for us?" I asked, my voice quiet, not wanting to ruin the moment.

"Your guess is as good as mine. It doesn't have to change anything if we don't want it to."

"Is that what you want?" I asked, unsure of myself.

"I don't know. I'm still trying to accept my feelings and what they mean," he admitted.

"Let's not pressure ourselves to be something we might not be. You said Holland's coming in the morning?"

He nodded, his body relaxing at my suggestion.

"Then let's go to bed and figure out one thing at a time. Neither of us is going anywhere; we don't have to express our love and cross a boundary we might not be ready for on the same night."

"You truly are brilliant, Max. Yes, let's do that. I need to check in with Grady, but I'll be back in a few minutes."

"He was down at the bar," I offered, pulling my hands away, the sudden loss of him bigger than it ever had been before.

"Figures. He's so twisted about her that he can't admit it. I'm willing to let him into our dynamic with her as long as he doesn't hurt her. I won't let him get away with his bullshit, leader of us or not."

Q released my hair, his hand traveling down my neck in a soft caress. Tingles I hadn't allowed myself to notice before ran through my body. He smirked as he stood, making me wonder if he'd done that intentionally. Was he flirting?

While he went to Grady's room, I pulled my laptop over and checked all the servers one last time. There was a message for the location of the meeting tomorrow and the protocol to get in. The information was like a bucket of cold water, reminding me of our reason for being here—to find a killer.

Shutting down my laptop, I changed out of my clothes and brushed my teeth, crawling into bed just as Quentin reentered the room.

"He's back in his room bordering on drunk and pissed he couldn't gather any new intel," Q relayed as he pulled off his shirt. My eyes tracked his muscles, the awareness intensifying inside of me new.

"Did you tell him about Holland?" I asked, looking away.

"Not yet. I don't want him to fuck it up for us before we have a chance to talk to her. She's already flighty as hell. I'll tell him after we've superglued her to us."

He walked into the bathroom, the sound of water turning on as he did his nighttime routine. I stayed sitting up, too curious to lie down yet.

While it wasn't uncommon for us to share a bed, our room often only had a king size; I didn't know how it would play out tonight. Would he want cuddles? Or just stay to our sides, and that was that? It felt more important than ever before.

The light clicked out, the Alamo room falling into darkness as his feet padded over to the bed. I watched his shadowed form as he neared, holding my breath.

"Scoot over. I want you closer to the window," he said breezily, not noticing how my heart was about to beat out of my chest.

Doing as he said, I moved over and under the blankets, my head on the far pillow. Quentin climbed in and covered himself, turning toward me. His arms reached out, pulling my body to his. I relaxed at his touch, loving how nice he felt behind me.

"I need to feel close to you tonight. I need the reassurance you're here. I promise not to cross any lines until we talk more. Is this okay?"

"Yes, of course." My voice croaked, but my heart slowed as his arms wrapped around me. We lay there, our breathing evening out as we relaxed together. Quentin's head moved, his lips brushing the bare skin of my neck.

"What are you hiding?" he whispered. "I know there's something you haven't told us."

Sighing, I knew I couldn't hold it in any longer and spilled everything. I disclosed the information I'd found on Ava Savage and my fear she'd be used in the war against the Savages.

"Are you mad?" I asked once I was done. He'd been quiet the whole time, letting me speak.

"Only that you thought I could harm an innocent

girl. We'll talk more about this at the briefing. Sleep. *Our girl* will be here soon."

His lips pressed into my skin, and my heart took off at his words and the gentle kiss, and I didn't know if I'd ever be able to fall asleep.

But somehow, my body relaxed, falling into a deep and blissful rest despite it.

CHAPTER 15
HOLLAND xoxo

I STARED AT MY COFFEE MUG, MY FACE RESTING IN MY HAND as I leaned against the kitchen island. It had been really late when I returned, and I'd only gotten a few hours of sleep. I needed the world's largest coffee today. I didn't have it in me to deal with anyone's shit.

Fingers snapped in front of my face, and I looked up, meeting Lacey's scrunched brows. "What's with you?" she asked, crossing her arms over her chest.

"Tired," I mumbled, bringing my mug closer to my mouth so I could sip some of its goodness.

"Besides that. There's something else."

I shrugged, not wanting to get into my time with Quentin and his possessive dick. Or that he'd claimed me and wanted to talk. But most definitely, I didn't want to talk about how alluring it was. Nope, I wouldn't give in to the relational pull and get all loved up. Because gross. That wasn't the life for me.

I had my girls. I had the list. And I had my fun.

That was all I needed in life—end of discussion.

"Joy!" Lacey bellowed, startling me on the counter.

"Holland is hiding something. Get in here and figure it out."

Groaning, I placed my forehead on the counter, hitting my fist on the surface. "No. I don't want to talk about it. I'm too tired. Last night's job took a lot out of me," I whined. I knew it was futile, but I had to try at least to persuade them otherwise.

Joy wrapped her arms around me in a hug, burrowing her chin into my neck. She rocked me back and forth, kissing my cheek as she started talking to me like a baby.

"What's wrong, Holsy boo? What's got my scaredy cat all coiled up this morning? Hmm?"

"I'm not a scaredy cat," I mumbled, but her soothing antics coaxed me into a false sense of comfort.

"Yes, you are, and Lacey is my grumpy bear."

Lacey grunted but didn't deny the classification.

"Then who are you?" I asked, trying to buy myself some more time.

"Hmm, I'm more of a Harley Quinn type. A bit of sunshine, a bit of crazy, and a great ass."

Chuckling, I lifted my head onto my arms, my eyes moving over to meet hers. Joy stared back, her pure heart in her golden-brown eyes as she waited me out. I flicked my gaze to Lacey, finding her sipping her coffee with a smug smile, her blue eyes alight with mirth.

"I hate you," I hissed, sticking out my tongue.

"No, you don't. And don't act like you haven't done the same thing. No one can refuse that face. It's why she's so great at what she does," Lacey said, blowing me a kiss.

Sighing, I sat up, the movement causing Joy's arms to fall from me. She took the stool next to me, again giving me her patient and loving smile.

"I *am* tired, and last night *was* hard. She was just a little girl." Tears brimmed my eyes, the horror of what I'd witnessed surfacing. On the job, I blocked it all away, knowing I couldn't focus on my feelings and get it done. But after, when it was all tied up in a neat little bow, then I'd fall apart as the reality of my actions played out in my memory.

Joy's hand squeezed my thigh, her thumb rubbing gentle circles. "You saved her, Hols. She's with her mom now, and she'll get the help she needs. We'll make sure of it."

I nodded, sucking in a breath to stop the tears from falling. Lacey handed me a tissue, and I took it, drying my eyes.

"What else?" she hedged, leaning closer to the counter. The three of us made a little triangle, the move creating a little bubble where it felt safe to share.

"I found Quentin last night." I cleared my throat, tracking back through my mind of everything that had occurred between us.

"And?" Joy prodded, nudging my leg. "Did you learn anything new?"

"Maybe the size of his dick. She clearly fucked him," Lacey said, taking another sip.

Rolling my eyes at her candor, I waved my hand,

acknowledging she was right. "I walked into the bar with the intention of honey-trapping him, and somehow, we ended up fucking on his bike off the side of the road behind some trees."

"Damn, girl! That sounds hot!" Joy fanned her face.

"How big is it?" Lacey asked, raising her eyebrows. "He seems like he'd have a big one and know *exactly* how to use it."

Chuckling, I nodded. I still felt sore between my legs, which hadn't happened since my first time.

"Oh yeah, he's packing. The things he said, the way he held me, and the heat between us… Holy shit, it's something else," I said, exhaling. Now that it was out in the open, I felt lighter.

"So what's the problem? You got some good dick. You should be cocky as fuck," Lacey said, her brow furrowing as she studied me.

"You're catching feelings!" Joy exclaimed, clapping her hands.

"Yeah, right," Lacey admonished before stopping and staring at me. "Wait, are you?"

"I… I don't know. There's something magnetic between us. Something I've never felt with a man before. But it's not just him. I felt it with Max and in my brief encounter with Grady. There's a pull between the four of us that I can't explain, and that's what's terrifying me. Well, that and the fact Quentin wants me to meet him this morning to talk about our," I paused, swallowing, "relationship with Max."

"Wait, hold up!" Joy started, holding her hands out

in front of her, bouncing on her stool. "He wants to what now?"

"He started spouting something about how I was his, and I told him very politely that I wasn't a one-dick girl."

Lacey snorted, knowing me better than that. "You told him to fuck off, didn't you?"

Cringing, I scrunched up my nose, a smile following. "I don't know if it was those particular words, exactly. Maybe something about having too many disco sticks to ride."

Joy cackled, slapping the counter, tears streaming down her face. Lacey even smiled, shaking her head at me.

"What did he say to that?" Joy asked, going all eager beaver to hear my tale.

"He got all growly, closed his eyes, and then said, 'Max and Grady only.' The whole time we had this conversation, mind you, his dick was still in my cabana, and he was oiled up and ready to go."

"Shit. That's hot," Joy said, fanning herself.

"So, what are you going to do?" Lacey asked, eyeing me.

"I don't know. I don't do feelings for this reason. It complicates things. Us three against the world is so much easier." I laid my head back down on my arms, staring at the wall, hoping a solution would jump out and bite me.

"It doesn't have to be all or nothing, babe," Joy said, lifting my chin with her finger. "You can have us *and* be in a relationship. Or relationships. We'd never want to stand in your way. You're not going to lose us. We're ride-or-die. That's for life, Hols."

"What Hallmark Barbie said," Lacey added, nodding her head. She was just as uncomfortable with feelings as I was.

"What if that means they find out about XOXO? They won't be here forever, so eventually, we'd have to figure that out, too. You know… there are just too many complications. It's better to ignore it and just leave it at great sex. Yeah. That's what I'm going to do."

I started to stand, sliding off my stool. Joy grabbed my arms, holding me in place.

"Stop running scared. You're a badass killer; don't let fear be the thing that conquers you. All those questions we can figure out together. We never planned to stay here, so that's a non-issue, and as for XOXO…" she trailed off, turning her head to Lacey. They exchanged something between them before Joy refocused back on me. "Maybe you should tell them. I can't stop thinking about Ava or all the other clients we couldn't take on because we're just three girls taking justice into our own hands. They might be able to help us."

I sucked in a breath, looking back and forth. "You're serious. When did you talk about this?"

"Last night, but that's not the point," Lacey said, knowing I'd focus on being left out of something.

"Then what is?" I asked, crossing my arms like a petulant child. Clearly, I still had some brat energy in me.

Lacey smirked, lifting one brow. "The point is, you have feelings for these guys," she said, the word sounding weird from her mouth. She stopped, licking her lips like even saying it about someone else tasted funny. "So we might as well kill two birds with one stone, so to speak."

"We're not saying you have to be with them, but even before we knew you liked them, it seemed like the logical solution to helping Ava. So, maybe test them out and get to know them and see if they're the good-bad guys or the bad-bad ones."

"Aren't we technically the bad ones?" I asked, pointing at the three of us.

"Not from our perspective. More like morally gray," Lacey said like it was that cut and dry.

And I supposed it was when it came down to it. Most people would have a problem with us taking justice into our own hands, handing out punishments we saw fit, and making people pay for the harm they'd done. So, yeah, we might be the bad guys to some, but I'd rather be us than their lazy good guys any day.

"When are you going to meet them?" Joy asked, not letting it go.

"Oh, about twenty minutes ago," I said, lifting my coffee to my lips. The mug was wrenched out of my hands before it made it there, a scowling Joy in its place.

"Get dressed!" she ordered, pointing toward my room.

"Yes, ma'am," I simpered, ducking under her arm

and scampering away to the safety of my room. Angry Joy was not one to mess with.

"If you're not out in five minutes, I'll drag you out in whatever you're wearing!"

"Yes, Mommy Joy!"

She cackled again. "Oh, I like that. Mommy Joy."

"Does that make me the daddy?" Lacey asked.

"Totes, babe. You got all kinds of daddy energy. And let's face it, Hols is definitely our bratty child."

They both chuckled, and I screwed up my face as I ignored them and rushed around my room to throw on clothes. Joy wasn't playing around. She might be tiny, but she was fierce.

With ten seconds to spare, I stumbled out of my room, hopping on one foot as I slipped the other shoe on. Joy handed me my purse and pushed me out the door, smacking me on the ass.

"Go get your men!" she shouted, waving like a loon as I started down the sidewalk.

I felt more centered as I walked into the Secret Keep Inn, the worry I'd lose my best friends gone. If they were by my side, I'd get through anything.

Stepping off the elevator, I jolted to a stop when I came face to face with Grady. His eyes sparkled for a brief second; then he looked as shocked to find me in his hallway as I did to come upon him. His eyes dropped down my body, taking in my jean shorts, rock t-shirt, and Converse. I slipped the sunglasses I'd been wearing on top of my head, my arms crossing over my chest as his gaze hardened.

"Why are you here?" he asked, the earlier light I'd seen evaporating. I guess he wasn't a fan.

"I was invited."

He stepped closer, eliminating the space between us, my back hitting the closed elevator doors.

"You need to leave. I don't know who you are, but I know you're up to something, and I don't want you anywhere near *my* men."

"*Your* men? You sure about that?" I taunted, my natural armor falling into place.

His lips pulled into a sneer, the look still making him look handsome, the jerk.

"They'll use and discard you, just like they've done to every other woman. You're nothing special. You'll be yesterday's news, and I'll still be standing here, watching their backs come tomorrow. So go spread your legs for them then. I hope you're better at it than you are cleaning."

His words stung, hitting my insecurities one by one. I didn't think as I reacted, and my hand flew up, smacking his cheek in a flash. His head turned with the force, the red handprint forming as he stared back at me in shock. My hand tingled, but I stood my ground.

"Stay the hell away from me, or next time, it won't just be a slap," I threatened, turning and hurrying down the hallway.

My body shook with rage, tears threatened to spring up, and all I could think about was getting to Quentin and Max and as far away from Grady as possible. Dammit. I didn't want to cry.

Sucking in a breath, I knocked on the door, my fist banging rapidly as my breathing came quicker.

Shit. I needed to get out of this hallway before I had a panic attack.

Thankfully, the door opened, and I rushed in, not waiting for the invite, and ran into Max's arms, taking him by surprise.

"Holland? What's wrong? What happened?" he asked, his arms holding me just like I knew they would.

His hand smoothed up and down my back, grounding me into place. I focused on his heartbeat, on the way his lungs filled with air, and I followed suit, my body slowly coming down from the adrenaline that had been whizzing through it from the altercation in the hallway.

Once I was calm, I stepped back and wiped my cheeks. I didn't want the evidence of my weakness to be seen. But Max's eyes watched me, never leaving my face, his goodness on display for anyone to see. As much as I knew I didn't deserve it, I wanted it. Wanted him.

I turned around, my face falling when I didn't spot Quentin.

"He went out into the hall. He'll be back," Max answered in response to my unasked question. Nodding, I sat on the edge of the bed and patted it for Max to join me.

As we waited for Quentin to return, Max talked with me about the odd tourist attractions and asked me what it was like to work in the Inn. By the time Quentin walked back into the room I was laughing and at ease, the calmness of Max having seeped into me.

There was no doubt in my mind that I could trust Max and Quentin, but there was no way I could trust Grady, which created a serious problem. Because as much as I felt for them, I didn't know if they'd stand by him or me in the end, and that terrified me more than anything.

CHAPTER 16
AVA SAVAGE

"AVA!" MY FATHER SHOUTED AS HE STOMPED THROUGH the house.

I rolled my eyes; it was doubtful that he needed me for anything. More likely, he couldn't let my peace and quiet go uninterrupted. Viper wanted to remind everyone he was the biggest and baddest asshole in the room and, consequently, the most important.

No worries, Dad. We all knew.

"Your presence is requested," he seethed, surprising me.

"Mine?" I squeaked, jerking back like he'd struck me.

"Are *you* questioning me, Ava?" my father asked, prowling closer.

I flinched in fear, just like he wanted. He smiled, happy his only daughter was terrified of him. Internally, I longed for the moment I could show him what I was truly made of. But it wasn't now. There were still too many things at stake.

"No, Papi," I whispered, dropping my eyes to the ground.

He lifted my chin with his hand, tightening his grip on me. "Get dressed. One of your potential suitors is here. He wants to check out the goods before he commits."

Ah, there it was. My father didn't like to be questioned, especially on his word. He'd promised all the deadliest families a docile and virgin bride… for a price, of course. My father had never wanted *me*, but he saw the potential to use me to his advantage. This was made even more abundantly clear when he took over for Grandfather and became the big boss.

My whole life, I'd grown up surrounded by burly bodyguards to protect the one thing I had of value—my vagina. It was both my weakness and strength. I'd never been considered an actual threat to my father because of it, and the only purpose I served was to broker an alliance.

No one ever asked what I wanted. Not that anyone would listen if they did.

Most of my life had been spent on the compound, with only killers to entertain me. I'd watched men murder one another and knew I wouldn't survive once my father's protection wore off. The things I knew… were too great to let me live a life outside of the Savages, even if my father treated me like I was too dumb to survive.

So I'd either join the ranks by killing an innocent.

Or marry whoever my father selected for me… with a future of being beaten and raped.

Yay, me! Yeah, I didn't like either one of those options.

Dipping my head in understanding, I hurried to my closet to change into something appropriate. I needed to look the part and hope the man with the best offer wouldn't be as ruthless as the Viper. It was a foolish hope, but without any contact from the XOXO killer, I had to play along and bide my time until I could escape.

Pulling on a white cotton dress, I pulled my dark hair back into a low ponytail. I dabbed on some perfume, slipped on my flats, and returned to my bedroom.

My father was no longer there, but my personal bodyguard was. He nodded, motioning for me to head to the main part of the house where we received guests.

I'd been fortunate to have Theo on my side these past few years. As far as ruthless killers went, he was the most decent. At 6ft, he was several heads taller than me, with broad shoulders and thick muscles. His beard covered most of his face, giving off a grizzly bear vibe. His brown hair was kept short, matching his chocolate eyes. I'd heard from some of the servants that he had a thing for my mom, making him a little softer toward me since I looked just like her.

Whatever the reasoning, I knew he'd shielded me from a lot of the darkness and helped me have as normal of a teen life as the Viper would allow. I'd been able to attend public school for high school, and his youngest son had been tasked as my accompanying guard as part of the Junior program. It worked to not draw attention to me with someone trailing me, letting me have a semblance of a normal life. Thanks to Lukas, I got to make a few friends, volunteer, and pretend like I wasn't a Savage for eight hours of the day. It was the best four years.

But since graduation, all the freedom I'd had vanished, and my father was fixated on my looming birthday and the subsequent trade he planned to make.

"How's Lukas?" I whispered as we walked side by side. I hadn't seen his son since graduation, and I missed him. We'd grown close over the four years, and he'd become my true best friend… maybe more if we'd been allowed to explore our feelings. But we both knew that wasn't in the cards for us… unless we managed to run away successfully.

Neither of us was placing our eggs in that basket just yet.

"He's made it through the program. He'll be graduating next week after he finishes his last job," he replied, his eyes watching me from the corner.

I nodded, not liking what I'd heard but knowing there wasn't anything I could do. Lukas and I were both powerless to our circumstances.

"He asked about you," he said, catching me off guard.

"He did?" I smiled, unable to stop the blush.

"There's not anything I need to know, is there, Ava? You guys haven't…?"

I shook my head even though he didn't finish the

sentence. "No. We never. It's not like that. I promise we never crossed the line."

Except that was a lie.

We'd kissed once when we were kids, and again on the night of my graduation, the night he left for the training program for senior mercenaries. It had been the best and worst moment of my life.

Theo watched me, nodding as he turned back to the front. I didn't know if he believed me, but he let it go for now.

The corridor came into view, and I spotted all the Savages present, the snake patch with a large S over it adorning their shoulders. I quickly looked around the room, trying to figure out which suitor was here. None of the options were good, but some were way worse.

A greasy man in his fifties smiled at me, his eyes tracking over my body as we approached. I could feel Theo tense next to me before stepping back along the wall with the rest of the men.

I lowered my head in reverence, staring at my feet as the man stalked around me. His hot breath skirted across my skin, and I had to control my body from shuddering in revulsion.

"How do I know she's a virgin?" he spat. "Maybe I should have a test?"

I jerked my head up, my eyes wide with fear. No. This was too soon. I wasn't ready.

"Absolutely not, Marquis! You know the rules, the same as all the other families. No one gets to touch her until they're married. I promise on her life that she is untouched and have the medical examination to prove it. You wanted to see her, and now you have. Do you have any *legitimate* requests?" Viper hissed, pissed off he was being questioned. "You're wasting my day with your obnoxious concerns."

The small man vibrated with anger, letting me know everything I needed. This man would not be kind to me. If he didn't beat and rape me to death, I'd end up killing myself to escape a future with him.

"I'll be in touch," Marquis said, storming out of the room.

My father stormed over to me, directing his anger at me. He gripped my chin so hard I knew bruises would be visible tomorrow. Good thing I didn't see anyone.

"If you've lied to me and made me look like a fool, you'll regret it. I'll kill every single boy at that school. I'll have all the animals slaughtered at that shelter. And I'll make you watch every single second of it before letting every Savage have their way with you until you're begging me to kill you. But I won't. I'll wait a month to see if you conceive; if you haven't, I'll let them all do it again until you do. Once you provide me with a replacement, then and only then will I kill you, letting you know I'll be raising your child however I see fit. Do we understand one another, *Daughter*?" His voice was ice-cold, hatred and ill-intent ringing in every word he said. There was no doubt in my mind that he meant every single thing.

I'd always known he felt this way, but having him say it in front of his top men sent the message home.

He had no feelings for me. Not an ounce of paternal love.

"Yes, Papi," I whispered, my voice wavering as tears gathered in the corner of my eyes. "I promise I'm untouched. The doctor verified it, remember?"

He grunted, dropping my chin as he turned and marched out of the room, not looking back. I wasn't worthy enough to deserve a response. He made the rules, and we all had to obey them.

A hand touched my shoulder, and I jumped, spinning around as I cowered. Theo lifted his hands, showing he wasn't going to hurt me.

"Let's head back to your room, princess," Theo whispered, using the nickname he'd given me as a child.

Wiping my tears, I nodded, walking back to my room in a haze. I had to find a way out. There was no way I could continue to live like this. I wanted so much more for my life than as a sex doll and incubator for a merciless man.

"I'm going to take a bath," I whispered when I entered my room. Theo nodded after checking my room, ensuring no one had snuck in during our absence. Once it was secured, he stepped out, shutting the door and giving me some space.

In slow motion, I undressed, my mind whirring with thoughts. I hung my dress back up, pulling out the burner phone Lukas had given me from my hiding spot. I turned it on, praying there would be a message.

When nothing showed, I sent one more, hoping this one wouldn't go unanswered.

XOXO,

It's worse than I imagined. I know it's a big ask, but I'm desperate. My father plans to sell me off to another mercenary family for the highest price. I only have a week until my 18th birthday. That's the night it will happen. If you can help, I have a few guards who might look the other way —ones who are sympathetic to my plight. If you can't help me, there's nothing left for me to live for. I'd rather die than live out the life my father has planned.

A desperately hopeless Savage.

CHAPTER 17
HOLLAND xoxo

Quentin watched me from his spot on the wall. He'd been standing there since he walked in, his jaw working as he chewed something over in his mind. Noticing the time, I swallowed, biting the bullet. I needed to get this started so I wasn't late to work.

"Um, so you said you had something to talk about, Q?"

He uncrossed his arms, his eyes bouncing to Max and then back to me. It looked like he was debating something. With a grunt, he strode across the room, lifting me into his arms and sitting back down with me in his lap. My eyes widened as I glanced at Max, unsure of what to do with Quentin's behavior. He shook his head, smiling, offering no help.

"Not that I mind my new seat, Q, but you're still not talking."

"You're ours. What else do we need to say?" he grumbled, rubbing his stubble against my neck.

"For starters, I haven't heard what Max feels about that. And if you think Grady's a part of this, then you didn't see the slap I gave him."

Max's brows furrowed at the same time that Q's head snapped up.

"Grady's who upset you?" Max asked.

"Yeah. In between telling me I meant nothing to you, and he hoped I was better at spreading my legs than cleaning." I crossed my arms, the anger returning as I recalled his words.

"He said *what*?" Quentin growled, sending shivers through me. It also calmed my racing heart that maybe Grady hadn't been right. Reinforcing that what I felt for Quentin and Max was different. Real, maybe.

I blew out a breath, my body relaxing. "If that's all this is, just tell me upfront. I'm fine with just fucking. You don't have to sugarcoat it for me but don't play me. It won't end well for you," I bit out, my breathing increasing.

Max reached over, uncurling my hand that I'd clenched unknowingly. Tiny half-moon indents appeared in my palm from where my nails had bit into the skin. Max soothed away the sting with his thumb.

"Holland, that's not what this is. I'm not one to do that." He cleared his throat, his cheeks reddening. "And Quentin doesn't say things he doesn't mean. I know you just met us, and we have to build trust, but I wanted you to know that. I'm sorry Grady said those things. They were uncalled for and out of line. We'll talk with him."

Max's face was so earnest and wholesome that I almost felt guilty for all the dirty things I wanted to do to it. Almost. I happened to have a kink for corrupting sweet guys.

"Are you sure? I don't want to come between you guys…" I laughed, realizing my choice of words. "Well, I would very much like to *come* between you two, but not in a bad way."

Max chuckled, his face redder if that was possible. I couldn't see Quentin, but I felt his warm body against my back. His lips moved across the exposed skin.

"That's just one of the things I want to do to you, Temptress."

I bit my lip, holding back a moan as frustration coursed through me that I had to work soon and therefore couldn't get any ideas. The hard-as-steel member beneath me apparently had other plans, too.

"So, um, what do you guys do? Why are you in Foolshope?" I asked, trying to change the subject.

The guys froze, instantly cooling my lust as I remembered their truth. Max looked over my head, his eyes sweeping back and forth as they searched for something from Quentin.

"We work in private security," Max said after a long silence.

"Private security? Like you're bodyguards?" I asked curiously, hoping to gain as much information as they would give me. Had to hand it to them; they were good. They gave me just enough truth that it sounded reasonable. But I was better and knew more than they were aware of.

"Sometimes. Though we mostly work on location and retrieval cases."

That piqued my interest. My eyes lifted, thoughts coursing through my head.

"Whoa, that sounds really cool. Do you have cool spy gadgets?" I asked playfully.

Max shook his head, relaxing that I seemed to accept what he'd said. "Not like you see in movies."

"So, are you here to find someone?" I asked, wanting to hear how they would spin this bit.

"Is that really what you want to talk about, Temptress?" Quentin asked, leaning down to kiss my neck, his tongue sweeping out along my throat. And there's the misdirection, the change of subject.

"Um, yes," I said, barely containing the moan. I shifted, making him groan as I brushed against his erection. "We're supposed to get to know one another. You guys already know what I do; it's only fair."

"Our job is boring. I'm usually stuck here while Q and Grady are out looking for our missing person."

"Missing? So, like they've been kidnapped?" Max's face flushed, his words stumbling as he realized what he'd let slip. I hated using him like this, but he was clearly the easiest of the three to gather intel from with his too-trusting eyes.

"Enough for now," Quentin demanded, stepping in. "When do you get off?"

"Five. Then Lacey, Joy, and I go out for drinks."

"Skip it tonight. Meet us for dinner instead," Quentin commanded.

The brat in me wanted to push him, but I knew when to pick my battles, and if I wanted to make it on time for my shift, I couldn't push buttons right then.

"Will there be dessert?" I asked, tapping my lips like I was thinking about it.

"The best kind," he whispered into my ear and licked it, not hiding what he meant by that at all.

I cleared my throat, fighting the urge to fan myself. I didn't need to give him any more ammo.

"Fine, but I have to change afterward, so text me where and I'll meet you there at 7 pm."

"Plan to stay here," he said, standing and spinning me in his arms. His lips crashed down on mine before I could respond, stealing my words as he devoured me. When my breath was officially gone, he pulled back and turned me to Max. My steps were wobbly as I attempted to regain oxygen.

Max pulled me gently into his arms, kissing my nose first, then my cheeks, before landing on my lips. This guy was almost too cute for words. I felt terrible for half a second for all the corruption I planned, but he was a grown man. He made his own decisions; I hadn't pushed him into this.

"Right. I'll see you guys later."

I waved, trying to regain some of my power as I left. I knew I couldn't walk away from them yet, I only hoped I wouldn't be the one to get burned in the end. Because there would be an end, and I prayed I was on the winning side.

But they didn't call this town Foolshope for no reason, and I was afraid I was about to be hope's fool.

The day flew by for once, and the three of us moved from room to room in a united precision, our minds on the latest message we'd gotten from our hopeless savage.

"You sure you don't want to tell them?" Joy asked for the third time.

"No. I can't. Not yet. Grady doesn't like me and is highly suspicious. I'm not sure he wouldn't turn us all in. I can't risk that. So, for now, I'm just Holland, the crappy maid." I gritted my teeth, his words cutting me to my core.

I'd once had a bright future and a plan to leave this town. The first time my dream was stolen from me was the summer before college, and my dad lost his job again. We'd never been rich, but my dad made decent money as a truck driver when he worked, and it provided us with enough to pay the rent on our crappy two-bedroom apartment and afford food from the clearance aisle.

But as usual, his drunkenness would catch up to him, and he'd fall off the wagon and get fired, losing our only source of reliable income and health insurance. The health insurance hit the hardest—especially for my little sister.

So, I stayed close to home to work a crappy job to

help support my family, still believing I could make something of my life if I worked hard enough.

What a kick to the gut that had been.

"You're not a crappy maid," Lacey huffed, pulling the sheets taught. "He's just mad he's not getting the Holland cream too."

"Shut the fuck up." I laughed, throwing a pillow at her head. She stuck out her tongue, picking it up to fluff and placing it against the headboard.

"Oh shit," Joy said, making us both turn to her.

"What?"

"Phantasm sent over more info on the kiddie circle. The guy's in town, and he's planning to meet up tonight with a broker."

"What the fuck?" We couldn't let this guy get his hands on a child. My heart raced as I tried to find a solution.

"He told us to stay hidden, and yet he keeps sending us shit," Lacey cursed, her go-to default to accuse everyone when she was scared.

"Yeah, well, it's not like we can take a sick day or vacation from unaliving bad guys. They sure as hell don't."

I paced back and forth. There wasn't enough time to make a good plan. This would need us all and the potential to be messy if things went haywire. I didn't think I'd be able to get away with a staged suicide for these guys. Because there was no way I was letting a buyer and a pedophile live to touch another child.

They'd both need to die.

"I need to cancel my date. This is our first priority, and we need all hands on deck," I said, a plan forming. "When's the meeting?" I asked, glancing at Joy.

"It's at 4 pm. He's probably grabbing a kid from school and selling them quickly to reduce the trail. You might be able to still make your date..." she trailed off, her unspoken words hanging in the air.

If we're not caught.

If we don't die.

If we're cleaned up in time.

Nodding, I pushed that aside for now. I could deal with them later once we saved a child.

"Do you have the location for the meetup?"

"Yes. What are you thinking?" Joy asked.

"See if we can contact the buyer and urge them to meet earlier. If we can head off the meeting and separate them, we'll have a better chance of success."

Joy nodded, already messaging Phantasm as she left the room. Lacey looked at the clipboard, checking how many rooms we had left.

"If we hurry, we can finish the last two and get Kerry to cover us until our shift ends."

"Yes. Message her. I'll start on the next one while you two do that."

While I cleaned, I prepared myself for the job, thinking through all the variables and the overall success rate of each tactic. My statistical brain came alive as it searched for patterns and solutions, finding the best cost-benefit analysis. I doubted any of my teachers ever thought I'd use math for murdering.

By the time we'd finished with our floor, I knew what we had to do. "Everything taken care of?" I asked, coming out of my mental fog.

"Kerry's on board. We owe her a case of ciders," Lacey said, hiding our cart in the back so it wasn't noticeable.

"The buyer can only meet thirty minutes sooner, so we have a small window before the second mark shows. We'll have to be quick," Joy added, checking over her shoulder as we peered around the corner.

Familiar voices headed our way, and I pushed us into a closet, keeping it cracked. I didn't need them to catch me leaving work when I was supposed to be here until five.

And this was why relationships were difficult when you murdered people on the regular. I didn't need a boyfriend checking up on me.

"I don't know what your problem is with her, but you need to let it go. Max and I like her, and we're not going to quit seeing her just because you can't accept your own feelings."

"Feelings?" the second voice scoffed. "The only thing I feel is pure annoyance that you don't see how wrapped up in some stranger you've become. This isn't healthy. It isn't you. You're supposed to be the emotional reader of our group. How could you let yourself become compromised by this slut?"

A loud thump had us jumping, our eyes wide.

"Out of respect for our history, I'll let that one go. But I won't hold back if you ever call her a name again.

Either get on board and get to know her or leave us alone. That's the two options, *chief*. She's not going anywhere."

"Fine," Grady gritted, the anger radiating from his one word.

"I'll check in later," Quentin said, his steps echoing as he walked away.

A loud crash sounded in the hall before the door to the stairwell slammed open, and feet ran down the stairs. When it was quiet, Lacey peeked out and nodded it was clear.

A trash can lay in the middle of the hall, spilling out. Sighing, the three of us picked it up and righted it against the wall.

"I take it back. He doesn't deserve your cream," Lacey grumbled, upset after touching the trash. It rated right under bugs on her list of things she despised.

"No arguments from me."

We managed to escape out the back and not run into anyone else. There was an hour and a half to change, grab our gear, and get to the location outside of town unnoticed. My heart pumped hard in my chest as we went through the steps, unease coating me for the first time.

Dressed in all black, I had a knife strapped to one thigh and a gun to the other. I didn't want to use the gun, but if it came down to it, then I would. I had a cloth with chloroform and pepper spray as well in case the man was difficult to take down. The girls were dressed similarly but with different roles.

"Alright, we all know our parts. We ready?" I asked, watching the parking lot.

Lacey had convinced the motel clerk to send the broker—whose name we got from Phantasm—to our room, stating she was surprising her boyfriend. The clerk hadn't honestly cared about the reason; the hundred was enough for them to agree. We'd gotten a room on the end, away from all the occupied ones and on the first floor, so it would be easier to move the bodies.

We knew it was our best bet to already be in the room to get the jump on the guy. Then Joy would take the child and leave, getting them to a safe location. That left Lacey and me to take care of both perps. Doing it during the day was risky, but we didn't have the option of waiting this time.

"We have movement," I whispered. The girls hid in their spots, and it felt like the three of us collectively held our breaths as the key was inserted into the lock.

Letting it out slowly, I centered myself as I pushed everything else aside and went to the place in my mind where I didn't question my choices and operated off pure instinct.

The door opened, and the light poured into the dark room. The door hid me from view for a few seconds as I waited for the broker to step in all the way. He was thankfully staring at the ground as he shut the door and didn't see us. Without hesitation, I jumped on his back as my hand covered his mouth. His body tensed, and he reared back, slamming me into the wall and bucking me off; my body fell onto the table, the cheap wood splintering with my fall.

Thankfully, the chloroform had started to work, his movements sluggish as he stumbled, reaching for something in his pocket. Lacey pounced, taking him to the ground and pulling his arms back, squeezing his hand until he dropped what he'd been going for.

"Shit," I groaned, sitting up, rubbing my lower back. Another reason relationships wouldn't work, I now had to explain a bruise.

"You okay?" Joy asked, running to me.

"I'll live."

She helped me stand, brushing off the wood splinters. We'd need to leave some money for damages, so we didn't raise questions.

"Here," Lacey said, tossing a set of keys to Joy.

She nodded, walking out the door and clicking it. A car beeped nearby, and she walked down the lot to check it out since he hadn't brought the kid with him.

"We waiting?" Lacey asked, and I nodded.

I didn't want to kill the wrong dude who had the misfortune of coming to our room. I picked up his phone; glad our gloves had touchscreen capabilities on them, so we didn't have to take them off.

"He was trying to call someone," I mumbled, peeking back out the window. Joy had a small child with her, waving that she was leaving.

"Joy's on to Operation Rescue," I said, sending a message to the contact with the room number. Once that went through, I slid a chip into the phone to copy the contents. "Let's get to work before the next one."

Lacey laid out the plastic, and we rolled the body onto the sheet. Releasing my knife, I debated how to kill him without it, weighing the fastest and cleanest ways. The decision was taken away from me when he reared up, reaching for my wrist that held the knife.

Out of instinct, I twisted, barely avoiding his grip. Slashing back at him, I nicked his arm, blood spraying outward.

"Bitch," he cursed, reaching to grab me.

Lacey jumped on his back, her arms wrapped around his throat to cut off his oxygen. While he fought her, I stabbed him in the gut, slashing a few times across his legs. I didn't stop until he quit moving, his body limp as he gave up the fight. Lacey fell backward, panting from the effort.

"Fuck. That was close. I hate messy kills," she huffed, trying to catch her breath.

"You good?"

"Yeah. Just need a second. He almost broke my arm," she said.

Blood pooled around him, quickly moving over the plastic. Cursing, I stood and rolled him up from one end, holding it tightly while Lacey came over with the duct tape. Once we had him secured, we cleaned up the areas where blood had sprayed and picked up the broken table. I checked outside, finding it empty, so I pulled the mask down and opened the door.

"Geez, he's a heavy fucker," Lacey cursed, zipping him into the black body bag.

"Right? Like, why couldn't the broker be a scrawny, short guy?"

"Probably because no one would take him seriously. Open the van, and I'll drive around until we have the next one, so they don't get suspicious."

Nodding, I hurried out and opened the van, using a cleaning cart to block the view. Together, we lifted the bag into the back of the van, huffing once we had the door closed. She saluted me and jumped into the driver's side as I repositioned the cart and closed the door.

I'd only been back in the room for a few minutes when someone knocked on the door. With a deep breath, I opened the door from behind it and let them enter.

Time to die, pervert.

CHAPTER 18
GRADY

I slammed out of the Inn, fury filling every cell in my body. This woman already had her claws in my men, and it had only been one day. The director wasn't going to like this. If I reported it, then he might pull us from the field, stating we weren't stable enough to go up against the Savages. But if he did that, then the last few years would've meant nothing.

That Camila had meant nothing.

I tugged at my hair, lacing my fingers over the top of my head as I paced back and forth. The sun was high in the sky, shining down on me as I tried to calm myself. Somehow, I had to get it together, or I'd lose everything. I couldn't go through that again. I wouldn't.

Falling back on my training, I cleared my mind and focused on the things around me.

A broken park bench.

A bird poop-covered light pole.

Litter scattered across the alley.

Graffiti marking the brick.

This town was a shithole, slowly driving me insane with its weird attractions and insanely attractive maids.

Fuck.

There it was. The thing I was trying to avoid but failing miserably at.

The hateful words I'd spoken ran through my head, and the feel of her hand slapping my face tingled in my memory. It had been well deserved, and part of me had relished in the pain.

My phone rang, and I grabbed it out of my pocket, answering before I looked.

"What?" I barked, assuming it was the director.

"Uncle G?" a small voice asked, my eyes shuttering in more self-loathing.

"Hey, baby girl. How's my favorite niece doing?" I asked, pretending like I hadn't just yelled at her.

"Oh, it is you! I got an A on my science test and made the soccer team. Mom's taking me out for froyo to celebrate," she cheered, her voice returning to the happy child I loved.

"That's awesome, sweet girl. I'm so proud of you. You've been working so hard."

"Thank you, Uncle G. I just couldn't wait to tell you."

"I'm so glad you called. I miss hearing from you," I said, my heart rate returning to normal.

"I miss you, too. When can you visit again? Will you bring Uncle Max and Uncle Q?" she asked, hitting me squarely in the heart.

The guys weren't just my teammates but my family. I had to fix this. I had to push my prejudices aside and figure out my crap like Q had said. He'd been right, just like he usually was.

"Soon, baby girl. I'll make sure we bring you a souvenir. Where I am right now, there's a giant toilet bowl that people go to just to flush." I laughed, the anger leaving me in waves.

"That sounds gross and awesome!" Her giggle filled the tiny speaker, and I took a deep breath to soak it in. "Here, Mom wants to talk to you. Love ya, Uncle G."

"Love you too, Bella."

Sounds of rustling greeted me as she passed over the phone, and my sister answered as the phone disconnected from Bluetooth, the wind picking up as they climbed out of the car, her locks engaging as it beeped behind her.

"Hey, baby brother. How are you doing? I know today is hard for you."

The second gut punch of the day hit me as I realized what she meant. It wasn't an excuse for my behavior earlier, but at least it made a little more sense why I'd reacted so strongly.

"Uh, yeah. I'm fine. It's fine." My voice strained as I tried to push away the memories that wanted to surge. I rubbed my jaw, the feel of my stubble grounding me.

"Uh, oh. I know that tone. Who were you an ass to?"

"What?" I spluttered, checking over my shoulder like I expected my sister to be there. Her sixth sense rivaled Quentin's at times.

"Listen, I know you don't like to talk about it. But it's been five years. You can't keep killing yourself with your job. You can only outrun your demons for so long before they catch up with you, Grady." Her voice was soft and caring, striking me in the chest. I didn't deserve kindness.

"Yeah. I know. I'm just so close."

"I know you feel you have to do this. But will it bring you the closure you desire?" Dora asked.

"I…"

Green eyes flashed in my mind, the color and depth so magnetic as Holland had pinned me beneath her stare. It jolted me back to life. She made me feel something, and that was why I pushed her away.

It didn't seem fair to feel something for another woman when I still hadn't redeemed the first one stupid enough to fall in love with me. I couldn't protect Holland anymore than I could Camila.

"It's all I have," I finally answered, realizing I'd been staring at the graffiti.

"You sure about that?" she asked with a hint of sadness.

My sister and I had always been close, and losing Camila had been just as devastating for her as it was for me. But I couldn't stay in our small hometown. There were too many memories and things that reminded me of her—of the life I'd never have again.

So, I'd left, joined the Shadows, and hadn't been back home for more than a night before I was off again.

I might've lost Camila, but my sister had lost us both.

When I met the guys and brought them home for a

visit, she seemed hopeful that I'd moved on and found new people to care about. And I guess, in some ways, she'd been right. But it was our focus and pursuit of the Savages that bonded us, pushing all three of us to hunt them down and make them pay for the pain they'd caused our families and so many others.

Dora knew I wouldn't let Camila's death go, but she had no idea the danger I constantly placed myself in to exact that revenge.

"The guys are angry with me at the moment," I mumbled, giving her a crumb so she wouldn't look too closely at what I wasn't saying.

"Hmm, that's interesting. You guys never fight. Which means it must be about a girl."

There she went again with that emotional intelligence, picking up on things I hadn't directly said. Trying to hide secrets had always been a nightmare growing up, but I thought I'd improved as an adult. Now I wondered if she'd been letting me believe that, waiting for the right moment to remind me I wasn't as clever as I thought.

"I'm not sure who's worse, you or Q," I grumbled, kicking a can further down the alley.

"Oh, definitely me. Quentin's nicer and doesn't call you out on shit as much."

I clicked my teeth, knowing she was right. "I might've said something to a girl they like."

"*They?* Did Max and Q finally admit their feelings?" she asked, surprising the shit out of me.

"What?" I spluttered again, my head feeling dizzy. What else had I missed?

"I swear you act like you're the boss and know everything about your team, but it doesn't seem you're as close as you believe. Those two have been dancing around each other for years, either too naive to understand their feelings or too afraid. Maybe a little of both. I wondered if it would take a woman they both liked to face it. So, are they going to be poly now? Or just a triad?"

"What the fuck are you talking about?" I hissed, not appreciating how much her words stung. Here lately, I wondered if I knew either of them. Perhaps I had been deluding myself. Putting up too many walls that even my team couldn't climb.

"Get with the times, Grady. Love is love. Don't be a square and stand in their way. If they're happy, that's all that matters. Who's this woman? She must be pretty special to make them both lower their guard and let her in, and in the process, open the door for them to be vulnerable with each other. I'd say I was surprised you haven't thrown your hat in the ring, but you're so walled up, a naked woman could be standing in front of you, and you'd look past her, wondering why everyone was staring."

My mind blanked as I let her words sink in. I wasn't in the mood to look too closely on today of all days, but it was also a nice distraction from remembering the worst day of my life.

"You're delusional. You need to see someone," I muttered, changing the topic.

"It's the 21st century, Grady. If you're not in counseling, *you're the problem*. Don't diminish what I said by attacking *my* mental health because it hurt your feelings."

Feeling properly reprimanded by my older sister, I sighed, rubbing the back of my neck. Shit. She was right. I *was* being an asshole.

"Fuck. Sorry. You're just bringing up a lot of things I haven't been ready to look at too closely. I hadn't realized what today was until you said it, and then it made sense why I've been acting so moody."

"Apology accepted, but I'm probably not the only one you need to make it to. And I'm sorry if I crossed a line. I want to see you happy, Grady. We miss you. Bella misses you. You're loved beyond measure. Don't forget that because it might feel a bit darker today."

"Thanks, Sis. I needed to hear that." I let out a shaky exhale.

"So, what's her name? At least give me that! Help a sister out!"

Chuckling, I felt lighter despite the heaviness of our conversation. "Her name's Holland. Quentin's convinced she's the one and wants to share her with Max. I'm unsure about the other things between them as they haven't shared that with me."

"Holland. She sounds badass. I approve. And you? Where do you stand with her? Would you be willing to be in that type of relationship?"

Where *did* I stand? That was a good fucking question and one I didn't currently know the answer to.

"That's more complicated. I might've crossed the line and said some things this morning."

"I hope she gave it back just as good."

"Aren't you supposed to defend your baby brother?"

"Um, no. Not when he's being a little shit," she said, her smugness evident through the phone.

"She might've slapped me and told me never to talk to her that way again," I mumbled.

"Excellent. I like her already. You need someone who will push against your barriers and not take orders from you. Promise me that you'll look closer if you feel even a speck of something for her. You can't keep yourself hidden from the world and expect to live it. I just want the best for you."

I swallowed hard; her words were more than I deserved. Yet, the love and emotion behind them drew me in, making me want them to be true. To feel worthy of love again. To have a purpose outside of revenge.

Because, again, she was right.

Revenge could only take me so far before I had to face the fact that Camila was gone and never coming back, no matter how many bad people I killed or put away.

"Yeah, okay. I promise to look closer."

"Alright, Bella is filling her yogurt cup with more things than I believe the scale will be able to weigh, so I better save the poor attendant whose eyes are about to bug out of her head. Call us back soon. We miss hearing from you."

"I will. Love you, Dora."

"Love you, too. Bye."

The phone disconnected, and my shoulders dropped, my heart aching at the things my sister had said. The hard part was knowing she was right, but I wasn't sure if I was ready to face it. I needed to make things right with the guys first and foremost.

My phone beeped, and I nearly jumped, forgetting it was in my hand.

Max: Something's up with the trap. The broker isn't responding, and the time's been moved.

Max: I didn't request it. I don't know who did. It's either our killer or the broker's double-crossing us.

Max: He just sent a room number. This feels off.

Grady: I can head there now.

Max: I'll drop a pin of the location.

Grady: I'll let you know if I need backup.

Max: Be vigilant. Our guy might be there.

Grady: Got it.

Walking around the Inn, I hurried to the car and

plugged the phone into the AUX cord to bring up the pin Max had sent me. The hotel was on the outskirts and would take me thirty minutes to get there.

Sighing, I pulled out of the parking lot as my mind bounced from Holland to the case. Clearly, I needed to confront my issues with her, so I didn't blow up the case.

I wasn't convinced I would join their little group, though, no matter what my sister said. Holland was attractive and had a fire in her that I craved. She made me feel alive, giving me something else to focus on. But that didn't mean I needed to let her into my heart. What was left of it.

When I pulled into the parking lot, I felt more settled and ready to focus on the job. Tonight could be the first break we had at apprehending this guy and finding out how he accomplished his kills without getting caught. If he weren't too far gone in the psychopathic realm, then we'd recruit him, hoping he'd be the tipping point with the Savages. If not, he could take a bullet to the head or rot in prison. I didn't care.

We just had to find him before the Savages did, or Viper would become even more dangerous than he already was.

Double-checking the room number, I parked a little way down so I wouldn't give away my arrival. An older car sat nearby, and I didn't know if it was the broker's or our killer's. But something told me it wasn't the XOXO killer. He was too smart to leave any trace of himself out in the open.

Creeping around the back, I checked the windows for any escape routes, finding them shut tight with no way to open them. I couldn't hear anything from the bathroom, so I snuck around to the side, but there was still no sound.

Surveying the parking lot, I didn't spot anyone, a feeling of unease crawling up my back. Pulling out my gun, I held it low and out of sight as I knocked on the door. It creaked open, not having been latched all the way. The dark room came into focus as the light from outside shined in.

At first, I couldn't make out what I was seeing. Two figures fought, both clad in black, as they tossed one another around the room. The shine of the silver blade in the light pushed me into action. But as my eyes bounced between the two, I didn't know who I was meant to save. Should I let them fight it out and then deal with whoever survived?

Neither paid attention to me, either too focused on one another or considered me a non-factor. A second later, the bigger of the two ripped the mask off the smaller one, and white-blonde hair toppled out as they fell to the ground. I blinked, sure I'd hallucinated her after thinking about her all day. But when she didn't disappear, her grunts echoing in my ear, I knew she was real.

My heart dropped to my stomach as I watched the bigger figure stab Holland in the thigh a second before she twisted her legs around his waist and flipped him as she rolled. Her hand gripped his forearm, smacking it against the ground to get him to drop the knife. His shirt lifted, allowing me to see the tattoo wrapped around his wrist, a large S at the tongue's end.

Suddenly, I wasn't standing in this crappy hotel room; I was back in the house I'd bought with Camila. I'd come home early, a bouquet of her favorite flowers in my hand as I walked in with a bounce in my step. We were officially sixty days from our wedding date, and I wanted to celebrate. But instead of my beautiful fiancé greeting me, I saw that same tattoo as he bent over Camila, stabbing her repeatedly as he whispered something in her ear. I froze, her eyes landing on me and the desperation I saw there as she pleaded with me to make it stop.

I couldn't back then, too frozen in shock to do anything other than rush to her, sliding in the pools of blood as I neared, the flowers dropping to the ground. I clutched her dead body to me as I called 911 while the man escaped out the back as he laughed.

That laugh had haunted me ever since.

Snapping back into reality, I knew I couldn't let the Savages take someone else from me—whatever she ended up being—especially not on this day, the anniversary of Camila's death.

Raising my gun, I shot off two rounds into the back of the man's head; his body went slack as he fell on top of Holland. The smell of irises wafted through the room, a warm presence enveloping me for a second before it evaporated, taking away some of the darkness and guilt I'd been carrying around for five years.

Holland groaned, jolting me out of my trance, and I rushed to her, pushing the dead body off her. Her green eyes were as vivid as I'd remembered, looking at me in shock.

"I always thought if I were dying, I'd envision some hot celebrity or something as my last wish to see before I crossed over. You were nowhere on that list. I guess it makes sense if I'm going to Hell," she groaned.

Her eyes fluttered closed, her face pale as sweat beaded on her brow, reminding me she'd been stabbed. Ripping off my shirt, I pressed it against her leg, where most of the blood was coming from. I smacked her cheek, getting her attention.

"Wake up, mi chispa. You don't get to die right now. There are too many things unknown. We still have lots to fight over, baby."

"Fuck... you... I'll die when I want," she whispered.

Laughing, I pulled out my phone and hit the emergency button, ringing Max and Quentin simultaneously.

"Hello?" Max answered first, followed by Quentin. "You get your head out of your ass?"

"Get to the motel. *Now*. Bring the med kit, along with body disposal. Hurry."

I hung up before they could ask questions. I didn't want them to know it was Holland yet, afraid they'd be reckless and end up dead on the way to get here.

I checked her over as best I could, finding a few other cuts, but most had stopped bleeding. While I waited, I tried to figure out why Holland was here and how she played into all of this. My first assessment that she was a Savage spy had to be wrong if she'd been fighting with a Savage.

But the only other conclusion didn't make sense. How could Holland be the XOXO killer?

Before I could ponder it any deeper, the door flew open as Max and Quentin arrived, stopping dead in their tracks when they spotted the blonde beauty lying limp in my arms.

"What the fuck did you do? This wasn't what I meant when I said to deal with your shit!" Quentin shouted, storming over toward me with murder on his face.

"Calm down. I didn't do this. But I did do that." I motioned with my eyes toward the dead body they'd ignored. "*He's* a Savage."

My team blinked, confused at what I was saying.

"But…" Max trailed off, his face white.

"She's not with him, considering he stabbed her. Speaking of which, how about you get over here and help me stitch her up so your girlfriend doesn't bleed to death on the anniversary of Camila's?"

My words vaulted them both into action, Quentin demanding I hand her over. Ignoring him, I focused on Max and helped him as he jumped into medic mode.

"Is it bad? Do we need to go to a hospital?" I asked.

"Luckily, he missed the femoral artery. She should be okay once I stitch it up. Everything else looks superficial or will suffice with some medical glue."

Max fell into his role, cutting away her pants and

efficiently cleaning her wounds. When he was done, I relented my hold on Holland, releasing her to Quentin as he carried her over to the bed, brushing her hair out of her eyes. Max sat with her while Q and I got to work on the body and clean up.

"Fuck, there's so much blood. We're going to have to call someone in," I muttered.

"Do it. Let's get her out of here," Quentin said, standing as he lifted the dead body over his shoulder. We'd rolled him up in the shower curtain, placing him in a Christmas tree bag. It worked surprisingly well to hold and disguise bodies.

Punching in my code, I requested a cleanup as the three of us walked out of the motel—one carrying a dead body, another cradling an unconscious woman to their chest, and the last with a mountain of grief and regret.

Something was going on in this town, and I was on the cusp of figuring it out. And I prayed, for the first time in five years, that my gut was wrong and Holland had nothing to do with it.

CHAPTER 19
HOLLAND
xoxo

My body throbbed with pain, and I cursed whatever truck had decided to back up and run me over, dragging my body for miles before I tumbled down a hill and landed on a pile of broken bottles. Someone jostled me, and I groaned, not liking the reminder of how badly my body hurt.

"Did you get the name of the driver?" I mumbled, hoping Lacey or Joy would know what I was talking about.

"What?" a male voice asked, taking me by surprise. I jolted up, ignoring the pain as I surveyed my surroundings. My chest heaved as I tried to figure out where the hell I was.

"Holland, you're okay. It's safe," Max's soft voice said from my side. I jerked, blinking as I tried to recall how I ended up with him.

"Max," I said, my mouth dry.

Licking my lips, I smacked them together as I stalled for time. I needed to remember what had happened. I peered down, taking in my black tactical shirt with the extra padding to help protect my ribs and throw off my size if anyone saw me. My pants had been cut on one side, giving me a short length on my left leg and pants on the right. My black combat boots still adorned my feet.

Okay, so clearly, I was still dressed for murder, sans half of one pant leg. Time to play it dumb and see how much they knew.

"What happened?" I asked, looking at him. His brows dipped, and he pulled out a penlight and shined it in my eyes. I swatted it away before my arm protested and I had to drop it back to the bed.

"Do you remember anything?" he asked slowly, putting the light down.

I blinked, trying to remember and figure out a lie at the same time. "Um, not really. Where're my pants?" I asked, gesturing to the summer shorts on one side. "I doubt this is in style."

Max chuckled, shaking his head as his shoulders dropped slightly. "Yeah, sorry about that. I had to cut them to get to your stab wound." He stopped himself, only giving me bite-size portions of information. Max, the cutie, was harder to crack than I'd anticipated.

"Stabbed?" I asked, making my eyes owlish. "Why was I stabbed?" I looked around, taking in the rest of the room and finding it empty.

Now was my chance to discover as much as possible before the other two returned. The part of my heart that liked Max pinged in self-hatred, not liking that I was manipulating him. I didn't enjoy it either, but it was a matter of life or death, and not just for me. I needed all the facts before I told them anything.

"We were hoping you could tell us." Max sighed, hanging his head. "Holland, I think we could help one another, but we've gotta trust each other to do that. So, how about I go first, and then you tell me how you ended up in the room of a child molester."

I bit my lip but nodded. "Okay. First, do you have my phone?"

"Yeah." He stood and walked over to the dresser, picking it up. "The screen got cracked, but I think it still works. It's been vibrating, at least."

I grimaced when I saw the state of the screen. Swiping my finger over it, I jerked back when I felt the sting of the glass. "Ouch!" I hissed, pulling my finger to my mouth to suck the blood. Max gave me a horrified look.

"That's not sanitary," he stammered, his hand reaching to pull my hand free.

"It's fine. I'll grab a bandage when I'm done."

He dropped his hand, his face grimacing as he stared at me disapprovingly. Sighing, I placed my finger under his nose, not wanting him to look that way at me. Max's eyes popped up, a smile spreading as he took it and opened a medical kit. Damn, he was dangerous.

While he fiddled with doctoring me up, I opened my messages with my other hand, being more careful to avoid the shards this time. I had several messages from the girls but couldn't read them on the cracked screen.

Taking the chance, I hit the button to call them, needing them to know I was okay.

"Holland! Are you okay? What happened?" Lacey rushed out, not giving me a chance to respond. "When you didn't text, I returned to the motel and saw your three amigos carrying you to their car. The room was trashed and covered in blood. We were so worried but figured it was best to stay back if they had you," she whispered, keeping her voice low.

"Yes, um, good call. I'm with Max," I said, trying to tell them without saying more.

"Do you need us to extract you?"

"I don't think so. I might not make it to work tomorrow. How did your appointment go?"

"Got it taken care of. No more creepy perv, and the little girl was reunited with her family," Lacey said but was soon interrupted by Joy.

"We'll cover for you, but I want proof of life, or I'm storming in," Joy exclaimed.

Chuckling, I felt better already, knowing they hadn't been seen and had been able to reunite the little girl with her family. I knew I had a decision to make, and I would protect them in this as much as possible. We were ride-or-die for a reason.

"Thanks, love you both."

They made some kissing sounds before the call ended, and I turned back to Max. My finger had a bandage, his eyes watching me as he held my hand.

"I was so scared when I walked into the room and found you covered in blood, Holland. I know we just met, but in those few seconds, I thought you were dead…" he trailed off, shaking his head, sucking in a breath. His eyes were wet when he peered back up. "It felt like someone had stolen all the light, and I was lost in the darkness with no way out."

My earlier resolve broke at his words and tears. It was too much sweetness for my damaged and battered heart. Max was pure, and I wouldn't sully him with my manipulation and lies. I owed him the truth.

"I'm sorry. I would never wish for you to feel that way, Max. And honestly, I should step away before I taint your goodness." I dropped my eyes, not wanting to see the agreement in his eyes.

"I'm not as good as you think, sweetheart. Let me be the judge of what I can handle, okay?"

"That feels like something out of a romance book," I grumbled, but secretly I rejoiced inside that he'd called me sweetheart. No matter how dark Max's deeds were, he was still pure in his soul. I'd long given up on mine. But if he didn't have enough self-preservation to keep himself away from me, I was enough on the dark side not to stop him.

"Maybe." He chuckled, the sound deep and hearty. "I think you could use some romance."

"Gag." I made a barfing sound in the back of my throat, and he laughed even more.

"You're cute when you're trying to push me away. I was already hooked, Holland, and now I'm even more enamored of you. I want to know everything about you if you'll let me."

I sighed, letting out a big breath, and picked at the comforter, fidgeting as I debated. "I like you too, Max. I'm just worried once you hear all my truths, you won't look at me the same way."

"Never, Holland. What I feel for you goes beyond the surface. Trust me?"

I let out the breath I'd been holding. Somehow cute and nerdy Max had lowered my barriers, and I was ready to squeal all of my secrets. If he wasn't an interrogator, he needed to be.

"Where are the other guys? If I'm going to share, I should tell everyone at once."

Max nodded, reaching out to cup my jaw and leaning his forehead against mine. His soft green eyes searched back and forth before his lips pressed against mine. They were tender and warm, sending shivers through me. Unlike the first time I'd kissed him, this one felt more powerful, punching me in the gut as elephants trampled over the ants in my belly.

"I'll be right back," he whispered, standing from the bed and walking to the door to the adjoining room.

He poked his head through, then stepped back and opened it wider. The other two members sauntered in, Quentin making a beeline straight for me. His hands shook as he tried to find a place to touch me. I rolled my eyes, reaching out to pull him to me.

"I'm not going to break, Q."

He fell on the bed, scooping me back into his arms, settling me between his legs, my back resting against his chest. Quentin's body rumbled beneath me, his muscles practically vibrating as he squeezed me to him.

Damn, he'd been scared. Like really scared.

"I'm okay," I said, trying to reassure him as I smoothed my hand over his forearm.

"No, you're not," he argued, his voice rough. "If you weren't so injured, I'd bend you over my knee and spank your ass until it was red. You scared the shit out of me, Temptress. Don't ever do that again."

"I can't promise that," I started, pausing when he growled in my ear, "but I'll do my best," I finished.

I glanced up, finding Grady watching me, his shirt covered in dried blood. A memory of him talking over me flashed through my mind. I swallowed, trying to come to terms with the fact that the asshole had saved me.

"I'm guessing I have you to thank for taking out that guy?" I asked, no longer pretending not to remember.

He nodded, his eyes glued to me.

"I haven't forgiven you for what you said, but…" I gritted my jaw, my nostrils flaring as I pushed out the words. "Thank you for saving my life."

Grady reared back like I'd slapped him again, his eyes wide with shock. His mouth hung open for a second; then everything returned to the resting asshole face he wore so well.

"Let's start with why you were in *that* room," Quentin demanded in my ear.

I debated how much to say. Did I admit I knew they were looking for me, or wait to see if they revealed that?

"I got a message that a pedophile was meeting with a broker in the area. There was suspicion that the child would be quite young. I couldn't let them harm a kid." I shook my head in disgust, letting my emotions show. "I paid off the clerk by saying I was surprising my boyfriend and had them direct him to that room." I paused, deciding to keep the others out of it for now. "But that man came in and wasn't who I expected. He should've been easier to take down, but he was trained. He evaded me and attacked. I honestly thought he was going to kill me."

The tears fell on their own accord as I replayed the fight in my head. It was one of the first times I'd been terrified. He was bigger and better than me and had taken me by complete surprise. I hadn't stood a chance.

"Have you ever heard of the Savages?" Grady asked, his voice strained.

I shook my head. Outside of their chatter and the message, I had no clue who they were or why they'd attack me. I wanted to know who they were to my three guys.

I mean, these three guys. They weren't mine.

"No. I've never heard that before."

"Why would you go up against a child molester? Do you do that often?" Max asked, changing directions.

"Oh, um..." Shit. Did I tell them I was the killer? I'd really hoped they'd give more information first, but so far, it had all been one-sided—time to change that. I furrowed my brows. "What happened to that man?"

Max looked at Grady, who nodded. "He won't hurt you again."

It was all he said, the words heavy with everything he left out. How would we trust one another if we were both holding back? But being the odd woman out, I didn't feel like I could cross that line first.

Quentin's arms around me tightened, his breath blowing my hair as he huffed. "This isn't getting us anywhere. Fuck it. I'm telling her." He turned me around so I was straddling his waist, our eyes connecting as the others protested. We both ignored them.

This was what I'd been wanting.

"Babe, we're part of an organization called the Shadows. We operate outside the purview of the government, catching bad guys and recruiting others with a certain skill set. The three of us were sent here to locate and assess the XOXO killer. We believed they were a white male in their mid to late twenties with a criminal history. So, imagine our surprise when you were in the room for the trap we laid for the XOXO killer. My mind tells me you can't be them, but nothing else adds up." He stopped, his eyes bouncing back and forth from mine. "So, Holland, are you the XOXO killer?"

I sucked in a breath, both hating and appreciating how he'd laid it out there. I sorted through the information he'd given me.

An organization called the Shadows.

They'd set up the buy.

They recruited killers.

"What does that have to do with the Savages?" I asked, not answering yet. It was the one piece that didn't fit.

Quentin blew out another breath, his nostrils flaring.

"The Savages are a ruthless mercenary gang that kills anyone who gets in their way, taking any and every contract regardless of the kill. They're one of the biggest threats in the US and have evaded law enforcement and the FBI on every charge thrown at them." His face hardened, his nostrils flared, and his hands flexed against me. "They're the ultimate bad guys and have taken someone from each of us."

That statement hung in the air, the grief and hatred for this group palpable. Quentin kept his eyes on me, reading every little emotional cue I gave. I had no doubt that he knew the truth but wanted me to say it. *Needed me to say it.*

"If they were following you, then you're on their radar, and that's not good. They won't stop until you're covered in blood," he said, softer now.

He wasn't trying to scare me but to prepare me for the truth. The Savages knew who I was and would come for me. Therefore, I had to throw myself at their feet for mercy and pray they were enough to keep the people I loved safe.

I couldn't lose anyone else.

Gulping, I held his eyes as I dropped my shields, letting him see the truth.

"I'm the XOXO killer."

CHAPTER 20
QUENTIN

THE WORDS I NEVER EXPECTED TO ACTUALLY HEAR FELL from Holland's mouth, hitting me in the gut like a freight train. My hunch had been adamant as it slotted the pieces together, but I hadn't been able to bring myself to believe it.

The moment my eyes landed on her emerald orbs, my world had been turned upside down. She was the other half of my soul, and a few hours ago, I'd thought I'd lost her—another victim of the Savages.

Grady didn't want to share who we were with her, but I was done keeping secrets. This whole mission had been a bust, mainly because we'd been operating off the wrong profile. Holland had been the one good thing to come from this town, and now she held an even more important role.

The one we'd been searching for. The one to join our fight against the Savages.

I held her eyes, searching them as I tried to understand how. My brave girl stared back, proving to me without a shadow of a doubt she was who she said she was.

She was our killer.

"How? What?" Max jumped up, tugging his dark hair as he paced. "But that doesn't make sense. Our profile—"

"Was wrong, obviously," Grady gritted out.

I could feel his eyes on us, but I wasn't ready to drop Holland's yet. She needed something from me. There was a small amount of fear present, something else she was scared of being discovered. Whatever it was, I'd let her keep her secrets for now, preferring for her to come to me. I wanted her to trust me implicitly, so I wouldn't disclose whatever she was hiding… for now.

"You're safe with us, Temptress. We won't let the Savages near you."

Holland let out a breath, leaning her forehead onto my chest. She'd fought that man just a few hours ago and was injured. We shouldn't be pushing her this hard, this quick. My protective need to keep her safe reared up and I held her tightly to my chest.

Max and Grady wanted more answers, but they could wait a fucking minute. Smoothing my hand down her hair, I gave her the moment she needed to collect herself. Holland took a deep breath and nodded, her body relaxing as she sat up. She went to move off my lap, and I growled. Holland grinned, patting my cheek.

"I'm just moving so I can see the other two, MF," she whispered.

"Still don't know why you call me MF," I muttered under my breath, letting her go so she could turn. I didn't miss the coy smile at the corner of her mouth. I'd have to show her later how she could use her mouth better. Once she was healed, of course.

"I know you both have a lot of questions, and I'll try to answer as best as I can, but maybe ask only the pertinent ones right now since, you know, I'm injured and all."

I hid my smirk in her shoulder, loving how she gave it to Grady. I was grateful he'd been there to save her, but I hadn't forgotten how he tried to push her away from us, either. He needed to figure out his shit and get on board before it was too late.

"Fine. Max, you can ask first," Grady offered, huffing as he leaned against the dresser shaped like a bar top from a western.

"Oh, um, hmm."

Max paused in his pacing, the cutest look coming over his face as he tapped his finger against his lip, his brows furrowed. Wait, cute?

"I guess I'm just curious how you fooled the profile. Do you do steroids? How strong are you?"

Holland chuckled, shifting in my lap. "I don't take steroids, Max. And I fooled the profilers because no one expects me. Simple as that."

She shrugged her shoulders, but I caught how her body tensed up at his question. There was another reason she was hiding. How likely was it connected to the thing she was fearful of us discovering as well? Pretty likely.

Max spluttered a protest, so I shot him a look, narrowing my eyes to drop it. He clamped his mouth shut, pressing his lips inward, and sat down on the bed, pulling his computer back into his lap.

"Why?" Grady asked, not wasting words when it was his turn. His arms were still crossed as he observed her, his ice-blue eyes narrowed and calculating.

Holland took a deep breath, her body softening in my arms. I didn't know if it was to calm herself or out of relief that he hadn't asked any of the questions she dreaded.

"A guy attempted to rape me one night," she told us, pulling me from my thoughts.

My hands tightened on her, a growl rumbling in my chest. With how I kept reacting around her, I was beginning to believe I had a wolf shifter in my bloodline. Holland rubbed my forearms with a soft touch, her fingers gliding over my skin and sending soothing ripples through me. She peered down at the comforter, picking at it with her fingers as she resumed.

"As I lay there, trying to figure out how to get away, hating how helpless and weak I felt, he had an allergic reaction. I'd eaten peanut butter earlier that day, and I guess it was still on my breath or lips." She shrugged, her voice utterly defeated. "I didn't question it. I scrambled out from under him and grabbed my clothes. As I sat there getting my breath back, I watched him struggle to breathe just like I'd been. He kept pointing to his pants, but my mind was too fuddled to realize he was telling me where his Epi-pen was. I watched him die and regained my power with each second he gasped for air. By the time he was done, I'd realized I could've called an ambulance, but it hadn't even crossed my mind. So, yeah, it was an accident, but it made me feel powerful."

The truth in her story rang true, and I knew she wasn't an unhinged serial killer. In a moment of desperation, she'd found a way to survive and used that to become something new. Not one of us in this room could say we hadn't done the same. We'd all faced darkness, letting some of it attach itself to us, and used it to justify our actions.

The three of us hid behind the Shadows, making us feel better because our kills had been sanctioned. Holland was at least more honest about hers.

"How did you go from an accident to choosing victims?"

"Life had never been sunshine and rainbows for me. I've seen more horrors than most people before I was twenty. Once I had that hit of feeling powerful, I wanted more. I saw all these horrible people thriving off the pain of others, and I couldn't let it stand any longer. So, I decided to do something about it. I found people on the dark web who needed help. I'd investigate assholes to make sure they truly were scum, and then I'd make a plan of attack. I learned how to defend myself, took classes in different fighting styles, and trained with weapons. No one ever expects me, making it easy to get away with a crime when you're not even considered a threat."

She took a deep breath, her head swiveling back and forth. "What now? I'm sure you think of me differently.

I understand if you don't like me anymore. I just need to know if you'll turn me in since I'm not this man you thought I was?"

The three of us all erupted, shouting out different answers.

"You're not going anywhere."

"No one will hurt you."

"You're safe with us."

Her body jerked at the explosion of noise. She held up her hands like a shield.

"One at a time, please. And inside voices. These rooms are *not* soundproof."

"Temptress, you're ours. Remember?" I answered, not waiting for the other two to mess it up.

"Even knowing what you do?" she asked, tilting her head back.

Max got up and sat next to me, taking her hand. His warm leg pressed into mine, and I enjoyed the added comfort of his presence.

"I know you won't believe me when I say this, Holland, especially with your aversion to romance." Max smiled, running his thumb over her hand and drawing her attention. I stared at him as well, loving this more confident and vocal side of him. "You're already embedded in my heart. Finding this out only makes me like you more. The three of us don't live a normal life, and none of us got into this line of work just to pay the bills. We all have a personal stake in this fight against the Savages. Your darkness doesn't scare us, sweetheart. It compliments ours."

"So, what does that mean?" she asked, licking her lips. She turned to Grady, somehow knowing he'd be the one to answer this part.

"You have no idea why a member of the Savages would be after you?" he asked, rubbing his jaw.

Holland opened her mouth, and I could already tell what she was about to say would be half a lie; her stomach had clenched up, her legs trembling.

Before she could answer, the door burst open, and a cacophony of things happened all at once.

I lifted Holland and threw her between the wall and the bed out of harm's way. She screamed at me, but I'd deal with it later. I'd rather she be safe and mad than dead. Fear gripped me as fury roared. I couldn't believe I'd forgotten to check the locks.

Max and Grady reached for their guns, raising them a few seconds before I could grab mine. Two girls, one short and one tall, shrieked, raising their hands as they stared at us with big eyes.

"Wait! Don't shoot. We're friends of—"

"Lacey? Joy? I'm going to kill you both," Holland muttered, pulling herself up. She glared at me, but I shrugged. I'd do it again. "Lower your weapons. They're my friends." She stood tall, her eyes narrowing at the three of us who hadn't lowered our guns yet. Max was the first to relent, dropping his arms.

Sighing, she rolled her eyes and peeked around the corner, spotting her friends. The second they saw her, they flew to her and looked her over like mother hens.

Huffing, I lowered and holstered my gun after

turning on the safety. Grady did the same, stalking to the door and shutting it, latching all the locks this time. He crossed his arms, his resting asshole face intact as he leaned against it.

"Seriously? You're going to use intimidation to keep them in here?" Holland asked, scowling.

Grady didn't reply, he just lifted his shoulders. It looked like they were back to not trusting one another. I was starting to believe it was an act of foreplay for Grady.

"Oh my God, I can't believe you were stabbed," the shorter one said, her hands hovering over Holland as she glanced around the room, and it wasn't to check if the room was clean. No, she was searching for something. Weapons? Exits? Cameras?

"What did you tell them?" the taller one asked, eyeing us. She had cataloged Holland's injuries quickly, moving on to assess us with a critical gaze. Her arms were crossed over her chest, her fingers twitching against something.

Pieces of a puzzle I hadn't known I was solving started slotting into place. Holland was clever and more than met the eye. I didn't take her for someone who'd be friends with idiots. These two girls had known she was with us. Grady and I had heard her on the phone tell them. What were the odds that her friends were also able to slip under the radar?

Three girls working together would throw off the profile. They'd always have an alibi and the necessary muscle to help pull it off. If they were as close as I believed, they'd easily follow Holland down her path of power and justice. And Holland would protect them by outing herself to us.

They were best friends, the type willing to kill and help bury the bodies. The kind most people only dreamed of having.

They were just like Max, Grady, and I. Maybe even closer.

This was what Holland was hiding—her friends.

I glanced up, Holland's green eyes meeting mine. I had a feeling she'd been watching me the whole time, knowing I'd be able to put it together with the correct information. And now she wondered if it was safe or if I'd out her to *my* best friends.

Knowing it wouldn't hurt either of them, I'd give her this, letting her tell them when she was ready. Nodding, I kept my mouth shut, dropping her eyes to look at the others. The tall one had been watching the exchange, a smile crossing her face. She didn't have the same reservations about keeping Holland's secret.

And like the best friend she was, she wouldn't let her friend go down alone.

"She's protecting us. I can tell she told you something, but I guarantee she didn't tell you everything."

"Lacey!" Holland hissed, moving to stop her. The shorter one blocked her, proving my point she was stronger than she appeared to be, too.

"No, Hols. The three of us decided to become the XOXO killer together, so the three of us will go down together. Ride-or-die, bitch, so stop trying to steal our moment."

Holland's eyes watered, a tear falling down her cheek as she stared at her two friends. After a few seconds, she nodded, opening her arms for them. While the three of them hugged, I assessed my teammates and how they were processing the information disclosed.

Max frowned, his brows creased as he watched them, solving a complicated math equation in his head. Grady's eyebrows were lifted, his jaw slack as he absorbed the news. His arms had fallen to his sides. Gripping Max, I wrapped my arm around his shoulders, pulling him into me. I needed the comfort of my friend, reminding myself I had people in my life who would do the same.

"There's three of them," Max muttered. "It's brilliant, actually. It changes everything, though. All the profile databases don't take it into account."

"Shh, Max. Leave the nerding out for later."

"Right." Max nodded, pulling himself together. His cheeks flushed when he realized my arm was around him; his body pressed tightly to mine in a show of possession. Grady moved around them, taking up his mantle on the dresser. All the fight had left him, all his assumptions about Holland were now proven wrong.

She wasn't only deadly but loyal. She was the perfect candidate for the Shadows, and he knew it.

The girls pulled back, and Holland wiped her face. "Sorry, I tried to protect these two, but apparently, I forgot the first rule of murdering with your friends."

"Damn straight you did, bish."

"What's the rule?" Max asked, wrinkling his nose.

"Those who stab together go down together."

"But not in a sexual way. Unless you're Joy, she swings both ways," the tall one said.

"I'm not sure I can handle all three of you together," Grady said, rubbing his temples.

"You wish, grumpy. You just better hope our girl here forgives you for being a twatwaffle. I was on Team Grumpy Ass until you pulled that shit. Holland barely stopped me from stabbing you."

"Okay, okay," Holland said, grinning. "Guys, the angry one is Lacey." She pointed to the taller one with dark hair and light blue eyes. Out of the three of them, she was the only one I would've pegged for a serial killer. Lacey nodded, lifting one eyebrow in question. She was crazy protective of my girl, and I instantly liked her.

"Hi, I'm Max, and this is Quentin. And Grumpy is Grady." He waved, laughing at the end. Both girls softened toward Max. It was hard not to. He just had that effect on people.

"Hi, Max," Lacey said, her voice softer.

"And our sweetheart is Joy. The brains behind our app."

"Hi. Sorry about busting in. We knew Holland wouldn't share everything, so we had to rush to save the day."

"Wait, app?" Max asked, ignoring what she'd said.

"Yeah, so about that." Holland cringed. "There's just

a bit more I didn't tell you. Could we sit? Again, stab wound over here. Not that anyone seems to remember since I just got thrown into the wall," she grumbled under her breath.

I instantly moved into action, extracting her from their arms and sitting her between Max and me on the bed. The girls laughed, taking the table and chair, and Grady stayed where he was.

"You guys are cute. I approve, Hols," Joy said, smiling.

Holland rolled her eyes but smiled. "Okay, to start, we have an app where we get our hits, and a few days ago, we got one from a hopeless Savage."

"What?" the three of us shouted. Fear returned, and my stomach sank as I tried to stay calm.

CHAPTER 21
HOLLAND
xoxo

Two hands squeezed my thighs, one near the stab wound, and I winced in pain. Max's hand flew off in horror, and he immediately scooted back like his presence might harm me. Reaching out, I tugged his hand, bringing him back toward me.

"Don't go. I'm fine."

Max nodded, his eyes worried as he trailed them over me. Grady moved closer, kneeling on the floor in front of me.

"What did the message say?" he asked, his voice soft.

"Joy?"

"On it." She pulled out her phone but paused. "First. Exactly who are the Savages? We've only found basic info that doesn't really tell us much."

The guys relayed what they knew about the Savages and how he'd been the man who'd jumped me and not the child molester we'd expected. Who was actually the guy posing as a child molester, to begin with? What a messed up mindfuck.

"Okay then, that tracks with our Hopeless Savage."

Joy read off the two messages we'd received. I leaned into Quentin's shoulder as she read, the fatigue of the day hitting me.

"It sounds like Ava," Max mumbled, drawing my focus.

"Who the fuck is Ava?" Grady roared before I could ask more delicately.

Max rolled his eyes. "This is why I didn't tell you yet. I didn't want you to rush in without thinking about the consequences. I'm even more certain now she's an innocent in all this. No more responsible for this than Camila."

Grady's nostrils flared, and he stood, his hands flying to the top of his head as he pulled the strands, pacing back and forth as he took in deep lungfuls of air.

"Is he going to be okay?" I whispered, leaving out the part I really wanted to know. *Just who was Camila?*

"Give him a minute. The Savages killed his fiancée, along with my mother, and Max's uncle. Grady's was the most recent, five years ago… *today*. Fuck, I forgot in the rush of you being stabbed."

Quentin glanced over my head at Max, his face paling at the information.

"I can hear you, assholes."

"You guys sure show your love in interesting ways," Joy said, hopping up on the windowsill, crossing her legs, and swinging one.

"Not to interrupt your man meltdown, but can you please explain to the rest of us who Ava is?" Lacey asked, cutting into the quiet.

"I'm sorry my personal tragedy is interrupting your gab time," Grady spat.

"Dude, from what I've gathered, everyone in this room has lost someone. It's not unique. Break down on your own time. We all have baggage."

Grady gave a dark chuckle but turned, looking at Max to continue. My nerdy, sweet guy swallowed but nodded.

"Right, she's seventeen and the daughter of Viper, the leader of the Savages. From what I gathered, she's been sheltered and allowed out only to do a few things. She volunteers at an animal shelter and has an interest in fashion. If your Hopeless Savage is Ava, then it sounds like things have escalated, and her normal life is about to expire."

"We want to help but didn't know how to broach something this big," I admitted.

"You're forgetting that her family knows about you and was able to follow you to that hotel room. We need to figure out how they identified you before we did," Quentin said.

"Did you grab his phone?" Max and Joy asked at the same time. They smiled at one another, making my heart happy.

"Yeah. But it's a burner," Grady said, pulling it from his back pocket. He handed it to Max, who moved away to grab his laptop. Joy hopped down and sat next to him. Max didn't seem to mind, and I smiled, liking they were getting along.

"What's this app you use?" Grady asked, focusing

back on me. Sighing, I sat back up, needing all my strength to take on the man in charge.

"Have you ever heard of the game Fuck, Marry, Kill?" I asked.

"Yeah," Quentin answered. "You name three people and place them on which list you would fuck, marry, or kill them."

"How the hell do you know about that?" Grady asked, peering at Q like he was an alien.

"I pay more attention than you." He lifted his eyebrow in challenge, waiting for Grady to comment. The boss man rolled his eyes, turning back to me.

"Yes, well, since the three of us don't believe in marriage, we changed it to steal. We used it to pass the time by picking out guests, tourists, townspeople, and the occasional celebrity to put on a list," I explained. "After that night, it became more than just a game. We met a woman staying as a guest with an asshole husband who beat her and their daughter. I no longer wanted to stay on the sidelines, so we did something about it. She thanked us profusely, joking that we should create a business called 'Asshole Dumpster' because there were a lot of evil men out there who needed to be taken out like the trash they were. "

Lacey and Joy laughed with me as I recalled that first time.

"How did you go from that to XOXO, then?" Max asked, glancing up from his computer.

"We realized she was right, and if we ever wanted to get out of this town, we needed to make more money than we got working at the Inn. It made sense to create an app that would give us a wide range and anonymity. Joy's a genius coder, so she created it to weed out the losers and people looking for petty revenge. We have strict criteria for all jobs we accept and put each case through an extensive background check before they even reach us, so we don't waste our time."

"How do people find your app?" Grady asked.

"Through word of mouth, mostly. They have to get it from someone with a password. If they pass the initial round of checks, they get the link to download. We're also posted in various spots on the dark web with some different checks in place," Lacey spoke, focusing on her nails like she didn't have a care in the world.

"How do you charge people?" Max asked. His eyes were focused, but I could tell he was running everything I said through his big brain as he tried to understand our operation.

"Some things we charge based on the task, others what they could afford. One of our first jobs led us to meet Phantasm, and he's been helping us out ever since. He's a dark web pro and will send us jobs he finds on occasion and keeps an eye out for any interest in us. With his assistance, we've created a network of people outside of regular channels we can trust to help people," Joy replied, a sweet smile on her face. She loved this.

"The night I was here, and Grady came in, he'd sent a warning that someone was onto us and to keep a low profile. I didn't know it was you guys then, but I overheard you talking about the Savages. It was the same day we got the first message, so I bolted, all of it seeming too coincidental."

"And he's who sent you to the hotel today?" Quentin asked.

Nodding, I looked at the guys, running everything through my head. "We chose XOXO because it's how we always ended our messages to one another growing up, believing at the time all you needed was a friend to hug and kiss it better. Then we all grew up, and our hugs and kisses became murder and theft."

"Your operation is impressive. And quite frankly, you would've gone unnoticed if these two hadn't fallen for you."

"Just those two?" I challenged, lifting my eyebrow. Memories of him cradling my head and telling me not to die had surfaced. Grady's blue eyes held mine, neither of us blinking.

"So we don't have to worry about the feds or local police knocking on our door?" Lacey asked, interrupting our stare-off.

"No. The Shadows exist outside of any law enforcement. You only got on our radar because we run algorithms looking for certain behaviors, and this area popped up. None of the deaths connect in any way, meaning anyone else wouldn't see a pattern, but we saw someone able to stay under the radar and operate without getting caught. Add in the information that all the casualties were known rapists, child molesters, and wife-beaters, and it seemed like our killer had a moral compass and the type of person we could use in our organization."

"Why?" I asked, realizing that while their explanation made sense, something else was missing.

"Because we've been building a case against the Savages for years. We haven't been able to get close. But this killer... They had skills unparalleled by any of our agents. Our hope was this person would be able to join us, our motives aligning, and take out one of the worst crime families in the northern hemisphere."

"And now that we want to rescue Ava..." I trailed off, running the information over in my head.

"It seems like our agendas line up even more," Grady said. Max and Quentin had gone quiet; their expressions were grim. But Grady smiled, his whole posture lighter than I'd ever seen it. He peered at me like I just might be the Holy Grail.

I didn't need the other two's reactions to know that didn't bode well for me.

Joy yawned really loud, the sound obviously fake, as she stretched. "Oh wow, look at the time. How about we break for now and reconvene tomorrow? We can plan and strategize more later once everyone has time for all the information to sink in."

"Ah, look, you can return to your man tantrum now," Lacey teased, standing and brushing off her pants.

Grady's jaw ticked, but he didn't say anything. Good call, Grady. Lacey would eviscerate him.

"Stay," Quentin said, not even bothering to ask. I rolled my eyes but nodded.

"I'll see you girls in the morning."

I stood to hug them, more glad than I'd admit that they'd barged in here and demanded I quit trying to protect them. Life was just better with them around.

Once they were gone, exhaustion weighed heavily on my shoulders. Slumping down on the bed, I yawned; my body ached, reminding me of the fight I'd been in earlier.

"Do you want to shower while we grab some food?" Grady asked, surprising me.

"Oh. Um. Yeah. That would be great." Thankfully, everyone ignored my inability to speak as I blinked owlishly at Grady. Quentin smirked and assisted me in standing.

"Come on, Temptress. I'll help you settle, and Max will re-bandage your leg."

Quentin followed his word, starting the shower and helping me undress. It surprised me how caring he was; not a hint of desire in his movements as he removed my clothes. If anything, anger coursed through his hands when he got near the wound, his fingers tracing over the bruises forming on my body.

"I'm okay, Q. I've been through worse. I'm just a little sore. After some rest, I'll be fine."

His eyes met mine, pools of darkness glinted back. Self-loathing mixed with fear swirled together, and his hands shook as they raised up to cup my jaw.

"The thought of losing you when I've just found you

terrifies me, baby." He rested his forehead against mine, breaths coming in sharp as he pressed us together. "I'm going to freak out for a bit and go crazy about security. Just let me, please. Can you give me that, Holland?"

Quentin shook, his fear a visible thing as he worked through whatever was plaguing him. I knew a flashback when I saw one. I'd had enough of my own.

"Hey, Q, look at me." His eyes snapped open; his head pulled back a smidge so he could peer at me easier. "Wherever your mind is going, it's in the past. I'm right here with you, and I'm safe. I'm strong and know how to handle myself. While I can't promise I won't be in danger again, I promise not to make reckless decisions. Okay? We're a team now. We do it together."

His body tightened, and he took a few deep breaths before he relaxed. Kissing me once on the forehead and then lips, he opened the shower for me and made sure I was enclosed before he walked out, not saying a word.

My heart fell to my stomach, worried I'd messed it up. But I knew I wasn't someone to be coddled. Power and control were things I needed. I wouldn't give that up for a man to protect me. I was no longer the damsel in distress, so I wouldn't pretend to be now to soothe his ego.

I could admit I cared for these guys, which in and of itself was a feat. It had been years since I let anyone outside of Joy and Lacey in. But I wouldn't change myself.

Stepping out of the shower, I dried off, avoiding the

wound on my leg. Now that I could see it better, it wasn't as bad as I'd first believed. It would leave a wicked scar—just another to add to my collection.

My hands moved over the small quarter-inch spots along my pelvis. They were so tiny most people didn't notice them, their silvery scar tissue easy to dismiss. I didn't have the luxury of forgetting. They were remnants of the old Holland, the one that still believed in miracles.

But that version had been wiped out with the death of Harper, my sister.

I'd given everything to save her—my dreams of college, my savings, even my bone marrow—but it hadn't been enough in the end. And I'd been left broken, the best part of this town gone, and all I had to show was a new sad girl moniker stuck in a town I loathed.

Holland Kyler—a girl too smart for this town.

Holland Kyler—poor thing with a deadbeat dad and alcoholic mother.

Holland Kyler—the one with a dead sister.

If it hadn't been for Lacey and Joy, I wouldn't have survived, the grief so vast I never thought I'd make it through. It was the real reason the game started—a way to give me something other than my pain to think about.

It had given me a purpose, a way to right the wrongs the world ignored and find my own path to the life I wanted. I couldn't stop, no matter how much it scared Quentin. I needed this to survive. There was no longer a Holland that didn't include killing bad guys. I'd gone from sad girl to badass killer, and she was here to stay.

"Holland? Do you need any help?" Max asked, knocking on the door.

"Yeah, but I didn't bring any clothes, so I'm naked. Enter if you dare," I teased, some of my darkness fading back at the sound of Max's voice. It was hard to imagine him having his own since he was pure sunshine to me.

"I'm not scared of a naked girl, sweetheart."

Smiling, I placed my hands on my hips, ready to test that theory. The door opened a crack, Max peeking his head in. He froze, his eyes dilating as he took me in.

"Okay, so that wasn't a joke."

"Nope. Still stand by your statement?" I asked, hopping onto the counter and spreading my legs. Max gulped but stepped into the room, his eyes working hard to stay on my face.

"Yep. Not scared. Turned on. But definitely not scared." He placed the med kit on the counter, stepping between my legs. Now it was my turn to swallow, the heat of his body giving mine ideas.

"You're beautiful, Holland. I'm having to hold myself back not to take advantage of you right now."

"Why would you be taking advantage? I'm a willing participant, *Maxwell*."

His eyes heated at me using his full name, and he licked his lips. His fingers flexed against my thighs, the rough calluses sending goosebumps over my skin.

"Hmm, maybe I should do a scan to verify. I need to

check you over from head to toe, so I know I didn't miss anything."

The fake protest died on my lips as he lifted my leg, and his lips and nose trailed over my calf. His fingers caressed my skin as he moved up, touching every inch of me as he went. When he neared my thigh, I sucked in a breath as he kissed the soft skin, his teeth nipping lightly. He pulled my lower half closer to the edge, my back naturally arching as I tilted toward him, bracing against the mirror with my hand.

"Mmm, you smell delicious, Holland. But I need to confirm for my own curiosity."

His nose trailed up my pussy lips, quickly followed by his tongue as it swept through my wetness. One leg propped onto his shoulder, the other he spread wide, careful of my injury. My free hand tangled in his soft curls, keeping him precisely as he was. Not that he seemed to have any intention of moving as he licked and sucked at my folds.

It was the most gentle tongue fucking I'd ever had and also the best. Max took great care to lick and flick his tongue, sucking and nipping with his teeth, sending flutters through me as my body responded in kind. As good as it all felt, it wasn't enough to send me over the edge. My body was caught on a ledge between ultimate bliss and dizzying desire, afraid of crashing down to the bottom.

"You're so wet, Holland. I can barely keep up with lapping your cream before you have more for me. You're being such a good girl for letting me lick you. If I give you my fingers, will you keep being good and give me what I want?"

Holy shit, Max's sweet praise was hot.

"What do you want, Max? I'll give you anything. I just need more."

"I want you to clench my fingers so tight, I'll be worried they'll be stuck inside you forever. I want you to gush all over my face so I'll be smelling you for days. I want you to scream my name so loud, everyone on this floor will know who you belong to. I want to give you an orgasm so strong your whole body quakes until you're begging me to fuck you hard with my cock. Can you give me that, sweetheart?"

My heart raced from his words as he turned it up a notch, my whole body on fire from desire. I'd never had words spoken to me that were so dirty yet so sweetly given, belying their promise. My pussy twitched, dripping my arousal down my legs like I'd never experienced. A tight ball inside me felt ready to unfurl, an unknown sensation primed to be unleashed.

All the pain and fear from the day were wiped away, and only Max and I were in this bubble of time and space. And there was no question or hesitation on my part—I'd give Max whatever the hell he wanted.

"Yes, Max. I will. Please," I begged, my body moving as I took in deep lungfuls, searching for the more it desperately sought.

"Now!" Max demanded, plunging three fingers into me, sliding in with ease as I coated him. He curved them up, hitting my g-spot, as he sucked my clit, sending me careening over that ledge, no longer worried about falling to the bottom as I flew heavenward.

"Aaaahhhh, Max!" I screamed, my body doing everything he wanted. My walls clamped down on him, my entire body spasming. My orgasm crashed through me, his name hoarse on my lips as I coated his fingers, my cum drenching him.

Stars lit behind my eyes, my body alive in a way I'd never encountered. As I lay there on the counter panting for breath, I caught the briefest glimpses of blue eyes searing into me from the open door.

Grady.

The reluctant and evasive boss had watched, and from what I'd seen, he'd been hungry, barely containing himself from entering.

It looked like I'd scored the hot guy trifecta after all.

My eyes fluttered closed, my body completely sated as I fell into Max's arms, trusting he'd keep me safe.

CHAPTER 22
MAX

I'D BEEN STARING AT HOLLAND ALL NIGHT, UNABLE TO take my eyes off her for a second while she slept. My feet were propped up on the end of the bed, my laptop in my lap as I leaned back in the lone chair in the room. Because it was made to resemble the Alamo, it was wooden, making it very hard. I'd long lost feeling in my butt hours ago, but not even that had deterred me from watching her.

Even the pull of research hadn't taken my focus, despite my excuse to Grady and Quentin to do it instead of sleeping. The truth was, I was nervous. What if I closed my eyes and when I woke up, this was a dream?

She'd be gone, and this time we wouldn't find her. Especially now that I knew who she was and what she could do. The three of them would vanish, never to be seen again. I had no doubt they could do it, and it wasn't something I was willing to risk.

"If you're going to keep staring at me like that, the least you could do is get me some coffee. The hotel stuff is shit, but it's better than nothing," she grumbled, lifting an eyelid at me.

I smiled, unable to stop myself. She made me so happy.

"Stop being so gorgeous, sweetheart, and I'll stop staring."

"Ugh," she groaned, rolling over into Quentin's hard body. "MF, Max is being gushy before coffee. Make him stop."

Her hands roamed over his tattooed and bronze chest, a fluttering I never let myself explore, flaring to life. I watched as she grazed each muscle until her hand dipped under the cover. I couldn't see what she was doing any longer, but I could take a wild guess. Quentin's hips rocked up a second later, confirming it as he growled awake.

"Temptress, I see you're living up to your name this morning. Not that I'm complaining."

She hummed, rising on her side, and dropped her mouth to his as she stroked him beneath the covers. Lust and heat overwhelmed me as I watched, hypnotized by how their tongues stroked one another and wishing I could see what was happening below.

Q's hand gripped her ass a second later, squeezing the thick globe before shoving his hand down the borrowed pair of boxers. As Holland squirmed and moaned, I had to move the laptop to the desk, my dick hardening at record speed.

My wish was granted a second later when Q hauled Holland onto him; the cover pushed down in the process. His cock sprang free, the thick member already leaking at the tip as Holland stroked it. Licking my lips, I felt my dick twitch against my leg as I watched.

Everything Quentin had said the other day raced through my head, and I wondered exactly where this would go. I hadn't ever thought about my attraction before, much less how my body responded. But now that it had been broached, everything was hitting me at max capacity.

Huh. My tired brain made a joke.

"Quit laughing at yourself and get over here, Max," Quentin growled, making both myself and my dick jump. As if on autopilot to follow Q's demands, I stood up, my legs shaky from their numb condition.

"I wasn't sure if I was invited," I admitted softly, crawling as tingles spread through as my limbs woke up.

"You're too cute, Maxy," Holland said, grabbing my neck and kissing me so thoroughly I actually forgot to think for once. She bit my bottom lip, dragging her teeth through it before she let go.

"I like to fuck, babe. *A lot.* So unless you're shy about watching me with someone else, which I don't think is the case since you both were game to bed me together the other night, odds are, you'll see me balls deep at least once a day. I'd much prefer if you joined in unless watching's your thing; then I can totally pivot to that. I do like a little exhibitionism."

Her words heated me from the inside out, spinning my head around as I grappled with everything she said.

Holland was definitely the most sexually free person I'd ever dated, and I loved how open she was about it. She didn't let anyone else make her feel bad about enjoying sex. I was just glad I got to be included. The way my dick twitched, leaking pre-cum against my joggers, my body was on the same page.

"Stop overthinking it, Max. Kiss our girl, touch our girl, make her feel good," Q said, snapping me back to what was happening in the room. Holland was naked now, sheathed on Q's dick as she rocked forward, her eyes watching me.

Not needing to be told twice, I captured her lips with mine as my hands roamed her naked body. The white gauze taped on her leg drew my attention for a second, but I decided to ignore it for now and just make her feel good. Tweaking her nipple between my fingers, I rolled my thumb over it as my other hand explored south.

When I came into contact with Quentin's abs, I paused and withdrew from the kiss. Holland's head fell back as she rode him, enjoying what he was doing to her. His eyes were locked onto me, his hands firm on her hips as he thrust up. Licking my lips, I sucked in a breath as I trailed my fingers over his abs and the hair there.

His pupils grew bigger with each touch, his mouth parting slightly as he continued to watch me, waiting to see what I would do. His confidence and trust in me, combined with the power I seemed to hold at this moment, encouraged me to keep pressing forward. As I flicked Holland's clit with my thumb, I bracketed two fingers around his cock. I could feel him as he pushed in and out, the slick member rubbing against me before he entered her.

"Fuck," he cursed, apparently liking that little extra touch.

Holland's hand trailed down my chest, dipping into my pants this time and stroking my cock. I dropped my head back as she wrapped her fingers tight around me, pulling me free.

Drunk on the lust, I reached around her with my free hand and rubbed Q's balls, stroking his taint as best I could. The way he bolted up, trapping my front hand between his body and Holland, halted my breath as I watched.

"Holy shit, Max. I think you're trying to kill me," he groaned.

I could feel his abs flexing as he took a deep breath, slowly pulling back. Holland giggled at his reaction, thrusting her hips forward more and placing her tits right in his face.

"Suck, Q."

He narrowed his eyes at her but did as she asked. Well, in his Q way. He stuck out his tongue and licked the raised bead, wrapping it around it.

"You too, Max," Holland moaned, jerking herself forward to hit my finger.

I kept massaging his balls and the expanse of skin beneath them, Q's legs trembling as he held on. Leaning forward, I took her other nipple into my mouth as she stroked me faster, her hand tightening and twisting with each upward movement.

Closing my eyes, I gave into the sensations as moans and grunts echoed around the Alamo, the sound of skin slapping a happy chorus. When a tongue touched mine, my eyes flew open, and I stared into the dark eyes of my best friend. His pupils were blown entirely, making his eyes the darkest I'd ever seen them.

Q's tongue peeked out, tentatively touching mine on Holland's nipple as he continued to watch me. My body vibrated as anticipation and need raced inside me. When I didn't pull back or stop him, he moved a little closer, his tongue tangling with mine more before his lips sealed themselves on my mouth.

Eyes falling shut as I gave in to kissing my best friend, I couldn't help but notice how different it was. Not in a bad way, but different. His lips were firmer, his tongue more demanding as he sought mine out. His stubble rubbed against my chin as he kissed me. The oddest thing of all was how natural it felt. Like we should've always been doing it.

But maybe that was because Holland was here, too. She made it feel… more. More full, more connected, more everything.

The three of us formed a perfect triangle, all melting into one another to where you couldn't determine where one began and the other ended. We were an endless loop of lust and want.

"Fuck, that's hot," Holland whispered as we drew back, both of us panting.

"She's gushing from our kiss, Max," Quentin purred, nipping her chin with his teeth as he grabbed her hips and pistoned up into her harder. My hand was truly trapped now, so I focused on moving my other one, more determined than ever to make my best friend come.

Never thought I'd think that.

"Wait, let's change position," Holland cried, stopping Q's movement.

"Are you sure? I didn't want your leg to hurt."

"I'm fine. Promise. I want to suck Max while you pound into me. That way, we can all come together," she told him, kissing his lips before pulling me to her, and the three of us attempted to kiss as one.

"That's pretty close to romance, Temptress," Quentin teased, lifting her and flipping her around to her knees before she could protest. I didn't miss how she was propped on his lap more than anything, his need to care for her riding him the hardest.

I moved over, kicking my sweats completely off in the process. Holland didn't get a chance to respond as Q sank his dick back into her. A long moan filled the room, followed by their skin slapping. Her lips wrapped around my cock a moment later, and I lost track of time as she proceeded to give me the best blow job I'd ever had.

Her tongue ran up the length flat before swirling around the tip, sucking out the drops of pre-cum. She hollowed her cheeks as she went back down, taking me further down her throat. I could feel her fluttering around me before she pulled back and repeated it all over again.

"I'm so close," she moaned, stroking the base before she took me back into her mouth.

"Max?" Quentin asked, his eyes searing into mine over our girl's backside.

I nodded, words unable to form in my mouth. I gripped Holland's head, just needing something to ground me before I spilled down her throat.

When she moaned around my dick, I couldn't stop myself from coming either. Liquid spurts shot out, hitting her throat as my cum filled her. My eyes fluttered closed as I held my hips up, my ass cheeks clenched as all the blood rushed to my cock. Tingles raced up my spine as the most cum I'd ever unloaded continued spilling.

Wiping it from the corner of her mouth, I felt my cock twitch as I watched her lick her lips, taking my thumb with a bead of cum on it and sucking it. Quentin roared then, his orgasm overtaking him as he stilled in her as she came again.

Heavy panting filled the room as we tried to get blood back to the right areas, our bodies languid and sated as the orgasm high-filled us. Glancing up, I froze as I spotted Grady standing at the adjoining door, his hands braced atop the frame as he leaned in, a massive tent in his pants.

His eyes were fixated on Holland's naked body, the lust and desire so apparent as he openly stared. Holland noticed my gaze and tilted her head toward him, not reacting how I envisioned. Brazen as ever, she smirked at our grouchy leader as she withdrew from Q's cock and sat back against the bed.

"Typically, I wear more clothes for team meetings, but I'm game to shake things up if you are. Go ahead. Pitch that tent in your pants so you match the rest of us."

Snorting, I couldn't even be embarrassed that my boss and closest friend had seen my girlfriend deepthroat me as her other boyfriend railed into her from behind. Or that my flaccid cock was still out, sticky with Holland's spit and my cum.

Quentin, as sure as shit, didn't care, lounging back on the bed once he threw away the condom I hadn't even seen him put on. He crossed his ankles and arms behind his head, staring at Grady while waiting for the man in question to respond. Taking a page from his book, I scooted back next to them, my cheeks only slightly red from embarrassment as I forced myself not to cover up.

Grady blinked, coming to his senses as everything trickled through his head.

"I'll just grab some breakfast and be back in thirty. Be dressed. This isn't a nudist colony or naked day at the office."

He cleared his throat, his eyes betraying his words as he dragged them over her again before spinning and shutting the door behind him. We could hear him curse behind the door as he leaned back against it, thumping his head as he groaned.

"How much to say he strokes one out before donuts?" Holland asked, chuckling.

"I'll bet you another orgasm that he manages to hold out. The man's so tightly wound, he asks Jackson for permission to shit," Q harped.

"Exactly my point. I'm pushing him over the edge. Just wait."

"As much as I believe in your pussy powers, I know Grady," Q argued just as a loud moan echoed under the door.

"Hmm, what were you saying about orgasms?" she asked, sliding off the bed and heading to the shower. "I think I might want one in the shower."

Q looked at me, his eyes wide, and motioned for me to check the cameras. It felt like a violation of his privacy, but considering he'd just watched us fuck, I guess that boundary was gone. Holland laughed harder as we clambered off the bed to the laptop. With a few clicks, I had his feed up, and the image was clear as day. Grady against the door, his head thrown back as he jacked himself into his fist.

"I'll be damned," Q whispered, his eyes lighting up as he met mine. He shut the laptop and grabbed my hand, pulling me to the bathroom. A lightness I wasn't used to seeing radiated out of him as he bantered with Holland about the parameter of her orgasms.

Thirty minutes later, one orgasm for Holland, and a steamy shower for all three of us, we were dressed and waiting for Grady to treat us with donuts. Lacey and Joy knocked on our door a minute later, and I ushered them into our room just as Grady entered through the other with donuts and coffee.

He didn't glance at anyone, his cheeks heating as he sat everything down.

"Okay, so here's the plan," he started, leaning back against the desk in full boss mode.

"Whoa, someone got over their man tantrum," Lacey exclaimed, grabbing a chocolate donut.

"Definitely. That's a face that's had an orgasm," Joy added, pointing to Grady. "Not to mention the room reeks of sex."

"Not by me," Holland chirped, making her friend's heads turn.

"Oh, deets," Joy said, jumping on the bed beside her.

"I already regret this partnership," Grady sighed when he'd clearly lost control.

"Gossip later. Let's talk Savages now," Q cut in, stopping the chatter.

"Damn, that's some sexy energy. I see what you mean," Lacey said, fanning herself.

Holland chuckled, rolling her eyes but sat up a little straighter, the other girls following suit.

"Where do we begin?"

And just like that, the merging of XOXO and the Shadows was officially off the ground.

CHAPTER 23
HOLLAND

IRRITATING GRADY WAS QUICKLY BECOMING MY FAVORITE pastime. His jaw ticked as he tried to gain control of the five of us, and I had a sudden urge to lick it. Blue eyes simmered as he stared at me, heating me from the inside. And for one second, I couldn't help but remember the moan I'd heard through the door, my cheeks pinking at the memory.

That simple response made Grady soften as he appeared to regain some of his confidence. He broke our stare off as he scanned the rest of the room, the three of us crashing his pow-wow.

"Right, I know you're not used to listening to me, but for the safety of all involved, it's better if there's a clear hierarchy."

"Is that your safe word?" Lacey whispered, causing Joy to snort. I even caught Quentin's lip twitching.

"How about you tell us your plan, then we tell you how we operate and figure out a way to work together. The very reason we're in the business of stabby-stabby is that men believed they could take our power." I leaned forward, my expression hardening. "We're not going to be eager to line up in an orderly fashion for you to take that from us. I respect your leadership and skills, but you can't treat us like your team and expect us to blindly follow you. You haven't earned that yet. We either collaborate with equal say, or this won't work."

Everyone else remained quiet for the first time in the room. Lacey and Joy were still, while Max and Quentin appeared to hold their breaths as they waited for their brother-in-arms to decide. I held Grady's gaze, lifting one brow. His gorgeous face was impassive as he stared, his eyes boring into me as he took my measure. When he nodded, the entire room seemed to take a collective exhale as sound and life returned to the occupants.

"We've been gathering intel on the Savages for years, but we've never been able to pinpoint their main base of operation. Our best guess is it's in a small town somewhere outside of Dallas. There are several outposts in surrounding states that we've been able to infiltrate, but the main compound is kept under lock and key. If I had to guess, they're holed up in a town where they control everything that comes and goes, and the town is either part of their crew, on their payroll, or too scared to ever cross them."

"Then how do you expect to get in?" I snorted. "Has this place not taught you anything? Say what you will about places like this, but their townsfolk are loyal. You spent the whole day chasing a ghost. If you hadn't known we worked here, I doubt you would've learned anything about me," I challenged, resting back on my hands and crossing my leg, kicking it out as I waited for him to respond.

Grady's jaw ticked, and I could've sworn I heard his molars crunch together.

"You're not wrong, Hols. But where we didn't know what we were coming into here, we've been gathering and plotting for years. I've narrowed it down to three places based on satellite images and traffic," Max explained, his voice patient and soothing.

"I know where they are," Joy said, lifting her head from where she'd been typing on her phone. All heads turned to her as she turned it around, an aerial view of a location on it.

"How?" Max asked, his voice croaking.

"I asked Ava and had Phantasm verify it." Joy shrugged her shoulders, pulling out her bubble gum and twisting it around her finger like she was bored. Knowing her, she probably was.

"Well, there you go," I said, smiling. "What's next?"

Max spluttered but got over it quicker than Grady, who still had his jaw hanging open. Max moved closer to Joy, whispering in geek speak, as he typed things into the computer. Lacey switched spots and took Max's vacant one, putting her on my other side. She nudged me when Grady still hadn't said anything.

"Did we break him? I'm starting to see why they need us."

Chortling, I coughed to cover up the sound. However, it did seem to knock Grady out of his trance as he cleared his throat and attempted to regain his footing.

"Great. Okay. So, the next step is to survey the area and identify the best way in. I've pinpointed three options with the best success rate at one of the outskirt operations."

"If it's the laundromat, they know there's a mole and have doubled their crew and replaced the original workers with their men," Lacey said, picking the lint off her jeans.

Grady froze, and I wondered if his mouth would fall open again. Standing up, I waved my hand in front of his face. He shook himself, blinking as he reoriented. I gave him a soft smile, hoping to minimize the crush of defeat he seemed to be feeling.

"Believe it or not, we're not terrible at this. We have a unique set of skills between the three of us, and we've gained a lot of contacts and resources online. Right now, it's amusing that you continue to be shocked by it, but eventually, it *will* get old. Just because you know we're women doesn't take away the fact we're the XOXO killer." I placed my hands on my hips, needing him to get this. We wouldn't work if he couldn't respect us.

"Sorry. I'm not trying to," Grady whispered, his eyes scanning over me. Something shifted in them, and I felt his genuine respect for the first time. He nodded as he swallowed. "What do you recommend?" he asked instead of mansplaining the art of undercover work.

"Lace?" I asked, turning back to her as I settled

beside Grady against the dresser. This close, I could feel the heat of his skin as it warmed mine.

"We're gonna need to use our best assets," she said, smiling wide.

I groaned, dropping my head to my hands and making Grady and Quentin turn to me in confusion.

"What does she mean, Temptress?"

Sighing, I looked up, meeting his eyes. "You're not gonna like it."

Q's jaw ticked, his nostrils flaring as he breathed slowly. "I can deal. I trust your skills."

Be still my heart. I think that was the most romantic and sexy thing a man had ever said to me.

"Lace," I said, motioning for her to explain as I stopped myself from moaning, or worse, swooning.

Smirking, she stood up and bent over, twerking her ass in the air before snapping back up and running her hand down her side seductively.

"Strippers, of course," she said when she was done making her point.

"Oh, yay! It's been a while since I've been on the pole," Joy chimed in, picking up the tail end of the conversation. She jumped up, and the two of them danced together, taking turns acting like one another was a pole.

Max swallowed, his eyes wide as he took in the scene. Q's eyes had closed, his fists clenched down on the bed. Lifting my eyes up at Grady, I was surprised to find him watching me and not the spectacle my friends were putting on.

"What?" I asked, my forehead creasing. I didn't understand his expression.

"Your operation really is brilliant. I can see that now. I don't understand why you need us. You could've kept quiet and never subjected yourself to our scrutiny."

I relaxed against the desk as the tension fled my body. I looked back at my two friends and the guys who'd somehow managed to make their way into my small circle of people I cared about. Nodding to them, I smiled as Joy attempted to pull Max up to dance, telling him to act as a bouncer. His cheeks were red, but he went along with what she said. Joy was hard to resist.

"Them. They deserve a choice if they want to continue down this path. Our plan was to stop once we earned enough money to leave this town."

"There sounds like a *but* there," Grady said.

Smiling, I nodded and turned to look back up at him. "I'm not sure I can. I like it too much. It gives me a purpose to help people who need it. Plus, I like making bad people pay. I'm not ashamed of that, but I'd never want to trap them in this. They have so many skills and attributes to show the world still." I paused, swallowing, my eyes flicking over to my friends before I returned to Grady's.

"There are a lot of things we're good at as XOXO. Being hidden in plain sight and underestimated are just two of them. But the things we don't have… manpower and tactical experience. We've never taken on an organization this large before. There are a lot of pieces to this and people at stake. I wouldn't be able to live with myself if I didn't accept that and seek out our best chance of succeeding. That's where you guys come in. I'm hoping you're the big bad power we need."

"Something tells me if you had to, you'd find a way to rescue Ava without us, though," Grady whispered, his eyes soft and warm, making something inside of me respond to him in a new way. A way I wasn't used to. He felt safe and like someone I could trust. He understood me in a way I hadn't realized I needed—as a leader.

The lives of Quentin and Max were on his shoulders, just as Lacey and Joy's were on mine.

Clearing my throat, I dropped his eyes like a scaredy cat and returned to the group. "Maybe. But I'd rather not gamble with their lives. We have a location and a way in. Now it's your turn to step in."

"Are we sure that's the best way?" Grady asked, pulling everyone else back into our conversation.

"As much as I don't like it, it does sound like the less risky way in," Max supplied, back to sitting on the bed with his computer. "The place is routinely looking for new talent and tends to steal girls from other clubs. It wouldn't look as suspicious to have them be new in town if they worked there."

"Plus, most of the Savages' crew frequent the club and pick their pussy for the night from the girls," Lacey said. "It's been a while since I fucked a bad boy," she mused, making the other three guys' eyes widen, protests forming on their lips as they turned their heads to me. It was surprising to see Grady be so possessive, and that part that had warmed for him earlier flipped in my chest.

"I'm not going to fuck anyone," I said, stopping them before they went all alpha male on me. "There are other positions at the clubs, but usually, we only need one of us with an in. The other is surveillance, and the other is getaway/cleanup. It's dealing with the other men and getting Ava out of the compound that will be tricky. So, Shadows, what do you have?"

I ignored my heart as the three of them ran through their plan. This wasn't just a simple grab-and-go. They wanted vengeance and planned to take out Viper and as many other Savages as possible. The bloodiness of it lit a fire in me, making me itch with the need to be part of it. I knew it was dangerous to give into that desire, to actively feed it.

But when your soul rejoiced at the decimation of people who preyed on those they deemed weaker, the only recourse was to dance in their blood, knowing the world was a little safer because of it. If that made me bloodthirsty, so be it. I wasn't worried about my soul.

"Holland, I could use your help finalizing a few things around town. We'll roll out at dusk."

I blinked, nodding before I knew what was going on. In my bloodlust, I'd missed the assignments.

"At least wiping the rooms should be easier since we have professionals," Max chirped as everyone stood.

"Just for that, I should make you clean the toilets," Lacey teased, tossing her arm around his shoulder as she pulled him with her.

Joy bounced over to Quentin, swaying back and forth as she smiled at him. He lifted one eyebrow at her, and she kept grinning like he was her new favorite toy. His face softened eventually; no one was immune to Joy's energy.

I was almost sad I had to leave with Grady, curious to see how my friends played out with my lovers. To be a fly on those walls!

But that piece of me that had slowly been unraveling inside was eager to get some time alone with Grady. He nodded toward the inner door, stepping through before I could say anything. I met Q's eyes before I followed, and he nodded, saying so much with the simple act.

You did well. Be careful. Don't give Grady too hard of a time.

Smirking, I waved my fingers and hoped he also got *my* message.

I'll try my best, but no promises.

Poking Grady was my favorite hobby, and it would only end one of two ways. With us hot and sweaty between the sheets or at war with one another.

It was a toss-up which one sounded more enticing to me at the moment. Something about fighting with the man really got my engine going.

The three guys on their team were all different, attracting me in various ways.

Quentin challenged me, meeting my strength with his own and showing me I could relax in his.

Max softened me, reminding me that there was still good in the world and to cherish it.

And well, Grady, he was showing me that my darkness wasn't anything to be scared of, and if anything, he would meet me in the shadows.

CHAPTER 24
AVA SAVAGE

PRESSING MYSELF INTO THE CORNER OF MY ROOM, I covered my head at the sounds outside. Something crashed close by as my father's yells escalated, hooting and laughter following. My body shook as I tried to make myself as small as possible. There wasn't much I could do, considering my door was locked from the outside, the alarm system was armed, and guards stood sentry at every exit. I just had to pray they wouldn't let anyone in, even my father.

I'd learned early on that if I hid, it made my father's punishment worse, so I didn't try now. But there was something about self-preservation that wouldn't let me stay in my bed, waiting. So I huddled into the corner, the shadows covering me and giving me the illusion of protection.

The lock clicked in the door, the only warning I got before it crept open. Though the fact it wasn't flung, slamming against the wall that stopped me from jumping up. It wasn't Papi.

Could it be? Had the XOXO killer finally responded?

"Ava?" a voice whispered, their steps soft against the carpet. "Angel?"

Sucking in a breath, I leaned forward, bringing my upper body out of the shadows. "Lukas?"

He turned at my voice, a smile breaking free as he spotted me. His long, dark hair was gone, shorn close to his head in the standard buzz cut of the newest members. Tears pricked my eyes at that, hating that he was as stuck in this place as I was.

With a few steps, he crouched before me, his hand hovering out in front of him as he debated whether he should touch me. Leaning my cheek into his palm, I closed my eyes at the contact. It was so simple, but it was the first non-violent touch I'd felt in almost two weeks. The tears I'd been holding fell down my cheek silently, hitting his hand before I could stop them.

"Shh, Ava, don't cry. Please, Angel."

"Oh, Lukas."

Before I could stop myself, I launched into his arms, wrapping my arms and legs around him. He fell back from his crouch position onto his butt, his arms clinging to me just as fiercely. I kissed his neck, needing that bit of affection to remind me there were still good things in the world.

And Lukas was all good.

A small groan left him as my lips touched, and his arms tightened around me. My hands swept over his hair, leaning back to stare into his familiar eyes.

"I hate what my father's done to you." I frowned, wishing we'd been born into a different family.

"It's not so bad." I knew he said that for my benefit.

"What's going on out there? How are you in here?"

"The final test was completed, and everyone got their assignments. Believe it or not, that's the sound of celebration." He chuckled, but it sounded off.

"Doesn't surprise me. Viper has gotten more violent as of late." I shuddered, remembering the last time he hadn't been pleased with me.

"Yeah. Well." He cleared his throat, his fingers flexing against where they touched me. It should feel weird to be this close, considering this was the most we'd ever touched before, but it never had with Lukas. It always felt right.

"Dad let me come see you." He swallowed, his eyes shiny. "I'm being sent out tomorrow."

I thought the worst thing to happen to me would be turning eighteen in a few days and being married off to whoever my father chose. But knowing I'd never see Lukas again after this felt a hundred times harder.

"No," I whispered, cupping his cheeks. The tears I'd been able to barely stop fell again, and I nuzzled his neck, letting them soak his shirt. "I can't lose you."

"I'll be okay, Angel. I'm not going to give up hope."

I shook my head, not wanting to hear what he said. It hurt too much. There was no place for hope in the Savages. Nothing but rape, grief, and heartbreak lived here.

"Ava, look at me."

Lifting my head, I blinked away the tears, his thumbs brushing them off my cheeks in the softest caress. My heart thumped in my chest for an entirely different reason now.

The air between us felt charged, like we were standing on a cliff as lightning struck down around us. I licked my lips, the saltiness from my tears making them dry. Lukas's eyes dropped down to them, tracking the movement.

"If I could go against your father and win, I'd do it in a heartbeat, Ava. But I know I can't yet, so I'm biding my time until the day I can get both of us out of here. Dad's helping as best he can. Just... don't give up, okay? I know what will happen in a few days, and I wish I could make it easier." He swallowed, his throat bobbing with the effort. "It won't matter to me, though. That's what I wanted you to know. It won't change how I feel. Do what you must to stay alive until we can be together."

"Lukas," I cried, tears falling again. Instead of telling me not to cry, he sealed his lips to mine, stopping me.

Our first kisses had been simple. All lips and no passion as two awkward teens shared a moment. It had been everything, though, to me—my first real choice.

But this... I didn't want to think that Lukas had been kissing a lot of other girls, but he'd definitely improved from the small pecks we'd previously shared.

His lips were still soft but firmer, and he knew how to press them into me just so. When his tongue peeked out, licking along the seams, I parted my lips with a gasp at the contact. His hands tightened on my hips, grounding me into him instead of floating away like my body wanted.

Passion scorched through me, heating me from the inside out, and I knew I wanted more. *More of him. More of this. More of everything, Lukas.*

Breaking apart, I gasped as I attempted to catch my breath, touching my swollen lips like I didn't believe it was real. But I knew there was no way I'd dreamed that.

"Don't forget me, Angel. One day I'll come for you, and we'll run away together where no Savages can find us. Promise me you'll fight with everything you have until then."

Clutching his hand to my heart, I nodded.

"I love you, Lukas. It might be stupid to say that, but I do. I love you. I think I always have."

"I love you, too, Ava."

He smiled, his eyes shining in the moonlight, and I tried to commit everything about this to memory, to have something to hold onto when it got bad. Because it would. Things were about to get so much worse.

"Please be careful. I'll keep fighting if you don't try to be a hero. I need you alive."

"Babe, that's like telling the sun not to rise. It's in my DNA. Plus, I gotta come in and be all heroic so I can sweep you off your feet."

"Lukas Dellota, don't you dare! My feet are perfectly fine on the ground. I just want yours with mine."

He smirked, his eyes heating to a playful simmer as he stared at me. "There's my sassy angel. I love when you go all Ava Savage on me." My cheeks tinted red, and I hid my face in his neck as he laughed. "How about we just promise to love one another and let the rest sort itself out?"

I nodded, kissing the spot behind his ear. "I like that."

The door opened again, and we both stilled. If it was my father, none of this would matter. He'd find us in a compromising position, shoot Lukas, and let the other guards have me without asking.

"Time's up, Lukas. The party's winding down. You got one more minute to say goodbye," Theo whisper-hissed, his eyes narrowing at our position. But like the good man he was, he didn't say anything.

"Yes, Dad."

I hugged Lukas tighter, breathing him in one last time and deciding to take a chance on fate. "I sent word to the XOXO killer. Maybe this will be over before it goes too far, and we're still the people we are right now."

Lukas squeezed me harder, nestling his nose against my neck and sending shivers through me. After a few seconds of feeling him breathe me in, he placed a feather of a kiss on my collarbone.

"And you say you're not an angel, Ava." Lukas shook his head, smiling at me. I giggled, the feeling lifting me and helping me to hold onto the hope he so desperately desired.

"I love you, Lukas."

"I love you, Ava."

He kissed me quickly, then stood and set me on my feet, turning to march out of my room. My heart dropped to my stomach, a sense of foreboding hitting me, and I grabbed my mother's angel pin off my vanity and rushed to him before he exited the door.

"Wait. Take this. That way, I know you have to return to me."

Lukas's hand wrapped around the delicate silver pin, nodding as he placed it into his pocket and slipped out the door, the lock engaging a second later.

The noise beyond had quieted, and I prayed we hadn't been too careless and used too much time. As much as I cherished every second of it, I'd hate it if it cost Lukas his life.

I just had to believe that Theo would've said something sooner.

Feeling brave and full of love, I ducked into my closet and shut the door as I pulled out the burner phone. I'd make one more plea for the XOXO killer to save me… us.

Opening the app, I almost dropped the phone when I saw that I actually had a reply. Sucking in a breath, I sent out a prayer to whoever would listen that it was good news and not bad.

Dear Hopeless Savage,

We're coming.

Hold on for a few more days, and your nightmare will be over.

We've gone over everything you've sent and formed a

plan, but there might be little to no notice we can access the compound, so any other information you can provide will be helpful. We're going to send one of our team into the Savage Garden as a stripper; if you have any allies that could help, now is the time to have them prepared.

Be ready to go, as there might not be time to grab anything, so always keep whatever you need on you.

Don't give up hope, Ava.

XOXO

I sucked in a breath as tingles raced down my spine. It was happening. I would finally be free. I quickly responded with Lukas's name and Theo, and that they were the only two I trusted. The rest were too addicted to drugs or so far up my father's butthole they wouldn't be helpful. I gave a brief outline of the schedule and guard routine, hoping it would be enough.

Deleting the messages, I cleared out my history and tucked it back into my hiding spot when my closet door was wrenched open.

Jumping back, I gasped as the silhouette of my father stood at the door, his hateful and evil eyes glaring at me.

"What are you doing in here?"

"Um, chan-ng-ing," I stuttered, my body shaking as nerves and fear took over. His lip sneered in disgust, my stuttering an insult to him.

"Your future husband's here. Put on something else and meet me in the foyer in ten minutes. Don't make me have to come back in here, Ava."

"Yes, Papi," I mumbled, dropping my head in respect.

He sniffed, and I tensed, praying I didn't smell like Lukas. "Why does it smell like a man in here?" he growled, stepping forward.

"That's my fault, sir. I stepped in when things got loud and crazy outside to ensure no one attempted to breach Miss Savage's room," Theo said from behind.

My father turned, his gaze calculating as he took in my bodyguard. He couldn't say anything to Theo, so he nodded and stomped out of the closet.

"Good. See that she doesn't reek of it. Her husband might not be as forgiving."

The door slammed a second later, and I dropped my shoulders. Theo gave me a look but kept his words to himself, shutting the door so I could change to meet my husband—oh joy. There was no point hoping the one he picked wouldn't be the most despicable.

I didn't care, though. Soon I'd be free. And that was the best feeling in the world.

Borrowing some of Lukas's hope, I decided to be a hopeful Savage instead of a hopeless one.

Just a few more days. I could hold out for a few more days.

CHAPTER 25
HOLLAND xoxo

I HAD TO GIVE IT TO GRADY; EVERYTHING HAD MOVED quickly and seamlessly once we had a plan. We'd been in Lundy, the town closest to the main base, for less than twenty-four hours, and Joy and Lacey already had interviews with Savage Garden. Since Max was on surveillance, Quentin the muscle, and Grady extraction, it allowed them both to go inside.

I didn't argue about them being selected. I knew it would be a lost cause based on how the guys had responded to the idea of me undercover as a stripper. Besides, I was glad they got to be together—being in pairs felt safer.

Max was occupied on his computer back at the motel, attempting to access cameras and security systems to give us an advantage. Quentin was surveying the local scene to learn what he could from the local bars. He blended the best and liked to work independently, thus leaving me with Grady.

Things with us had shifted so much that I almost didn't know how to act around him now. Long gone was the animosity and vitriol he'd spat at me a week ago. In its place were respect and a brewing attraction neither of us had spoken of out loud since Q had proposed the four of us be in some quad-ship.

"Anything?" he asked, shifting in his seat. We'd been quiet for the past hour as we watched a few places Viper visited. The information they had on the Savage's operations was extensive, or at least at the outpost level. There was little to nothing on the main place, which sucked when it was where we needed to break into.

"Nothing interesting," I sighed, dropping the binoculars.

"Take a break; the camera will pick up anything we miss. Max has a program to sort through the feed later."

Nodding, I stepped away from the window I'd been vigil at and propped myself against the desk, the lone piece of furniture in the vacant office we'd snuck into.

My legs brushed against his, heat searing me from the brief contact. The fire had been simmering for so long there was no doubt that if we gave into the heat, it would burn bright. The question was whether or not we'd catch the whole world ablaze with us.

Grady didn't pull away, leaving his leg pressed into mine, and I looked up, meeting his eyes.

"So, you get the boring jobs, Boss?"

He snorted, shaking his head. "I thought we were co-bosses?"

One side of his mouth lifted, immediately sending flutters to my chest. I felt like a schoolgirl with a crush and wasn't sure how to handle that response. I liked it better when we were at odds with one another. That was easy.

"Don't let it go to your head. It was an honorary title out of respect. We both know I'm the real boss here," I teased, shifting so his leg fell between mine.

Leaning forward, I braced my hands on the desk chair and watched as he reacted. Grady's Adam's apple bobbed, his blue eyes darkening as lust overtook them, and a tiny bead of sweat appeared on his brow. I didn't know if that was from me or the humidity of the room, but I enjoyed it all the same.

"I'd like to argue, but we both know you're right. You're amazing, mi chispa."

The term and admittance knocked me off balance, my body tensing at the uncharted territory. So naturally, I had to throw some snark at it.

"Did you just call me chives? I'm not something you can dip your chip in."

Grady chuckled, leaning forward and bringing our faces only a millimeter apart, his breath fanning me as he spoke.

"There's something else I'd like to dip in you, mi chispa."

He licked his lips, his tongue grazing mine in the process. I wanted to suck in a breath or back away, but I couldn't do either, or I'd lose the upper hand.

When I stayed, it made his smirk grow wider. Or at least from what I could tell. His cheeks tilted up higher, and his eyes creased more. We were so close I couldn't really see much else except him.

"You can push me away all you want, Holland, but I'm tired of running. Tired of playing games and denying myself for something I couldn't control five years ago."

Grady swallowed hard, real emotion entering his eyes and voice. His hand came up and cupped the side of my face, his thumb brushing a piece of hair behind my ear, and I melted.

I. Fucking. Melted.

No guy had ever done that before, and it seemed I was a goner for it.

"We're so alike, you and I, but we could improve each other, too. We need to stop hiding behind the shields and armor and realize we're still worthy of good things. Of this," Grady whispered, sending my heart galloping.

I couldn't deny my body's response anymore or the fear that wanted to crawl up my throat. Hearing Grady, the man who'd been nothing but a thorn in my side since the second we'd locked eyes—showing a similar darkness within— that he felt something for me, I knew this moment had been inevitable. Even if I hadn't realized it.

Closing my eyes, my body trembled as I physically felt myself drop the last of the walls that I'd been clinging to.

"Look at me, mi chispa."

Taking in a shaky inhale, I opened my eyes and let him see me. All of me.

The parts I'd hidden.

The pieces I was scared of.

The things I felt shame for.

But also the love I had for my besties and the bond forming with his teammates.

"You're so beautiful, Holland. Every single part of you."

I didn't think I was capable of it, but I felt myself swoon at those words. I guess my heart was a romance fanatic, after all. But I'd deny it if anyone said it.

"If you're trying to get into my pants, you don't have to try this hard," I teased, though we both could hear how flat the words were. I swallowed when he didn't immediately respond.

"I want that more than I thought possible, but I want it to be real. What I don't want is this thin layer of mistrust still between us. I'm letting you in, Holland. Will you do the same?"

If there was ever a more loaded question, I hadn't heard it before. Everything within my being wanted to run far away from this. I'd let my guard down. But for what? I didn't do emotions. I didn't do feelings.

But you have. With Joy. With Lacey. Even Quentin and Max. Why are you holding back from Grady?

I knew that answer even if I wasn't willing to admit it—he had the most power to destroy me.

"Tell me about your fiancée," I said, surprising us both. "I want to know what you were like before the Shadows."

Grady nodded and released my cheek, moving back to his chair. I immediately hated the space but felt more myself at the same time, the surrounding air not feeling as suffocating.

"Camila was the best part of me. I was still my controlling self, but I definitely smiled more. When I found her…" Grady stopped, clearing his throat as emotion clogged it. "I never felt so angry and scared in my whole life. It felt like the sun was sucked out of the sky. Finding the men who did it was the only thing that got me up that first year. Max and Q became like brothers to me, and we all connected through our shared hatred of the Savages."

"Do you ever fear that you'll wake up one day and that burning rage won't be there anymore?" I whispered, apparently shocking him, his brows raising.

"Every damn day. If I'm honest, it's what scared me about you at first. When our eyes connected in the elevator, for once, I wasn't focused on revenge, and that terrified me. It's hard to remember who I was without this unquenchable need to make the men who took her from me pay."

Feeling on equal ground once again, I slid off the desk and dragged my hands over his thighs as I lowered myself. He didn't stop me as I unzipped his pants, his eyes searing into mine just like they'd done that first day.

"I can't replace your fiancée."

"I don't want you to," he answered quickly, shaking his head simultaneously.

I nodded, swallowing down my emotion as I cupped his dick through his boxers. Grady groaned, his head falling back for a second before he jerked it back to stare, wanting to see what I would do.

Slowly, I stroked him, licking my lips as I kept his eyes held with mine. Dipping into his boxers, I swiped my thumb over the tip, smearing the pre-cum already gathered there. Grady moaned, and it was heady, setting my heart racing as goosebumps broke out. It was the sound of a desperate man and apparently my kryptonite.

With my eyes, I gave him the thing he wanted. I let him in.

Sliding down to the floor, I stuck out my tongue and licked away the bead, the saltiness exploding in my mouth and causing my eyes to flutter closed as I moaned. I took his cockhead further into my mouth, sucking him as I licked up his length and tried not to freak out at how big it was.

Grady was thick, like *really* thick.

Spitting on it, I widened my lips as I took him deeper. Grady's hands softly tangled in my hair, and I knew right then I was over the soft and demure Grady. I needed his fire, his darkness. I wanted him to show me the parts no one else understood. Popping off, I twisted him with my hands as I met his eyes again.

"I'll also never ask you to forget her or to stop hunting her murderer. If we don't get Viper here, I promise to help you track him down until you do," I whispered, the conviction thick as I swallowed him down in the next breath.

Grady's eyes were blown, his hands tightened in my

hair and gave me that bite of pain I desired. Moaning as he tugged, I barely had time to react as he hauled me into his lap and sealed his lips to mine, his arms banding around my ass as he held me pressed to him.

It was greedy and sloppy as we fought for control, licking and nipping at one another. The stubble of his beard rubbed my face, and I moaned again, loving it.

"You keep making sounds like that, and I'll come in my pants."

"I'd much rather you fuck me against the desk and come inside me, but your choice."

"Joder, mi chispa," he cursed in Spanish, making me wetter.

Nuzzling my neck, he sucked and nipped at the skin as he marked me. Suddenly, he stood up and placed me on the desk as his hands greedily roamed me, unzipping my jeans and lifting my shirt over my head until I was left in only my bra and panties.

"Merda, how are you so fucking sexy in every goddamn thing? I owe Q an apology."

Leaning back, I dipped my fingers into my pussy, spearing myself and spreading my wetness over my fingers.

"Should I go get Q, then? Are you not up for the job? You're doing an awful lot of talking now that you decided not to hate me. I almost prefer the jackass Grady," I taunted, gasping as I flicked my clit.

Grady's brows narrowed, and he wrenched my hand out of my panties, bringing my fingers to his mouth and wrapping his plump lips around them. He moaned, his eyes closing as I wiggled on the desk, no doubt leaving a wet spot in my wake.

"This belongs to me. Do you understand?"

"Could've fooled me."

It was the last straw as Grady tore my bra and panties from me and flipped me around, my knees landing on the desk with my ass up in the air. A second later, his mouth descended onto my wet heat, and I sighed in relief as I finally got what I wanted. I watched between my legs as he ate me out, pushing down his pants with his other hand. He gave his cock a few good strokes before he reached down and plucked a condom out of thin air.

Watching him open and roll it on with one hand while spearing me with his tongue was fucking hot. I gripped the edge of the desk as I watched, pressing myself back into his face, needing more friction. The second he was fully sheathed in the condom, he moved his head and plunged into me in one go.

"Shit, ah, yes," I moaned, my head whipping up as he filled me.

A string of curses fell from Grady's mouth in Spanish, too quickly for me to follow before he moved and sent us both gasping again as we moaned.

There was a slight burn as my body adjusted to his size, but once he was covered in my wetness, nothing but pure pleasure raced through me.

The desk rattled with each of his deep thrusts, his hands gripping my hips as he held on. My own were carving indents into the soft wood, and I had half a mind to request we take this desk back with us for sentimental purposes.

"You feel better than I even imagined. Watching you ride my friend while sucking the other was one of the hottest moments of my life. I hate that I'd put a wall between us, stopping me from being able to join. But not anymore, mi chispa. Do you understand?"

"If it means I get your monster cock, then I'm all for it," I gasped, my words coming out in pants with each of his thrusts.

"It's yours, mi chispa. All yours."

His arm wrapped around my stomach, and he lifted me, the blood rushing to my head suddenly. The angle changed, and I gasped, but he swallowed it as he covered my mouth with his, doing some short thrusts as he held me to him, my legs trembling as everything came to a crescendo within me.

I didn't want to admit it, but I'd never come so fast before. And it had nothing to do with the way he held me, or caressed me, or made me feel like the most beautiful thing in the whole world.

Nope. No fancy schmancy romance was allowed here.

"Fuck," I screamed, the edges of my vision going dark as a second orgasm overtook me, Grady thrust forward one more time as he let out his own sound of release as he came deep in me.

"Joder. I'm not going to get tired of that anytime soon."

"It's cute you cuss in Spanish when you're all

aroused," I teased. Grady laughed, his sweaty forehead falling to my naked back.

"They're the only words I know, that and the sweet ones, mi chispa." He kissed my skin, sending goosebumps.

"How?" I giggled and ignored how light I felt or how smitten I sounded. I wasn't. So stop getting ideas.

"Camila and the town we grew up in had a large Hispanic population. All my friends taught me the naughty words, and then I looked up the sweet ones to impress Camila but ended up calling her my piglet. After that, she taught me the real ones."

"I can't believe you called her that." I laughed, his dick slipping out a bit with the action.

"Yeah, well, I've at least grown since then, mi chispa, my spark," he whispered with so much adoration. He gave me another kiss on my back before he pulled out, giving me time to cool my cheeks from his declaration.

Grady managed to find something for me to clean up with after he disposed of the condom, and we went back to our surveillance, the atmosphere much friendlier now that we'd gotten the elephant in the room out of the way.

And by elephant, I meant his cock. Not his dead fiancée or my walls. It was definitely his dick. I was going to have to start calling him Grady Tripod... or Dumbo.

Pet names are a surefire way of saying you like someone...

Shut up, brain; no one asked you.

Shit. Now I was arguing with myself.

I didn't know which was worse. The fact I might like Grady, and he made me feel squishy inside, or making myself crazy by talking in circles.

It really was a toss-up at this point.

After a few more hours, we decided to check-in with the others and headed back to the motel. It was time to move on to the next phase of Operation Liam Neeson.

CHAPTER 26
QUENTIN

Checking my phone, I was relieved when I spotted the text from Grady to return to base. Typically, I enjoyed profiling the town by myself and found it easier to focus when I didn't have someone else to think about.

But that was before Holland—my temptress.

Not only did I constantly notice her presence missing when she wasn't around, but my mind kept wondering what she was doing, how she was feeling, and whether or not Grady was being an ass to her.

I'd never felt this level of obsession before. It went beyond needing to know she was safe and into the "I want to know everything" stratosphere. I was utterly fucked.

But I didn't know if I cared.

Holland brightened my world and resuscitated the dead organ in my chest. It scared the hell out of me but also excited me. I hadn't felt that emotion in so long; it had thrown me off the first time my heart had beat in happiness.

Tossing some cash onto the counter, I slid off the

barstool and headed for the door. The ghost of Holland had been with me every step, wondering how she would find information and what outfit she'd wear this time. It had sent my mind spinning so much that I'd almost forgotten why I'd come in the first place.

Knowing I'd get to see her soon lifted some of the tension I hadn't noticed in my shoulders until it was gone. Holland had me so twisted up, and I never wanted to be untangled ever again.

Climbing onto my bike, I nodded at a few guys lingering around as they talked shop and backed out of the row of motorcycles. The ride to the motel wasn't short enough, and I was practically vibrating out of my skin by the time I disembarked from my motorcycle and stored my helmet. I had to stop myself from skipping to the door, but the joyfulness was there.

Knocking on the door of the guy's room, I bounced on the balls of my feet as I waited. Anticipation and longing filled me.

"Password?" Max chirped, also setting my pulse on fire.

How I hadn't noticed the effect my best friend had on me all these years, I didn't know. It had to be an emotional numbness I'd been in or something until Holland crash-landed in my heart and opened me up to possibilities.

"Hullaballoo."

The chain was dropped as Max opened the door, a ridiculous smile on his face that made my heart flop over and my insides feel light and fluttery.

"Hi," he said, his cheeks pinking.

Before thinking too long about it, I bent down and kissed him. It lasted for only a few seconds before I stepped back. I watched as he blinked, his hand going up to his lips as I walked further into the room. Smirking, I discreetly shifted my cock as it grew heavier from that simple contact.

Tossing my jacket onto the chair, I'd barely turned when the inner door to the girl's room burst open, and Holland ran through.

"You're here!" she yelled, taking off and jumping into my arms.

Instinctively, I caught her as Holland wrapped her legs around my waist. She kissed me, her hands holding my cheeks. It felt like everything was right again, the two pieces of my heart safe with me.

"I missed you, Temptress," I whispered when she pulled back.

"I'll say," she teased, then dropped her eyes to my crotch. My cock had fully hardened with her body pressed against me. "Though I don't think I'm the cause of all of it." She smirked, lifting a brow.

I glanced over at Max, his eyes heated as he watched the two of us. He peered up when he felt my stare, giving me a soft smile.

"No, you're not wrong," I admitted, making Max's cheeks turn a lovely rose this time.

"Do you think we have time—" Holland started.

"Nope," Grady said, entering the room and shutting down her question. Holland pouted but didn't retort, and I noticed my usually scowly boss was less 'mad at the world' than he'd been a few hours earlier.

Interesting.

There was even a slight smile on his face as he took his position leaning against the dresser, his eyes heating as they trailed over our girl.

Lacey and Joy joined us before I could interrogate Grady, but I wouldn't forget to grill him later.

"Alright, gang, gather round, and let's get this debriefing started. We've all been up for a while, and tomorrow will be all hands on deck."

I sat on the bed and shifted Holland in my arms so she sat between my legs. She leaned back against my chest and reached for Max to join us. He slid onto the other side and curled up to my side, my body releasing the last of the tension I held as I was cocooned by both of them.

"Holland and I got ample footage of the comings and goings of the businesses. Once Max runs it through his program, we'll have the key players and areas of weakness. Joy, Lacey, what did you discover at the club?"

Joy sniffed the air and then crossed her legs on the other bed. "And here I thought Lace and I would smell the most like sex. Add in the stick up your ass being gone, and I'm gonna guess you finally got some. So, how was it?" she asked, turning to Holland.

Grady's mouth dropped open, and his head swiveled to Holland.

"It was—"

"Don't answer that," he huffed.

"—hot. He totally has some Daddy Dom energy with a side of praise. Hit all the buttons," Holland said, ignoring Grady.

"I could see that," Lacey said, leaning back on the bed. "How—"

"Enough." Grady's face was beet red as he growled. "I get that you're used to doing things differently, but can we not?" He sighed, rubbing his hand over his face in exasperation.

The girls twittered but mimed zipping their lips.

"Joy?" Grady provided when she didn't finish answering his question from earlier.

"Oh, right. We have plans later with two guys we met. Hello, new fuck pool."

"I also got us on the list for the party tomorrow. I'll be serving while Joy's performing. Not that my outfit is much better," Lacey said with all the enthusiasm of a root canal.

"Anything else?" Grady asked hesitantly, like he was scared of what would come from their mouths.

"I think the kid Ava mentioned is there. I didn't get a chance to verify. Two other Savages were talking about him. His dad is Ava's personal guard."

"That must be Theo," Max added.

"At least he's there. It makes it easier to pull him. Do you think he'll go easy?" Holland asked, the girls listening to her so much easier.

Grady huffed but didn't stop them since he needed the information, too. I felt terrible for keeping Holland

in my arms since it seemed everyone paid more attention when they were side-by-side, but he could suck it
up since he got to have her earlier.

"No clue. If I have to, I'll drug him," Lacey said,
shrugging like it was an everyday occurrence. Shit,
maybe it was with them.

"Max, were you able to get access to anything?"

"Yes, and no. The main system is separate, and I'll
only be able to get in for maybe ten seconds before I'll
be kicked out. If I'm there, I could get in for longer, but
still not as much time as I'd like."

"No," I said before anyone else could say anything.

"Is it something Joy could do?" Holland asked,
turning to stare at Max and soothing my arms. I didn't
realize they'd tightened around her until I felt the
tension relax as she touched me.

"Maybe." Max grimaced and then looked at Joy,
spouting off some computery nerd shit I didn't understand after the first word.

"Hmm, maybe. I'm not as familiar with that type of
back-end."

"You sure about that?" Lacey snorted.

Joy winked and asked a few more questions before
shaking her head no.

"How much of an advantage would it offer us?"
Holland asked Max, much to my annoyance.

I didn't want Max anywhere near danger. It wasn't
that I didn't trust him. He was trained, but I never
wanted him to have to use it. He wasn't the type of

person who could keep moving forward like nothing happened if he did.

Max glanced at me, his eyes meeting mine. I watched as his throat bobbed as he swallowed before answering Holland.

"It could be the difference between getting out alive or not."

Fuck.

Closing my eyes, I tried to fight off the impending panic that wanted to swarm my body. The thoughts rolled around, telling me I was going to lose him.

"We'll come back to that," Grady said, listening to the rest of the intel.

"Q? What did you find?" he asked a few minutes later.

I opened my eyes, blinking as I adjusted to the light of the room. I hadn't heard anything else that had been said, only him saying my nickname had gotten through.

I cleared my throat. "There's talk of a big merger happening tomorrow. The husband chosen for Ava is part of the Black Angels."

"Shit," Grady cursed, dropping his head.

"So the rumors are true. They're getting into human trafficking."

I nodded, my jaw cracking as I attempted to keep my fear at bay.

"The wedding party is our best and only way to get them out then," Holland said, determination lining her words.

"Alright, that's all for now. We'll meet back in the

morning to finalize everyone's movements. Um, be safe?" he said to the girls, his brow wrinkling like them going out to sleep with people was the world's most difficult math problem.

"We can take care of ourselves, Pops," Lacey said, patting Grady on the arm as she walked back to her room.

"Don't forget to check in," Holland said, getting a nod of promise from Lacey. Joy bounced over and hugged Holland, including me, since she was in my arms, and I wasn't letting her go anytime soon.

"Have fun and help him work out some of that. It's not good for anyone to carry around that much worry," she said, kissing Holland on the cheek and then patting my cheek.

I wanted to be annoyed, but there was something so ethereal and pure about Joy that you couldn't help but let her get away with anything.

She blew kisses at Max and skipped out the door, closing the adjourning door on her way out with a bolt sliding into place a second later, letting us know their side was secure.

Grady shifted on his feet as he looked between the three of us on the bed. "Well, um, do we need to talk about this?"

Holland snorted. "We had sex. It wasn't a marriage proposal. Get off my dick already, dude," she teased.

Grady's face flushed as he fiddled with his hands, unsure how to respond.

"Do you plan to sleep with anyone else?" I asked. Holland's body tensed, but she remained quiet.

"Hell, no," he scoffed, giving me a look like I was asking the dumbest question. But based on how Holland responded, I knew it very much needed to be uttered.

"Then it's settled. The four of us together. No one else. Holland gets all the dick she wants, whenever she wants, and we get her. No jealousy. No miscommunication. We talk shit out just like we do to work. Everyone agrees?" I asked.

"I'm in," Max chirped, smiling wide.

"Me too," Grady added, clearing his throat.

"I mean, I guess," Holland teased, tilting her head back and winking. "I'm the real winner here, so if you're all good, I am. Let's seal it with a foursome," she said, sitting up and ripping her shirt over her head.

Instantly, all of our eyes were on her as she moved to the center of the bed on her knees, unbuttoning her shorts and pushing them down. She was completely bare beneath her clothes, and I gulped as I took in her naked form. She laid back on the bed, propped on her elbows as she looked at the three of us, biting her lip as she dragged her eyes over us.

"I'm…" Grady started but stopped.

"If you don't want to participate, just watch then. We all know you like that part," Holland said, before he could place his foot in his mouth. "But I think if you give it a try, you'll like this part just as much," she purred, running her fingers over her breasts.

"I'm not into guys, though," he said, making her roll her eyes.

"No one is asking you to be. They like each other. So what they do together is up to them. But I didn't hear MF say you had to join them too," she taunted, lowering her hand.

"Oh," Grady said, his eyes following her every move. "Right."

"No offense, Boss. But my dick only gets hard for him," Max said, shocking us all.

"Same," I growled, turning my head to Max's and slamming our lips together. The thought of him wanting any other dick infuriated me. He was mine. Simple as that.

"I think I could get off just watching them kiss," Holland said in a breathy whisper as a moan left her.

Pulling back from Max, we panted, our lips swollen and red from the kiss. His pupils were blown and his cheeks red as he stared at me. Wiping my thumb across his lip, I gripped the back of his neck and turned his head to our woman.

"I want to hear Holland screaming your name as you fuck her with your tongue."

Max nodded eagerly, pulling his shirt off as he crawled over to her, unbuttoning his jeans and pushing them and his boxers over his ass as he lay on the bed, pulling her legs to his mouth. I helped him remove them the rest of the way as I ran my hands up his body.

I'd never been attracted to a man, but looking at Max's body did it for me. Watching him eat out Holland was the sexiest thing. Them together was my favorite image.

Grady moaned, reminding me he was in the room as I stood and took off my own clothes. I lifted my eyebrow, asking him if he was staying. He held my eyes for a while before letting out a deep breath and giving me a nod. I knew he was being stupid, keeping up the last barrier between him and Holland. But it wasn't needed.

This would only work if we were all in. We needed to be a cohesive unit. It would make us stronger. That I believed.

With Grady dealt with, I focused back on the two before me. Max's ass beckoned me to touch, so I did. It felt freeing to do it, rubbing my hands over the globes of his ass, and squeezing them in my hands. When he moaned into Holland's pussy, I smiled, and my cock twitched, liking the reaction from him.

I moved closer, running my hands over the muscles in his back and then through his hair. When I had a good grip, I lifted his mouth from Holland's pussy, his face glistening from her. Pulling his lips to mine, he shared them with me, our tongues slowly rolling over each other and spreading the taste of her.

"It's time, MF," Holland said, sitting up and touching our shoulders. We broke the kiss, turning our heads to her.

"For what?" I asked, my head spinning from the kiss.

"No more barriers. No condoms. I want Max in my

pussy and you in my ass, and Grady, you can choose my mouth or hand. I'm not picky," she said, turning back to him.

My brain had gotten stuck on the no condoms part and then froze entirely on the "in my ass."

"I think you broke him, sweetheart," Max said, making Holland giggle.

"He'll catch up, lover boy. On your back. I need my dick carousel!"

"So greedy," he purred, kissing her as he lowered to the bed, pulling her with him.

"Too sweet," she countered, making him smile. "But show me how dirty you can be, lover."

She pushed his chest down and straddled him. She gave him two strokes, his eyes fluttering closed at her touch. The rest of the room waited in silence as we watched her notch his cock at her entrance and then lower down.

Fuck. That was hot as hell. Her greedy pussy swallowed Max whole, and they both groaned as she bottomed out on him.

"Holy shit, that's amazing," Max breathed.

"Mmhmm," Holland muttered, her fingernails biting into Max's chest. "I wouldn't dawdle, MF. I won't take long," she taunted, opening her eyes and keeping them on me as she started to rock forward.

Leaping off the bed, I grabbed the lube from my bag at record speed and was back as I watched Holland ride Max. It was the best show I'd ever seen, and if my cock weren't leaking to be in her ass without anything between us, I'd just sit back and watch.

Squeezing lube on my fingers, I pressed one into her opening, massaging around as I helped spread her. Holland's movements slowed as I worked her over, letting me press two fingers in, scissoring them in and out as I went. Once I got up to three fingers, she and Max were moaning so loud from how good it felt that I couldn't wait any longer to be in her if I tried.

Lubing up my dick, I notched the head at her hole, taking a deep breath as I pressed in.

"Deep breaths, Temptress. I got you."

She whimpered but didn't pull away, trusting me to take care of her. If that wasn't the sexiest thing ever, I didn't know what was.

Halfway in, I paused, the tightness and heat of her almost bringing me to my knees. Squeezing her hips tighter, I pressed in more and didn't stop this time until I was completely seated. We both sighed in relief, adjusting to me being inside.

"Move," she pleaded.

"Hold tight."

I pulled out and slammed back in, making all three of us groan in unison.

"I can feel you," Max groaned, his eyes wide as he stared at me. Holding his gaze, I pulled back again and slammed in, my cock twitching with the effort. I could feel his jerk in response, and I groaned, desperately trying to keep my eyes open.

Finding a rhythm together, I was on the brink when

I realized Grady had moved over at some point, his dick now in Holland's mouth. Each thrust I made pushed her further onto him, his cock slipping down her throat. I felt like the ultimate force as I orchestrated our orgasms, everyone at the mercy of my requests.

That spurred me on; I picked up the speed and slammed a few more times into them, reaching down to hold one of Max's hands as I unloaded my cum in Holland's ass.

"I'm coming," I moaned, my eyes finally closing against my will.

"Me too," Max shouted, pushing up and stilling in her as he shot out his own release. It was the oddest sensation, feeling it as he sprayed her walls with his cum.

"Shit, I can feel you," I groaned.

"Fuck," Grady shouted, holding Holland to him as he came down her throat.

He fell back onto the bed when he was done, his cock softening against his leg as he did. Holland trembled between Max and me, the aftershocks continuing in her body, her walls continuing to flex around us both.

"I want to add that we should do that as much as possible," Holland panted. "At least once a week, but I'm always open for more."

Snorting, I pulled out and watched as my cum trailed out after me. I didn't know why, but it was hot as hell, a primal urge being met.

We all cleaned up, ordered some pizza for dinner, and then talked and worked on the last details before crashing into bed. Grady stayed in our room, taking the other bed as the three of us cuddled up, Holland between Max and me.

The panic had ebbed, and I prayed it wouldn't return. I needed more of this and not the fear that it could all be taken away from me.

CHAPTER 27
HOLLAND

Waking up between two of my boyfriends was becoming my favorite way to start the morning. Especially when they were rock-hard, their morning wood rubbing up against me in the most delicious way. Blinking, I smiled when I met Max's green eyes. His dark hair was messy from sleep, the curls sticking up in every direction, and I had the intense urge to mess it up some more.

Leaning forward, I took his bottom lip between my teeth and gave him a little bite before sucking on it. Pressing my tongue into his mouth, we kissed one another languidly as the morning sun poured into the room. Roaming my hands over his body, I pulled him closer to me so I could whisper in his ear.

"Want to help me wake up, Q?"

I pulled back, watching as his eyes dilated a little more at the thought. He nodded, swallowing.

"Yeah."

Placing a soft kiss, I rolled over to face Q, checking the other bed and finding it empty. The light from the bathroom was illuminated under the door, the faint sound of the shower on. Smirking, I scooted down under the covers with Max following me. Quentin didn't seem like the type to sleep this deep, which meant he either felt safe for once or was faking it for our benefit.

Crawling over to his other side, I met Max's eyes before I reached out and wrapped my hand around Q's hard erection, standing proud. Giving it a few strokes, I stuck out my tongue and licked the tip as a bead of pre-cum fell into my mouth. Sucking him down once, I let go and nodded for Max to try.

His eyes had watched me the whole time, heating as I sucked on his friend's dick. Max raised his hand and wrapped it around Q. His larger palm contrasted so vividly with my smaller one. He gulped as he stroked, tentatively sticking out his tongue to lick the tip like I'd done.

Leaning forward, I licked down one side, hoping he'd feel more comfortable if we did this together. He followed suit, matching my licks, and we stroked him together, my hand resting over his.

The tension fell away from his shoulders when Q's hands landed on both of us, encouraging us to continue. The cover was lifted as he stared down as we alternated sucking him down.

"Fuck that's a sexy sight," he hissed, lifting his hips as I took him further. "Temptress, I think I can find you a better seat. Come up here," he demanded, his tone pure seduction.

Max moved between Q's legs as I shifted to his

head. I didn't have to be told twice when he pointed to his mouth. Lifting my legs over his face, I lowered my dripping wet pussy to his mouth and returned to licking him, now just from a different angle.

With us both working together, Max was more confident and comfortable; it didn't take long for the three of us to all come, Max gripping his own cock as he sucked Q with me, his cum spilling over onto his hand and Q's leg. That set Q off as he sprayed down my throat before pushing me over the edge, my pussy spasming around his fingers and tongue.

Panting, we all lay there for a minute as we caught our breath, the bathroom door opening in the process.

"Do you guys ever take a break?" Grady asked.

"Be nice, Grady, and I'll let you fuck me in the shower," I retorted, sitting up and shifting off Quentin's face.

Grady stilled, his eyes heating as he licked his lips. I sauntered to the bathroom, grabbing his hand and pulling him with me, the two on the bed cackling as he easily followed.

A few minutes later, with Grady's cock deep inside me as I braced myself against the shower, I knew I could get used to this. Who knew three cocks at the ready was the magic number to make me a relationship gal? And what nice dicks they were, too.

I guess the men they were attached to weren't too bad, either. They made me feel safe, beautiful, and desired. But I'd deny it if they ever asked.

I couldn't go and ruin my badass rep just yet.

"Joy and Lacey have entered the compound," I whispered, staring at the screen over Max's shoulder. We'd managed to use some of Joy's tracking devices to find our way to the Savage's compound. It was completely off the grid, meaning there were no maps and the only way in was through one access road with several levels of security. It was no wonder no one had been able to locate them or penetrate their base, even if they did stumble upon them.

Thankfully Max had located a secondary drain pipe system, the ones only used in case of a flood or hurricane. They were far enough away from the base that we could park without being noticed and give us a secret way in. The problem was, Max needed to be closer to access their systems, which meant he had to go in the pipes as well, and it was a gamble if he would be able to access it still while below the surface.

It also wasn't a complete route to Ava. Outside of one drain opening, the rest didn't go as close to the house, making it risky to use as we'd be in the open for a period of time. I had to give it to Viper. His compound was nearly impenetrable between the fence, armed guards, and security system.

And for once, our plan wasn't foolproof, and that frightened me. But we were out of time and ideas. The odds of getting another chance like this were slim. It was now or never.

"I don't like this," Quentin grumbled, not for the first time.

"It's our best opportunity, and you know it," Max countered, not scared of Q's wrath. Quentin gritted his teeth as he attempted to rein in his panic. Max reached out and placed a hand on his back, his other still typing as he focused on his laptop screen.

Q's tension lessened, and when I moved around him, placing my hands on his cheeks and bringing our foreheads together, it melted altogether.

"I know it's scary. My two best friends are inside that madman's house, the man whose group has killed people close to all three of you. But if we don't trust in each other's skills, then we're all dead."

Q held my eyes as he sucked in a breath, letting it out slowly. When he nodded, I kissed his lips and backed away. Grady watched us but said nothing. His face had been blank from the moment we'd headed out.

I think all three of them had been able to ignore that we would be facing the Savages today, focusing on rescuing Ava as the first agenda. But they couldn't deny it any longer as the girls weaved through the crowd. Years of anger and revenge came down to this moment.

"I can't believe you placed one of those on me," Grady grumbled, his cheeks pinking slightly at being caught unaware. It was the first sign of emotion, so I welcomed it.

"Only the audio one," I said, winking.

He shook his head, more of his tension falling away,

and I felt good for the part I played in that. I was slowly finding my role in their team dynamic.

"Guests are beginning to arrive. Now's our chance," Max said, looking up.

The four of us nodded, taking one last chance to say goodbye before we broke off into teams. I kissed Grady and Max, trying not to think about them not returning to our room tonight. I wouldn't let myself entertain it and hoped it meant it wouldn't happen.

Positive manifestation or something, the shit Joy was always spouting.

Quentin and I climbed down the ladder and turned left down the drains to put us at the back of the compound while Max and Grady headed to the front. Our steps echoed around us in the space, bouncing off the walls as we journeyed. Neither of us said anything. What was there to say at this point?

It was time to focus and not be distracted. Too many lives depended on it.

Quentin and I were on the rescue mission while Grady would deal with Viper. The grand plan was for Joy or Lacey to get him alone, and Grady to pull him into the drain before anyone noticed. The girls would then go back into the party until they could safely escape, grabbing Lukas in the process.

The whole thing balanced on timing, and ensuring we effectively hit each target before the next domino could fall.

If not, then it was game over as the whole plan collapsed with us in the center of it.

A few miles in, my legs ached, and sweat poured down my forehead, the tunnels getting to me. Even my lungs burned as I tried to inhale enough oxygen.

"Almost there," Quentin said, glancing at his watch with the layout on it. I nodded, unable to say anything, pushing myself to keep going.

Fuck, I hated running. If I was going to sweat this much, I preferred being pounded by several dicks than the hellish torture running was.

Quentin slowed as we neared our exit point, and I bent over, trying to catch my breath. The fucker wasn't even winded, just a mild sheen of sweat on his forehead, looking sexy as fuck. Which meant I had to poke him a little to even the score.

"How was your first blow job by a guy?" I asked when I finally had words back.

Q lifted his brow, stalking closer to me until I was pressed up against the wall. "That really what you want to talk about right now, Temptress?"

Letting out a slight noise, I nodded. "Yup. Sure is."

Quentin smirked, his hands grabbing my hips as he pressed his body into mine. "First of all, it wasn't a blow job by a guy. It was Max, which is different. And second of all, do I really need to answer, considering I filled your mouth with my cum? Maybe I need to remind you later so your smart mouth will remember."

"Nah. It's good. Maybe you should remind Max, though. Just blow each other in the van if you want. Whatever. You don't even need me," I rambled, my anxiety and insecurity getting the better of me.

He lifted his brow, searching my eyes.

"I didn't take you for being self-conscious, Temptress. The things between Max and I are new. We hadn't even acknowledged our feelings until we both realized we liked you. I do love him, and he loves me, and that makes our relationship strong. But we're not trying to be boyfriends. Being together adds something to our experience with you. We get to share that moment and feel even closer. I don't foresee us being sexual with one another outside our joint time. We're both comfortable going with what feels right, and that's always with you, baby. *You're* what brings us together. You don't have to feel insecure or worried that we'll leave you out."

"Oh."

I didn't know what else to say. One, because that was one of the longest speeches I'd heard from him, and two, he'd hit every fear and thought I had on the head, squashing them out of existence. I licked my lips.

"You're really good at the emotional stuff. Way better than me," I admitted, cupping his cheek.

"I had to be growing up, and now I can use it for something good. It's my main role on the team. Grady leads us, and I'm attuned to everyone's emotional state. It's why I tend to work alone. It's distracting when I'm with someone else, and I need that time to recharge."

"So why did you want to partner with me?" I asked, feeling guilty.

"Because I realized yesterday that being apart from

you was way worse. I thought about you constantly and wished you were there."

I smiled, lightness lifting in my chest, flower petals feeling like they were floating around me. Wait, what?

"You did?" My cheeks reddened as I tried to get the romantic feeling out of my body.

"Yeah." Q smiled, kissing me softly before pulling back. "Let's go rescue someone, and then I'll show just how much I think about you back in the motel."

"Yes, sir!" I saluted him, his cocky smirk growing as he turned me around and patted my butt to go up the ladder. "You just want to stare at my ass," I teased.

"And?"

Snorting, I took one more deep breath and went to that place in my head where I turned everything off and only focused on the mission ahead. By the time I'd climbed the ladder, I was ready to get my unaliving on.

Yeah, it might be a rescue mission. But sometimes, you just had to get a little stabby. Them's the rules.

"On my go," Q whispered, both of us hanging onto the rungs as we watched the countdown clock.

The second it hit zero, I flew into action and lifted the lid, peering out into the dead space. When I didn't encounter any movement, I pulled myself out of the hole and scanned the area as I waited for Quentin to join me. Once we were both out, I nodded in the direction we needed to head.

We were in an old barn a short distance from the back of the house. It gave us the best cover and position for Ava's room. Sticking to the shadows, our black outfits hid us as we made our way to the house. Hopefully, if anyone spotted us, we looked similar enough to the Savages that we should pass a first glance.

That was until they realized I was a woman. But hopefully, it wouldn't come to that.

"Almost there," I whispered, nodding to the window Ava said was hers.

She was going to hang an angel in it so we'd know for certain. Waiting for a guard to pass, Quentin and I crouched down low as we hurried the last few steps to the spot. Under the window, I glanced up and spotted the marker, sighing in relief that we'd made it to the correct one.

Quentin stared at his watch, waiting for Max's signal that the alarm had been disabled, giving us a few seconds to open it and slip into her room.

"Go," he hissed, and I popped up and pushed it open, happy it didn't make a sound. Quentin followed, closing it just as the timer went off. We both sighed in relief just as a gasp caught our attention.

"You're here!" a young girl in a wedding dress said, rising from the bed she'd been sitting on. "XOXO?" she asked, and I nodded, pulling my hood off so she could see I was a female. She immediately relaxed, just as I knew she would.

"You ready?" I asked, just as a loud commotion broke out in the hallway.

Ava jumped but ran and grabbed a bag she'd hidden behind some stuffed animals and hurried over to us. I wrapped my arm around her as the noise grew closer.

Quentin tensed, his anxiety ramping up the longer we waited here with no word from Max that the alarm was off again.

The door burst open, and a man in all black, similar to us, appeared. On instinct, Q and I raised our guns at him. He didn't seem surprised to see us, dismissing our weapons as he addressed the girl shaking in my arms.

"You have to go now, Princess. Your father knows they're coming and plans to make an example. There's no more time."

"We're waiting for the alarm to be off," I said, hoping this was the personal guard and our ally.

"You'll have to go a different way. Come," he said, motioning for us to follow.

I glanced at Q, his jaw tight as he debated. It wasn't part of our plan, but we didn't have time to argue. If the alarm wasn't off, we'd be giving them our location immediately.

"You can trust him. He's been more of a father to me than Viper," Ava whispered, unzipping the dress and letting it puddle at her feet. Underneath she had on leggings and a tank top, and thankfully, tennis shoes. She pulled on a hoodie next, pushing her hair back and helping to slightly disguise herself.

Once she was ready, we followed the guard, and Q trailed behind. His fists were clenched, and his jaw clicked as he ground his teeth, but he didn't argue. I tried not to think about why we couldn't get out the window or the fact Viper knew we were here and instead focused on our part of the plan.

They're all trained and experienced. They'll be safe. I won't lose anyone else I love.

If I kept repeating it, maybe it would make it true.

The guard opened a panel in the wall and motioned us through. "Go down the stairs, take two lefts, and enter 63284 into the keypad. Hurry. There's not much time."

He hugged Ava, kissing her cheek. "Your mother would be proud. Get Lukas and live a happy life, Princess."

Ava nodded, tears tracking down her face as I pulled her after me; Quentin had already descended the stairs. The panel sealed behind us just as other feet rounded the corner, voices infiltrating the space we'd just left as we hurried down.

"Why am I not surprised it's you?" a man spoke, full of pure venom. "You were always too soft with her. If I didn't know better, I'd think you were in love with her. But no, that was my wife who you fancied."

"You're not worth the explanation," the guard responded, his voice the last thing we heard as we rounded the last corner. Quentin already held the door open where he'd entered the code. Just as we passed through, the pop of gunshots overhead rang out, making me flinch.

Theo had sacrificed himself for Ava, making him a hero in my book. I'd ensure we had Lukas if it was the last thing we did. His sacrifice wouldn't be for nothing.

Ava's tears fell faster, but she kept pace with us through the tunnel. It wasn't the same as the drain pipes, so I had no idea where we'd come out, but it wasn't like we had a lot of options at the moment, so I'd trust the man who was willing to put himself between a gun and our escape.

Thankfully, it didn't sound as if they'd followed us. So either they didn't know about this exit, or they'd be waiting for us at the other end.

Sweat dripped down my back and into my eyes as I panted, trying to get enough oxygen. That was now twice I'd run within an hour. Fuck my life.

"You'll need to do more cardio if you join the Shadows," Q teased, earning himself my middle finger.

A door loomed in front of us, the three of us quieting as we neared it, unsure what lay on the other side.

Testing the knob, I was shocked when it turned. I pressed my ear against the door but couldn't hear anything on the other side. Not that a waiting mob would be loud, per se, but it gave me hope. Lifting my gun, I eased the door open. When nothing immediately made a sound or popped out at me, I stepped through into the space.

It appeared to be an empty storage room, with only a few boxes along one wall, the rest coated in dust.

"Clear," I whispered, motioning for them to join me.

"What now?" Ava asked, her eyes scanning the area.

I glanced around the room, spotting a door off to the side in the large, empty space. I went through the same routine, shocked even more when it opened into an empty hallway. The three of us crept along the side, listening for any noises. But it appeared to be a vacant house or building for all intents and purposes.

Light filtered through a window up ahead, so I slowed as we came into view. I could make out a desk and some old dental decorations, making me think we were in an abandoned dentist's office. I guess gangs didn't care about their dental hygiene.

The street we exited was just as empty as the building, since most businesses were closed for the night. Quentin pulled out his phone, lifting it to his ear as he called in our location. I withdrew my new one as well, hoping the maps app would give me some indication of where we'd ended up and how to get back to our crew.

The text that flashed on the screen chilled me to the bone, and I blinked, confident I'd read it wrong.

Lacey: They got Joy. I'm sorry, Hols.

The device fell from my fingers, smashing into the ground as I tried to remember how to breathe. Quentin was there in a flash, his hands bracing my face.

"Breathe, baby." His eyes swam into focus, and I mimicked what he was doing.

I nodded, not hearing his words but following anyway. Eventually, my heart rate returned to normal, and the edges came back into focus.

"Joy," I whimpered, but he only nodded, wiping my tears, the worry evident in his eyes.

"Come on. We need to get out of sight and devise a new plan." Quentin took my hand and Ava the other,

her face soft with worry. I reminded myself I needed to hold it together for her. Joy was a badass and would be okay. She would.

Somehow, Quentin got us closer to town, and we managed to hail a taxi, covering Ava's face to keep her hidden from any cameras. Arriving at the motel, I'd never been so happy to see the shitty place. Quentin led us into his room, the space dark and stale, like no one had been there for a while. I showed Ava the bathroom, allowing her to change and take a moment.

The door in the middle of the room burst open, light spilling through as Grady took us in. He relaxed for a microsecond as he checked us over for injuries. "Did you get her?" he asked when he didn't spot Ava.

"Bathroom," I whispered, all emotion gone at this point.

"We have a situation. Where's Max?" he asked, looking behind us like he might be hiding there.

"I thought he was with you?" Q asked, his body instantly going taut.

"No. We had to separate. He was going back to wait for you guys."

"We couldn't escape that way," I said, patting my pockets for my phone until I remembered it had cracked again when I dropped it. Quentin was already on his phone, calling him, pacing back and forth while it rang.

A loud groan rang out behind Grady, and I froze. "That's the situation. The boy was injured helping Lacey escape."

He didn't meet my eyes as he said it; I knew he was leaving out the fact that Joy was still at the Savages compound.

"Lukas?" Ava whispered behind me, having heard the last of the conversation. He nodded, stepping back as she flew into the room. I peered in, spotting Lacey pressing towels to a teenage boy, red seeping through them at an alarming rate.

"We need to call someone," I said, meeting Lacey's blue eyes as I entered. They were filled with tears, and I shook my head. It wasn't her fault.

A loud crash sounded back in the other room before Quentin stormed in, his face pale and stricken.

"They have Max. They have them both."

How were we supposed to survive this? Max and Joy were the best of us, and that was one domino I wasn't willing to let fall.

CHAPTER 28
MAX

The ringing in my ears was the first clue that something wasn't right, followed by a sharp pain in my skull. I moved my head, wincing when it felt more like a bowling ball and not the thing generally attached to my neck.

"Ow," I moaned, attempting to lift my arms to no avail. They were heavy against my sides, almost like something held them down.

"Max," a soft voice whispered, pulling me to the surface.

Blinking, lights swam in my vision as everything spun, the sound echoing around me like a rave was happening inside my body. I was not a fan.

"Turn it down," I mumbled, squinting until my eyes adjusted to the light. Everything was out of focus for a minute until my vision righted itself.

"Hey, Max," Joy said, giving me a lopsided smile.

I relaxed at seeing her, but something still didn't feel right. Like, why did I hurt so much? Taking her in, the memories of what we'd been doing rushed forward.

Shit. I'd been captured. The one thing I'd told Quentin wouldn't happen.

And it seemed Joy had been too.

"Holland? The others?" I rasped, hoping they were okay.

She shook her head. "I don't know. I was grabbed and thrown down here. When they brought you in, you were unconscious, and they tied you to the chair, leaving me on the floor. I guess they don't consider me the threat." Joy smiled, all teeth, and I snorted with her.

Out of the two of us, she was by far the scarier one. While she wasn't tied up, she was practically naked. Which I just realized as I became more aware of my surroundings, clearing my throat and turning my head so I wasn't staring at her nipples. My cheeks heated, my whole body turning up ten degrees as all the blood rushed to my face.

"You're too cute. But don't be shy. We gotta work together to get out of here. So, take a look. They're great tits and deserve to be admired; then we'll have the awkwardness out of the way and can move on. And don't worry; Holland would say the same."

Chuckling, I shook my head, feeling slightly better. But I still couldn't bring myself to stare directly at them, regardless of what she said. It felt like Medusa, and if I stared at them directly, I'd be turned to stone.

But Joy was right about one thing. We needed to work together to survive. I was glad I wasn't alone, even if it meant she'd been captured, too.

"How long has it been?" I asked, trying to

remember what time it was before I'd been taken. When the second alarm didn't disable, I'd left our tunnel to head to Quentin and Holland's in case they needed help. I'd sent Grady a message since he hadn't returned yet with Viper.

"Maybe a couple of hours. Time's weird down here."

"Fuck, did it all go to shit?" I shook my head in disbelief. "The second alarm. I couldn't deactivate it. There was a block or something," I rambled as my thoughts jumbled together.

Joy nodded, a contemplative look on her face. "That makes sense. I'd just gotten Viper to follow me, Lacey behind him, when he got an alert on his phone. His head had snapped up, and he told the guards to lock everything down and to grab me. Arms had wrapped around me from behind before I could do anything. Lacey had almost stepped in, but I shook my head for her not to. She needed to get out. One of us had to. That was when all hell broke loose and everyone scattered. I saw her slip out the door just as they carried me out of view."

"If they're not here too, then maybe that means they got away," I whispered, not wanting to mention that they could've been shot and were already dead. I wouldn't let myself go there yet. "Do you still have your dot camera?" I asked, my head snapping up when I remembered.

"No, they stripped me." She motioned down her

body, only a tiny thong on. Gulping, I nodded as I ran scenarios through my head.

"Are you cold? Do you want my shirt?" I asked, noticing the goosebumps on her skin.

"I thought about it but didn't know if the guards would notice." She shrugged.

"Might be worth the risk. It's cold down here."

"You really are too sweet, Max-a-million. How did you get into this line of work?" she asked, standing and walking over to me. I kept my eyes down as she worked my button-down shirt off my body, only my nerdy t-shirt left.

"Oh, you know. A bullied nerd uses his smarts to get payback, gets caught, and then is offered a different type of job. Add in that my uncle, the man who raised me, was killed by the Savages, and you have my whole story." I shrugged, my cheeks red as she sat back down, her body covered more now.

"Somehow, I highly doubt that's the whole story. But I'll leave you with your secrets."

"And you got into this for Holland?" I asked, curious.

"Yes, and no. It started that way, but it was fun thinking of ways to create the tech and go unnoticed. Punishing people is a high that's not harmful to my health. Add in the sex, and yeah, it wasn't a bad gig. I enjoyed each day, got to spend it with my besties, and helped women in the process." She shrugged, dismissing what she did, but I could see the pure joy radiating off her. I then snorted at my pun.

"What?" she asked, lifting her brow, a soft smile on her face.

"I thought about how you radiate pure joy, and then yeah, realized your name. I did the same thing the other day with mine. Something I guess we have in common." I smiled as she chuckled with me.

"See, too cute." I blushed for an entirely different reason this time. Joy noticed and continued back into her spiel.

"I'd love to be able to create more things. I also like doing undercover things. Do you think there's a spot in the Shadows to do that?" she asked, her voice soft.

I swallowed, realizing how serious she was. "You'd really want to? I don't think Holland knows that."

"Yeah, I know. She thinks she's the only one who enjoys the darkness, and as usual, she sacrifices herself to save someone she loves," Joy sighed, rolling her eyes. "So, is there?"

I nodded. "Definitely. The Shadows would love to have someone like you on board. Honestly, you could probably have your own lab to create all the tech you wanted."

"Really?" she asked, sitting up in excitement, her eyes shining.

"Honest."

"Well, alrighty then. We definitely have to make it out of here alive, Max-a-million."

Before I could respond, the door opened, and the man I'd wanted revenge on for years strolled through without a care in the world. His eyes were hard and evil, nothing kind in them at all. He stared at me, no ounce of recognition for the man he took from me.

But what did I expect? My uncle was just one of many he'd killed to prove his dominance and take over the Savages. I spotted his tattoo, the Viper with an S prominent on his hand and wrapping around his arm. Everything about him screamed 'evil villain' from his outfit to his hair, and I wanted to laugh. Thankfully, I had enough self-preservation left in me, despite the possible concussion, to not do it.

"Where's my daughter? Who do you work for?" he asked, staring only at me.

Joy rattled off something in a language I didn't know, gesturing frantically between her and me. I might not understand her words, but I could grasp her message.

She insisted she had no idea who I was, all the while informing me to play dumb as well. I instantly realized how freely we'd been talking and hoped there hadn't been listening devices in here.

Shit. The concussion had made me lax.

I'd trust Joy's judgment, though, and her experience in these types of situations. Plus, Viper didn't seem like the type to want any footage available, even if it was only local. No evidence meant it was easier to deny.

"That true? You don't know her?" he asked, making me jump out of my thoughts as his steely gaze assessed me.

"Me? I'm nobody."

"I don't believe that for a second. You were able to

bypass my system. That means you're valuable. So, who do you work for?" he asked as he leaned down, the threat clear in his evil-murdering eyes.

I swallowed, sweat beading on my forehead despite the chill. I prayed with everything I had that no matter what happened, I didn't pee myself. That seemed like something I wouldn't be able to walk away from. The ultimate low.

"No one. Just your neighborhood hacker who likes trying to break into impenetrable places. Sorry, I didn't mean to cause an alarm."

He smiled, the action making him scarier, and I braced myself, knowing something bad was about to happen. Men like him didn't smile for normal things. His hand struck out, slapping my face and sending my head flying, not helping the concussed feeling as the ringing returned and my vision swam.

Fuck.

"You're funny," he seethed. "I don't like funny."

He gripped my chin in his hand, squeezing my face hard. Tears threatened at the corners of my eyes, and I could hear Joy in the background, saying something in that language again, but I could only focus on the threat before me.

Viper took up my entire vision, and I prayed his ugly, evil mug wasn't the last thing I saw.

"My daughter was taken. So, try again. Who. Do. You. Work. For?"

"Sorry, man. No one."

Since his face filled my view, I hadn't noticed the

knife in his hand until he stabbed my thigh, barely missing my femoral artery. Wincing, I screamed out in pain as he drew back.

"You get one more try, and then I start taking body parts."

He stalked out of the room, his men following him and leaving the knife like a dumbass. Not that I wanted him to pull it out since I'd be more likely to bleed out, but he'd just given Joy a weapon.

Like I said, Dumb. Ass.

"Max, you okay?" Joy asked, smacking my cheeks. "Stay with me, sweet boy."

"I'm not a boy," I slurred.

"Okay, sweet man. Is that better?"

"Yep." I nodded, instantly regretting it. "Ow. Make it stop spinning."

"You were so brave, Max-a-million. Hols and Gruffy Cinnamon Roll will be so proud of you," she said, patting my cheeks and pushing my hair back on my forehead. Her cool hands felt nice on my face. It took me a second to realize what she'd called Quentin.

"Gruffy Cinnamon Roll?" I asked, chuckling.

"He's all Silent McGruff on the outside but a big cinnamon roll on the inside. You're his gooey center. Which, welcome to the rainbow, cousin."

"Rainbow?" I asked, trying to ignore the pain as I panted.

"You and Gruffy, you're a thing, right?"

"Oh. Um. I don't know what label we are. More like

we love one another and enjoy being intimate while exploring our relationship with Holland."

"That's cool. You don't need to label yourself to have my support, and if you have questions, I'm here for you. If I can't answer it, I know someone who can."

"Thanks, Joy. That's really sweet." I smiled at her, happy to have met her. "So, do you have a plan? I don't know how much more torture I can take. It's not my area of expertise." And it really hurt already. I was quickly on the verge of pissing myself.

"I have an idea, but you're gonna have to push through the pain if we have any hope of escaping. Where were you when they grabbed you?" she asked, her eyes moving fast as her mind calculated risks.

"Um, I was in the barn. I'd gone to look for Holland and Quentin when the second alarm didn't disable. It was dumb. I should've stayed where I was."

"Shh, it's okay. That's good, though. It means our escape route might still be open. We just have to make it to the wine cellar. It's only a few rooms down. But I can't carry you." Her eyes watered at the acknowledgment, and I tried to soothe her this time, forgetting my arms were still tied.

"It's okay. If you have to leave me, do it. I know you'll come back."

"Holland would never forgive me for that. We go together or not at all."

I sucked in a breath, biting through the pain. I wasn't in good shape, but if it was push through or let him keep torturing me, then I knew what I had to do.

"I can do it. Um, we need something to tie around my leg."

"Right. Here, let me untie you. I don't know how much time we have until they return, so we gotta be fast."

"Rip part of my shirt off to use as a bandage, and use my belt to stop the blood flow before you pull the knife," I advised.

Joy did as I instructed, giving me something else to focus on. She untied my feet, but the ones on my hands were too tight, and we'd need the knife to cut them loose.

Once she had all the parts in place, I counted off for her to pull the knife free. "One, two… Ahhh," I yelled, biting my tongue to stop the noise as she pressed the cloth against the wound and tied the strand she'd torn off in quick succession. Joy was all business as she moved, cutting my hands free a second later.

Tingles spread through my limbs as blood rushed to them. With the knife in one hand, she helped me stand, my legs wobbling as I pressed down on them. It didn't help that I'd been sitting in one position for who knew how long.

Hobbling along, I pushed through the pins and needles as they ran up my leg and followed her to the door. She gave me a look like she was asking if this was what I really wanted to do, and I nodded.

I knew it was a risk, and we'd likely be shot if found, but I couldn't take the chance of being here any longer. I would rather die on my feet running than be strapped to a chair as a madman tortured me.

"It's go time, Max-a-million."

Taking a deep breath, I swallowed the scream that wanted to escape and followed Joy into the dark hallway, praying I'd see the people I loved again. I'd even let Quentin wrap me in bubble wrap if it meant I got to be with them.

I just had to make it back. I had to.

CHAPTER 29
HOLLAND
xoxo

Watching Quentin fall apart made my own panic subside, and the baller part of me took control. I could do this. I could be the strength we both needed.

Lacey was just as freaked out, guilt radiating off her. I knew there must have been nothing she could've done, but until we had Joy back, she wouldn't be able to hear it.

A calm sense of control washed over me, pushing the fear and panic to the back. My mind whirled as I put together a plan. This was what I was good at. My big brain could sort through information quickly, and I used that to my advantage as I listed all the areas of crisis we currently had.

First, we needed to tend to Lukas.

Pulling out my phone, I sent a message to Phantasm, letting him know what had happened with Joy and Max and asking him to send a doctor to our location. There was a whole network of people who worked off the books, and he knew how to get a hold of them.

"Lace and Ava, keep pressure on the wound. The

doc's on their way. Do you need someone to trade out places with you, Lace?"

"No. I got this." She made eye contact, letting me know she meant it. I watched as she took a deep breath, taking comfort in my calm, no-nonsense demeanor. Kissing her head, I walked over to the men.

Quentin was trashing the other room, and I'd need to deal with him, but first, I had to get Grady out of his shell shock. He was just as pale as Lukas, and I didn't think he'd been shot. Using my hands to ensure none of the blood was his, I sighed in relief when there weren't any wounds. He kept staring at the kid on the bed and the blood, and I had to guess he was having a flashback.

This probably wasn't the best way to get him out of his head, but I didn't have time to question myself.

Slapping his cheek, I watched as his glazed eyes returned online, his shocked expression fading as he noticed me.

"Snap out of it. The doc's on his way. You need to call in the extra team. Get over your rivalry with them and do it. Call the big boss, too. We need all hands on deck, Grady. They have two of ours; we're not going in silent this time. You got that?"

He swallowed, nodding as color returned to his cheeks. It seemed that once he had direction, he knew what to do. Grady pulled out his phone and immediately called someone, pacing in the corner while he spoke to them.

The knock at the door had us all freezing, but I figured it was the doctor, so I rushed over and checked, sighing when I spotted the familiar signal on their hand —an O with an X over it. It looked simple enough that no one questioned it, but it gave us all a way to identify we were allies.

"We're having such good weather," I said when I opened the door, the last test before I'd let them in.

"Much better than last week. Clear skies tomorrow, too," they replied.

I nodded and stepped back now that I knew they hadn't been followed, the "clear" being the keyword. Joy had created the code years ago, her brilliance once again shining through. A sharp pang hit me at that, but I wouldn't think about losing her. I couldn't.

Now that the doctor was here and Grady was busy making plans, I slipped into the other room where Quentin now sat on the floor between the beds, rocking back and forth. Most of the furniture was splintered, and a lamp was smashed to pieces. All the bed sheets and comforters had been torn off and tossed aside. It looked like the Tasmanian Devil had been through here.

Kneeling between his open legs, I cupped his face and lifted his head. Tears streaked down Q's face, and his eyes were so small I worried I wouldn't be able to get him back. It was terrifying to see Quentin like this, but it also showed me we all had various sides. No one was always strong. No one was immune to pain.

I didn't think I could slap Quentin and have the same response as Grady; instead, I went with a softer approach. Pushing his thighs down, I sat in his lap and wrapped my legs and arms around him, just holding him to me as I cooed soothing things, rubbing the short, buzzed part of his head.

"Come back to me, MF. I need you. They both need us. We're gonna get them back. We will. And then we will make them all bleed for taking the best of us. I won't stop until every inch of that place is dripping in blood. After this, they'll have to call me the crimson killer because it will be my favorite color."

Okay, so maybe they weren't soothing things for everyone, but I hoped they were what Quentin needed to return to me.

Slowly, his arms tightened around me, his lips pressing into my neck as his body shook. After a few minutes, that also stopped, and we held one another, pouring our strength and worries together, not being alone in them.

I didn't realize I'd been crying too until I pulled back, my face damp with my tears.

"I'm sorry," he croaked, his voice rough from his rampage.

"Don't be." I shook my head, wanting him to know I didn't care. It was part of him, and I accepted it.

"It's not something I like to show. But…" He shook his head, hiding his eyes. "I have a problem."

"Q," I snapped, my voice making his face jerk up. "Don't you fucking apologize for loving that man. Don't you dare!"

"I," he started, but I narrowed my eyes, shutting his mouth.

"My sister died a few years back. It's why I stayed

here for college. Our parents were trash. My mother was an alcoholic, and my father was the same, just your typical deadbeat. They mooched off everyone else and never tried to actually make their lives better, and by some fucked up miracle, they had me and Harper. And despite our messed up parents, she was pure light. The absolute best." I blinked, tears returning to my eyes now that I'd started to talk about my baby sister.

Wiping my face, I took a deep breath before continuing.

"My sister was diagnosed with leukemia when she was fifteen. It was the shit cherry on an already fucked up sundae. Of course, our parents didn't care. And we didn't have the necessary medical care to cover anything. So I stayed to help. I couldn't leave her with them. But it didn't matter. I was a bone marrow match, but because they were so negligent, it was already too late by the time she was diagnosed. Her body rejected it, and that was that. After Harper died, I closed everything off. Lacey and Joy were the only two people I didn't push away, mostly because they're stubborn jack-holes who wouldn't let me. They saved me."

Sucking in a deep breath. I braced myself for the rest.

"I didn't realize how much I'd cut people out until you three barged into my life, not letting me go. You awoke something in me, chipping away at the ice I'd put around my heart. I thought keeping people out made me stronger, but it didn't. This week, I've felt more like that Holland I used to be, the one who had a sister who thought she'd hung the moon. I liked feeling that way again. It's scary, but it's real. I didn't know how hollow, how vacant my life had become. The game filled it, but it was only for a little while. Intimacy and connection, that's been the thing I've been missing. "

Quentin's hand flexed on my ass; his hands had moved over me, soothing me while I spoke.

"Don't ever apologize for caring so deeply for someone that the thought of them gone wrecks you because it's exactly what I needed to be reminded of. It's rare and beautiful, and we're not letting that asshole keep them. I will rain down hell if I have to and burn down the world in the process to get them back. The only thing I need from you is to know whether you'll be there by my side."

"Where you go, I go, Temptress." He placed his forehead on mine, his eyes clear and full. "Thank you for pulling me back from the ledge. I'm here with you and will walk through the fire with you. Your strength's so fucking beautiful, and I don't think you understand how amazing you are, Holland. You might've been numb, but you weren't as hollow as you believed. You saved so many people, giving them the hope and miracle they needed. I get that now. And I see you, baby. *I fucking see you.*"

It might've not been the right time, but after a man said that to you, the only correct response was to smash your lips together.

Slamming my mouth to his, I soaked in everything he'd just said, sharing my fear and panic with him and my strength. This was what I'd been missing, this recip-rocal connection from a place of true intimacy. For so long, I hadn't let anyone in other than Lacey and Joy, but now that I had, I knew I couldn't go back to how I'd been.

I was combining the rage and loss of control I'd felt for years with the power of connection. It felt like an unstoppable force, pushing me to hope for the first time.

We *would* get them back, or the world would mourn with us as we obliterated anything that got in our path. That was a motherfucking guarantee.

Pulling back, we stared at one another, the same mission and fierceness reflecting back in Quentin's eyes now.

"Not to break up the moment, but I hope you both know how much I echo everything you said. The three of us... we were floundering and trying to paste together a brotherhood built on revenge."

Grady had walked into the room, kneeling down by us as he finished, pressing his forehead to ours and letting out the tension in his shoulders as he wrapped his arms around both of us.

"You give us a deeper connection, mi chispa— a true purpose. We'll do this together. All of us."

Quentin nodded, squeezing the back of Grady's head as the last of his fear drained away. Grady sat back, and I spotted Lacey standing in the doorway, tears in her eyes. I motioned for her to join me, needing to hug my best friend, too.

She eagerly rushed to me, throwing her arms around me as she buried her head in my neck, not caring that Q was right there, too. I didn't plan on moving, not that he would let me if I tried.

"I'm sorry if you ever felt you couldn't let your guard down," she whispered, confirming that everyone had heard my confession.

"Shh. You saved me—you and Joy. Without you two, I wouldn't be here. It's as simple as that. I'm sorry I didn't realize how closed off I'd become."

"You lost your sister. We understood."

"Still." We cried-laughed together, knowing that if Joy were here, she would've told us to suck it up, kiss, and then dance it out. Wiping our faces, we pulled apart, but Lacey didn't move far, keeping her hand in mind.

Grady gave us a soft smile. We all needed a little healing-honesty and connection. It made my need to get the other two pieces of my heart back flare to life.

"How's Lukas? Any updates?" I asked, turning in Quentin's lap. He barely gave me the space to do so, keeping his arms snug around me.

"Doc was able to stabilize him and set up a drip. He should be okay in a few days. He's sleeping now," Lacey said, squeezing my hand.

I sighed; at least one thing had improved, and our promise to Theo remained. "Did Ava tell him about his dad?" I asked.

She nodded, her face slack. Sucking in a breath, I let it out slowly. Fuck. It felt like all we were doing was failing. I turned to Grady, and he squeezed my knee, the four of us so close on the floor between the beds; I wondered for a second how we would get up.

"Ryan's team will be here in an hour. We're getting Max and Joy back, whatever the cost."

"Even if that means Viper gets away?" I asked. I didn't plan on that happening, but I needed to know where his loyalties lay. The three of them had been hunting him for so long that I didn't know if he could let it go.

"They're more important and the priority. If Viper escapes, then I'll keep chasing him."

"We will," I amended. "He won't know what hit him with the XOXO killer on his tail."

Grady smiled, all teeth and predatory. "It shouldn't be as hot as it is when you go all murdery."

"And that's my cue to leave before it gets X-rated in here," Lacey said, attempting to stand in the small space.

"Nonsense. Like that's ever made you leave before," I teased, causing her to snort. "But as nice as that sounds, we should clean up, change, and eat something in the hour we have. Once they're here, I want to hit the ground running. Viper won't expect us to retaliate so quickly, and I want to use that."

"I can help," Ava said from the doorway.

"We just got you out of there. You're not going back," I said, not even considering it.

She shook her head, lifting it high and showing her strength. I admired that.

"You're right, I never want to step foot back there. But I can give you a better outline of the place, where the weakest access points are, and his routines. Viper thought I was stupid, so he never hid anything from me. I can help."

The steel in her eyes would do her well. I nodded, accepting her offer and knowing how much she needed to do something.

"Okay. Everyone get cleaned up and eat something. Let's make it thirty minutes, so we have plenty of time to plan before they arrive."

"Yes, Boss," Grady said, kissing me with a smile. I couldn't help it and returned it, liking how it made my heart flutter and my insides melt.

I could get used to that sound.

CHAPTER 30
GRADY

SOMEHOW, DESPITE TWO OF OUR OWN BEING CAPTURED, I felt lighter than I had in years. The bitterness I'd been carrying around was gone, replaced with a sense of acceptance and hope. It was terrifying to want something new, but I couldn't stop myself from craving Holland, even if I tried.

Gone was the desperate drive to kill a man—one who didn't even know my name—and in its place was a solid comfort of connection… of belonging. I had no clue what would come of the four of us, but it felt like we were on the brink of creating something solid and real. Something whole.

I felt like a new man, so much so, that even the arrival of Ryan and his team didn't piss me off.

"Grady," the man in question nodded after I opened the door. He looked me over, his brow creasing. "Something's different about you? Did you have surgery?"

"Surgery?" I asked, tilting my head. Why would he think I had surgery?

"Yeah, for that stick up your ass?"

Lacey and Holland snickered behind me, and I

couldn't even find it in myself to be mad at Ryan. Hearing Holland laugh was a reward within itself.

"Right. Yeah. As a matter of fact, I did." I grinned, smacking him on the shoulder as he entered, his face comical at my reaction.

"Okay, who body-snatched Grady?" he asked, taking in the two women now with more interest. "Wait, who are you?" Ryan spun on his heels, his face hard as he stared at me. "I'm all for you getting some, especially if it's the cause of this," he said, waving his hand in front of me, "but that doesn't mean you throw out protocol and invite your booty call to a debriefing. Fuck. I gotta call this in."

"Does this mean we'll be zapped like in *Men in Black*?" Lacey asked, leaning over to whisper to Holland, but didn't keep her voice low.

"Ooh, do you think that's real? I could use that on a few people. Though you might need to demonstrate *your* skills to Mr. Debriefing first. We don't have time to deal with the police or the cleanup crew today," Holland said, swinging her leg back and forth on the bed like she hadn't just insinuated killing a fellow Shadow.

"I'd like to debrief him alright," Lacey purred, licking her lips.

Ryan stopped, staring at the two women with his phone held halfway to his face. Taking pity on him and agreeing with Holland that we didn't have time, I walked over and clapped him around the shoulder, squeezing a little tighter than necessary.

"Ryan, this is two parts of the XOXO killer. The other is in the Savages' possession along with Max. *Not my booty call*. And I'm pretty certain they could kill you before you blinked, but let's not test that theory."

"*They're* the asset?" he asked, swallowing as he lowered his phone.

"I have an ass you can hit," Lacey teased, winking at him.

In all of my years, I'd never seen Ryan so flustered before. His cheeks brightened, and he cleared his throat, fumbling with his phone before it reached his pocket. I wanted to laugh, but since I had the same response to Holland, I wasn't one to judge.

"Right. Okay. My team's outside, and we're ready to roll out when you are." He glanced around the space, most likely trying to look at anything other than the two gorgeous women on the bed.

They hopped up at his words, all business now that we were headed into battle. Holland walked over to the door and did a series of knocks before Q opened, peeking his head out.

"It's time," she said, and he nodded, poking his head back to say something before stepping into our room. He waited to hear the lock engaged and then greeted Ryan.

"Ry."

"Quentin."

"Someone on your team needs to stay back to guard the room next door. No one is to enter or exit while we're gone. If, for some reason, we don't make it back, then a secondary team will come to collect them. They'll have a codeword that the inhabitants of that room know."

I love how Holland didn't ask but gave the order with the understanding that it would be followed while also not giving anything away, fully protecting Ava and Lukas.

Ryan looked at me for a second, but I just lifted my brows, letting him know she was in charge. He scrubbed his face as he thought, eventually nodding.

"Yeah, okay. Can I know who it is?"

"Nope." Holland didn't elaborate, strapping on a knife holster to her leg, finishing off her badass killer look.

Lacey and Holland both had on vests Joy had made that were apparently superior to Kevlar. Add in the black pants of the same material, guns, and knives strapped to them both; they made a deadly duo.

How Ryan didn't recognize them as killers the instant he entered the room spoke of how long they'd been able to go undetected.

No one ever suspected them. They might be the most valuable asset to join the Shadows to date.

Jackson would be thrilled, and we'd finally get that vacation. It felt dirty using them for that, but I couldn't deny the appeal of having time off with Holland after this. Perhaps a nice beach or lake would be in the plans. But first, we had to get back our teammates.

"Fuck me," Ryan whispered as Holland sauntered out of the room, not realizing the pile of shit he'd just stepped in. Quentin growled, his face hardening as he stepped forward. I barely managed to stop him, my own need to claim Holland raring to go in me, but it was Lacey who managed to de-escalate the situation.

"Anytime, hotshot. But *she's* already taken. You might want to keep your eyes to yourself unless you plan to lose them," she said, kissing his cheek and sashaying her own butt out the door. Ryan glanced back, noticing the killer expression on Quentin's and maybe my face, and gulped.

"Sorry. Didn't mean anything by it. Shall we?" he asked, clearing his throat and stepping out, his voice a higher octave as he left.

"Is it just me, or is that the first time we've gotten one over on him?" Q asked, his rage simmering down.

I snorted but nodded. Ryan was usually so flippant and disorienting, coming in to save the day, that I hated every second with him. But today, it had been fun seeing him be the one with his tail between his legs.

The rest of his team was gathered around a large truck, and it didn't surprise me as we approached that Holland had taken command. Ryan stood next to her, but it was clear who was in charge. If anything, he looked a little taken aback that she'd taken over but was too nervous to say anything about it. His men had fallen in line quickly, apparently able to identify the real threat better than him.

That, or all the guns and knives strapped to her and Lacey, had warranted some respect. So, maybe just smarter.

"You," Holland pointed at the guy in the back. He looked around himself, despite being the last of the crew.

Eventually, he pointed at his chest, his eyes wide like he didn't believe she was talking to him. My cock took notice, thickening against my leg at the most inappropriate time. But my girl was hot when she scared the shit out of everyone.

"No, the ghost next to you," she said, rolling her eyes. He jumped to his left, like there really was a ghost, gulping when he realized she was joking.

"Seriously, *this* is the best the Shadows have?" she asked Lacey, who shrugged her shoulders, then walked over to the men, looking them up and down as she assessed them. They instantly straightened like they were being inspected. Holland's eyes danced, enjoying the discomfort they brought the gathered men.

I cleared my throat, knowing she'd want to get to the compound quickly. "He the one to stay back?" I asked, drawing her attention.

"Yep. Can you tell him what to do and how not to fuck it up?" she asked, smiling at me.

I nodded, cupping Ben on the back of the neck and leading him over to the rooms. He shook, nodding at everything I said and planting himself in a chair before the door.

By the time I returned to the group, everyone had dispersed into vehicles, and we were ready to roll out. I had to hand it to Holland; she was efficient.

Sliding in beside Ryan, I centered myself as we

reached the entry point. Ava had given us the ideal location to breach the property, which hadn't even been on our maps. Apparently, Viper had connections all the way up to the NSA that kept his property off the satellites, limiting the information available and distorting anything that made it through before it reached the public.

Taking him out wouldn't be easy, but I was determined to try. He was the type of man who brought only fear and pain into the world, and I was sick of it.

"Your girl's kind of scary," Ryan said a little while into the drive. "But, also, hot. Is, um, her friend available?"

"Lacey?" I growled, reminding myself I couldn't kill him because he thought Holland was hot.

"Um, yeah. That her name? I didn't really get it."

"Yep, and as far as I know, she's single. Not that Lacey does relationships. More of a 'love 'em and leave 'em' situation."

He sighed, a wistful smile crawling over his face. "What a way to go, though."

I snorted, shaking my head, not that I could blame him. It had taken me far longer to realize I wanted Holland, despite my dick's instant reaction.

The vacant lot we pulled into was exactly as Ava described, the lone door jutting from the ground. This was her father's escape hatch, and because it was a secret only he and a few guards knew of, it wasn't guarded to keep the whereabouts of its location secret—hubris at its finest.

Which worked perfectly for us.

The still of the early morning surrounded us as we stepped out of the vehicles, our boots crunching on the gravel as we all circled the back of the semi. It was a mobile command station with monitors, weapons, and supplies. Ryan's team was typically sent in to completely wipe out a target if they weren't deemed worthy or able to be of use to the Shadows, but they also did rescue missions, making them the best candidates to help us on this job.

"Alright, the XOXO team will head through the tunnel; a secondary unit will follow ten minutes later. The third unit will head in that direction to catch anyone trying to leave the compound, and the rest will monitor from here. Time is of the essence. They've already been with Viper for over two hours." Holland steeled her jaw, her face taut. "If he's touched a hair on either of them, he'll regret it." She took a breath, letting out the anger as she focused. "The secondary team will escort out housekeepers and any staff first. Once we have Max and Joy, we're leveling this place to the ground."

Her teeth were gritted, the pure killer she could be was evident on her face. If there was ever any doubt I wouldn't find that attractive, my dick took that away as it thickened against my leg... *again*. At this rate, I would need to buy extra tight pants so I didn't tent up each time she walked into the room.

Or opened her mouth.

Or got sassy.

Or bossy.

Yeah, I was addicted to all things Holland, and I wouldn't deny it.

The men broke into their units, their respect for Holland clear as day. Ryan turned to me with the same look reflected in his eyes.

"I'm not trying to mack on your girl," he started, lifting his hands. "But I never knew I found women who killed things for fun and knew how to command a room so sexy before. I think every single one of these guys would follow her into the pits of Hell if she asked. Just saying."

Snorting, I nodded, entirely in agreement with him.

"I know I'm not your favorite person, but this is a good look on you, Grady. Don't mess it up."

He took off after that, not giving me time to respond. But what did one say to that, anyway?

Thanks for noticing I'm not a giant asshole anymore?

Nah. Better to keep it as it was between us. I didn't need the dynamic shifting amidst Ryan and me too much. There was only so much change a man could take at once.

Meeting Lacey, Holland, and Quentin, I did a quick scan to make sure everyone was fully equipped and ready. When I noticed Holland doing the same, my lips twitched up into a smile. I'd always needed control, but it felt nice to share it with her. Being on a team with her friends, even if Lacey and Joy annoyed me and tried their damndest to get under my skin, felt good. It was comforting in a way, like having little sisters or something. But I wouldn't tell them that just yet.

"Everyone ready to rescue our family?" I asked, shocking them.

"Yeah," Quentin said, giving me a nod and a clap on my shoulder. "Let's retrieve our family."

"First dibs on cutting off some appendages," Lacey said, spinning and skipping to the door.

"She's been hanging out with Joy too much," Holland grumbled, pivoting herself. "Lacey, I'll rock-paper-scissors you for dibs. You can't just call it like that."

"Why not? I want it, so I take it."

"This is like how you lick all the good chocolates in the candy box, leaving the rest for us. Haven't you ever heard that sharing is caring?" Holland continued, planting her hands on her hips as she faced off with her best friend.

"Fine," Lacey groaned like it was the most inconvenient thing ever. "We can both be stabby. Did you bring your favorite knife?" she asked, perking up.

"And here I thought the skipping was the oddest thing," Quentin muttered.

"I'm just glad to no longer be on the end of their knives."

"Let's fuck, steal, kill, bitches!" Lacey hollered, raising her fist into the air.

"You're not really going to fuck someone in there, right?" Heath, Ryan's second-in-command and leader of the retrieval unit, asked. Despite his question, his pupils were dilated, and his cheeks rosy as he watched Lacey, licking his lips.

"As if you wouldn't watch," Lacey teased, blowing him a kiss and winking, causing Henry, the last member of Ryan's team and leader of the command team to swallow hard, his breathing uneven as he watched her. It didn't surprise me he was right next to Heath, the two of them together so often that everyone called them H-squared.

"But no. We're gonna fuck them up, steal our girl *and* guy back, and then kill them all," Lacey answered as her eyes went dark, voice full of venom. And even I had to admit to being a little scared of the unhinged look on her face right then.

"Couldn't have said it better, babe." Holland grinned, then pulled the door open, stepping into the dark entrance, her mission clear.

Rescue our people, and make sure Viper never had the chance to take them, or anyone else, again.

Matching Holland's grin, I followed without any hesitation. The Savages had messed with the wrong people, and it would be the last mistake they ever made.

Only one crew was walking out of here alive today. Us or them.

CHAPTER 31
HOLLAND xoxo

Nervous energy rattled my bones, and the need to unleash it pushed me onward as we neared the entrance. Just a few hundred killers lay between me and rescuing Max and Joy.

Time to have my cake and eat it too.

I glanced over my shoulder, taking into account everyone's position, before I armed the door with an explosive device that would unlock it and turn off the alarm system. Not necessary for us since we wanted them to know we were there, but for the other team so they could get out all the innocent people. That had been Ava's request, stating that the house staff were just as much victims of her father's cruelty, and didn't deserve to die.

As much as it sucked to use people to rescue more, I knew it was the right thing to do, and I wouldn't make families deal with that loss if they didn't have to. I had a heart; it was just battered and mostly black.

"One, two, three," I whispered, stepping back into Quentin's chest as the device fired, letting off a pop as it sent shockwaves or some magic shit through the door to disengage everything. I didn't really know how it worked, just that it did. Joy was a freaking genius. A small plume of smoke rose, but otherwise, it was contained.

No words were spoken as I kicked open the door, my gun held at the ready for any guards that lingered on the other side. A man jumped up, dropping the phone he'd been holding in the process, an earbud falling out of one side. That at least explained how he hadn't heard us.

Unfortunately for him, he was dead before he had time to raise his weapon, my finger hitting the trigger and nailing him right between the eyes within seconds.

One down, ninety-nine, something or other to go.

"I'm up," I teased Lacey, the competitiveness helping to distract from the fear we were too late.

"Not for long," she sang, firing two shots and taking down two more guards.

Grinning, we continued advancing, more men taking notice as their friends fell to the ground around them.

By the time we reached the next door, I was up to ten, and Lacey was at twelve. Grady and Quentin had yet to fire. Slackers.

Reloading while I had the time, I motioned for Quentin to set the next device. Smirking, he did as I asked, blocking me as it fired.

"My turn," he whispered before stepping through the door first and firing off his own shot.

Fuck. That was hot.

"Why do I suddenly envision you fucking your men in the blood of your enemies?" Lacey asked, laughing as I only shrugged. I'd never deny it hadn't crossed my mind.

This room was heavily guarded, and it took all of us shooting and ducking for cover as they returned fire to clear it out. I lost count of my kills but shrugged it off, thankful the vest had held. It had taken a few hits, and I'd have bruises to show for it tomorrow. Holstering my gun, I pulled my knife free as we neared the last door into the house. With the close quarters of the hallways, I wanted to be able to slice and dice as I moved and not accidentally shoot myself with a ricochet bullet.

Been there, done that, had the scar to prove it.

The hallway was eerily quiet as we tiptoed out of the hidden door. There was no way our arrival hadn't gone unnoticed, especially since we hadn't been trying to keep quiet. Slinking along the wall, my heart pounded in my chest as the adrenaline spiked. We were so close now.

Despite killing over a dozen men already, my thirst hadn't been quenched. I needed to feel their blood as it seeped out of them, to watch them squirm and their eyes turn to fear when they realized the only way out was death. It might sound morbid, but it was the truth.

Until I had that, I wouldn't be satisfied, not after what these assholes had done.

We made it another few feet without spotting another soul. Where were all the men? My spidey senses tingled that we were about to walk into a trap.

"This isn't right," Lacey whispered, echoing my own fears. "Maybe we should split up?" she suggested, her eyes darting in every direction as she calculated the distance and risks.

"No," Q and Grady said before I could even form thoughts. Not that I disagreed, but sometimes their possessiveness went to the extreme.

Who was I kidding? I loved every second of it and claimed them back just as hard.

The hallway opened to a big room lying on the other side of the wall, and I had a gut feeling this was where Viper was taking a stand. From our angle, we couldn't see into the room, and I wasn't dumb enough to walk right out into the open. Unclipping a round silver ball, I tossed it in my hand a few times before crouching to roll it into the open space.

The ball could be heard as it rolled over the floor, but no one made a sound on the other side. Either I was wrong, and they weren't there, or they were the quietest mercenaries I'd ever met.

It didn't matter which scenario as the ball stopped, and it began a countdown of beeps, growing faster as it neared the end. And there it was, a faint squeak, a shift of a foot, the rustling of clothes. Someone was antsy.

A loud beep rang out in the quiet space as the ball opened at the top and released a mist. The four of us had pulled up our neck gaiters, blocking the sweet smoke as it permeated the room in record time. Coughing and furniture moving as people collapsed were the cues I needed before I rolled from my crouched position into the middle of the room, flicking my knife at the first thing that moved.

It landed in the shoulder of a Savage, his gun dropping as he clutched his arm. The others followed, though they stayed on their feet, guns popping off as they took out the rest of the men. Retrieving my knife, I kicked the guy who was still alive before kneeling next to him. Holding the blade to his throat, I glared at him.

"Where are the hostages?"

He shook his head, his eyes wide as he pleaded with me. This man might not be the killer the rest were, but there was no way of knowing. The only Savage that Ava had vouched for was Theo, and since he was already dead, I didn't particularly have a lot of grace when it came to the rest.

Had he stopped to consider his actions? Did he care when others had been killed? I highly doubted it, and therefore I wouldn't waste my time worrying whether or not he deserved death.

Here in this house, if they were a Savage, then they died. They'd made their decision, and I was good with that reasoning.

"Last chance, where are the hostages?" I pressed the blade into his throat, a line of blood dribbling down in the process.

"They escaped," he choked, urine permeating the air as it soaked his pants. Rolling my eyes, I asked one more question.

"Viper?"

He shook his head, the blade cutting him deeper in

the move, and the hot, sticky liquid ran over my fingers, sending a thrill through me. The smell of copper overtook the stench of urine, alighting the darkness in me.

"Coward," I hissed, slicing across his throat the rest of the way. Standing, I wiped the blade on my pants and stepped over his body, already forgetting him as I calculated the next move.

"They've escaped." Hope bloomed in my chest, and I prayed it wasn't misguided. "Stay on alert, and let's clear out each room. Viper doesn't get to leave this place alive."

The three of them nodded, falling into place as we worked together to clear out the rooms along this side of the house. I spotted some of Team Two leading people out of the house through the window, and I mentally sighed in relief that my plan was working. I hadn't meant to step in and take over full control, and actually liked how Grady and I worked together.

But it was like we both knew only one of us could lead while inside, needing only one set of commands to follow. Otherwise, it could lead to sloppy mistakes and miscalculations, which neither of us was willing to play around with.

We came to the last door, and I had a feeling we were about to find our target. It was the most secure room on this end, making it the perfect hideout. I nodded to Lacey, and she pulled a gadget off of her belt and slid it under the door. Opening her phone, she directed the miniature drone to walk up the wall and give us an aerial view of the space.

The second Viper came into view, I had to stop myself from rushing in. He had Joy on her knees, a gun cocked to her head. A few men were standing before him, but it wasn't the force I expected. Either we'd killed more than I realized, the men were hiding out somewhere, or they'd run when shit'd hit the fan earlier.

I wasn't sure which option was preferable.

"Where's Max?" Quentin mouthed, making me take a second look at the screen. He was right. He wasn't in there.

"Where would he go?" I asked, but I already knew the answer. If he were still alive, which I would believe until I saw his body, he'd risk his life to gather as much information as possible. "The security room."

Quentin nodded, shifting to his feet. I knew he was torn between wanting to go after Max or staying for me.

"Go," I whispered. His shoulders dropped, and he nodded, kissing me on my forehead before he jogged off back to the other side of the house.

"Ready, Boss," Lacey said, her harness on and the grate to the air vent already off. Moving with Grady, I helped her into the high vent on the wall and tied the end of the rope onto a doorknob. It wasn't the best solution, but it would be enough to give her a way out if she needed it.

"What's fucking taking so long? One of you, go," Viper hissed, pointing to one of his men to head to the door. "You ready to tell me anything useful, bitch?" He slapped her with the gun, and I had to hold myself back from bolting in there before everything was in place.

"Êl síla erin lû e-govaned vîn," she retorted, not at all scared as he seethed above her, blood dripping down her face.

"What did she say?" Grady whispered, and I had to shake my head to stop laughing. It helped ease some of the bloodlust, knowing that even when captured, Joy was still Joy.

"Sevig thû úan! Dôl gîn lost!"

"What language is that?" Grady whispered.

"Elvish. Joy's a closeted nerd. She's obsessed with LOTR."

Grady grinned, the action lighting his blue eyes, and if we weren't about to murder some people, I'd take a moment to really kiss him.

As it was, the door opened, and the man sent to check on our whereabouts emerged and stopped dead when he spotted us on either side. Lost in our moment, I'd forgotten about him. Oops.

Before he could sound the alarm, Grady elbowed him in the throat in a move so slick I had to grab the wall to hold myself up as my knees went weak. Because damn, that was hot.

The Savage sputtered, grabbing his throat as he tried to breathe and leaving himself open for my knife. With a few quick stabby-stabs between his ribs, I nicked his lungs, spleen, and kidney as he fell forward.

Unfortunately, the whole thing had alerted the room

to our presence, and bullets whizzed out the door, landing in the guy and wall.

"Well, hello, who do we have here?" Viper called, his voice maniacal as he cooed out to us. "Come out, come out. You can watch me kill this stripper," he barked, his voice changing to menace. Joy's protest echoed around my brain as I planted my feet, waiting for Lacey to get into position. As it was, we were outnumbered, and their guns would take us out in seconds.

"Nah, I'm good. Not a fan of guns," I yelled, tapping my knife against the doorframe.

"Tsk tsk, bringing a knife to a gun party. Amateur move," he boasted, chuckling like he was having the best day.

"Hmpf," I snorted. "That's where you're wrong." Dropping into a crouch, I slid a smoke bomb and knife across the floor to Joy.

By the time Viper realized what I'd done, Joy had rolled out of his grip with the knife in her hand as she took cover.

The next few seconds happened quickly, and I wish we had it recorded so I could watch it on replay over and over again.

The Savages shot at the space Joy had been in, one of them grazing Viper in the process. The smoke bomb turned into a firecracker as pops sounded, sparks flying as smoke filled the room. Visibility became nonexistent to them, each one shooting off at anything that moved and inadvertently hitting one another.

"Stop," Viper yelled. The shots halted, but it was already too late.

In the chaos, Lacey had opened the vent in the wall, her gun pointed directly at Viper, a vicious smile on her face just as the haze cleared.

"Say cheese," she bellowed, shooting the last of his men in the room, each falling to the ground with a thud.

Viper finally looked scared, jumping as I stalked toward him. He lifted the gun in his hand, and it trembled as he removed the safety.

"Who the fuck are you?" he spat, gritting his teeth.

Throwing my two shurikens—small blades in the shape of an X—at his wrists as I entered the room, I watched in satisfaction as he dropped the gun right into Joy's hand. She'd moved over, ready to snatch it so it wouldn't go off.

Again, been there, done that, learned the lesson. Don't mess with flying bullets.

Both his wrists bled, my X's hitting his flexor carpi tendons and stopping him from bending his wrists. He stared down at his bleeding hands, shock on his face. I bet it wasn't every day that this man felt so disarmed, much less by a woman, and I'd done it in a few seconds with the flick of my wrists.

You didn't need to have a dick to exhibit BDE or be the biggest threat. There was no doubt in Viper's eyes now who that belonged to as he learned that lesson.

Me. I was the biggest dick and threat because I wasn't alone.

I had my girls, and I had my guys. Anyone who

thought they could take us would meet the same fate as this scumbag.

"If you haven't figured it out by now, I'm not sure you deserve to know," I taunted, standing before him with Joy at my side and Grady at my back. Lacey hopped out of the air vent and joined us, the four of us painting a menacing picture as we glared at Viper.

"You're the worst type of man. You underestimate women and see them only as property to be used."

I jutted forward, slashing two long marks on his legs and making him fall to his knees as more blood dripped down, satiating my need.

"Grady, do what you need to," I said, stepping back with Joy and Lacey to give him space.

The man I'd been falling for the past few days was gone, and in his place was a cold-blooded killer. His face was void of any emotion outside of hatred and malice in his eyes as he stalked toward his prey.

"I doubt you even remember the woman you took from me, but I've been waiting for this day for five years."

He reared his fist back, punching him in the face, and Viper's head snapped back as Grady broke his nose. He rained down punches on his body before finally taking the knife I held out for him. A noise at the door had us spinning, guns raised as we prepared for an attack.

"It's us," Max said, leaning on Quentin as he hobbled into the room on one good leg. Seeing him alive broke the last of my resolve, and I flew toward him, wrapping my arms around his neck as tears fell.

"You're alive," I sobbed, kissing him between the snot.

"I wasn't ready to leave you yet, sweetheart." Max clung to me and Quentin, both of us needing to feel his weight against us.

"Gee, thanks. This one gets a weepy hug, and I didn't even get a hello," Joy teased behind me, breaking the tense emotional moment.

Wiping my face, I kissed Max before stepping back and pulling Joy into my arms next, so thankful she was okay.

"I'm sorry. You know I go all Scary Spice when I'm unaliving people."

"I know, Hols. I'm glad to see your heart is still soft because yours is the biggest I know."

Hugging her tighter, I widened my arms when I felt Lacey join in. The three of us clung to one another, our bond surging through us now that we were back together.

"Now give me a kiss, and then let's blow this popsicle stand. Literally. Momma's feeling bombey."

Giving her a big pucker, I laughed as I stepped back and wiped my face again for the second time in minutes. I hadn't cried this much in years, and while it freaked me out a little, and I'd deny it if anyone asked, it also felt nice. A bit cathartic.

I glanced over at Viper, not surprised to see Quentin and Max had joined Grady, taking their turns to get their pound of flesh. Not an inch of him was left unmarked, his face barely recognizable.

"Joy's feeling bombey, and I'm suddenly craving a milkshake. Who wants to stop on the way back?" I asked, breaking up the slaughter-fest. All three men turned to me, blood splattered all over them. They smiled when they met my eyes, making me almost lose my balance.

"Oh no, we need to go. Holland's got her sex face on," Lacey said, breaking up the lust.

I rolled my eyes but didn't deny it. Once we were all clean—okay, maybe even before—I planned to show the three of them exactly how hot they were.

"I should probably see a medic, too. I kinda got stabbed," Max said, bringing the mission back to focus.

"Right, put a bullet in his head so there's no Freddy returns moment, then let's go. Max needs medical attention, and this place needs to be wiped from existence. What were you doing in the security room anyway, Max?" I asked as we headed out the door, a shot firing off in the background.

"This," he said, pulling a flash drive around his neck. "It's the mother lode."

"And it's back; we gotta hurry, people," Lacey yelled, making me laugh as she pointed at my face.

Somehow we made it out to the second team, who confirmed everyone was clear of the house. The semi and trucks had been brought around to the gate so they could take all the innocents out and offer medical attention to those who needed it. I ensured Max was seen while we did one more sweep of the compound with a drone to rule out any other heat signatures. When it was negative, Joy prepped her bomb and secured it onto another drone. The smile on her face as she rubbed her hands together in delight made me glad we were friends—sweet but psycho, that one.

Once we loaded the trucks and pulled out of the driveway, she hit the button for it to detonate. A massive explosion sounded, and a fireball flashed in the sky as the sun started to rise on the horizon. A fitting end to our mission. I swear I could hear Joy's cackle of glee in the distance, too.

Resting my head against Grady's shoulder, I let myself relax for the first time in twenty-four hours. It was done. The Savages had been obliterated, our hopeless one and the rest of our family rescued, and we'd removed another monster.

I didn't know what the future held from here, but I hoped it was somewhere warm with fruity drinks because the XOXO killer had earned a vacation... and their way out of Foolshope for good.

CHAPTER 32
HOLLAND xoxo

I RAN THE TAPE GUN OVER THE BOX, THANKFUL IT WAS THE last one. Setting it off to the side, I wiped the sweat from my brow as I surveyed the house. Everything was boxed up or shoved into duffles, laundry baskets, and crates. Seeing the remnants of my life so sufficiently reduced to this was odd.

"Your lover boys are backing in with the truck," Joy yelled as she skipped into the room. "I think I even spotted Ryan and one of his guys with them. Who knew we could attract so much muscle?"

She plopped down onto the bare mattress, bracing her head on her hand. "Well, I guess I knew. We're a sexy threesome. Bonus to having less work for us. I need to step up my game in the muscle department. While I was captured, Lacey managed to snag herself a hottie."

"Mm, I'm not so sure she feels the same. He keeps following her around and hoping she gives him another ride on the Lacey coaster. Based on the noises I heard from her room, it was one helluva night. Not surprised he didn't want to let her go." I glanced out the window, spotting Lacey as she pretended to ignore Ryan. "Have to hand it to him, though. Ryan doesn't give up and takes rejection well."

"It's like foreplay for them at this point," Joy agreed, nodding. She fell back, staring up at the ceiling. "I'm gonna miss this place, as weird as that sounds. We've been working for years to get out, and now that we are, I'm kinda sad."

I sat down next to her, grabbing her hand.

"As much as we hated it here, we went through a lot in Foolshope. The three of us became a family, a team in this house. But that's not changing. We're moving, but we're not leaving each other."

"Damn straight," Joy said, rolling over to wrap her arms around my waist. "You sure you want to live with us still, though? You got your three hotties now."

"Definitely. I might not sleep in my bed many nights, but I'm not ready to move in with three guys I just met."

"Ah, young love," she sighed.

"Ew. Stop. It's not love. I'm in moderate-like with them."

"Uh-huh."

Joy made kissy faces, tickling my sides.

"Stop," I said, around a giggle, jumping away and falling onto the floor. "Brat."

"Nah. That's you, babe, and Lacey is such a Domme. I'm more of a vers, but if I had to pick one. Hmm." She tapped her lip in thought. "Depending on my partner, I'm probably a cross of a pleaser and tester." She nodded at herself, sitting up with a pleased smile.

"I don't even want to know," I said, laughing.

Joy shrugged, hopping off the bed when the front door opened. I wrapped my arm around her shoulders and led her out into the main area.

I couldn't help but keep hugging her at times, just so happy to have her back unharmed with us. Joy didn't appear to have any lasting damage, but I'd insisted she and Max do a few sessions with the trauma specialist. They only agreed to go if we all went, so once we got settled into our new place, the six of us would go to group therapy together. I already felt bad for that therapist.

The Shadows considered it team bonding and a way to ensure everyone was fit to work in the field. It made my skin crawl, but I'd do it for the others. Besides, I knew how to make the leader disappear if they hurt anyone.

The aftermath of taking down the Savages had been immense. It had taken a week to find new identities for the prisoners there and places for them to go. We'd been able to sneak Ava and Lukas out to our contact at least, so they were off the grid and able to move on with a normal life. It had been emotional to say goodbye and exhausting by the end with the added back-end bureaucratic shit I never had to deal with before.

I guess that was why many serial killers didn't go corporate; the paperwork was brutal.

But ultimately, I still got to do what I loved with the people I cared the most about.

"That nerd is here again," Lacey grumbled, giving Ryan the stink eye.

He smiled brighter, if possible, flashing her dimples as he listened to Grady tell him which boxes to grab first. Lacey shook her head and spun away from the besotted man with the biggest crush.

I didn't know the other guy's name with him, but I remembered him from the Savage compound. And I'd bet money Ryan wasn't the only one following Lacey with heart eyes. Why else would he volunteer to help three girls move? Sus, was all I was saying.

Max spotted me and made a beeline, picking me up as he neared and spinning me around. I'd been the most worried about him, but he'd proven us all wrong by bouncing back the strongest. He really was one of a kind.

"Hey, girlfriend. I missed you, sweetheart." He kissed me, setting my heart racing and my toes curling.

"I missed you too. Though, it was only one night," I teased, lifting my brow.

"Too long. I can't wait to get to the beach. Ten days with nothing but you and mixed drinks... Ah, bliss."

After a long debate with the girls, they assured me they wanted to join the Shadows, too. We'd all been offered a spot in the upcoming training class, though Grady felt we'd be schooling all the recruits by the end. Joy was excited to work on more gadgets, and Lacey apparently had a passion for profiling. I was glad we'd still be together, even if we weren't the XOXO killer anymore. Well, officially.

The app would stay viable, but the jobs would now be filtered through the Shadows. It was the one concession I had. I didn't want the people who reached out to us to lose that resource, and once the leaders of the Shadows saw our operation, they were willing to negotiate, especially if we shared all of our secrets.

It was the price to pay to go semi-mainstream, but I'd be willing to do it if it meant no more looking over my shoulder, waiting for someone to discover us and lock us away.

So this way, I got to kill people and punish the bad, and the Shadows gained three valuable assets. Tack on the salary they were willing to pay us, and I wondered why more people didn't become professional killers. Though, if I had to guess, that damn paperwork. That shit would be the death of me.

But before we became official Shadows, we had two weeks off. Ah, vacation—where I didn't have to clean up other people's shit or condoms.

"Oops, I might've forgotten to pack clothes," I teased, Max's eyes lighting up at the notion.

"Well darn. I guess I'll have to cover you with my dick."

Barking out a laugh, I kissed him again before making him set me down. "I think I have a solution for your mouth, too," I taunted, his cheeks red at the indication.

Oh, yeah, this trip was going to be so fun.

Three hours later, the house was completely emptied and cleaned. Everything had been loaded onto the truck, and Ryan and Heath—whose name I learned—were driving them back so we could all leave on our trip.

Lacey grumbled about it, but I think it was more to do with her ego and that they were doing something nice, wanting to get to know her beyond sex. But I would never say that out loud to her.

The girls followed behind them in Ryan's rental car and would get the apartment set up before meeting me and the guys on the beach. The first four days would be for us, and the last six we'd get to spend together. It felt like the perfect plan to me. But I wasn't sure how it worked since I'd never been on a real vacation.

"See you in a few days," Lacey said, hugging me. "Get all the group sex out of the way before we get there because there are so many things I want to do, and if I have to hear you say you can't because your vagina is broken, I will strap you to my back, and make you do it anyway."

"Okay, okay." I laughed, kissing her cheek. "See you in a few days, freak."

Joy hugged me and only told me to have fun, her parting words less threatening. Quentin wrapped his arm around me as a feeling of melancholy surged up.

"It's okay to miss them," he said, kissing my cheek.

"I'm fine," I argued, even as a lone tear slipped down my face. Thankfully, Q's emotional intelligence meant he didn't push it, and he let me stay in my denial bubble for a second.

"Next stop, paradise," Max cheered, pulling the sadness away and boosting my mood. Climbing into the car, I glanced back at the house one last time and said goodbye to the girl I'd been and the killer I'd become. It was time for a new chapter, and that felt exciting in a way nothing had for a really long time.

I guess the universe could grow as well.

"Holland, wake up," Grady whispered, pulling me from the sleep state I'd fallen into. Between late-night packing and traveling across time zones, I'd been exhausted.

Wiping my eyes, I blinked as the early morning sun rose, the colors painting the sky pretty purples and pinks as it woke up.

"We're here?" I asked, stating the obvious.

"Yeah, Temptress. We're here," Quentin said from the backseat. Instantly I was awake and bolting out of my seat, only to be snapped back as the seat belt pulled me back.

The guys laughed, and I played it off as I unleashed the thing and jumped out of the car. The instant my feet touched the sand, I felt something magical shift in my body. A feeling of expanding my capabilities by merely being in this spot in the world. It was the furthest I'd ever been from Foolshope, and I couldn't wait to explore more. An itch was opening inside me, a yearning to branch out from the confines I'd been placed in and see more of the world. *To feel more of the world.*

"It's magnificent," I said, swallowing the awe in my throat. I always hoped I'd get to travel this far, had dreamed about this moment, but hadn't ever believed it would actually come true.

Murderers didn't get happy endings.

So it was a good thing I'd gone legit—or as legit as someone who liked to punish horrible people could go —because I wasn't ever giving this up. Deserving or not.

"Come on, let's check out where we're staying," Quentin said, pulling me over to a bungalow I hadn't noticed. Focusing on anything else with the beautiful ocean before me was hard.

Climbing up the wooden stairs, I blinked to ensure I was awake.

"This is ours?" I asked.

"For the next four days at least. Then we're meeting the girls at the hotel in town."

I glanced around, not spotting any other cars, people, or houses. "Are we the only ones?"

"We better be considering I paid for privacy," Grady huffed, but when I glanced at him, I found a soft smile on his face; the corners of his eyes creased as he watched me.

A wicked grin spread at the realization of our predicament. "Well, okay then."

Lifting my shirt, I tossed it at Grady, then flung my bra at Quentin and my shorts and panties at Max. They stood stunned, my naked body fully displayed in the morning light.

"Come and catch me," I taunted, taking off as I ran through the house.

Sounds of feet followed, and I giggled at the thought of being chased. Hello, primal kink unlocked.

I ducked and turned around furniture, making it onto the deck where a giant hot tub and pool bed lay. Arms wrapped around me before I could step onto the sand, spinning me around as lips crashed down onto mine.

I wasn't surprised Q had gotten to me first. Mostly because he was the most primal-driven one of the bunch. His hard cock pressed into my belly as I wrapped my legs around him, falling headfirst into his kiss. Quentin had a way of kissing that always made your toes curl. He left me breathless as he pulled away, leaving smaller kisses down my throat. His whole being went into his kiss, and I never wanted to not be on the other end of it.

"You're so goddamn beautiful, Temptress. I could worship your body from sunup to sundown, and it still wouldn't be enough. I crave you every second I'm not near you. My dick weeps when it's sliding in and out of your pussy. How do you drive me so wild and crazy?"

"You do the same, Magic Fingers," I said with a smile, finally letting him know what it meant.

"And here I thought MF stood for motherfucker," Quentin teased, kissing me softly.

"Depends on the day, really." I rolled my eyes but without any of the usual bite. Another body pressed into my back. Soft hands and lips met my skin, alerting me to Max's presence.

"Do you know how hard it is to run with an erection?" he teased, sliding his hands over my ass.

"Worth it," Quentin mumbled, making me laugh. I looked over to the pool bed, finding Grady there as he watched us. He'd undressed, laid back on the surface as he watched the show we were putting on for him. His cock was hard, his hand stroking it slowly.

"I have an idea," I breathed, throwing my head back on Max's shoulder as Quentin sucked my nipple into his mouth. "But it requires some... *finagling.*"

"Why do I feel I'll be the one... *finagling*?" Max asked as Q snorted.

"Because you're the prettiest," I cooed, leaning back to kiss him.

Where Q was all heat and passion, Max was sweet and seductive, a slow crawl as he drew me into him a little each time. Quentin demanded your attention immediately, while Max won it over bit by bit. Together, they were a dangerous combination.

Add in Grady, who fought me tooth and nail, and I was a goner.

While I was kissing Max, Quentin had managed to

direct us over to the bed. I blinked in a daze as I unlocked my lips with Max, trying to remember why we stopped.

"You had an idea?" Grady teased, still just stroking his cock lazily like he had all the time in the world.

"Right." I grinned, then turned to Max and Q. "Undress."

They pulled off their clothes and then waited for my next command. However, the smirk on Q's face told me not to get used to it. I'd only have control for so long.

"Q on your back and cradle Max in your arms." They both panicked for a second, and I realized why. "No, I'm not suggesting you dive into anal with each other. It will just make it easier for me to take you both… in the same hole."

Their eyes widened as lust took over, their pupils dilating as my words sank in.

"As in," Max stuttered, his cock twitching at full attention.

I winked as I turned to Grady. "Got any lube? Because I want you in my ass."

He gulped, his eyes tracking over my body as he digested the words before leaping off the bed and sprinting into the hut. A moment later, he flew out the door with a bottle of lube in his hand and a smirk on his face. It had a Post-it note, and I knew exactly what it said before he even read it.

"Lacey?" I asked, chuckling.

"Yep. How did…" he started but stopped, realizing I

knew my besties very well. "And a strap-on from Joy, but I left it."

"For now," I hedged, giving him a wink before I turned. I wasn't certain, but I swear his eyes dilated at the thought, his cock twitching.

Well, well, well. Maybe I'd get to peg someone after all.

Q embraced Max on the couch, the smaller man lying on his chest with his legs sprawled over Quentin's darker ones. Q stroked their cocks together side by side in his strong grip, and the sight of them like that had my pussy gushing as I kneeled on the soft mattress. They might not want a sexual relationship outside of me, but their love and connection for one another was a thing of beauty all on its own.

"Do you need to get warmed up?" Max asked, gesturing toward me, his cheeks pinking. Taking his hand, I placed his fingers inside me, moaning as he pushed them in and out. "Fuck. You're drenched," he gasped.

I dropped his wrist, and he drew his hand back. I expected him to suck his fingers, but when he put them in Q's mouth instead, my legs wobbled as I held back my moan. Shit, that was hot.

"You ready to try this?" I asked, and they both nodded, licking their lips as I straddled their legs. I wrapped my hand around both of them, stroking up and down together as they tossed their heads back, enjoying the slow torture. Glancing at how thick they were together, I gulped as some anxiety at being able to take them entered my head.

"One at a time, Temptress," Q said reassuringly.

Nodding, I let go of Max and placed myself over Quentin, sinking down slowly on his cock. His width stretched me as I bounced up and down, feeling full. But I wanted to feel the three of them together; I needed it.

"Okay, ready," I whispered, helping Max notch himself next to Q. It was a lot slower as he pushed in next to his friend's cock, my walls stretching to their max as I welcomed him in.

A giggle escaped me, and the three of us groaned as the vibrations tightened my walls around us.

"Shit, don't do that," Max hissed, making me laugh more.

"Grady, hurry," Q gritted out.

Leaning forward, I kissed Max and Quentin while moving my hips slightly. It was torturous and blissful. Tortiss? Blisture? Eh. Torture bliss.

Cold liquid hit my backside as Grady prepped me, working one finger, then two, into my ass. My body trembled from the added pressure, my orgasm growing higher as sensations bombarded me. Max sucked on my nipple, flicking my clit with his finger as I kissed Q. It was weird and amazing having them like this, like a two-headed boyfriend with four arms and two cocks. Okay, that math was too much. My hands trailed over their bodies, taking in every inch I could.

"Fuck. It feels so good sliding against you," Max gasped, "and now I can feel Grady's finger. I'm not going to last long," Max whined, his jaw tight.

Grady pushed the head of his cock against my rim, pressing down on my back and shifting the other two cocks already in me. The three of us groaned at the new angle, the pressure growing as Grady continued.

"Breathe," Grady commanded, reminding us all to do it. Max held one of my hands while Q held the other, the three of us panting as we waited for the torture bliss to end.

When his thighs met the back of mine, we all let out a breath as we adjusted to the new feeling.

"How does this feel so good?" Max groaned, shifting his weight and causing Quentin to moan next.

"Someone move," I gasped, my body vibrating with need, and I seriously questioned myself about this idea.

Grady pulled out and slammed back in as the two men in front alternated. It was the perfect orchestration, keeping me full of a cock at all times—my favorite state. Sheer perfection.

After a few thrusts, I was over the edge, crying out as my body let go of the orgasm that had been building, tingling from my toes all the way to my scalp as it crashed over me. My muscles tensed, my walls clamping down on three dicks as I came so hard, I blacked out for a second.

When I came to, it was to the roars of Max and Q as they came together, their cum flooding me, followed quickly by Grady, who grabbed my hips and fucked me so hard into the bed I knew I'd have finger indents for days.

As the four of us lay there, out of breath and trembling, I knew I'd found my tribe. I never thought I'd settle down, but I could for these three.

"So, I think I love you, dumbasses. Or whatever. Don't make a big deal out of it or anything. Just thought you should know."

After a moment of shock, the three of them pounced on me, kissing me all over as they shared how they felt and filling me with hearts and shit. It was gross, and I wanted to punch myself in the face for being so ridiculously happy about it.

In the end, these three had been my ultimate fuck steal kill.

They fucked my brains out, stole my heart, and accepted my killer side. What more could a girl possibly want? Well, a dress with pockets and shoes that didn't hurt, but they weren't magicians—just three guys who happened to be perfect for me.

And for the first time in forever, I couldn't wait to fuck, steal, and kill with them every single day. Now that was what I called a happy ending.

CHAPTER 33
HOLLAND xoxo

FIVE MONTHS LATER

I strolled through the lobby of the Shadows headquarters, my steps the only sound outside the show playing on the guard's iPad. I nodded toward him as I passed; my presence at this late hour was not uncommon, nor was the fact I was the last one here.

My hatred for paperwork was well-known. As was my avoidance of doing it, which was why I'd spent the last two hours finalizing it before midnight when it was due. The guys had left hours ago, heading off to do their various interests while I sulked in my office, staring at the stack of memos and wishing they'd magically do themselves.

I knew it was my own fault since I waited until right before the deadline, but I could never make myself do it beforehand.

The guys had initially stuck around and waited with me, but after a month, they realized how boring it was to watch me and that no amount of bribery on their part sped up the process. So Max went off to play his online video games with his squad, Quentin typically went to the gym to get in a few rounds of sparring, and Grady would visit his sister and niece or try out a new recipe he discovered.

Our life had become adoringly domesticated, and it was almost sickening. Almost. There was still the unaliving of foes and all the fucking, so maybe not so domesticated. I didn't see us posing for one of those Christmas cookie tins anytime soon.

Which was a shame, really. I looked killer in red. No pun intended.

Mark, the front door guard, looked at his watch as I neared, sighing loudly.

"Dammit," he cursed.

"I'd be hurt you bet against me if I hadn't also done it myself," I teased, causing him to belly chuckle.

"Come on, Holland. You can stick around for five more minutes, and then I can finally buy that new TV I've been wanting," he pleaded, rubbing his hands together.

One guess who'd set up a monthly pool on when I'd do my paperwork, offering odds and wagers on whether I'd make the deadline or not.

If you said Lacey, you would be correct.

"Ooh, sounds tempting, but I already emailed the reports. You know the betting pool uses them as the timestamp. I'll try harder to fail next time."

Shaking his head, he laughed some more as he waved me off, opening the doors for me. "Night, Holland."

"Laters, Mark!" I waved over my shoulder, the smile on my face not even fake anymore.

Despite my hatred of paperwork, I loved everything about being part of the Shadows. Every day was different, and I got to see my besties, punish bad people, and work with my guys. To top it off, I no longer had to clean people's rooms to make ends meet. And weirdly enough, people respected me here.

I wouldn't say I was a completely different person; I still tended to stab first and ask questions later. But I no longer actively wanted to do that to everyone. It was progress for my morally gray heart.

My phone vibrated with a text from Lacey and Joy, halting me in my tracks as I read it.

> Lacey: The amount of people that bet against you never fails to astound me.
>
> Lacey: Mostly that you've convinced that many people to root against you.
>
> Joy: It's all the yelling.
>
> Joy: And the throwing.
>
> Lacey: Oh! And the one time she stabbed a stack of paper and sent it back to Jackson.

Okay, so maybe I'd exaggerated how much I'd changed. But I was working on it.

> Holland: And yet, every month, I always make the deadline.

Lacey: And me a lot of money. I'll be able to buy that new motorcycle I want soon.

Holland: Like you can't already afford it.

Joy: Oh, she can; she just wants to brag about it.

Lacey: And name it HolsAss. Get it?

Holland: Ha. Ha.

Holland: I'm seriously considering trading you in. Molly seems nice. Maybe I'll ask her to be my new bestie.

Lacey: All lies. Besides, she's terrified of you. You love that I'm not.

Holland: Debatable.

Joy: What about Ava? She's been wanting to hang out since she joined the intern program.

Lacey: JOY!

Lacey: I've never felt so betrayed before.

Joy: What? I didn't say I was replacing you, and Ava is cool.

Lacey: Fine. You're forgiven. She's alright.

Joy: She's the little sister you always wish you had. Admit it!

Lacey: Never.

Ava and Lukas had joined the Shadows a few months ago. After two months on their own, they both realized they were bored and wanted to help people like themselves. Jackson created an intern program for people like them who'd been victims of their circumstances. It gave them scholarships for college and a place to feel useful by sharing their knowledge on how organizations like the Savages worked. Both of them had bloomed into amazing young adults already, and I saw bright futures for them. Killers could have awards, too, you know.

> Holland: No one is replacing anyone, and Ava is a little sister to all of us. Stop acting like you don't care about her.

Lacey: I hate you both.

Joy: It sounds like Lacey needs to play the game.

> Holland: Speaking of FSK, did you give in to Ryan yet? He your boyfriend now?

Ryan and his team still followed Lacey around like a lost puppy. She said she hated it, but she'd been working with their team a lot more recently, so I wondered if that had been changing. I didn't know if they hooked up after the first time since she ignored him and his team when in public, but it seemed almost too much protesting, and I had a feeling my dark and stabby bestie had caught feelings and didn't know how to deal with them yet.

> Lacey: Who?

> Joy: The cute guy who's your shadow. Omg. Get it; he's a Shadow, who is your shadow?

> Holland: Don't forget H-squared. They're both just as bad.

> Lacey: Have you been sucking the helium again, Joy?

> Joy: No. Why?

> Lacey: Did James and Mallory give you special brownies?

> Joy: Nope. It's all me, baby.

Joy had met a married couple on one of her dating apps who were looking to add a partner. She hit it off with both the husband and the wife and had been happily coupled up with them ever since. I was happy for Joy. She was a rare light that the world needed more of. Now, if we could only get Lacey to pull her head out of her ass, then I wouldn't feel so guilty for leaving her alone.

> Lacey: Either of you coming back to the apartment tonight?

Joy: We're having a slumber party. Gotta try out the new strap-on I made this week.

Lacey: Pretty sure the Shadows don't want to fund your sex life.

Joy: You never know when it could be useful on the job.

Holland: I'm staying over at the guys. They said they had something for me.

Joy: Do you think they're popping the question?

Holland: Ew. God no. They better not. I still haven't changed my stance on marriage. I'll have to stab them if they do.

Lacey: Are we still having drinks tomorrow for your birthday?

Holland: Yep. Girls' day first, and then everyone for tacos and tequila later.

Joy: Yay! I miss seeing you both.

Lacey: You saw us at lunch today. You literally talked to us for thirty minutes about the new lipstick you were making.

Joy: Gosh, that was so long ago!

Holland: Miss you too, Joy. Have fun at your sleepover, and let me know how the toy works.

Joy: XOXO

Lacey: Since I have the house to myself, it's time for some Lacey naked cleaning and dancing.

Holland: Thanks for the heads up. I will avoid the house until tomorrow. Night.

Lacey: XOXO

Holland: XOXO

Grinning, I finished walking the rest of the way to my car. It was surreal sometimes to think this was our life and that we'd ended up here. The city was so alive, and our lives were fuller with all the new people we'd added. It felt like our life was significant in a way it had never been before. And despite working for the Shadows, it seemed we'd actually stepped out of them into the light.

As I approached the parking garage, a tall, dark, and handsome man was leaning against my car. His blue eyes heated up as he spotted me, his cocky smile lifting the corners of his mouth.

"I've killed men for doing exactly what you're doing."

"Hmm. That sounds like a fun game to play," Grady teased, pulling me into his body and kissing me.

The kiss was languid as his tongue swirled with mine, heating up my insides.

"Mm, I've missed your taste."

"Then let me remind you. We can pop back into the building."

He chuckled, shaking his head. "No can do. We have a present for you."

"A present? I told you guys I didn't want anything for my birthday."

"This, I think you will." He nodded to a black van, linking our fingers together as he pulled me over.

Lifting my brow, I opened the back door and found Quentin and Max with a guy tied up in rope. It took me a second to realize who he was, but once I did, the grin on my face grew so wide I thought my face might break.

When the man spotted me, he screamed, begging for me to save him. Wrong person to ask for forgiveness, honey.

"You got this for me?" I gasped, clutching my hands to my chest.

"Happy Birthday, Temptress. This one's off books."

"So, no paperwork?" My eyes widened as I smiled bigger.

"No paperwork, sweetheart," Max confirmed, causing a tear to run down my cheek.

"You really do love me," I gushed.

"I think we finally found the way to romance our girlfriend," Grady said, wrapping his arm around my waist and kissing my cheek. "Happy Birthday, mi chispa."

Wiping my face, adrenaline rushed through me as I rubbed my hands together and stared at the man from the XOXO app. He'd been abusing his wife and son for years, to the point his wife was considering suicide. She'd attempted it, but her son found her in time. The request had come in from the aunt, her sister. We hadn't been able to locate him, though, and I worried he'd get away before we found him.

"It's the best birthday gift ever," I raved, making the guy tied up squirm a little more now that he realized I wasn't his savior.

Unsheathing my favorite knife, I flicked my wrist a few times and made the blade catch the light, the asshole's eyes growing wider. Jumping into the back of the van, I relished in the man's fear as he openly cried when I read of his crimes and gave him a little stabby-stab for each one.

That feeling never got old. But the best part? The three men I'd fallen in love with didn't even blink an eye as the blood ran down his body, covering me—and them—in the process.

"It should probably weird me out that I find it hot when she punishes people, right?" Max whispered.

Quentin smirked, taking Max's hand and placing it on his crotch, his hard cock pressing against his leg. Max gulped but relaxed his shoulders as he accepted his attraction.

I stared at the man and knew I could drag his torture out a little longer, especially with how awful his crimes were. But this unaliver was learning that some-times there were more important things than killing.

Not much, but there were. And these three were at the top of that list.

"How about we call my clean-up crew to take care of this, and then I can show you how happy your gift made me?"

"You don't have to tell me twice, but first, let's hit the showers. Blood is hard to get out of the upholstery," Grady said, opening the doors and leading us to the secret locker room on this garage level.

Tossing our clothes into the incinerator and rinsing off all the blood, the four of us headed back to my car twenty minutes later, as fresh as daisies. The van was gone, as was any trace of the man. And the best part was no paperwork.

"How about we stop for food on the way?" Max asked. "Watching you work makes me hungry."

"You are making this the best birthday ever. I'm not sure how you'll top this next year."

"I'm just glad there's a next year," Max said, giving me a smile.

Yeah, me too.

My book might be covered in blood, but it wasn't the only thing about me. In fact, it wasn't even the most interesting. Not by a long shot.

CHAPTER 34

JOY
xoxo

ONE MONTH LATER

Unlocking the door to the Moore's house, a smile graced my face as I took in the person that greeted me with a grin and nothing but a silk robe. One that I'd gotten her a few months ago.

"Well, hello. This must be my lucky day to be greeted by such a beautiful woman at the door."

"Every day is lucky with you, Joy," Mallory whispered, pulling my face to hers to kiss me. Dropping my bag, I threaded my fingers through her long auburn locks as her tongue tangled with mine. Her body pressed into mine, all her soft curves melting into me as we kissed. Mallory's hands roamed over my body, squeezing my ass as she tugged me even closer.

My heart sped up as arousal grew, my heart thumping loudly in my chest. Butterflies swirled, and I prayed that this feeling never ended. I was falling head over heels for these two.

I knew my odds weren't good. Coming into an already-established couple would always put me at a disadvantage to being the odd one out, but I really liked our dynamic. It was almost perfect.

"Welcome home, darling," Mallory said once she released me, her words surprising me. "I missed you."

"I missed you, too." I pecked her lips again and retrieved my bag from where I'd dropped it. She took it from me before I could protest, tucking me under her arm as we walked further into the house. Mallory was tall for a woman, making me the shortest of the three.

"James and I have a surprise for you *and* a proposition."

"Oh, that sounds intriguing."

I looked up at her; her cheeks were a perfect shade of rose, and I wondered if I'd ever met anyone as beautiful. James and Mallory were a few years older than me, in their mid-thirties. They'd worked hard on their careers for years, and when they'd been ready to start a family, it hadn't been possible. But they didn't let that stop them. They decided to explore more of themselves and use this time to develop stronger bonds with each other.

They were both bi-sexual and had discussed adding someone to their bedroom activities, leading them to join Trice, where we met. That had been five months ago, something I didn't think any of us foresaw. But the three of us worked well, and it had become more than just sex. Though it *was* some of the best sex I'd ever had. They never made me feel like a third wheel in their marriage, and if anything, I seemed to balance them both out well.

We spent most of our time together as a triad, but I also did things with only James and only Mallory—in and out of the bedroom.

Walking into the open-concept living room and kitchen, I was shocked when I spotted not only James but his best friend, Tyler. He was several heads taller than me, putting him well over six feet. He had dark blond hair with natural honey highlights, most women would kill to have, with a slight wave. Every time I was around him, I itched to run my fingers through it to see if it was as soft as it looked—like silk and cotton had a baby.

His eyes were the deep green of grass after a hard rain, which bore into you like he could read your thoughts with one look. Tyler was quiet, which made me extra chatty to offset his calm exterior and stop myself from asking if I could climb him. The man was stacked. I knew he and James worked out together daily, so I could only imagine the muscles he kept hidden beneath his button-down shirts.

I'd been secretly crushing on him for a few months since he would often tag along to things the Moores did and inevitably put us together. He didn't speak much to me, so I was confident he hated me or thought I was a nuisance. He was the first man not to flirt with me, which also threw me off my game.

Glancing at James, I noticed his chocolate brown hair was slightly askew, like he'd been running his fingers through it for hours. His hazel eyes lit up when he spotted me, and he stood from the couch. He was dressed as casually as Mallory in a pair of gray sweatpants and nothing else, his dick pressing against his leg and giving me a delicious outline.

His abs were on full display, his Adonis belt causing me to lick my lips as it flexed and moved with each step he took. His golden skin was peppered with a light dusting of chest hair and his happy trail, making my fingers eager to touch him.

Where Tyler was silent and stoic, keeping his emotions in check, James was as open as I was, wearing his heart on his sleeve. His smile was wide as he neared, lifting me under my butt and bringing me closer to his height as he kissed me. Wrapping my legs around his waist, I fell into the kiss as he gripped my thighs. I loved how enthusiastic he was, not caring who was around as he kissed me.

The best part of being shorter than Mallory and James was that they were always picking me up, and I loved it. It was nice to feel delicate and protected by them, even if I knew four different fighting techniques.

Breaking the kiss, we both panted as we pulled apart. His hair was even messier now, my hands having run through it as our lips locked.

"Hey, baby doll. I'm so glad you're here." He smiled, his eyes twinkling as he looked over my face.

I never thought I was one for words of affirmation or praise, but with how these two doled it out, I lapped up every bit of it I could. It felt nice to be in their presence, and it wasn't just about the top-notch sex. They were just truly nice people, not an evil bone in their bodies.

I giggled, kissing his lips again as he nibbled my ear. "Mal and I feel so fortunate to have met you, Joy. We couldn't imagine our lives without you."

"I feel the same," I said, looking for Mallory. She was still standing where we'd stopped, so I reached my hand to her, pulling her into our huddle. I'd forgotten about Tyler, but he was used to their PDA with me, so I didn't think twice about him being here. Mallory's hands drifted up my and James' backs, teasing us with her touch.

"We were hoping you'd make this official with us. Become part of our family," Mallory said, tears in her eyes as she said the words.

I sucked in a breath, my mind racing as I processed it.

"You mean it?" I asked, choking down my own emotions as I glanced between the two. "I don't want to ruin anything you have here. We all knew it was just temporary."

James shook his head. "Not anymore. We don't want anyone else. You're it for us, Joy. And you couldn't possibly ruin anything. You make us better. In fact, there's a second part of this."

He turned, dragging Mallory with him as he faced his best friend. James placed me on my feet but kept his arms around my shoulders, his wife at his side and my back. Tyler stood at our movement, and I wondered if he was getting up to leave. While that meant sexy times were coming, something in me felt saddened that I wouldn't get to see him longer. It was a sick game I played with myself to see if I could get him to crack, to show me something true of himself.

"It seems Tyler has been keeping a secret to himself." My brow creased, not having expected James to say that.

"What do you mean?" I asked when no one else said anything. Tyler swallowed and stepped closer. James' hands flexed on my shoulders, his cock twitching against my back as his best friend approached, making my eyes widen.

"Tyler wants to join us," Mallory said, rubbing her hand up my arm. "He's been harboring a crush on James for years, too nervous to say anything. Meeting you and learning about our new dynamic gave him the courage to speak up. Go on, Ty, tell her what you told us."

Tyler fidgeted, shuffling his feet as he stared at James and me. His calm exterior was gone for the first time since I'd known him. His eyes were heated, and his pupils were dilated, making the green eyes even darker. Tyler cleared his throat, meeting my eyes and showing me more emotion than I ever thought he had.

"I'm not great with words, so excuse my bluntness. I've been so jealous these past five months since you entered their lives and, by proxy, mine. At first, I thought it was just because you got to be with James, when I never would. But as I got to know you, Joy, it became more. I was jealous of your connection with my best friends, but also that they got to be with *you*."

"You like me?" I asked, my voice high as I tried to process everything.

He nodded, licking his lips. "Yes, I think you're the most beautiful woman I've ever met. I think about you constantly and go crazy when you're not near. I wonder what you're doing, how your day is, and what crazy new gadget you've created. Sometimes I fantasize about you and James and me. I've jacked off to the thought of the three of us more than I care to admit."

I scrunched my nose in thought, realizing he hadn't mentioned Mallory. "But not Mal?" I asked, linking my fingers with hers. She was the best, and I felt protective of her.

"Not sexually, no. Mal and I are best friends, but it's never been more with us."

"And I feel the same way," Mallory said, squeezing my hand and letting me know she wasn't upset.

"So, what do you think?" James asked, his heart beating fast against me.

The yearning on his face was unmistakable. He wanted to explore things with Tyler, and I couldn't deny I was also curious. I was definitely attracted to him, and I could tell the sex alone would be out of this world. But with the relationship we were building, I didn't know if it was worth blowing that up for.

"I think you're hot as fuck, and I'd be lying if I didn't say I've thought about what you'd look like naked. But I don't want to mess anything up with these two."

"And I get that," Tyler said, stepping forward to touch me now that I hadn't said no.

His hand was warm against mine, his thumb sweeping back and forth and sending shivers through me. "But can you honestly say that any time the four of us have been together has been awful? It wasn't until you slotted in that I felt that all of our pieces matched. Together, we're whole."

Deep down, I knew he was right, and the missing thing that kept this from being perfect was him. If it all fell apart, it wasn't what we thought it was to begin with.

Instead of answering, I pulled his shirt down to bring his face to mine and sealed our lips together. His stubble rubbed against my face, his pouty lips soft as I pressed harder into him. Electricity sizzled in me at the contact, and I knew this was it; this was the real deal.

My hands climbed up his neck, tugging at his long strands, my fingers finally touching his silky smooth hair.

"Fuck, that's hot," James whispered behind me, kissing my neck as I devoured his best friend's mouth. Mallory's hand roamed over me and James, and the sensation of all three of them touching me made me so wet I knew I needed more.

"I want to climb you like a tree," I panted, making them laugh.

"Do it, baby. We wanna watch," James encouraged,

letting go of me as Tyler pulled me into him, and I jumped up, wrapping my legs around him.

"Damn, you're tall," I squeaked as he chuckled into my neck, moving back to the couch.

"And you're short."

"Nah, I'm fun size."

He snorted, his hands roaming over me as he settled onto the couch. Our mouths crashed back together, and I rocked into him now that I straddled his lap. His cock pressed against his jeans, and I moaned as I felt it. He was huge.

Mallory pulled my shirt over my head, exposing my naked breasts to Tyler, who gulped as he took me in. James unsnapped my skirt, tossing it to the side and leaving me only in my thigh-high socks. Tyler's hands rubbed my thighs, and he groaned as I sat before him naked.

"You're so beautiful."

Smirking, I shoved his shirt over his head and uncovered his chest. It was just as delicious and cut as James', but Tyler's was also covered in tattoos.

"Hot damn. I always wondered what you looked like under your shirt. You far exceed my imagination," I breathed, rubbing my hands up and down his muscles.

Tyler moaned, lifting me so my breasts were in his face. He sucked a nipple into his mouth as I unzipped his pants and pushed his jeans down as best I could. James came up behind me and sucked on my neck, reaching down to help me undress his best friend. Watching him lick his lips as Tyler's monster cock jumped to attention made me so wet that I squirmed, needing some friction.

"My turn next," he whispered, kissing me before kicking off his sweatpants and sitting beside Tyler, their thighs touching. Seeing these two men, who were both mine, side-by-side was its own type of aphrodisiac.

Mallory dropped her robe to the ground and joined James on the couch, taking his cock and notching it at her entrance as she sank on him with her back to his front. They groaned as they moved together, focusing on the two of us.

Stroking Tyler, he moaned around my breast as I pumped him, my fingers barely fitting around him.

"Condoms?" I asked, stopping myself before I sank onto him.

"He's clean. I have his results," Mallory said, reaching out to touch me. Linking our fingers together, I nodded as I notched Tyler at my entrance. He cursed as I slowly sank down, his fingers gripping my hips.

"Jesus fuck. You're so tight, dragonfly. You grip my cock so well. And damn, you're so wet, I could slip in and out of you so easily, despite my size. You feel better than I imagined."

"Ah, fuck. He's a dirty talker," I moaned, making Mallory laugh.

"He might be better than you," James moaned, sucking his wife's neck as he flicked her clit. Most people assumed they were bored of each other or didn't love one another the same way anymore since they'd invited me to be their third. But it was the complete opposite. They loved one another so fiercely that they wanted to share it.

I added to their love, not took it away. And now it seemed Tyler would do the same.

"You like some dirty talk, dragonfly?" Tyler asked, apparently getting his bearings now. I nodded as I bounced on him, his cock hitting me so deep I was already seeing stars.

"Didn't expect Mr. Quiet to be good at it, though," I teased, tugging his hair. He grinned, sending a thousand butterflies to life as they took flight inside me.

"Kiss James," I challenged, my eyes heating at the thought.

Tyler only smirked, turning his head and sealing his lips to James'. Watching them kiss while James fucked Mallory was apparently my new kink because my orgasm slammed into me out of nowhere.

"Fuck, I'm coming on your big dick," I yelled, grabbing Mallory and sealing my lips to hers as she followed.

I barely managed not to black out, using Mallory to ground myself. From there, we shifted partners and took a few breaks for food and water. But none of us could go long without jumping someone.

Currently, Mallory lay on the floor before me as I licked her pussy and fucked her with a silver dildo. I made one that heated and vibrated and expanded its girth once it was inside. I loved pleasing Mallory and often had her in mind when I invented new things to bring her the ultimate pleasure. She moaned and writhed on the ground, her slickness running down her thighs as I continued to lick and suck her clit, thrusting Mr. Silver into her.

"Look at how good I fuck you, Mal. Your pussy is so hungry for Mr. Silver," I cooed, making her moan. "You're such a good girl, Mal. You're my good girl."

She groaned again, making me wetter in the process. I loved pleasing others and got almost as much pleasure out of it as I did being the one receiving.

The guys watched, propped up against the couch, having taken a break after the last round of lovemaking. But the more they watched, the more their cocks hardened again, and I knew exactly what I wanted to do. This was when my tester side came out to play.

"James, I want you to fuck me while I fuck Mal and let Ty fuck you."

They looked at one another, the lust evident in their eyes as they stared. Mallory moaned, clearly wanting to see her husband be fucked by another man.

"Yes, James. Let Ty fuck you," she cooed, encouraging them.

James nodded, swallowing slowly as he got up and grabbed a bottle of lube. While I continued to torture Mallory with pleasure, we watched as Tyler prepped James.

James wasn't a virgin to ass play, and I'd pegged him a time or two, but I knew he hadn't ever had sex with a man before. It was something he'd wanted, but they hadn't been able to find a suitable guy candidate that they'd meshed with.

Honestly, it was probably because he was in love with Tyler and hadn't been able to say it. So, now, they could have their moment.

When Ty had James ready, they moved closer to us, and James decided to play a little with me. He breached my rosette, and when he thrust one finger in, I trembled so hard I almost fell on top of Mallory.

"Shit," I cooed, pressing my butt back at him.

"Turnabout is fair play, baby doll," he teased, kissing down my spine as he continued to prep me. When he was ready, he squirted a lot of lube on himself and me before lining up and pressing in. I focused on Mallory, who was petting my hair and telling me how good I was doing. I loved how much of a cheerleader they were for each other and now me.

His thighs met my ass, and I sighed in relief once he was entirely in. He stilled in me as Tyler lined up, pressing his monster cock into James' ass.

James pulled me up, kissing me deeply as his ass was breached. Mallory also kneeled, lining her front with mine and running her hands over the two of us. Pulling apart from James, I kissed Mallory and then had them kiss. I reached back and grabbed Tyler's hand, feeling us all connected.

"Ready?" Tyler asked, his voice strained. "Fuck, your hole is so tight, James. I'm not going to last long."

"Me either," James gasped, his hips thrusting forward into me.

Somehow the four of us moved together as I fucked

Mallory with the dildo, James fucked me in the ass, and Tyler him.

Our moans filled the room, and our skin clapped together as we all rocked toward our orgasms. Mallory was the first to go, her body convulsing as she came around my fingers and Mr. Silver. I knew I'd made her squirt again when she gushed over my fingers.

"Yes, Mal. You're a fucking queen. Covering my fingers with your cum," I cooed, making both guys moan.

"Shit, that's hot," Ty whispered. "I'm so close." He dropped a kiss on James' shoulder, and that was all it took for him. James stilled as he gripped my hips, his cock shooting off his load in my ass and filling me with his warm cum. My orgasm rippled to life as I tensed around him, Mallory's fingers helping as she rubbed my clit and flicked my nipple.

"I'm coming," I screamed, tensing my walls as everything went black this time.

Coming to in a naked pile of arms and legs, I sighed contentedly as the person nearest to me rubbed my back in soft caresses. James and Mallory were the bomb at aftercare. I always felt cherished and loved. Speaking of…

"I love you, guys," I whispered, realizing it was true.

"We love you," Mallory and James said together like they often did.

"And me?" Tyler asked, rubbing my face. I blinked, staring into his eyes.

"Halfway there, maybe more," I admitted, kissing his lips. He smiled, and it lit my heart on fire.

Our relationship wasn't conventional, but I'd never wanted one that was. This was what my heart needed, and I was here for the long haul.

"What would you guys think about trying for a baby?" I asked, leaning up to look at Mallory and James.

Mal's eyes watered as she nodded. "Really?"

"Yeah. I want everything with you guys. I don't know if I can, but I'd like to try. I want to give you that."

"But you want it too, right?" James asked, scanning my face as he stared at me.

"Yes. I didn't think I did before I met you both, but now, I couldn't think of anything that could make me happier."

"Is that something I can be part of?" Tyler asked, his voice small.

"For fuck's sake, Ty. You're in this now. Your sperm or my sperm, I'll love that baby. It will be *our* baby. Can you say you won't?" James challenged.

"No. I would. You're my family. Always have been."

"And you ours," Mallory added, squeezing his hand. Despite them not being sexual with one another, I could see the genuine love they had for each other, and I knew this would work.

It might be wild, and it might be out of the box for most people, but it was exactly what I wanted.

"We should do brunch with my best friends.

Holland has three boyfriends, and Lacey is in denial about the guys she likes. It will be fun."

"Sure. Invite them over tomorrow. I'm excited to meet them," Mallory said, leaning up and kissing me. "Let's move to the bedroom. Us old people can't be as comfortable on the floor, anymore," she teased.

"Plus, in our excitement, we forgot to show you the surprise," James added, giving me a wink.

"There's more?" I asked, leaping up and running down the hall. Pushing open the door to the primary bedroom, I stopped and gaped at what I saw. "How is that possible?"

"It's custom-made. And now the four of us can sleep comfortably."

Laughing, I took a flying leap as I jumped on the humongous bed, giggling as the three of them joined me. My heart was full, and I felt utterly like my name-sake… Joy.

CHAPTER 35
LACEY xoxo

MY PHONE BEEPED, AND I GOT ANOTHER TEXT FROM JOY about doing brunch tomorrow to 'officially' meet her lovers. Unofficially, Holland and I had stalked, researched, and verified them after her second date to ensure they weren't psychos.

Fortunately for Joy, they weren't. Unfortunately for Holland and I, they were boring upper-class workaholics with too many throw pillows.

Though, some people might say that made them psychos. Who needed that many tiny pillows? All they ended up doing was being tossed to the floor, and then you had to rearrange them again later. They served no purpose outside of collecting dust.

So, clearly, they were psychos. But not the kind I could kill. Shame really.

I was happy for both of my friends as they found people they could share their lives with. And based on the hickeys I saw on Joy's body, great sex, too. Seriously, I was thrilled for them. I'd give them a round of applause if they were here.

But they weren't. They never were anymore.

I basically lived alone, which was fine by me—meant more time to do naked cleaning and naked yoga—and I essentially walked around naked any time I wanted because I could.

I hadn't always been a nudist, but since I hated my neighbors, it was the perfect way to torture them. It was a little game I'd started playing about a month after we'd moved in. Both girls were out, and I'd been enjoying sharpening my knives on the porch. That was until he walked by, ruining my peaceful bubble.

Ryan fucking Sykes and his cocky little followers: Heath and Henry, also known as H-squared since they did everything together. *Everything.*

Frustrated that they'd infiltrated my safe place, I knew the only way to survive living here was to get payback. And since I couldn't kill him—again, damn shame—I had to find other ways to torture him… well, them. Ahem.

Of course, I hadn't expected the aftermath that had followed, pulling me into this game to the point I now craved it… and them.

But I'd deny it if anyone asked. Because, unlike my sisters in crime, I didn't do relationships. Nope. Never gonna happen.

It had been a few weeks since our last tussle, and with brunch on the horizon, I needed a distraction—time to get naked.

Blinds and curtains open, I undressed in the bathroom, tossing my clothes into the hamper. Pumping my roots up in the mirror, I turned and checked myself out.

My dark hair was halfway down my back, the dark magenta ombre at the bottom fresh and laying perfectly against my pale skin. I pulled the front up into a small top-knot, leaving a few strands to fall around my face.

My blue eyes shimmered, the dark eyeliner and shadow making them stand out more. My lip stain had faded, so I applied a new layer of the shimmery nude color I loved after a quick mouthwash rinse. Adding some deodorant and a few spritzes of my perfume in strategic areas, I felt ready to strut around the house naked.

For myself, obviously. The primping was all self-care. Totes.

My rib tattoo stood out against my skin as I turned and hit the light while padding across the soft carpet. A thrill of excitement zinged through me as I stepped out into my bedroom. The freedom of being completely bare was a high I never knew I needed. Though, with my exhibition kink, I shouldn't have been surprised.

Picking up a few things around the room, I moved through the house and shifted items from one spot to the next. From the corner of my eye, I spotted my first viewer. Grinning to myself, I entered the kitchen, where the floor-to-ceiling window was in front of the dining room table.

I grabbed the eggs and butter from the fridge and spotted a second viewer when I reached for the sugar and flour. Preheating the oven, I leaned up on my tiptoes as I stretched over the stove for the chocolate chips. It didn't make sense to store them up there, but having to reach for them was always a crowd-pleaser. And sure enough, by the time I bent over for the glass bowl to dump everything into, the final guest had arrived.

Smirking, I turned on my playlist and danced as I mixed the ingredients. I enjoyed baking so much that, at this point, I usually lost focus on the game and just had fun, which was good since no one liked salt mistaken for sugar in their muffins. Dropping the batter into the muffin pan, I placed them in the oven and set the timer just as the knock came.

The window across the room was dark, the three men gone from view and right into my trap.

Opening the door, I scowled at the three guys standing there. I crossed my arms under my breasts and waited for them to say something. I couldn't be too eager, even if they'd done exactly what I wanted.

"Yes?" I asked, leaning against the doorframe when they didn't say anything.

I had to give it to Ryan; he always kept his eyes on my face as he beamed his perfect smile at me. I couldn't say the same for Heath, who blatantly checked me out, heat and lust clear as day in his eyes, and Henry's face was too red for him to stare at me for long, the southern gentleman coming to the surface.

This was the first time all three of them had come over together. Typically, it was Ryan *or* H-squared.

"Whatcha baking, babe?" Ryan asked, giving me one of his charming smiles.

His classically handsome looks had taken him far in

life. He had honey-brown hair with golden highlights that shimmered in the sun. This was fitting, since his eyes were the color of the sky, so blue and pure that sometimes it hurt to stare at them for too long. He had a prominent chin with light stubble, that charming smile always on his lips like he had the world's best secret.

It pissed me off to see it. Though my body reacted differently as my pulse raced, my arousal ramped up as he directed it at me. His lips were pillowy and soft, and he knew exactly how to use his tongue. *Everywhere.*

"None of your business. Did you need something?" I sighed, staring at my fingernails.

"You on my dick," Heath mumbled, causing Henry to cough as he spluttered.

"The three of us thought it was time to talk. To put an end to this little game we've been playing."

"I'm not playing any games. I hate you three. If that's all, you can go."

I stepped back to shut the door, my heart beating so hard in my chest. The bluff game always got me hot and bothered. The risk of it all. Was it too much or just enough? Who would fold first? I never wanted to fold first.

Ryan's arm stopped the door as he stepped into the gap, his face a mere inch from mine. His intoxicating scent wrapped around me, and I had to focus to not shiver from it. Damn. He smelled good.

His hand landed on my naked hip, his thumb brushing up and down, leaving goosebumps in his wake.

"Lace, we just want to talk."

"Yeah. I don't do that. If you want to fuck, come in. Otherwise, see yourself back to your own house. I have more naked cleaning and a date with my vibrator and favorite smutty book."

"Fucking hell," Heath muttered as Henry groaned. Ryan just smiled wider, like he knew I was full of shit.

And that was the problem. Ryan knew me too well at this point. I hadn't meant to repeat our tryst after taking down the Savages. He kept following me around to the point it made me crazy, and I gave in to him again. Once I had, I couldn't stop. The push and pull was too intoxicating, so I started the game to give myself some clear boundaries and keep it clean. I kept ignoring the three of them and pretended to hate them when it was anything but.

Even going as far as lying to my best friends.

Because if they knew, then it was game over, and my heart was truly and utterly lost to them. And that was a price I didn't know if I could pay.

Ryan took another step, forcing me to move back and give him more room in the door or let him into my space.

Stepping back, he kept pushing forward until all three of them were inside, and I was pressed against the kitchen island, his hands on either side of me.

"Fine. You got your way, and you're inside my home. Say what you have to say and then leave."

"Heath shut all the curtains. Henry, lock all the doors and remove the muffins in three minutes."

"On it," they said, following his commands without question.

His blue eyes bore into me, the heat and lust swirling with an emotion I didn't know. Something deeper, something resembling reverence. But I couldn't let myself hope or fall into his easy embrace. If he won, then I was done.

No more, Lacey. No more...?

I wasn't even sure what anymore, just that it terrified the fuck out of me to lose.

"As much as we love your naked cleaning, there are easier ways to get our attention, Lace."

"I don't want your attention. You're the ones coming over here," I argued, making Ryan smile wider. It was insufferable how handsome he was and how easily he rolled with everything. He only tended to bring out his bossy side during missions or when I pushed his buttons just so.

And I'd gotten really good at pushing his buttons.

"We both know how this ends, Lace. Do you honestly want to fight me?"

I snorted, rolling my eyes. "We both know I'd beat you in a fight."

He growled, his smile slipping as he pressed more into me. His cock strained against his pants and pressed into my lower half. I bit my cheek to stop from moaning at the touch. My heart beat faster, the thrill of pushing him over the edge spurring me on.

So, I had a thing for pushing limits as foreplay. Sue me.

Licking my lips, I moved so my nipples rubbed against him, torturing myself with that brush. Leaning next to my ear, I played my last bluff.

"We both know this has run its course. There's nothing left to be gained here. Now be a good boy and go home."

He growled, his hands landing on my hips as he squeezed and lifted me onto the island. The move was so sudden; I didn't fight him as he spread my legs and held them down as he attacked my center with his mouth.

"Fuck," I moaned, gripping his hair with my hands to hold him. His tongue speared into my pussy, my center so slick that it instantly covered his face and offered no resistance as he plunged in two fingers.

After a long lick, he drew back, his eyes piercing me as he stared into mine.

"You're fucking *mine*, Lace, and I'm done with you pushing me away. Pushing *us* away. If you won't talk, then you can listen as we show you how this can be. How it is."

Before I could respond, he stepped back, releasing me and taking his fingers with him. Gasping, I didn't have time to yell at him as Heath stepped into view.

While Ryan was classically handsome, Heath was the exact opposite. His hair was as dark as mine and hung to his shoulders. It naturally had a slight wave that I spent hours trying to achieve. And the asshole looked good with it down or pulled back. He was the most buff of the three, with yummy muscles in all the right places. His back, his thighs, his abs. Everywhere. Though, his arm muscles were a thing of beauty and covered in black tattoos.

His dark eyes heated as he took me in, smirking as he licked his lips and clasped his tattooed fingers on my thighs. Heath lifted me, tossing me over his shoulder as he carried me out of the kitchen and to my bedroom. His big hand slapped against my ass, making me moan more than scream.

"There's my naughty girl," he teased, his finger dipping into my cunt as he groaned. "So fucking wet already, baby."

"It's not for you," I taunted.

He chuckled, slapping my ass again as he palmed my cheek before tossing me on my bed. I bounced, gasping from the move.

"Keep telling yourself that, Ace."

Henry wrapped his arms around me from behind, trapping me to the bed. Not that I was fighting it at this point. I'd gotten exactly what I wanted. Henry dropped a kiss to my shoulder, his warm breath skating over me.

"Hey, suga." His deep voice coated over me, his southern accent thick with desire.

I never knew how he and Heath were joined at the hip because they were complete opposites. Henry was soft and sweet, often bashful. He didn't have any tattoos but did have several piercings. Including one in particular on his cock.

His chocolate brown hair was curly and short, his green eyes soft and playful. He worked out but wasn't stacked like Heath. His muscles were lean, and he preferred running and swimming versus Heath's more aggressive boxing option. Yet the two of them together was magic. They were completely in sync in bed, balancing out one another and bringing me pleasure I never knew existed.

Heath tended to be harsh on his own, and Henry was too reserved. But together… they hit all the right spots.

Ryan shut the door and joined Heath at the end of the bed. They stood side by side, both of their intense glares on me. Squirming, I knew why they had Henry hold me now. He was the one I'd be least likely to hurt.

"Fine. If you want to talk. Talk."

"Oh, that's passed now, little warrior. Henry," Ryan said, nodding to the man behind me.

Henry handcuffed my wrists and draped them over his neck. I was pressed against his chest, his cock hitting me in the ass. His hands spread my thighs, holding me to him.

Again, if I wanted, I could break his hold, but we all knew I didn't want to.

Heath rubbed his hands together before stripping out of his clothes. And just like every time I saw him naked, I gasped as I took in all the art on his body. His cock jutted up, thick and hard as steel as it leaked with pre-cum. He stroked it once while he held my eyes, licking his lips as he stepped closer to the bed. He laid on it, his face right at my pussy. Blowing air across the sensitive flesh, I moaned as he thrust two fingers into me, coating them with my wetness. He moved them down, Henry lifting me so he could access my ass.

When his tongue met my hole, I screamed, not expecting it. Together, they worked me over as Henry fondled my breasts, pinching my nipples and kissing my neck as Heath breached my ass, rimming me. I was squirming in minutes and ready for more.

"More," I groaned.

But instead of giving me what I wanted, they both stopped.

"The three of us want to be with you. We've seen how Grady's team works, and since we're better than them in every way, this will be a breeze. This is to show you how great we could all be together," Ryan said, pulling my attention to him.

While H-squared had been working me over, he'd undressed, fisting his cock in his hand. The two on the bed moved before I could respond. Heath laid down on the bed, his head toward Ryan. Henry lifted me so I could straddle Heath. Feeling needy, I didn't fight him as they notched me over his cock, and I sank lower. My cuffed hands fell forward as Heath pushed up from below.

It distracted me until I felt Henry at my ass; I didn't have time to think as he pushed in one go, his piercing rubbing against me. My body came alive as they moved together, giving me that balance of hard and slow, soft and fast.

My body trembled as Henry kissed down my neck, his hands roaming over me as he pistoned in and out.

Heath fucked me hard from below, his tattooed hands holding onto my thighs, leaving bruises.

"Yes, baby. God, you fuck so good, Ace. You feel amazing wrapped around me. I love being inside you. Fucking you is my favorite thing," Heath said as he worshipped me, his words bringing me closer to my release. I loved a vocal lover, and Heath was the dirtiest.

Henry caressed my body as he plunged into me, a dichotomy only he could pull off. His piercing hit me just right, and my orgasm crawled up my spine, ready to erupt. I was on the edge, so close to falling over.

Ryan moved closer, gripping my chin and forcing my eyes to his. Both guys promptly stopped, my orgasm halting, and they stayed perfectly still, their heavy breathing the only thing I could feel and hear. I whimpered, my eyes begging Ryan to let me come.

"Are you going to be our good girl and admit you like us?" he asked.

"Never," I hissed. His hand moved to my throat, squeezing it slightly.

"Quit fighting, little warrior. We're not going anywhere. You belong with us. Let us in."

"No." I shook my head, his fingers flexing with the movement.

Ryan's eyes heated, and he licked his lips as he stepped closer, bending to whisper in my ear. "What are you so scared of, baby?"

My eyes shuddered closed, a whimper falling from my lips against my will as my body fought the sensations. I needed to move, to feel something, to let go of all the stress. But they wouldn't let me. Henry held my upper half, while Heath had my lower. With my hands still cuffed and my throat in Ryan's grip, I'd never felt more vulnerable in my life.

"We got you, suga," Henry whispered. "You don't have to fight us anymore. You've tossed everything at us, pushed us away, and tortured us so we all had blue balls for weeks. And yet, six months after meeting you, the three of us are still as head over heels for you as the first moment we met. You waltzed out of that hotel room with all the confidence in the world, hollering about fucking, stealing, and killing like you didn't have a care who heard. You were magnanimous, and it knocked us all off our feet."

He softly kissed my body, his warm lips sending chills through my taut body—the anger and roughness I could handle. But when Henry busted out his sweetness, I was always a goner.

"Let us take care of you, sugar. Let us be your guys. Say yes," he whispered, his breath fanning over my skin as he bit into the space between my neck and shoulder.

It set me off, my head falling back as my orgasm rushed to the surface from the place it had been waiting. Ryan's hand tightened, adding to my release as my entire body spasmed, the edges of my vision going black as every nerve ending in me lit up with the most intense orgasm of my life.

"Yes," I screamed, not knowing if it was to them or the orgasm and not caring because they were all right.

I wanted to be with them; I was just too scared to depend on someone other than the girls.

H-squared moved with me, their releases following mine as my body continued to careen through the after-shocks. My brain shut off as bliss filled me, my body feeling light as a feather as soft hands ran over me.

"You with me, baby?" Ryan asked, hovering over me.

I'd been placed on my back, Heath curled around me on one side and Henry on the other, both touching and petting me. Blinking, I nodded as everything came back into focus.

"Yes," I whispered for the second time. And this time, I meant it in the way they all wanted to hear.

Ryan kissed me, smiling as he dropped his body to mine, sliding into my pussy in one thrust. His love-making was slow as he took his time kissing and thrusting into me. It was sweet and a far cry from anything we'd done before. My arms had been released from the cuffs, and I squeezed Henry and Heath, feeling connected to all three of them at that precise moment.

Wrapping my legs around Ryan, I pulled him closer, his pelvis hitting my clit and sending tingles through me.

"Yes, Ry. That feels so good," I moaned, lifting my neck for him to suck. I tilted my head toward Heath, so I pulled him closer, kissing him as Ryan fucked me. It felt scandalous and delicious, and I knew this would work.

I'd been so worried that I wouldn't be enough, I'd

grow bored, or worse, they would. But Henry had hit the nail on its head, showing me that despite everything I'd done to push them away, their attraction and passion hadn't wavered.

Add in the fact that I hadn't slept with anyone else that whole time, and I knew I was as obsessed as they were. I'd just been in a bit of denial about it.

Okay, maybe it had been more of a delusion considering how hard I pretended not to care. But in the end, it brought us all here, so I couldn't bring myself to feel ashamed about it.

"Look at me, little warrior," Ryan demanded, and my eyes snapped to him. A second later, another orgasm flooded me, and I shook as my body wracked with pleasure.

"Yes, baby," he moaned, stilling as he flooded me with his cum.

I woke up again, having missed some time, spooned between two hard and warm bodies.

"You back with us, sugar?" Henry asked, tracing his finger over my face.

I blinked, nodding and leaning into his touch.

"How long was I out?" I asked.

Heath, the hot body behind me, leaned over, practically draping me as he peered into my face.

"Too long," he groaned like the man-child he was. "My dick's ready for round two." To emphasize his point, he thrust up, his cock sliding between my ass cheeks. "He likes knowing that you're ours, Ace. Ours to love, ours to fuck, ours to cherish."

I coughed, smiling at Henry. "Love, huh? I don't remember that being part of it."

"Don't worry, sugar. We already have a five-step plan to make you realize you love us."

Chuckling, I shook my head, nudging Heath's cock. He groaned, kissing my neck and leaving a love bite.

"You're too tempting, babe. I need a month's vacation so I can fuck you in all the ways I fantasize about at night."

"He's very creative," Heath added, making me giggle. The sound was so foreign that I paused, my eyes growing wide.

"Here, eat this," Ryan said, plopping onto the bed and shoving a piece of pizza at me. The smell of cheese and greasy meat had me sitting up and taking it.

I moaned around the bite I shoved in my mouth; the guys laughed around me as I devoured four slices. By the end, I had sauce all over my face, but I didn't care.

"So, this is what it's like to be taken care of?" I asked, picking at the blanket.

"It's just the start, little warrior," Ryan said, squeezing my leg. "What did you think?"

I shrugged, smiling. "I guess it wasn't so bad." I met all of their eyes, letting myself relax in their presence and not trying to push them away. "How do you feel about brunch?"

"It's food. I'm down," Heath said, tracing and connecting my freckles. He rarely ever stopped touching me, and I didn't hate it.

"If you're there, I want to be there too," Henry said, kissing my hair.

"What time do we need to leave?" Ryan asked, smiling softly at me.

"Um, ten?" I asked, biting my lip. This felt too easy.

"Perfect. Plenty of time for a few more rounds," Ryan said before diving toward me as the four of us fell into a pile of naked arms and legs.

And while the sex knocked my socks off, the laughter and intimacy in between were becoming my favorite.

"You didn't say you'd protect me," I whispered sometime around two in the morning.

Heath snuggled into me, yawning around his words. "That's because you don't need us to protect you. I fully expect you to be my bodyguard from here on out. All those grabby girls at work are gonna have to watch out."

"What girls?" I growled, the hair on my neck standing up.

"Shh, you can go all stabby tomorrow. Sleep now, Ace," he whispered, pressing my lips together.

Warmed by his words, I let him pull me into his chest and listened to his heartbeat as I fell asleep.

In the end, even the rebel slut from the wrong side of the tracks was deserving of love. It had just taken me a while to believe it. But now that I had, I'd hold on to them with everything I had.

And if anyone tried to come for them, they'd have to

go through me, and I always stabbed first and asked questions later.

Try me.

I wasn't afraid to be a little psychotic, *especially* when it came to them.

CHAPTER 36
HOLLAND xoxo

"You ready?" I asked Grady, his ass up in the air and perfectly prepped. I'd never wanted to fuck someone so much in my entire life as I did right now. The thought of pegging Grady had become an obsession, and I wanted to bring him to his knees.

"Yes." His voice was strained, but he kept his ass up, his legs spread. "I trust you, mi chispa."

Smiling at his nickname for me, I notched the head of the strap-on at his hole and slowly pressed in. His hands tightened on the sheets, his face red as he gritted his teeth.

"Breathe out," I reminded, stopping as I waited. When he did, I pushed through the first ring of muscles, and he relaxed. When I brushed against his prostate, he moaned, his body softening.

"Fucking hell," he cursed. "Don't stop."

Gripping his hips, I pushed the rest of the way in, my thighs meeting his ass.

"I'm in. How does it feel?"

"Weird, but good. Move, baby. I want to feel you moving."

"Why is that so hot?" Quentin whispered to Max as they waited for me to get Grady comfortable.

"It's Holland?" Max said, shrugging as he watched. He smirked, hitting a button and making the vibrator inside the strap-on go off, sending flutters through me.

Faltering, I fell forward for a second before I regained my stance and pulled out. With each thrust, Max hit the button, sending the pulses through me as I fucked Grady. I found a good rhythm as Grady moaned, his hands gripping the sheets for a different reason this time. Quentin moved behind me, ever the impatient one.

"You ready for me?" he asked, kissing my neck.

"Yes," I moaned, trying to focus on my thrusts as Quentin pulled the plug out of my ass. I felt my ass clench and unclench as the plug was removed, feeling empty as I waited. My pulse jumped as I continued to move in Grady, my thigh muscles burning as I rocked into him. He panted beneath me, groaning and moaning into the comforter, completely blissed out now.

"Shit," he mumbled. "I'm so close to coming." He gripped his cock between his legs, tugging it as he clenched his eyes closed.

I grew tired as I continued to ram into Grady, appreciating the athletic ability guys had to fuck hard. I'd definitely be feeling it in muscles I hadn't used in a while tomorrow. But I looked forward to it, knowing it was from making Grady a weeping mess and wholly wrecked.

Quentin pressed his cock into my ass as I plunged forward, halting my movements as he filled me.

"Oh, god," I moaned. He held my body to him, tilting my head to kiss me.

"Don't stop," Grady groaned. Max hit the pulse again, and my legs shook.

Quentin held onto my hips, pushing me forward with his thrusts, helping me gain some power behind mine. I went deeper, dragging the dildo over Grady's prostate with each thrust. My heart raced as sweat beaded on my skin, and every inch of me flushed as need rushed through me. I was close and knew it would only take one more pulse from Max, and I'd crash over the edge.

"So close," Grady groaned, squeezing his dick hard as pre-cum leaked over his hand.

"Take it, baby," I demanded as I pushed forward, Quentin following me as he did the same. I lost track of my movements as I rocked my hips back and forth, fucking Grady with everything I had as I grew closer to the edge.

"Fuck," he screamed as I hit his p-spot one last time. His cum spilled over his hand as he stroked himself, his ass tightening around the strap-on as I moved in and out. Max hit the pulse, and I detonated, squeezing Quentin as I came. My body shook, my walls clenching tight as everything in me exploded.

Grady fell to the bed as Q held me to him; his hips made small thrusts while I came. When I was done, Max moved to me and helped me remove the strap-on before I took him in my mouth. Max fucked my throat as Quentin gained his rhythm, pounding into my ass with deep and hard thrusts.

I hummed around Max as another orgasm built. Quentin squeezed my hips, pulling me up and off Max as he kissed me, spilling his seed in me as he shuttered.

"Fuck, Temptress. That was amazing."

"My turn," Max said, pulling me from Q. He kissed the scowling man before wrapping me in his arms and laying us on the bed on our sides. Lifting my leg over his hip, he gently pushed into me, giving me slow and deep thrusts as my body recovered.

When he noticed I was ready, he pulled us closer, kissing me as he picked up speed. My body was so boneless, and I held onto him as he snapped his hips, pistoning his dick in and out. Moaning, I dropped my head back as I clawed his back, my body vibrating with pleasure.

"Yes, god, yes, Max. Right there," I cried, feeling every flick of his hips and twitch of his dick. It didn't take us long to find our release, and I fell over the edge, tumbling into the abyss as the orgasm crashed over me.

"That was amazing," I wheezed. "Grady?"

"Yeah, mi chispa. It was better than I expected. I'd definitely let you do that again."

"Yeah?" I asked, tears pricking my eyes.

He smiled, kissing my lips as he pushed my hair back from my sweaty face. "Anytime, Holland. Love you, baby."

His words settled in my heart, and I basked in their warm feeling.

"Next time, you should peg Quentin, and I'll let him top me," Max said, shocking us all.

"Um, no," Q said, shaking his head.

"It's good," Grady said, shrugging his shoulders. "Your loss for being scared."

"I'm not scared," he scoffed. "I'll top Max, though, if he wants."

"Only if you're also being topped, Q. All is fair in love and anal," Max teased, making us all laugh.

"Maybe," Q said after it had been quiet.

"It's a start," Max mumbled, pulling me closer. Feeling empty without one of them in me, I stroked Max since he was behind me until he was hard. Lifting my leg, he pressed in, kissing me as he stilled.

It was the ultimate form of intimacy for me, something I hadn't known I'd like as much as I did. I was glad the guys didn't seem to mind the cockwarming either, since I often hopped from one to the other throughout the night as we spooned like a Goldilocks of dicks.

But after sex, I always wanted more, the need to feel them in me so I wasn't so empty. The act made me feel connected on every level, keeping our bodies intertwined and together until morning.

It often led to more sex, but not always. And with how tired we all were tonight, I didn't see it happening, but it was lovely... like our genitals were holding hands.

"Night, sweetheart," Max sighed, nuzzling into me as he held me.

"Night," I yawned, barely able to keep my eyes open.

Kisses woke me the following day, a hardness still between my legs. Pushing back on the owner of the cock, I moaned as it shifted and hit my G-spot.

"We gotta get ready for brunch," Grady said in front of me, the owner of the lips kissing my neck.

"Fine," I pouted, tilting my head back to find Quentin sleeping.

"Don't even think about it," Grady warned, grabbing me and pulling me off Q before I could have fun. I moaned at the loss of him, giving Grady a bigger pouty lip. He pulled it down, nipping it as he held my lip.

"You can hang a bucket off it now," he teased, not falling for my pout. "After brunch, we're stopping by Dora's. Bella made you something. So, no time to dawdle."

Sighing dramatically, I let it go and got ready, knowing he was right. Grady's family was great, and I loved spending time with them. It made me feel like I had my sister back in many ways. Add in Ava and Lukas, and I had all these people I cared about now. It was weird, but it made my life full. Murder and sex weren't the only things in my life anymore.

An hour later, we pulled up to the address Joy had sent. It was a grand house, one I never thought any of us would live in. It proved how far we could go now that we weren't bound to Foolshope.

Knocking on the door, I wasn't surprised when it was immediately opened, and Joy jumped into my arms.

"You're here, Hols!"

"Of course. I'm excited to meet them," I said, kissing her cheek. I loved seeing Joy this happy. She was the brightest and most joyful person I knew, and I wanted her to have people who appreciated it.

"I have news," she said, beaming. "But it looks like I'm not the only one." She jumped down, and we turned together as Lacey walked up the sidewalk, two Shadows behind her and one holding her hand.

"Do my eyes deceive me, or is Lacey holding hands?" I gasped.

"Oh, good. You see it, too. I was worried I'd smoked too much weed this morning." Joy giggled before pouting. "Damn. I thought moving in with my married couple and their best friend and trying for a baby would be the day's biggest news."

"What?" Lacey and I shouted together, our eyes wide as we stared at our best friend in shock.

"Best friend?" Lacey stuttered.

"Baby?" I added, raising my brows.

Joy nodded, smiling as she swayed side to side, not giving us a clear answer. "You hungry?"

"I brought muffins," Lacey mumbled, pointing to the container Henry held.

"Hi, Henry," I said, liking the quiet man.

"Good morning, ma'am," he said, his southern accent warm and soft.

"Back off, Grigson," Quentin muttered, wrapping his arm around me possessively as he scowled.

"He just said hello," I sighed, letting Q pull me to him.

"Ryan," Grady said, nodding. "Heath. I guess it's time to lay down the competitiveness between us. Our women are best friends, so we'll always be in each other's lives now."

"No need to lay anything down, Grady. Consider it our foreplay," Ryan chuckled, slapping him on the shoulder as they headed into the house.

"I'm beginning to regret inviting you," Lacey mumbled, Henry and Heath wrapping their arms around her as they moved inside.

Squeezing Max's hand, we walked in with Q, closing the door behind us, and followed the noise into the kitchen, where we met James, Mallory, and Tyler.

Despite being shocked by Joy's news, it was apparent how much they all cared for each other. They were the only ones here not in the business, which oddly made it enjoyable. I wanted Joy to have something away from the Shadows. She was too bright to be kept hidden. Plus, she'd be the best mom. It didn't hurt that it would also keep her more on the sidelines.

Lacey gave me a look, one I knew well. This was good for Joy, so we'd support her and buy her all the baby shit she needed.

But we'd draw the lines at diaper changing. She had three lovers; they could figure that shit out themselves. Literally.

As I watched my two best friends and all of our lovers mingle together, I had a weird sensation blooming in my chest. Rubbing my heart, my brows furrowed as I concentrated on the feeling.

"How do you feel about a baby?" Grady asked.

"Don't even think about it." I rolled my eyes as he laughed, but it helped the feeling lessen.

"You love them. Your lives may go in different directions, but it doesn't mean you'll grow apart. You three are intertwined forever. There's not one without the other two, even if that's with a little distance as you make your own families."

"You're very wise, Grady," I whispered, kissing his cheek.

"I'm only reporting on what I observed. You three, it's one of the most real connections I've ever seen. Nothing will break that. Hell, murder didn't even crack it, so a baby won't." He lifted his brows, making me smile. I knew he was right. What the three of us had went beyond words.

"Thanks." He wrapped his arms around me, hugging me to him.

"So, does this mean we could convince you to officially move in now?" he teased.

"Maybe." Smiling, I pulled him along as we filled our plates, talking with Joy's lovers like the rest of us weren't cold-blooded killers as we shared brunch.

Once all the plates were cleared, Ryan and Max volunteered to help clean up while Heath and Quentin went to the garage to check out Tyler's car. Grady was in a deep conversation with Mallory while Henry and James discussed some country music singer they'd seen in concert.

Nodding to Lacey and Joy, the three of us slipped out to the back deck, the peace and quiet outside settling around us.

"Can you believe this is our lives now?" I asked, leaning against the deck railing.

"It's better than I ever imagined," Joy gushed.

"I fought it for a while. Worried I didn't deserve it. But last night, the guys wore me down, telling me they weren't going anywhere and that I could let them in, too. It shifted something in me. To know other people other than you two saw me... who got me... And maybe even loved me," Lacey whispered.

Joy and I moved to her, putting her in the middle as we hugged her.

"Ah, Lace. You're so worthy of love. I'm glad you finally caved. In fact, I think I might've won this pool," I said, giggling.

"Wait, what?" she asked, pulling back.

"You didn't think you were the only one who could coordinate a betting pool, right?" I teased, making her jaw drop as she lost all her words.

"I had you folding a lot faster," Joy admitted, shrugging.

"How much did you win?" Lacey asked, narrowing her eyes at me.

"Enough to buy me a motorcycle and name it Leather N' Lace."

"Bullshit." She laughed, shaking her head.

"No, you're right. Lace of Base is better."

"I hate you," she said, grinning.

"No, you don't." I bumped her shoulder.

"No, I don't."

"I think we need a new game," Joy said, grabbing our attention. "We've outgrown fuck steal kill."

"What do you suggest?" I asked, curious.

"Burp, change, or rock?" Lacey said, laughing.

"Dash, pass, or smash," I said, joining in.

"Oh! Lick, stick, or kick," Joy added, and we all broke out into laughter, bending and holding our stomachs as tears ran down our faces.

The game had set us on this course, giving us an outlet for our darkness and a way out of Foolshope. But unlike our friendship, we'd outgrown the game, not needing it anymore to pass the time.

And that was okay because life never stood still, but good friends, they'd always keep you rooted, growing right along with you.

"I love you both," I said once the tears had dried from laughing.

"Love you, too," they both said, grinning.

The rebel, the sweetheart, and the brains—we made one badass killer, but even better friends—the kind you'd kill for.

XOXO.

The End

LETTER FROM THE AUTHOR
XOXO

This book was such a joy to write, and it wasn't because I got to punish bad people doing bad things. (Though, that was a lot of fun being stabby.) It's because the friendship in this book lifted from the pages and pierced my soul. These characters were so flawed, but they loved hard and I think that's what endeared them to me.

I've never written a book where I smiled as much as I did with these characters. Holland, Joy, and Lacey are the type of friends I hope you have. Their love and friendship was inspirational and made me want to hug my best friend, so I hope you had a similar feeling by the end of the book.

I'm most impressed that I was able to write a true standalone. If you've been a reader of mine for a while, you know I tend to leave something open, but for this story, I truly feel it's closed. Of course, there will be people who want more, but at this time, I don't see that happening. They're off living their best unaliver lives with their lovers. What more could they ask for?

I'm thankful for the ladies who surround me, giving me feedback and support on a daily basis. I hope you were able to feel some love from this book and our friendship.

Emma, you're the best friend I never dreamed possible. We didn't meet until late in life, but I couldn't imagine doing the rest without you. I always have my shovel ready for your call.

Heather, Megan, Melanie, and Lindsay, thank you for reading through this and giving me your insight and encouragement. And Maya, as always, you do an amazing job. You're an invaluable part to my writing process.

To my ARC readers and street team members, thank you for reviewing and sharing this book. Your encouragement, love, and enthusiasm help me keep pushing through when it feels overwhelming and that no one will care. So, thank you!

And if you're a new reader, thank you for taking a chance on me. Not all of my books are this bloody, but they all share the themes of emotion, connection, and healing. Plus the spice, can't forget that part. Check out my back catalog on the next page and you just might discover your next favorite book.

Thanks for reading,

XOXO.

Kris

For the most up-to-date look at my releases. Check out all my books here: https://authorkrisbutler.com/my-books

BEAUTY AND THE CLEATS

#baseball #standalone series #heartfelt

The Cleat Retreat (Blake's prequel)

The Pitch Slap (Blake's book, MMFMM)

No Balking Way (Bryce's book, MMF)

Whiff it Real Good (Ledger's book, MM)

LUX BRUMALIS (COMPLETED)

#hockey #girlboss #nonbinary sibling

3 guys, no MM

Penalty Box

Dead Lift

Breakaway

THE COUNCIL SERIES (COMPLETED)

#figure skating #secret past #dark elements

7 guys, lots of MM with bi-awakening

Damaged Dreams

Shattered Secrets

Fractured Futures

Bosh Bells & Epic Fails

The Council Boxset

THE ORDER DUET (COUNCIL SPINOFF)

#secret agency #spy + hacker games #fashionista

4 guys, light MM (book 2 only at the end)

Stiletto Sins

Lipstick Lies

DRESSED TO KILL SHARED WORLD (STANDALONE)

#female assassin #quirky & curvy #twins

4 guys, no MM

Raven

F*CK STEAL KILL (STANDALONE)

#morally gray #bestie unalivers #sassy

3 guys, biawakening, (FF in Joy's chapter)

F*ck Steal Kill

DARK CONFESSIONS (COMPLETED)

#mafia #therapist #foster kids + dogs #tattoos

5 guys with MM

Dangerous Truths

Dangerous Lies

Dangerous Vows

Reckless (Cami's Novella)

Relentless (Nat's Novella)

Dangerous Love

TATTOOED HEARTS DUET (COMPLETED)

#tattoos #penpals #music #curvy fmc

3 guys with MM

Riddled Deceit (Part 1)

Smudged Lines (Part 2)

Open Road (Road trip Novella)

Tattooed Hearts Completed Duet

MUSIC CITY DIARIES (TATTOOED HEARTS SPIN-OFF)

#motorcycle club #age gap #TW #cam girl

4 guys, no MM

Beautiful Agony

Beautiful Envy

VACATION ROMCOM

#romcom #social media experiment #besties

3 guys, no MM

Vibing

SINNERS FAIRYTALES (STANDALONE)

#Rapunzel retelling #dance #TW

3 guys, no MM

Pride

ABOUT THE AUTHOR
XOXO

Kris Butler writes under a pen name to have some separation from her everyday life. Writing has become her second love, providing a safe place to normalize mental health, trauma, and healing through her characters.

Kris enjoys writing emotional books with flawed characters, sassy heroines, and all the book boyfriends she loves to drool over.

You can find her at home most nights reading with her husband and furbaby, trying to maintain her nerdy sock collection, or playing tabletop games with her friends. Kris loves to talk with readers about her books, even if it's just them yelling at her for that cliffhanger.

If you enjoyed her book, please consider leaving a review. You can find her in her reader group or on social media.

www.ingramcontent.com/pod-product-compliance
Lightning Source LLC
Chambersburg PA
CBHW061901310726
48972CB00004B/1119